A DANCE CALLED AFRICA

BOOK ONE OF THE 'JOHN ROSS' TRILOGY

A DANCE CALLED AFRICA

They rose from the dust of Africa,
One, a warrior king, the other a man of magic
While one created a mighty kingdom,
The other warned of what was to come

ISABELLA BLESZYNSKI

A Dance Called Africa
Book One of: THE JOHN ROSS TRILOGY
© Isabella Bleszynski 2015. All rights reserved.

www.stravaig-books.com

ISBN: 978-0-9933461-2-5

Requests to publish work from this book should be sent to:
Isabella@stravaig-books.com

Cover design: JD Smith Design
Interior Design: Maureen Cutajar

Published by Stravaig Books

To my sons, Nick and Tim,
for walking the long road with me.

Prologue

Act i

1799. *Somewhere between the White Umfolozi and Mhlatuze Rivers, south-east Africa.*

In the strange hush that comes before the storm, the kingdom of the eLangeni waited while the immortals played their deadly games of dice on high. Now here, now there, flash of thunderbolt, battle commencing.

A boy stood alone with his back pressed up against the stakes of the cattle enclosure. Blood oozed from a deep wound on his cheekbone. A flying stone had narrowly missed his eye and laid the flesh open to the bone.

Squinting against the pain, he cast a wary glance around the wind-swept patch of land. Ever since he'd come to live in the village of iNguga, a group of older boys had been making his life a misery. Life here was like a piece of stone, no warmth in this land of strangers.

His blistered lips throbbed. By forcing him to lick a red-hot spoon straight from a pot of maize porridge simmering by the fire, his tormentors had shown him the depths of their contempt.

'*Nyale!*' he muttered, wiping away smears of porridge. 'One day, I will make a big surprise for them… and no one will escape me.'

At that moment the ten-year-old couldn't decide who he hated most – his father, Chief ka Senzangakhona, who had brought this trouble down on their heads or the rabble of *utivi* scum to whom they had been forced to appeal for shelter.

Lightning forked silently away on the far horizons, serpents' tongues of incandescent fire, malevolence in their caress. All was still; only the Devil's children playing with their silent fireworks out there on the vast rim of the world.

A faint but insistent noise reached him, soft at first then gathering in strength. The boy cocked an ear, listening. It seemed to be coming from beyond the dragon-toothed mountains far to the south. *Ki-si-ki-si* it seemed to be whispering, like the hissing of deadly mambas slithering away from the coming storm or the rustling of a million leaves.

A vivid flash of lightning startled the cattle. They milled around, raising dust and clattering their curved horns together. Instinctively, the boy made soothing noises to calm the restless beasts.

It was so dark now, he could hardly see. A wind had risen and with it came the evocative smells of raw earth, moist and pungent. The rustlings and whisperings were coming closer. Now they were just beyond the flat-topped thorn trees a mile or so away. Nearer and nearer they came, blotting out the last of the glassy light.

Without warning, another stone caught him in the small of the back, breaking the skin and exposing raw flesh. He cried out in pain and shock. Blood trickled down and collected in the crease between his buttocks and the hand he put to it came away red and sticky.

The unexpected blow had made him bite his tongue. Leaning over, he spat a gobbet of blood-streaked mucus on to the ground. Shrieks and howls of glee told him that his tormentors were back, eager for more sport.

Somnamuzi, the leader of the pack, stepped out of the dusky light and strutted forward, arrogance in every step. As he looked at the younger boy, his eyes gleamed with malice. Jeering, he called out to his friends: '*Ake ni-bone umtondo wake! Ufana nom sundu nje!* Look at his penis – as small as an earth worm!'

The boy flinched as if physically struck, the member in question shrivelling up into his groin. A hot flush rose to his face.

Adolescent voices shrieked in joy. One of the conspirators strutted forward, boldness in every line of his skinny body. He put his hands on his hips and stuck out his buttocks, waggling and strutting in the grotesque parody of a woman openly flaunting herself. Before turning away, swaggering, he made an obscene gesture with his fingers, its meaning not lost on the younger boy.

A thin coil of red-hot anger rose from somewhere deep inside him. For his mother, Nandi, to be so insulted was something he would not, could not tolerate…

An enormous crack split the air, a great vibration of sound and fury. Its energy crackled all around him, metallic and acrid. The cattle in the enclosure reared up, bellowing in fear. Above the noise, he could hear the yells and taunts rising in pitch.

His eyes searched the brooding sky above his head as if looking for an answer. It was vast and grey-black, like the scarred skin of the great *ndlovu*, anger in its trumpeting and grumbling belly noises.

Whose power was up there? he wondered. Did it belong to sorcerers as some claimed, or was it just the wind and the thunder? A rolling crack made his ears ring. Flickers of lightning lit up the clearing in shades of silver and black.

'*The name Zulu means "the heavens"* his mother had told him. '*It is where we, the People of the Heavens come from, and what makes us strong.*'

The words echoed in his head, reminding him who he was and the people he came from. A low growl came from somewhere nearby. It was followed by a soft breath of air, as if someone had just passed close by. The hairs on the back of his neck stood up.

Could it really be Zulu, his ancestor, or Jama, one of the Powerful Ones his mother had told him about? Though their earthly bodies lay at rest in eMakhosini, the Valley of the Kings, he knew their spirits still ruled the living and were always close.

The thud of feet drumming on the rock-hard ground brought him back to his present predicament. Desperation clutching at him, he lifted his eyes to the fury raging in the skies above him.

'I am of the Zulu…' His ten-year-old voice wavered then held. 'Help me fight – '

Suddenly, all was deathly still. Even the cicadas ceased their chirping. A surge of energy winnowed around him, surprisingly gentle, yet with a core of ferocity at its heart. The boy felt it touch his face, his eyes, his hands…

His heartbeat steadied.The warm snake of blood from his wounds slowed down then stopped. A great calm came over him. Now he was on a pinnacle, somewhere inside of himself, alone and free, afraid of nothing and no one.

The pack was very near now, closing in. As he turned to face them, his fingers brushed against the thorns studded along the length of the stick he'd used for herding the cattle…

Somnamuzi's grin was bold and insolent, his teeth white against his dusky skin. The chorus behind him chanted his name, confident of victory. Then, in a blink of an eye, everything changed.

The ten-year-old stepped forward and spat into his face. A glob of blood-streaked saliva hit Somnamuzi straight between the eyes. Wiping it away with the back of his hand, he stared at the younger boy in disbelief. Shock gave way to outrage.

The insult would be repaid, and in full. The little bastard, whether a king's bastard, or not, would not be allowed to live…

The blow from the herding stick came out of nowhere, a sharp, hard crack that made his ears ring. He clutched his head, dazed and disorientated. The stick descended for a second, then a third time. Thorns snagged on his flesh and left angry streaks of red from shoulder to wrist. Howling with pain, he covered his head and tried to protect himself.

A searing flash of light coursed from the sky. A tree split in two and gouts of orange flame sprouted among the dusty foliage. Someone was screaming nearby, the voice high and strained. Humiliated, he realized that it was his own. The storm rolled and throbbed overhead, as if taunting him.

Shouts burst from his small mob of followers. They jostled forward through the smoke, intent on personal revenge. But when they realised it was their leader, and not their intended victim who lay on the ground with his arms frozen protectively over his head, they faltered. Looking from one to the other, they were confused, unsure of what to do next.

Sporadic flashes lit up the kraal. In the eerie light they could make out the rise and fall of a knobbed stick across their leader's head and shoulders. The boy wielding it turned towards them, his face twisted in a scowl. He looked taller and somehow different from the fatherless boy who had been such an easy victim. Now it seemed as if another persona, blown in on the storm, had come to stand in his place.

The wind shook the tops of the trees and bent them low, stirring grit, dried grass and twigs into a brew which spiralled across the ground. In the sky, the dark gods and their cohorts rode high and wild. Clad in streaming black and silver, shot through with gold and scarlet, they were full of sound and fury- and very, very close.

The boy glowed, absorbing strength and power from the storm. Out of the corner of his eye, he saw a curtain of rain advance through the bush, blotting out visibility. His bare foot increased its pressure on the back of Somnamuzi's neck and ground his face into the hard, red earth of the compound. Crooking a finger, he challenged the others to come closer.

They hovered uncertainly, caught off-guard by the unexpected turn of events. Retreat was unthinkable. They would never live it down if news got out that they had backed away from a fight, especially with the despised one, *i-tshaka, the beetle.*

The group bunched together for support then advanced, slowly at first. Fanning out to encircle him, their ragged cries were almost lost in the howling wind as they closed in on him.

Some time later, the sting of icy rain brought them back to their senses. They were huddled together like a bundle of new-born puppies, shivering, bruised and bloody. The stink of burning hair and singed flesh would linger in their nostrils for days and many nights afterwards, while ferocious roars and growls continued to stalk them in their sleep.

They never talked about what had happened that day, not among themselves, and especially not to their families. Terrified of being considered bewitched, or possessed by an evil spirit, they decided to bear their fears in silence.

Some would swear they had been tossed bodily into the air, ripped by the talons of demons while others were convinced it was the terrible, screaming noises that had been responsible for turning their limbs to water.

In any case, whatever they believed, they would keep their mouths tightly shut. The truth was that they were terrified the rest of their peers would find out that *"i-tshaka, the beetle"* the outcast, the bullied and despised one, had somehow got the better of them. And, most galling of all, they had absolutely no idea of how he had done it.

Forked lightning still tore from the crown of the sky in displays of steely light, but it was sporadic now, the thunder growling in the distance, its fury muted.

The boy tilted his head back. Turning round slowly beneath the downpour, he raised his arms and allowed the water to run clear and clean off his body, the gentle rain taking with it his father's rejection, the sneers and taunts which had haunted his dreams, and especially, *especially,* the pain of having no place to be happy, for feeling small and powerless in a land of strangers.

He laughed into the face of the dying storm, loving its ferocity and rage. Drops of rain beaded his eyelashes and the tight curls of his hair and dripped off the end of his nose. For the rest of his life he would revel in the feel of fresh water on his skin, that and the smell of it... *nuka manzi*.

'I see you, eLangeni!' he shouted above the hiss of falling rain. 'One day, I will return! You can be sure of it!'

Sucking his tongue hard, he felt the coppery taste of blood flood into his mouth. Bending over, he spat blood and saliva into the rivulets of water at his feet and watched as the scarlet threads mingled with the soil of his native land.

When the boy, whose name was Shaka kaSenzangakhona, stopped to pick up his thorn sticks, he saw that the cleansing rain had washed away the blood of his enemies. Laying them across his shoulder, he set off across the compound and made for home, whistling as he went.

There had been no gesture of reconciliation afterwards as was common among Zulu boys after a fight. Usually it ended when blood was drawn, with the victor then expected to wash the loser's wounds.

But this had not been just an ordinary skirmish. There had been far more at stake than that. And because of it, the boy Shaka had learned the first and greatest lesson of his young warrior's life, one he would never forget.

To strike an enemy, you must do it fast, without mercy – and up close.

As he passed Somnamuzi who was still lying on the ground, moaning, he feigned a kick at his head. The answering cringe made him laugh out loud.

'*Undidi we mpisi! hyena's arse!*' His mocking laughter would one day be remembered by the eLangeni when Shaka of the Zulus returned to keep his promise.

Act ii

Five years later. Esi Klebeni.

As he surveyed the crowds of people milling about in the arena below, the scowl on the face of King Senzangakhona of the Zulus deepened. Stifling a groan, he fervently wished that he was somewhere else, preferably in a place where disaster was not about to fall on his head.

An important ceremony was about to take place that day. The formal presentation of the *umutsha*, the traditional short apron presented to adolescent boys around the ages of thirteen or fourteen, marked the end of their childhood and entry into young manhood. Unfortunately, it was one ceremony that he, as King, could hardly refuse to attend.

Trickles of sweat coursed their way beneath his kilt of grey monkey tails. Although his genitals itched, he restrained the maddening impulse to relieve the irritation. Now was not the time to be seen scratching himself like a warthog...

He stared morosely into the oval parade ground below and saw that it was beginning to fill up with eager participants and their fathers. The *izinyanga*, the traditional medicine men, were already there, preparing for the ceremony.

Senzangakhona closed a bloodshot eye and squinted up at the sky. It was still the same peerless blue as the last time he'd looked at it, except for a solitary white cloud lurking far out on the horizon.

A red haze of dust hung over the crowds. With no breath of cooling wind to dispel it, the stink of sweat and body odours was beginning to drift up the hillside and foul his nostrils. He wrinkled his nose in distaste.

Somewhere below drums began to beat, a low rhythmic pounding which did nothing to relieve the dull ache in his head, the result of the copious amounts of *tshwala* beer consumed the night before. Suppressing a groan, he shifted his fleshy buttocks into a more comfortable position, and silently cursed the *amadhlozi,* his ancestors.

Why were they still punishing him for that single lapse of judgment in his youth? Long, hot afternoons by the river, the temptation of a young girl's willing flesh, a reckless moment or two...

Both he and Nandi, the youngest daughter of an eLangeni chief, had been fully aware of the strict rules of *ama hly endlela,* 'the fun of the roads.'

On the face of it, it seemed an eminently sensible arrangement. Providing full sexual intercourse did not take place, a certain amount of love play was allowed between young, unmarried men and women. It did not, however, give any guidance on what to do when temptation proved irresistible.

The pregnancy that followed had been as welcome as a hyena in a chicken roost. The royal court had been thrown into turmoil when the girl's swelling belly was brought to their attention by her irate father.

Senzangakhona shook his head. Even after he'd taken Nandi as his wife and brought her to esiKlebeni, the spiteful remarks had continued. If only she had just been a little more tearful, more apologetic – but headstrong and impetuous, she had stood her ground and lashed out with some ferocity against the whispered jeers and snubs.

It could only end one way. When *i-tshaka*, the five-year old boy of the union allowed one of his father's pet goats to be killed by a dog, Senzangakhona seized the opportunity to eject both his wife and his children from the royal kraal.

Nandi was left no choice but to throw herself on the mercy of her father's people, the eLangeni. After a few years of living a brutalised and fearful existence in the village of iNguga, when famine and disease began to sweep the land, they were once again driven out.

A rootless existence followed until Ngomane, a chief of the powerful Mthethwe tribe, took pity on her and welcomed her small family into his kraal.

Now, more than a decade later, Senzangakhona's past had returned to haunt him. The boy, *itshaka*, was now of an age to receive the *umutsha* from the man who had fathered him.

The questions burning holes in Senzangakhona's brain were, on the face of it, quite simple, although the answers were proving to be somewhat problematic.

What if he refused to take part and simply washed his hands of the whole affair? Everyone knew he had cast out the boy and his mother years ago, so why should he be forced to acknowledge someone who was a stranger to him? Sweat dripped down his face. Unfortunately, such a course of action would have repercussions, far-ranging ones.

The clan elders would strongly condemn such a move, claiming it would undermine the kinship and ritual that held families and nations together. The ties of blood could not be shaken off so lightly. Not even a King would dare disobey the age-old laws with impunity.

And this was exactly why, some ten years later, he was sitting there on a blistering hot day waiting for disaster to strike. Any rash action on his part could unleash the deeply-hidden antagonisms lurking at the heart of Zulu society. It had long been riddled with treachery, subversion and murder; brother killing brother; cousin killing cousin, sons killing their fathers in the pursuit of wealth, cattle, or high position. But that was not all...

Scheming women were also known to seek out a witch or evil shaman to lay a curse on anyone standing in the way of a favourite.

Senzangakhona shuddered. His former wife, Nandi, was more than capable of resorting to such tactics, if provoked. And what of the boy himself? To have his blood father refuse to offer him the *umutsha* would deliver a blow of monumental proportions. Who knows how he might react?

He rolled his eyes in frustration. If the boy possessed even a sliver of his mother's stoked-up fury, it was more than likely he would retaliate – if not now, then most certainly sometime in the future.

Senzangakhona gazed unseeing down the length of esiKlebeni, deep-seated guilt and resentment prodding at him like an aching tooth.

'I should have had the whelp and his mother disposed of long ago,' he muttered. 'Once this business is over, I might just consider it.'

On presenting himself with a possible long-term solution to the problem, he allowed himself to relax a little. After a bit, he noticed that it felt a little cooler, more comfortable.

Glancing up, he saw that the white cloud had not only grown in size, but had moved to a more commanding position. A thin veil of opalescent mist now covered the face of the sun.

On the far side of the arena, the young woman called Jabulile undid the ends of the piece of cloth wrapped round her upper body. Leaning forward so as not to dislodge the baby nestling in the curve of her back, she gently brought him round to her naked breast. She smiled as the child's tiny mouth groped for her engorged brown nipple.

At her side was a small boy. About four years of age, his only adornment was a string of red beads around his protruding little belly. Unusually for a boy of his age, his hair had been allowed to grow long and fell to his shoulders in a nimbus of tight curls.

Lost in concentration, thumb in mouth, his dark eyes were fixed on the drummers as they began to beat out their rhythms on the huge tribal drums.

After a while, his thumb came out of his mouth. He bent his small legs at the knees and began to bob up and down. Soon the rest of his body took up the rhythm, his small round buttocks and stamping feet compounding the beat and making his mop of hair bounce on his shoulders. A delighted smile stretched from ear to ear.

People nearby laughed and called out to him in encouragement. His young mother glanced down at her four-year old son.

'Eh, Langani,' she said, flashing him a brilliant smile. 'See how well you dance! If I wasn't feeding your brother, I would join in – so you'll just have to wait for your father to come.'

Just then, a plump woman with hair standing out around her head in stiff plaits stepped out of the crowd. Wreathed in smiles, she greeted the young mother, clucking and smiling over the baby at her breast.

Ruefully, Jabulile rubbed the small of her back. The child, six months old already, was getting heavier by the day.

'We should sit down while you are feeding him,' her friend suggested. Jabulile's grateful smile signalled her agreement.

Four-year old Langani, with eyes and ears only for the beat of the drums, did not notice that his mother had moved away a little. Caught up in the spell of the insistent, pounding rhythms, he went on dancing.

Senzangakhona shot a sideways glance at the *umutsha* which lay at hand ready for presentation.

The softest of calf skin had been used for the *ibeshu*, the rear flap covering the buttocks, while the front part was decorated with luxurious 'tails' of animal pelt; in this case twisted strips of Samango monkey fur and spotted civet. By anyone's standards, it was a fine piece of craftsmanship.

He'd grudged using such fine materials, but accepted that he had no real choice in the matter. Eyes would be on him, probing for any signs of weakness or abuse of traditional Zulu customs and tribal law.

As always, his sister Mkabayi had been his most outspoken critic, openly voicing what others would not dare say to his face.

'Play the game with as good grace as you can,' she'd said, leaning towards him, her musky smell overpowering at close quarters, 'then either rid your mind of the accursed boy and his mother – or find a way to rid us of them for good.'

Her black eyes had bored into his. 'One way or the other, *i-tshaka* must be handled carefully, or the entire house of Zulu will live to regret it. Take heed of my words, brother King.'

Senzangakhona had flinched at the use of the derogatory term used to describe the boy who was, after all, flesh of his flesh and blood of his blood. But, as usual, he'd made no attempt to remonstrate with his fiery sister.

'*i-tshaka*' was a term commonly used to describe a parasitical intestinal insect. Coined in a flare of resentment against the ill-planned babe still in his mother's belly, the shameful name had stuck to the infant as burrs cling to an animal's coat.

He turned his head to where Mkabayi was sitting a few yards away in the shade of a fig tree. With her dark lustrous skin and hair arranged in extravagant, stiff-plaited coils, her bearing was poised and regal. Sister or not, though, the picture that instantly sprang to mind was of that fast-striking and most deadly of snakes, the black mamba.

Scanning the faces of those around her, he sniffed in contempt. Very telling, just who was there, and who wasn't. Usually, very few of the royal clan, including Mkabayi, would have bothered to attend such a ceremony, but today – *snarling jackals to a bloodied carcase*, he thought sourly.

A frenetic burst of drumming heralded the start of the ceremony. His attention shifted to where the *izinyanga* stood flicking their fly whisks, ready to begin. Wisps of smoke from burning herbs rose into the still, hot air.

Senzangakhona had made it clear that under no circumstances would he come down to the arena to present the garment in person. He would remain seated at the brow of the hill and the boy would have to approach him to formally receive the *umutsha*.

Sitting back, he congratulated himself on suggesting such a cunning move. Not only would he neatly achieve what was expected of him, both as a father and a king, the boy would not be disgraced, and the risk of him becoming a threat in later life greatly reduced.

A sly smile tugged at the corners of his mouth. In order to receive the prized *umutsha*, though, the boy would be forced to run the gauntlet beneath the scathing gaze of the royal family from whom he'd been banished.

Surely the unfortunate youth would be so overawed by their aura of power and authority that it would prevent him from trying to challenge the royal house of Zulu in the future? Senzangakhona relaxed into the pliable softness of the rush matting. *If only it weren't so damnably hot!*

From behind the veil of cloud, the sun continued to shrivel the air and suck out every drop of moisture. Even the dust and the flies seemed to have settled, too exhausted to rise.

When he next glanced up, he noticed that the wayward cloud was much larger, and its underbelly had changed to a sullen dark grey shot through with red.

Out on the edge of the crowd, the small boy called Langani had wandered a little way off from where his mother was laughing and talking with her friend.

Although he could still see her, his world had contracted into a very small space, within it only the insistent beat of the drums, the feel of the earth beneath his feet and the moving and swaying of his child's body. His small head with its mop of tangled curls nodded and shook in time to the rhythms.

If anyone had been watching him, they would have seen that his eyes were closed and he was smiling, as if he were listening to something far away, something that made him happy.

The heavy silence and lack of frenetic drumming snapped the king back into wakefulness. His head jerked up. Bleary eyed, he looked around.

Muttering, he struggled into an upright position, resentment stabbing at him. How long have these fools been watching me snore open-mouthed, dribbling down my chin like an infant, he fumed. For a moment he was tempted to get up and storm out, putting an end to it all.

Down below in the arena, the izinyanga were hovering nervously, their fly whisks twitching. The tribal drums had fallen silent, their sweating drummers waiting for the royal signal to continue.

Realising it was much too late for any futile gestures on his part, Senzangakhona waved a petulant hand. The sonorous voices of the medicine men rose and fell as the rites of passage which would herald the passing of the symbol of manhood from father to son got underway.

His heart beat a tattoo against his ribs. Very soon now, the boy he hadn't seen for years would appear. What would he look like? Who did he take after, his mother or himself?

Anxiety clutched at him. What if the boy's mother, that head-strong bitch from hell, demanded he be given his rightful place at esiKlebeni? He could just hear the words fall from that large over-generous mouth of hers.

'*After all, haven't you, his blood father, publicly acknowledged his right to receive the umutsha from you? And if so, why should he not be allowed to take his place at your side?*'

In such an eventuality, a massive family feud would break out. The stability of the whole Senzangakhona clan would be threatened. First, there would be bitter confrontation between himself and Bukusa, his eldest son and heir apparent.

After that, his sister Mkabayi who had always hated the boy, would most certainly fly into one of her rages and try to gouge his eyes out. And then there was Mudli, his brother, the one who had crafted the cruel name of *itshaka* in the first place –

Suddenly the world around him shrank and became darker. Panic licked at him. *My eyes…my eyes! Have I gone blind?*

Seconds later he realised that nothing cataclysmic had happened to his eyesight. What *had* changed, however, was the colour and position of the previously static cloud. It was now an ominous black colour and stood almost directly overhead, blotting out the sun. Even the light had changed to a strange bronze, overshot with red.

The *izinyanga* ceased chanting. An eerie quiet had settled over the heart of esiKlebeni. Senzangakhona felt a shiver of superstitious dread run through him. Was it just his imagination, or had the brooding shades of the ancestors edged closer?

He dashed a swift glance down into the arena. Empty now of eager participants, only the medicine men remained.

It was then he became aware of eyes on him, drilling a hole in his skull. Turning his head, he intercepted the venomous look directed at him by his sister. She was not known as '*impika,* the wild cat' for nothing, he thought. The angry scowl on her handsome face reminded him of the ferocious, spitting creature after which she'd been named.

She made an abrupt gesture towards the empty parade ground. *Where is he? Where is your misbegotten offspring?*

Then he saw her body go rigid, her eyes riveted on someone who had just appeared out of the crowd below. His eyes swivelled back down to the arena. A strangulated croak broke from him. *He should have known the she-devil would not be far from her cub. . .*

Nandi, his former wife, had timed her appearance well, knowing that all eyes would be on her, especially his. Senzangakhona felt his heart contract, as if squeezed by a giant hand.

Against all expectations, the mother of his children was still a beautiful woman, tall and full breasted – a tawny lioness with rather sharp fangs and claws, as he recalled.

Though not dressed in Mkabayi's finery or adorned with brass ornaments and cascades of beads, Nandi's bearing and the set of her head was no less imperious.

At her side was Nomcoba, his daughter, the second of their children. The small boy holding her hand was obviously the product of another marriage.

His glance slid back to his former wife. She was probably aware he was watching her, but her icy stare gave nothing away.

The crowds stood silent, waiting with bated breath for the next step of the drama to unfold. Tension began to build.

When a tall, well-built youth stepped out of the crowd and strode to Nandi's side, a rustling sigh murmured its way through the crowds. A stab of pain lanced through Senzangakhona's eyeballs, and the sour taste of last night's beer rose in his throat. He regarded his alienated son with mixed emotions.

About fourteen years of age, the youth was naked except for the traditional *umncedo*, the sheath covering the male genitals. His body was well-developed; his arms, shoulders and legs muscular and rippling with health, his skin gleaming in the sultry light.

For a moment, a flicker of male pride stirred in Senzangakhona's breast. Angrily, he thrust it aside, resentment warring with paternal instinct. As he looked at him more closely, his heart sank.

Trouble oozed from every line, every pore of the youth's body. The whelp was not the only son he had sired, Senzangakhona thought sourly – but surely the most difficult and aggravating of them all.

When Nandi took hold of her son's arm and tilted her head towards him, her lips moving rapidly, it was with some satisfaction that he noted the stiffening of the youth's body and the stubborn way he shook himself free of her grip.

His eyes flicked to his former wife. Oh, how well he knew that set of the head, the squaring of those magnificent shoulders. *So, bane of my life, you are not having everything your own way!*

A spurt of humour bubbled up in him. The glance he shot at the boy could almost have been construed as paternal. His mood much improved, he gestured to the *izinyanga* to begin. The drums began a slow beat, a thrumming background to the start of the ceremony.

When the youth was summoned to come forward, he did all that was asked of him, kneeling down and bending his head as if praying.

The King's attention gravitated back to where Nandi was standing on the edge of the crowd. His eyes lingered on the generous lines of her bosom and shapely hips, the full lips that promised so much. *Aiii, still so much a woman, in spite of your fractious nature…*

Memories of their better times, the times of passion began to filter through his defences. It was only when the tempo of the drums changed abruptly that the Zulu King snapped out of his lust-fuelled reverie. As he looked around, a frown creased his sweating brow.

The ceremony seemed to have come to an end. His eyes raked the empty arena, looking for the boy. Where was he?

It was only then he realised what was happening. Not only had the youth left the arena before the ceremony was over but was actually striding up the hill, heading straight towards him.

He snorted in anger. How dare the impudent young dog turn his back on the ceremony! His irritation was short-lived, however. Something relentless in the way the figure was forging its way uphill made itself felt.

A ripple of disquiet ran through him, making his nostrils quiver. *Lucky you've nowhere to conceal a weapon – otherwise I might think you were planning to kill me…*

Chiding himself for being a fool, he glanced quickly around to reassure himself that his personal guards were at hand. Only thirty yards or so separated them now. The youth drew level with the Senzangakhona family members sitting in the dappled shade, but passed by without a sideways glance.

The Zulu ruler's lips twitched. The snub to the family had not been lost on him. Undeniably, he was a Senzangakhona – the handsome features, the determined set of the mouth, the scowl. No denying the blood line, the stamp of the royal house of Zulu.

Again, a grudging flame of pride sprang to life. The boy was no coward. Stories had come to him over the years of how he had protected the cattle in his care; killing snakes and warding off hyenas, even sending a whole pride of lions scuttling for cover.

Senzangakhona flicked a sideways glance at the prized *umutsha*. Best do it quickly, he thought. After that, it is done, my final duty to you.

The youth was only a few yards away now. He was taller than Senzangakhona had expected, his body more developed, muscles rippling below the well-oiled skin. *Almost a man...*

For an instant, he considered getting to his feet to greet him, but pushed the treacherous thought away. Instead, with a flick of his hand, he indicated a nearby aide to instruct his son to pay the respect due to him as his King, and prostrate himself face down on the ground.

To his consternation, the boy ignored both the aide and the command. The eyes that raked his face held no trace of fear, anger, or even much curiosity.

A sudden, quick intake of breath came from people close enough to see what had happened. Never in their lives had they seen anyone defy the Nkosi, let alone raise their eyes to his without being bidden!

A flush of hot blood rose to Senzangakhona's face. Stabs of pain skewered his left eyeball, making his head throb. Outcast son or not, had he forgotten where he was, or who he was? He had no rights or privileges here. With a snap of his fingers, he could have him beaten or dragged away by the royal slayers –

Somewhere below, a cockerel crowed, its raucous shrilling piercing the hush which had fallen over esiKlebeni. A ripple of superstitious fear ran through the people in the royal entourage.

The Zulu ruler forced himself to look directly at Shaka, his son. The brief brief responsive flicker in the black eyes alerted

him to the emotions lurking beneath the youth's outward composure. He found it hard to look away, his gaze imprisoned by the
uncanny strength of will he saw reflected there.

A shock of alarm ran through him. In a few years time this
outcast would be a force to be reckoned with. What he had seen
in his eyes was more than just a flash of fiery temperament; more
than the age-old clash between father and son. No, there was
something else there, an extraordinary power, an indomitable,
ruthless force.

Senzangakhona struggled off the pile of mats and heaved
himself upright. *This had to be ended, and quickly...*Snapping out a
curt order for the *umutsha* to be brought to him, he snatched the
garment from the terrified servant.

The tension surrounding father and son was palpable, quiver-
ing on the air. Reluctant to make further eye contact, he mumbled
the few words he could remember of the ceremony. Then, with as
much dignity as he could muster, thrust out the garment in the
youth's general direction. All was still, the air sultry and tasting of
old, stale fears. The first stirrings of unease began to filter down
from the royal family on the hill.

Senzangakhona waited, beads of sweat trickling down below
the circlet of padded leopard skin. *Take it, take it,* he prayed, hoping no one would see his hands trembling. *Take it and be gone. . .*

Long moments ticked by. Still the soft calfskin with its fine, twisted tassels of animal tails remained unclaimed. The King shook the
garment irritably and addressed the boy for the first time.

'What are you waiting for?' he hissed. 'You have come far
enough to receive it. *Take it, now – and go!*'

The youth called *i-tshaka* said nothing, merely continued to
observe his father as he would a stranger, his eyes remote and
cold. Then he shook his head, his lips forming the silent, single
word of refusal.

Stunned, the Zulu ruler stared at him in disbelief. Near-naked
and bearing nothing in his hands, the boy presented a stark image
of the dispossessed, unwanted prince that he was.

Why then did Senzangakhona, the absolute ruler of the Zulus, clothed in the leopardskin and regalia of his high rank, have the feeling that he was the lesser of the two, his power inferior to that of this stubborn boy who also had his blood and that of their Zulu ancestors running through his veins?

The young man looked steadily back at him, his black eyes riveted on the man who, father or not, also held the power of life or death over him. Then, in an unmistakable gesture of rejection, he brushed his hands together, as if wiping away something offensive, every line in his body re-inforcing his contempt, both for the garment and the man offering it to him.

Senzangakhona stood as if frozen, the rejected *umutsha* clutched in his sweating hands. Gasps of disbelief rose around them. It was unheard of for a youth, *any* youth, to refuse the garment of manhood, but for the son of a King to do so –

A burst of wailing broke out, and women began to cover their heads in fear.

Then the youth, who had been so cruelly named *itshaka, the beetle,* smiled an open, generous smile, his teeth white against the gleam of oiled skin. Shaking his head, he brushed his hands together once more, in a gesture of final and utter dismissal of both the prized garment and the man who had fathered him.

'*Indaba ipilele,*' Shaka said softly. 'It is over, finished.'

Turning his back on Senzangakhona, his courtiers and servants alike, he set off back down the hill, each step taking him further away from the crippling humiliation he had so successfully managed to reverse.

He did, however, slow down long enough to run a dispassionate eye over the members of the Senzangakhona family who were gathered in the shade. A nod of the head to each of his blood relatives was followed by a swift glance of appraisal, almost as if he were committing their stunned faces to memory.

His blood aunt, Mkabayi, shot to her feet, her bracelets and necklaces clinking, ready to claw his eyes out, but his gaze passed over her, dismissing her as easily he had all the others.

Then, with the mocking smile still on his lips, he went on his way down the slope to look for his mother in the dust bowl that was the heart of esiKlebeni.

Nandi melted away into the crowd with her children, not knowing whether to laugh or cry. Two maddening male creatures, the young bull and the old one butting heads with each other; only it was much more serious than that.

In some ways, what her elder son, Shaka, had done was worse than she had feared – in other ways, much less.

As his mother, she was all too familiar with the simmering hurt raging inside him as he struggled with a renewed sense of manhood. The idea of being presented with its symbol by a man he despised more than any other, had only served to inflame his sense of injustice and inner questioning about who he was and what he stood for.

Up to the last moment, she had pleaded with him to shun the ceremony altogether and refuse to allow the cursed Senzangakhona clan another opportunity to humiliate him. But never for a moment had she suspected what his plan had been. Laughter bubbled up inside her.

Eh, I wish I had been close enough to see the look on the old goat's face, she thought, not to mention his 'wild cat' sister!

One thing was very clear, however. She would have to get her children back to the safety of Mthethwe lands as soon as possible.

In spite of the heat, a chill of premonition ran through her. Her first-born son had turned out to be stronger and more powerful than she had ever imagined, but where his degree of certainty came from, she was not sure.

All she knew was that the man he was fast becoming would refuse to run from danger if it came looking for him; nor would he brook any interference if someone tried to stand in his way.

The storm came without warning out of a clear blue sky – clear that is, except for the towering cloud of cumulus, which had been growing larger as the day progressed. Now it was moving to menace the noon-day sun, a dark rider of the gods' displeasure.

Suddenly, there was no more blue sky. Within moments, all the light had disappeared, sucked into a vortex of darkness. An eerie dusk had fallen. A gigantic clap of thunder split the heavens, a monstrous crack which made the ground tremble. People clapped their hands to their ears while small children sobbed and clutched at their mothers.

Dazzling flashes of lightning tore out of the skies above esiKlebeni, fizzing, crackling and jumping along the hard-baked ground like demons. Terrified people rushed here and there, not really knowing where to go to find safety.

Cattle grazing by the river bellowed in terror and set off galloping clumsily, their udders swinging. The herd boys raced after them, oblivious to their own safety. The beasts had to be protected at all costs, for they were the backbone of their people's wealth and security.

By the time Shaka reached the parade ground there was no sign of his mother and the younger children, and he knew she would have already moved with them to a safer place, preferably outside the gates of esiKlebeni.

He looked up at the streaks of jagged light and smiled. Senzangakhona was no doubt cowering beneath the storm, sulking and licking his wounds, no danger to them as yet.

On the far side of the arena, the small boy called Langeni had stopped dancing. His eyes fluttered open, and he looked slightly dazed, as if he'd just wakened from a deep sleep. He cast a wondering glance around him as if seeking the vanished rhythms, but the drums had been abandoned, the drummers gone, running for shelter like all the others.

A vivid blue flash lit up the parade ground. Startled, the little boy blinked and looked up as if to see where it was coming from.

Oblivious to the chaos around him, his chubby hands reached up as if to catch the display of naked power tearing the skies apart.

A great wind came spiralling out of nowhere, bending trees and snapping off branches. People were bowled over and tumbled like spindrift across the dusty ground, shrieking in fear. Torrents of rain and bullets of hail came slanting down, bouncing off the ground as icy and sharp as needles.

Spasms of superstitious horror ran through the fleeing crowds. *The amadhlozi are angry, but with whom – the father, the son, or both?*

Another thunderous clap and a forked streak of blinding light descended to earth. The small boy laughed out loud, delighted by its spectacular sound and fury. His bare feet splashed up and down in the mud, a dance of innocent abandonment, rain drops clinging to his lashes and beading his mop of ringlets.

His young mother, Jubilele, frantically pushed her way through the fleeing people, calling out his name, her voice snatched away by the winds. 'Langani! Langani, where are you?'

A terrified woman jolted into her, causing the swaddled baby on her back to scream as it sensed the fear and panic.

By then, Shaka was halfway across the arena. With his eyes half-closed against the rain, he was heading for the main gates of esiKlebeni, fully intending to be well clear of the accursed place by the time the storm lessened.

A blurred movement ahead caught his eye. Something about its size and shape made him stop. Wiping the rain water from his eyes, he peered into the gloom.

Through the sluicing rain, he could see it was a small child, a boy. He was quite alone, probably separated from his mother in the crush of fleeing people. Over and above the sound of the hissing rain, Shaka heard what he took to be the sound of crying or stifled sobbing.

Concern for the lost child over-rode his desire for a speedy retreat from esiKlebeni. Changing direction, he strode towards the small figure.

Standing with his hands above his head, naked except for the string of red beads around his belly was a boy about four years of age, his unusually long hair forming a spiky nimbus of wet ringlets.

Shaka wiped the water from his face and took a closer look at him. The *toto*, far from crying, seemed to be actually enjoying the crackling flashes of light and earth-shaking thunder.

What he'd taken to be cries of distress were, in fact, chuckles of laughter. And what was more – the child was actually *dancing*, dancing and clapping his hands while the mud spattered around his small body.

Intrigued, Shaka laughed aloud, his teeth a flash of white in the dusky light. Moving slowly so as not to startle him, he moved into the small boy's line of vision then squatted down so that their eyes were almost level.

The child, momentarily distracted by his sudden appearance, stopped in mid-dance and stared back at him. The large dark eyes searched Shaka's face and lingered curiously on the crescent-shaped scar on his cheekbone. After a few moments, Shaka held out his hands.

'*Ninjani, mdodo.* How are you, man? *Uthandau kudansa nami?* Would you like to dance with me?

Langani surveyed him for a moment longer. Then a quick smile lit up his chubby face. Reaching out, he shyly placed his hands in those of the youth who had so recently spat in the eye of the powerful man on the hill, the man who was the King of the tribe to which they both belonged.

Shaka said, '*Woza*, come, let's dance.' A white-toothed smile of sheer joy lit up the little face.

In the eerie dusk, Shaka, the fourteen-year old who had just come into his own and the lively little boy with the mass of curling hair and a string of scarlet beads around his belly, began to dance.

They had no need of drums to create the rhythms. The atmosphere pulsed with the energy generated by the massive storm raging overhead. The air was full of super-charged ozone which seemed to crackle and spit as it was discharged into the atmosphere. Caught up in the excitement of the moment, they stamped their feet on the ground, laughing and hooting as gouts of mud leapt up and spattered their bodies.

'*Asihambe*! Let's go!' Shaka caught the child up bodily in his arms, twirled him upside down a few times for good measure then set him on his shoulders. Bouncing him up and down, the small buttocks thumping on his shoulder blades, the child's shrieks of laughter rang out over the bedlam. The dance went on, both youth and small boy revelling in the moment and the rhythms of the storm.

Drawn by the sound of their laughter, Langani's mother stepped blindly out of the sluicing rain, peering this way and that, the baby on her back drenched and sobbing. Catching sight of her little one perched on the shoulders of a near-naked stranger she let out a high-pitched shriek of fear and clapped her hands to her mouth.

When Shaka swung around, her fear turned to hysteria. When she saw who had hold of her child, she clutched her head in her hands, and wailed in high-pitched terror, setting the baby on her back screaming.

Shaka stopped in mid-dance with Langeni perched on his shoulders. At first he was puzzled. Why was the young woman, who was clearly the *toto's* mother, so afraid? Her son was safe.

As understanding began to dawn on him, his brows drew together in a frown. So, not only was this young mother afraid of the storm and of losing her son, she was also afraid of *him* – or rather, of who he was, or what she believed him to be. He could well imagine what was being said about him following the confrontation with his father.

Shaka looked at the despairing young woman then nodded to show her he understood. Gently, he swung her son's rain-soaked little body down from his shoulders and set him on his feet. Squatting down beside him so that their eyes were more or less level, he took the child's cold hand in his.

'Eh, little brother,' he said, giving him a nudge in his mother's direction, 'you must go with *umama* now, enough dancing for one day.'

The child's lips begin to quiver, his face falling in disappointment. Gently, Shaka disengaged the small fingers which were clutching at his, not wanting the game to end.

Her eyes dark pools of fear, Jubilele bent down and pressed her child against her trembling body. Still sobbing, she smoothed the wet hair off his face before stumbling hurriedly away, clutching him by the hand.

Langani turned and glanced back to where Shaka was standing in the slanting rain. Taking his thumb from his mouth, the four-year old gave him a small wave.

Then he smiled, a tremulous, tearful smile of remembered joy, before trotting away with his mother, leaving Shaka with only the flickering lightning and the dying storm for company.

Part I

One

The white man, his horse and his gun were the first of their kind to be seen in that distant part of Africa. The horseman, who was called Robert Cowan, had stopped briefly at a remote mission station on his way north.

Afterwards, as they stood watching the figure in the saddle dwindle away into the mirrored distortions on the horizon, one of the Christian brothers was heard to remark that Cowan had 'the faraway look in his eye of a man in a hurry to meet his destiny.'

Africa is very rarely as uninhabited as it would seem. Observant eyes follow most comings and goings, especially those of strangers. Consequently, Cowan's arrival in the lands of the Hlubi people caused no great surprise because runners had already gone ahead with the news that a frightening stranger was heading their way.

The village headmen feared he was a wizard, a superior kind of sorcerer or a chief of diviners who possessed magic powers. Perhaps he would make rain pour from the sky or bring down thunder and lightning on those who displeased him.

The superstitious villagers fled, leaving an ox behind as a sac-rificial gift, hoping the stranger would pass on by. Next day, they found the ox grazing by the side of the track, unharmed. And, wonder of wonders! Where the strange man had lain down to sleep, they found glass beads in all colours of the rainbow, also brass necklaces, bracelets, mirrors and other trinkets.

Chief Bulane of the Hlubi people, being an astute man, made the stranger welcome in his village. The bearded *abelungu* was regarded as a marvel, and people came from far and wide to peep at him from a safe distance.

The village children would stare wide-eyed at him for hours on end, taking in in every inch of his pale, sun-reddened skin, his bushy beard and moustaches, and the breeches, laced-up leather boots and sweat-stained hat with the wide brim. They circled his black stallion, exclaiming on its size and smell, laughing and giggling when it lift-ed its tail and left great dollops of dung on the ground.

Most fearsome of all, however, was the man's magic stick. It could spit fire and thunder from its long mouth and if he pointed it at an animal or bird, the creature would fall down dead, even if some distance away.

A man called Godongwana also lived in Chief Bulane's village. A few years earlier, he had fled there for sanctuary after his father, the king of the powerful Mthethwe tribe, had wanted him dead. The mother of the king's second son, Mawewe, had come to the old man whispering that Godongwana was secretly plotting to kill him and seize control of the tribe.

After being accused of such a heinous act by his own father, the man now called Godongwana had no choice but to flee his homeland.

When he returned to the village after a day's hunting, he was in-trigued to find Cowan there. Being intelligent and open-minded, Godongwana whiled away many pleasant hours with the white man, the *abelungu*. Though they did not speak each other's lan-guage, the two men learned a great deal from one another by gestures, snatches of speech and drawings scrawled in the dust with the point of a stick. During their long, companionable silences, they smoked or enjoyed a pinch of snuff.

Some of the bolder village women were also full of curiosity about the *abelungu*. They would make ribald comments, and giggle behind their cupped hands, cackling and shrieking when their audacity reached new heights.

'Hau! See his fine buttocks, round and fat like water melons,' they would shriek. 'See how his body hair pokes out of his clothing on his chest. What do you think, sisters? Is his *umtondo* covered with it, like that of the baboon?"

It was just as well the man did not know the meaning of the words, Godongwana thought, as he scolded the women, threatening to beat them, until they ran off, screaming and laughing, to the comparative safety of their huts, their naked breasts bobbing as they ran.

When the disowned son of a chief learned of Cowan's people far to the south, he was intrigued to hear about their great King who lived in a far-off land across the sea.

Godongwana felt the hairs on the back of his neck rise when Cowan told him of the soldiers belonging to this King-across-the-sea who wore bright red coats with buttons of shining brass and carried fire sticks, just like the one Cowan carried, which spat out fire and death.

Strange and wonderful vessels enabled the white men to travel long distances over the sea. These silent demons were driven by the power of the winds filling their great white wings. They also spat out iron balls of fire. Godongwana's mouth dried in fear when he learned that these terrors could be unleashed without the *abelungu* ever setting foot on dry land.

However, he put all these pieces of information carefully to one side for future reference. Something more urgent had begun to claim his attention.

After he reclaimed his tribe from his father, Chief Jobe, as he fully intended to, he would enter into trade with another group of *abelungu*, the Portuguese, who lived to the north. The people of the King-across-the-sea were too far away for him to trade with – but the Portuguese were not.

They would provide him with supplies of the beautiful beads, brass bells, mirrors and trinkets he had received as gifts from his white man, Cowan.

These wonderful things would add to his prestige and provide him with a powerful bargaining tool.

All too soon, the time came for Cowan to leave. The children ran on their skinny legs alongside his horse, while packs of flea-bitten dogs snapped and barked in excitement.

Godongwana was sorry to see Cowan go, because he had enjoyed his company, but his mind was racing ahead, calculating how he could make contact with the Portuguese who lived beyond the Lembombo Mountains.

The people were sad as they watched the rider and his horse disappear into the distance. Soon all that remained of him were his horse's hoof prints on the dusty road and the gifts he had left behind.

When he was brought news of Cowan's death, Godongwana was angry, and suspected that he had been killed by the Qwabe for the wonderful things he had in his possession.

And then he thought that since he, Godongwana, had been the true friend of the white man, it was only right that the fire stick should belong to him. This being so, he took it as an omen that the ancestors were on his side, and that the time of *isipiwo*-destiny, was upon him.

So he retrieved the gun and returned to his own land. His father now being dead, he deposed his brother Mawewe and became King of the mighty Mthethwe nation. After that, he took back his real name, which was Dingiswayo.

At last he could start to live the vivid, all-encompassing dream, which had stayed with him during his years of exile. It was to first unite, and then forge into a single political system, all the Nguni-speaking clans to the south and west of the Black Umfolozi River.

In his vision, Dingiswayo saw only one great leader standing at the heart of this empire. And naturally, there was absolutely no doubt in his mind as to who that person should be.

Among the lesser entities, however, was a small and insignificant clan known as Zulu, the People of the Heavens. In the first flush of success, Dingiswayo could not possibly realise the significance this would have for the future of south-east Africa.

Nor could he know that it would be his destiny to play a vital role in the subsequent rise of an even greater power than he.

Two

Five years later

It was the end of a hard day's march. Beyond the Tugela River, the setting sun was a glittering ball striking fire from the tips of the warriors' spears.

The straggling lines of men trailed back for a long way. Dust hung over the columns, thick and acrid, clogging eyes and throats. The rank smell of sweat was in the air and clouds of flies buzzed around the men, drawn by the sickly-sweet smell of blood and pus.

Already the shadows of evening were creeping in from the horizon. Very soon the evening star, *Komotsho*, would appear above the tops of the bee-hive huts visible in the distance.

The first star of the night was always a welcome sign; a harbinger of cool night air, the smell of wood smoke and the promise of ease and rest. Inevitably, there would be those to whom the evening star would bring no joy, and the wailing and keening of the mothers, wives and sisters of those who had not returned would fill the air with sadness.

King Dingiswayo, at the head of the *Izi-cwe* and *Yengondlovu* regiments, felt both sorrow and pride for those they had to leave behind on the plains. Silent mounds in the long grass, covered by their shields, their bellies slit open so that their spirits could roam free.

The familiar shapes of the bee-hive huts appeared, dark against the rose-tint of fading skies. A pack of stringy dogs rushed forward, barking, yapping and stopping to scratch in excitement.

The rituals of bathing and purification would come first, for it was forbidden for warriors to resume normal life until they had been cleansed in both body and spirit after so much spilling of blood. The comradeship around the fires would ease their weariness. There would be sorrow and shaking of heads over lost comrades, the telling and re-telling of their brave deeds, and how they had died.

The main feast would be followed by celebration and dancing to commemorate their recent rout of the Buthelezi army. A sense of urgency spread down the lines.

In spite of the long day's march, Dingiswayo looked every inch a king. A tall, dignified man in early middle age, his face bore the stamp of one who was open-minded and fair, a diplomat of the first order.

Flanked by his commanders, he moved on through the press of warriors. Ahead of him a group of cadets stood with their eyes lowered, waiting for him. A smile flickered at the corners of Dingiswayo's mouth when he saw them. 'How pleased I am with these fearless young lions,' he remarked to his aide, 'they are indeed true warriors.'

Although the compliment was sincerely meant for all of them, his eyes came to rest on the one he was really looking for. Aged about twenty summers or so, the young warrior stood several inches over six feet, the sweeping plumes of the black widow-bird feathers of his headdress adding to his impressive height.

The face below the band of civet skin and dark feathers was strong, even in repose. In the hand held loosely by his side was a short spear, more like a stabbing sword than the usual long, throwing assegai favoured by the army generals. Unlike the others, he wore no ox-hide sandals, preferring to fight barefoot. But it was neither the lack of footwear nor the weapon that held King Dingiswayo's attention.

In this young warrior, he believed he had found someone incomparable, someone with an unusually high degree of intelligence and courage, an undeniable leader of men.

In the final phase of the recent battle, Dingiswayo had advanced his regiments to within a hundred yards of the massed ranks of the Buthelezi. In the time-honoured way, he had dispatched a messenger to demand their immediate surrender.

According to custom, the opposition replied with a stream of abuse. This was the signal for any outstanding warrior to step forward and engage in single combat, as a prelude to the main battle. This would be a test of champions, a ritual only for those with the necessary courage to fight to the death.

Almost immediately, a tall, muscular Buthelezi, a seasoned warrior bearing many battle scars, strode out and stood with his feet apart, taunting the enemy. Holding his shield and spear aloft in dramatic and provocative pose, he pivoted around on the balls of his feet, baring his body defiantly. Apart from the *umutsha,* the short loincloth, his only adornment was the string of leopard's teeth around his neck, visible proof of his bravery.

A groan passed through the ranks of the Mthethwe. Heads began to turn this way and that, searching for a warrior brave enough to rise to the Buthelezi challenge.

Seconds later, a tall, powerfully built figure pushed its way through the ranks of the Mthethwe and into the no-man's land between the two armies. Bar the *um-ncedo,* the foreskin cover, which all males over the age of puberty were obliged to wear, he was naked, his sole concession to battle trimmings being long strips of ox hair around his upper arms.

Undeterred by the thundering of spears on shields and the cat-calls and jeers of the enemy, he took up his place facing the Buthelezi. In one hand, he held a short, stabbing sword; his only protection a small ox-hide shield.

The unknown warrior took a few paces forward and directed a glance of contempt at the Buthelezi champion, his features twisted in a scowl. A ripple of shock ran through the ranks of the Mthethwe. This was no seasoned champion, a warrior of proven experience on the field of battle. The challenger was young, and judging by his lack of insignia, a mere cadet.

Questions as to the identity of the challenger buzzed like agi-tated bees around the regiments. *Who is this young fool who dares to challenge the Buthelezi? Will he bring us victory... or only disgrace?*

An *induna* brusquely cleared a path so that Dingiswayo could have a clear view of the proceedings. The Mthethwe king leaned forward on his shield and keenly surveyed the scene.

Caught by surprise at the lack of the usual courtesies, the Buthelezi champion jerked into action. Stepping forward, he drew back his arm and threw his long spear directly at his opponent, according to protocol. It was immediately deflected by the Mthethwe challenger's small shield, while the man behind it re-fused to flinch or step aside.

Instead, he bent down, calmly untied his sandals and swiftly kicked them aside. Then, ignoring the usual courtesies, he sprint-ed forward, his bare feet flying over the rough ground, impervious to stones and thorns.

A tremendous roar burst from the throats of the Mthethwe army as their hero began to close the distance between himself and the Buthelezi. Only thirty yards or so separated them now.

As he closed the gap, the near-naked figure roared out a defi-ant challenge. Easily deflecting a second spear, he charged towards the startled champion without losing pace or slackening his speed. Now they were almost face to face.

Deftly, he hooked the Buthelezi shield aside with the edge of his smaller one, exposing the man's vulnerable belly. Using his short assegai as a stabbing weapon, he plunged the blade up through the rib cage.

The incredulous Buthelezi forces watched as the sharp tip of the blade pierced their man's back and protruded through his ribs. A moan of horror rippled through their ranks. Their champion's knees buckled. He began to fall, his hands clutching the shaft of the lethal weapon.

A gush of bright arterial blood pumped from the dying man's mouth. He slumped to the ground, his hands still desperately trying to pluck out the fatal blade. Moments later, he was dead, his shocked eyes staring sightlessly into the ground.

A single war cry issued from Dingiswayo's warrior, chilling in its ferocity. The near-naked victor leaped astride the body, and turned it over. Placing a bare foot on the dead man's chest, he grasped the shaft of the weapon with both hands and pulled it from the still-warm flesh.

Blood dripped down the shaft and spattered on the ground. Turning to face Dingiswayo's regiments, shield in one hand and bloody assegai in the other, he raised them both in triumphant salute.

'*Ngadla!! I have eaten!!*'

Now the identity of the young man became clear. Buza, the commander of the *izi cwe* regiment, expelled his pent-up breath in a loud hiss of approval.

Shaka kaSenzangakhona, who else could it be!

Again the thundering war cry rang out. At that moment, it was unclear if the horrifying blend of meaning was made on behalf of the weapon, or the man wielding it. But there was more to come.

Not even allowing the stunned Buthelezis time to retrieve the body of their champion according to custom, the defiant figure turned the full glare of his attention on the massed regiments facing him.

The hubbub of noise died away. The eyes of the new Mthethwe champion scanned the front ranks, probing for signs of weakness. He stood, unmoving, only the tendrils of the oxhair around his upper arms stirring in the hot air.

Dingiswayo swore below his breath; not in anger but in admiration. Fierce anticipation ran like a forest fire through the ranks of the Mthethwe.

With a savage cry, his warrior streaked towards the bewildered Buthelezi. In a state of suspended belief, they stood watching as the relentless figure who had so summarily disposed of their champion raced ever nearer.

Three more figures broke from the ranks and sprinted forward. Dingiswayo recognised them. They were Mgobozi, Nqoboka and Mdlaka, close friends of the young cadet, Shaka. Others began to follow suit and surged forward.

For a moment or two, the Buthelezi front ranks continued to hold. In the face of such opposition, they broke ranks and fled, hotly pursued by the four young warriors and the remainder of Dingiswayo's army.

Standing in the glow of the setting sun, battle-stained and weary, King Dingiswayo gestured towards the young warrior. Buza, the commander of the *izi-cwe* regiment, answered respectfully, 'The men call him '*Nodumehlezi, Sitting Thunder*'. He is the best of my cadets – but a law unto himself, I fear.'

Dingiswayo nodded. The degree of self-command and disregard for danger, the intensity with which he wheeled and ran, far outpacing the others, always intent on some inner plan of his own, was truly inspiring. There was also something else about the young warrior, an uncommon power, a coiled and arresting spirit which had held his attention from the start.

He suppressed a groan. His body was stiffening, and he badly needed to retire to the *isigodlo*, where the women would ease his pain with their soft hands and soothing oils. But it would have to wait.

'His name?' pursued the perceptive Dingiswayo, with an impatient frown. 'I need his true name, man, and that of his tribe.'

'Shaka kaSenzangakhona of the Zulu,' was the answer.

Dingiswayo nodded. He had already heard stories of the young Shaka. Gossip and rumour ran rife in the women's quarters. Apart from that anything else of note came to him through the many confidants and spies who formed an integral part of his court.

The ill-fated presentation ceremony was well-remembered, not only for the unprecedented refusal of the symbol of manhood, but also for the severity of the storm which had broken out almost simultaneously.

Dingiswayo noted with some amusement that Shaka still refused to wear an *umutsha*. His nakedness was covered only by the *um-ncedo* which was the foreskin cover of palm leaves, the minimum requirement for males over the age of puberty.

Not only was this Shaka strong-willed and full of temper, by all accounts, he was also fiercely brave. When he was sixteen, he had killed a black mamba, the most deadly and fast-moving of snakes, after it had bitten a prize bull he was tending.

On another occasion, a leopard had launched itself at him out of a tree. Surrounded by a pack of snarling dogs trying to snap at the cornered beast, he had stood his ground. Then, stepping in close, and holding it off with a club, he had rammed his spear straight into its heart.

Afterwards, he had presented the prized leopardskin to the chief, Ngomane, as a token of his gratitude for giving his family a place to live. By all accounts, his mentor had been totally astonished by the touching generosity of this usually scowling character he'd given sanctuary to.

So, my young lion, Dingiswayo thought. You appreciate loyalty and reward it fittingly, the mark of a decent man.

It came to him then, in a flash of knowing. It was like seeing a version of his younger self during the lonely years of exile he had spent among people not his own. Despising a father who had hated him enough to want to kill him, wandering from place to place, waiting for a sign so he could go home and claim his heritage – in that strange and lucid moment, the eyes of Dingiswayo and the young warrior met. It was unheard of for anyone, let alone an insignificant young warrior, to look into the face of a king directly, if at all. But Dingiswayo held the gaze.

As he looked deep into the bold and fearless eyes, he saw an answering reflection in them, a ripple of energy and raw power, earthed as yet, held in waiting. Too well do I remember that feeling, Dingiswayo thought. There is little, my friend, that I have not already shared with you.

Sensing a slow dawning of recognition in the other, Dingiswayo felt his scalp prickle. His keen intuition told him that his own destiny was somehow linked to that of the young man whose name and legend he now knew.

A cold shiver passed through him. The shades of the young Zulu's ancestors were at his heels, omnipresent and very close. 'I see you, Shaka ka Senzangankhona of the Zulu, I see you,' he said, in the classic gesture of acknowledgement and respect.

The young warrior fell on one knee and bowed his head over his shield. A ripple of envy, quickly subdued, spread through the ranks. King Dingiswayo turned aside and smiled to himself.

Tomorrow, he would see to it that Shaka be given double honours; first, the privilege of leading the warriors in the *giya*, the victory dance; and secondly, promotion to the rank of Captain. It would mean a hundred men at his disposal and a free hand to forge them into warriors after his own heart.

Also, he would approve the praise name the men had given him – '*Nodumehlezi, Sitting Thunder.*' As a final seal of royal approval, he would add another praise name '*Si-gi-di, Greater than a thousand.*'

His friends would also be given promotion and a selection of prize cattle for their part in the rout of the Buthelezi.

These four young men would form a most formidable military leadership, although Shaka of the Zulu would stand head and shoulders above the others, in rank as well as ability.

As he was making his way to his quarters, Dingiswayo glanced up at the night sky. *Komotsho,* the evening star, was glowing steadily against the vastness of the African night, other constellations scattered like diamond dust across the broad expanse of the heavens.

But they were not what caught and held his attention. Beyond the flat-topped acacia trees outside the camp there was a small lake. Mirrored in its placid surface, was the mesmerising reflection of a young full moon rising blood red out of the bush.

He suppressed a shiver of superstitious fear. Beyond the protective fences of thorn and wattle, a horned owl hooted, a long and mournful sound.

Three

T
he kraal of Ngonyama, the Lion, lay in a wild and lonely valley in the lands of the Mponambi. The morning was gloomy after the night's rain, and shrouds of mist rolled eerily through the forests surrounding the clearing.

The tall man's footsteps were muffled as he stepped out of the trees. Black crows cawed out a warning at the approach of the stranger who had travelled far to see Ngonyama, the Lion. Although the man known as the Master of the Blades had the reputation of being the finest smelter and blacksmith in the area, the local people shunned the place as they did all of those reputed to be meddling in the occult.

However, Shaka ka Senzangakhona wanted only the best, and the sinister reputation of the brotherhood suspected of using human fat in the forging of their keenest and most powerful blades had not deterred him from his quest.

Young women surreptitiously observed him from the shadowy interiors of the huts. Their eyes lingered on his well-developed body and the youthful lines of his face. '*Aaii,* but he is truly a giant of a man, so young, so strong.'

By his bearing and powerful physique, he was undoubtedly someone of importance. The three heavy spears he was carrying were also interesting. Both the man and his weapons had an aura of menace and unpredictability about them.

Clad only in a ragged goatskin apron, Ngonyama was squatting before his hut at the opposite end of the kraal, his gnarled hands busy with the burnishing of new spear heads. Only after the stranger was standing before him did he look up.

The Lion's eyes were startlingly youthful, bright black buttons brimming with humour and curiosity, his cheeks and brow bearing the cicatrices of his tribe. Putting the spear heads to one side, he folded his skinny legs beneath him and sank down crosslegged, like an aged stork. He gestured for the stranger to sit down facing him.

Shaka did as he was asked, then greeted him politely. '*Sakubona, baba.*'

Ngonyama's black eyes slid away under his steady gaze and lingered for a moment on the spears the stranger had in his possession.

The customary formal enquiries concerning health and wellbeing followed without either party touching on the matter in hand. Formalities over, Shaka waited for the next stage of the proceedings to begin.

Without appearing to place him under undue scrutiny, the wily blacksmith had carefully taken stock of the stranger who had entered his village. He could be a potential acolyte looking for instruction in the ancient skills, or even a renegade seeking sanctuary where no one would dare to come looking for him. It was wise to be careful.

After an appropriate silence, Ngonyama provided the opening Shaka had been waiting for. 'Have you travelled far, my son?'

'I am one of King Dingiswayo's warriors,' Shaka answered truthfully, though careful to omit his true rank. It did not do to reveal too much in such a situation. 'And I am of the tribe of Zulu,' he added. He then outlined what he desired of the maker of the blades.

'So be it, Zulu,' answered Ngonyama, his decision made. He reached for the spears Shaka had laid before him. After a brief examination of them, he added, 'But it will take time. A new furnace must be made and equipped with the best materials to make sure the iron is superior. The blade must be tempered with the strongest fats.'

Ngonyama flicked a swift glance sideways at his visitor. For a moment, his eyes glinted red, a sinister reminder of his true calling.

Shaka met the sudden slant of inherent evil with the cold contempt he reserved for purveyors of the occult. He nodded, dismissing the matter of cost as being of no significance.

The canny eyes of the Master of the Blades scrutinised the man before him. *By the look of you,* he thought, *I doubt you would fear much in this world – or even the next.*

His senior wife came forward to place food and drink before them as it was their custom to offer hospitality to strangers. Shaka contained his impatience and nodded his thanks to the woman.

After he had eaten, he wiped his fingers and proceeded to the details of design and weight he required for his new weapon, the cost of the blacksmith's services and the length of time he would have to wait.

'The usual throwing spears are too light,' he explained. 'There is always the risk of them breaking. And as for the others...'

He rose to his feet and picked up one of the heavy-bladed spears.

'They are too long and heavy to be used up close,' he explained. 'To thrust a blade between the ribs, or into the stomach or throat of an enemy, I need a new kind of blade, one that is light, but deadly.'

A gasp of horror came from the watchers in the shadows as he brought the blade close to Ngonyama's throat to demonstrate. Oblivious to the on-going drama in the background, Shaka continued his discussion with the master of the blades. The blacksmith nodded, saying nothing, allowing him to speak.

Aaii, my fine warrior, he thought. *You speak wisely. Your assegai blades are only of base metal, things with no spirit or force of their own.*

It was an ancient, yet well-known belief that the fats of animals held supernatural potency if applied in the correct way. However, to those who dabbled in such mysteries, it was universally accepted that human fat was even better.

Ngonyama deviously proposed several alternatives, although hoping this warrior of the Zulu clan would settle for no less than he had suggested at the outset.

Shaka had long since made his decision on that point. 'I have decided. You will make me your finest tempered blade, the very best you can make.'

The eyes of both men met; those of the young warrior and the old, experienced blacksmith.

'Use all the magic you can summon from the very heart of your great skills,' Shaka said, softly. 'I demand no less.'

It had been raining intermittently during the day. As night approached, the dying light shafted through the ridge of black clouds sweeping in from the mountains to cast a leaden glaze over the village.

An air of nervous expectancy hovered over the smiths as they worked the red-hot forge. Shaka, alert as ever to subtle nuances and shifts in behaviour and atmosphere, cautiously moved away from them. Ngonyama remained squatting, fidgeting uneasily with his hammers. Now and again, he cast tense glances into the undergrowth behind him.

Suddenly, the forge spurted. Gouts of flame blazed from its mouth. A low keening rose from the shadows. The blacksmith's assistants moaned in terror and covered their heads with their leather aprons.

Rustling noises and low, throated growls made the hairs spring alert along Shaka's arms. An obnoxious stench, a foul carrion smell of blood and decay drifted out of the darkness.

A long silence followed. Beside him, Ngonyama shook and shuddered, mumbling incoherently. The forge spat out a vicious shower of sparks. The hot air sucked at them, making them glow fiercely.

Beads of sweat burst out on Shaka's forehead. As he suspected, it was time for the final part of the ritual. The Nameless One, the shaman responsible for bringing the secret ingredients surrounding the consecrating of the deadly blades, was very close.

A burst of demented laughter ran round the clearing, making the cattle stir restlessly in their enclosure. The noise ceased as suddenly as it began. Then a voice, as ancient as the black streams that run beneath the earth, croaked out.

'I smell a hidden person. Who is he and what is his desire?'

The rustling came nearer. The stench was stronger now, almost tangible in its cloying thickness. The presence was close now, very close. Impatient to complete the final part of the ritual, Shaka swung round to face it.

A shapeless apparition stood a few feet away from him. Clad in animal skins, the creature's face was hidden by long, matted tufts of hair. Male or female, it was impossible to tell, though Shaka suspected it was male because of its height and the bulk of the shoulders. In its right hand, it carried a stout, polished knobkerrie, and in the left, an ancient goatskin bag.

A pair of keen eyes watched him through the matted hair. As his eyes bored into those of the evil-smelling figure, Shaka made no effort to hide his repugnance.

He suspected that it was one of the dreaded *inswelaboya*, the society of secret murderers and procurers of human fats, livers and other parts that provided the potions and medicines used by many dealers in the occult. Ignoring the stench, he moved closer.

'You, who are called the Nameless One, already know why I am here. I am Shaka and seek a keen blade, ready for the battles to come.'

The voice which answered was smooth, ancient and powerful, like dark water running over the stones, roots and bones buried deep in the earth.

'*Yebo, I know who you are – or will be. Shaka, the greatest Nkosi of them all.*'

The words and the riddle within dropped like heavy stones into the silence. Even the assistants had stopped moaning, Shaka's unexpected confrontation with the shaman having stunned them into silence.

The voice continued. 'You have spoken of the battles you must fight, Nkosi. The day will come when your warriors will spread out across many lands. They will be as the great herds of buffalo and the ground will tremble at their passing. I see a King whose name will be whispered in awe and shouted out in terror by those whose path cross his. The name of Shaka will live forever.'

On hearing this, Shaka's heart leapt with shock. Before he could make a response, the voice croaked, 'The Master of the Blades will make you the weapon you desire. But take heed, because from the first to the last, it will also be your destiny…*to live by the sword and then die by it.*'

A small bundle, wrapped in deerskin was thrown on the ground. It rolled and twitched like a small animal before coming to rest at the feet of Ngonyama. Shaka expelled his breath in a long hiss.

For a moment or two, the sinister figure seemed to hover above the ground, not even touching the earth. One minute it was there, the next it had melted back into the forest leaving only the rancid odour behind.

Ngonyama began to open the small package while carefully shielding what was inside. Shaka caught a brief glimpse of twisted bones and fragments of globules of fat, streaked with blood, before the blacksmith hurriedly hid it in the folds of his leather apron.

In the near darkness, the forge glowed, casting an eerie glow of coppery light around the clearing. The face of Ngonyama was thrown into deep relief, the grooves of age and strain mapped out on it. He snapped out instructions to the assistants still cowering below their aprons

As they scurried off to do his bidding, Shaka spat on the ground to clear the bad taste from his mouth. The stench left in the wake of the purveyor of the unspeakable still hung in the air, cloying and redolent of evil.

The long night passed in the final shaping of the blade to Shaka's satisfaction. Time and again, he insisted on each tiny imperfection being erased, until at last he was completely satisfied.

In his eyes, it was a thing of beauty, with great strength and power in its sweeping lines. Now, all that remained to be done was the final tempering of the blade and its consecration.

A deep hush fell on the clearing. Ngonyama began an incantation using strange words which Shaka did not understand. A lump of dubious-looking fat was placed on the granite anvil by one of the assistants. When the blade was passed over the writhing mass, the fats sizzled and sputtered and oily globules rose into the night sky in gouts of ill-smelling smoke.

Ngonyama completed his chanting then addressed Shaka. 'The spirits are pleased. Listen to the hissing of the flesh, Zulu. It acknowledges the timeless bond between the spirit of the blade and that of its bearer.'

As the blade cooled, the sizzling slowed down. After a while, Ngonyama announced, 'The spirits are satisfied.'

So was Shaka. His eyes lingered on the clean lines of the blade, caressing it as he would a lover. The magic rites were all but over. Only one more remained. He waited, staring into the darkness.

Ngonyama refined and tempered the blade until just before cockcrow. The intricate tapping of his tiny hammers echoed in the silent forest. At last, pale daylight crept through the trees. By the time the first raucous crows stirred in the forest, the blade was ready.

Shaka nodded then rose to his feet, saying nothing. Exhaustion was etched deeply into the face of the Master as he stood back, his work over. The blade gleamed dully in the raw light of dawn, a thing of power and infinite strength. As Shaka grasped the hilt, vibrations ran through his fingers, making him tremble.

He watched as the blade was fixed to a temporary shaft. Almost as much care and attention would be paid to the new shaft as had been lavished on the design and weight of the blade itself. One of the fine hardwoods would be used, to a specific length of his choosing.

A hole would be drilled into it with a red-hot piercing tool then filled with the sticky juice of a bulbous root. The shank of the blade would be inserted into it and firmly glued into place by the same strong juice before strips of tough, pliable bark were bound tightly round it to hold it in place.

Last of all, the skin of the tail of a freshly-slaughtered ox would be pulled over the entire shaft then left to dry and shrink to an iron-hard consistency.

Shaka strode swiftly out through the gates and up to the top of the ridge overlooking the valley. The sun had not yet risen above the horizon. In the east, ridges of gold-tipped clouds spread like ripples of water across the sky.

Holding up his new blade, he examined it closely in the growing light. His eyes followed the long sweep of tempered metal, admiring its symmetry and grace. The metal was cool to the touch, its power not yet awakened.

Finding a suitable name for the blade had not been easy. Because the weapon was unique and the first of its kind, he could find no single word in his language which satisfied him, or seemed to capture its essence. So Shaka of the Zulus had created one.

'*iKlwa*,' he said aloud, and then repeated it. '*Iklwa.*'

The name slipped easily from his lips, his throat contracting with the soft, guttural click sound of the Zulu language. He smiled. No other combination of sounds so perfectly reproduced the sucking sound made when a weapon was being withdrawn from living flesh.

Although the hills were wreathed in soft hues of rose, blue and gold, the new commander of the *izi cwe* regiment thrust the beauty of the morning to the back of his mind and focused on his future plans.

Now he had the weapon he wanted, he would begin to work on a more effective deployment of his warriors. In his mind's eye, he saw his army form the shape of one of the most aggressive beasts of the plains, the black buffalo.

His regiments would be divided into three parts. The main, central body would represent the virtual chest or head of the animal. Close behind, would be closely packed reserves of fresh troops ready to step forward to take the place of those who fell.

Meanwhile, out on the flanks, in the shape of the buffalo's great curved horns, would be the strongest and fastest of his warriors. Once the battle began, they would advance at devastating speed to spread out, encircle, and cut off the enemy. Disciplined, well trained and ruthless, with this tactic in place his army would be invincible.

Shaka drew in his breath with a hiss of satisfaction. Just as the Nameless One had prophesied, one day the earth would tremble with the menace and power of his Zulu *impis*.

In spite of his elation, however, a faint irritation lurked at the back of his mind. Recently, his father, Senzangakhona, had deliberately spurned him in favour of one of his younger half-brothers.

Although Shaka had long since acknowledged that his father would never forgive him for the humiliation he'd suffered at esiKlebeni, the bitter irony was that he, Shaka, by merit of being placed so highly in King Dingiswayo's favour and also one of his most trusted military commanders, had become a man to be reckoned with-and especially now that the Mthethwe king was now the overlord of the Zulus.

The creator of the blade called *iKlwa* looked out over the rolling hills of his native land and filled his lungs with the clean, cold air of the high lands.

Time enough in the future for all of it, he thought. The *amadhlozi* are on my side and nothing will change that.

The power that had touched him on that long ago night in the eLangeni village had stayed with him through the years, and he had learned many things from the time he'd stood alone against his tormentors.

Physical strength and power, along with superior co-ordination of brain and body, fast reflexes and great reserves of stamina was already his. But these alone were not enough. Courage, tenacity of mind and soul, the ability to endure and the bitter heat of hardening resolve must become an integral part of who he was.

He stared into the distance for a few moments. Then he drew the tip of his newly-forged blade in a symbolic arc across the sky, from horizon to horizon, east to west, north to south.

The sun inched upwards and spilled its crimson fire over the edge of the world to bathe both the blade and the man who raised it to the heavens in a brilliant light. Across the divide, Shaka issued a silent message.

Beware, royal house of Zulu – because what is proposed is not always what comes about. I am Shaka, born of the royal line, and I send you these words, both as a warning, and a promise. My day will come... so be very afraid.

Four

Many miles away, the swift-arrowed flight of swallows crossed the Black Umfolozi River, winging their way towards the warmth of a northern summer.

Below them lay the domain of the powerful Ndwandwe people. During the next few months, the stars would hang low and sparkle icily over frost-rimed grasses ushering in the traditional season for the resolution of tribal grievances, and the struggles for supremacy that commonly led to open clan warfare.

That day, Zwide, the Ndwandwe leader, was in a belligerent mood. He stared, unblinking and morose, out over the central enclosure of the royal compound. His thoughts that day were not on the looming battles with his greatest enemy, the Mthethwe, but on the unpalatable belief that most of his present troubles were entirely due to women.

Take the old dog, Nowawa, for instance. He glared down at her as she lay moaning and trembling at his feet. The eldest of his dead father's many wives, she was constantly trying to run his life and interfere in things she had no right to. Only the presence of his birth mother, Ntombazi, stopped him aiming a kick at her defenceless head.

'Why are my footsteps dogged by women such as this old fool?' he had complained to her earlier. 'She should have been put out for the hyenas long ago.'

His mother, not a woman to be crossed, had defended the old woman with spirit. 'Nowawa was merely trying to stop you making a fool of yourself – *yet again*,' she'd reminded him forcefully. 'Your insistence on doing battle with King Dingiswayo so soon after being thoroughly routed by him was not a good idea. The most junior of your warriors could have told you that.'

After his previous ill-fated campaign, he had been taken prisoner and brought before Dingiswayo. Instead of being honourably executed as befitted someone of his status, he had been sent home with his tail between his legs and a gift of cattle for his trouble!

In one mistakenly magnanimous gesture, Dingiswayo had effectively reduced him in the eyes of his people from a gallant leader slain in battle to a cowering village dog, patted on the head then kicked out.

Zwide ground his teeth in silent rage. But even he dared not defy Ntombazi, for she had the 'shadow', the ruthless spirit and dominating character which made her feared throughout the kingdom.

As a child, he had cowered away from her touch. Even now, he tended to approach her with caution. One area he especially tended to avoid was the infamous hut in which she kept her museum of skulls.

The more he brooded, the deeper his frustration became. Was ever a man as unlucky as he to have such women at his heels, dogging his footsteps? As if having a witch for a mother was not enough!

Zwide rocked to and fro trying to blank out the details of the old woman latest ploy. In an effort to stop him going to salvage what was left of his honour by launching another attack on Dingiswayo, she had broken one of the most sacred taboos of the tribe. While rallying his men for the battle to come, she had rushed wildly into the large oval enclosure in the centre of the kraal, a place where women were forbidden to set foot on pain of death.

Then, in full view of his troops, the old woman had stripped off all her clothes. Stark naked, with her dried-up breasts sagging to her waist and making no effort to cover the straggles of pubic hair visible between her stringy thighs, she had wailed and cried, kissing his feet and begging him not to go to war.

As a result, the old fool's scandalous behaviour had ruined any chance of snatching back even a modicum of victory to ease his humiliation at Dingiswayo's hands. His men had seen the old woman's actions as a fearful omen of impending disaster. Rather than have a full scale rebellion on his hands, he had been forced to call off the intended attack.

Zwide was almost beside himself with rage. *Somehow, he had to diminish Dingiswayo's power…the only question was how?*

As he seethed with discontent, his eyes happened to fall on the hut directly opposite where he was sitting. The figure of his mother swam into focus. Sitting cross-legged in the shadows, her face was almost indistinguishable from the pyramid of hollow-eyed skulls arranged behind her.

The colours of the grim pile varied from the base upwards. The lower ranks were brown, cracked with age and the smoke and dust of the years, while the upper mass of vacant-eyed horrors leered out from rows of clean-picked bones, luminous in the gloom.

But the heads all had one thing in common. They had once sat on the shoulders of those who had stood in his way. Only Ntombazi could say to whom they had once belonged. Zwide glanced instinctively at the upper reaches of the pyramid. His heavily jowled face broke into a smile at the clean, shining pates of the most recently dispatched.

His flash of macabre humour was short-lived, however. Last night, his messengers had brought him some more bad news.

Spies in the Mthethwe camp had reported that Dingiswayo had been alerted to his recent activities, and was planning to bring him to heel again much as he would a scurvy dog.

Three regiments, each six hundred strong, were already marching north towards the Black Umfolozi River. Once they forded the river, it was only a few days' march to Nongama, where he was sitting at the present moment, brooding on his misfortunes.

He shot a glance at his mother. Her smooth, unlined skin was stretched tightly over her facial bones, a mask of pale brown ivory. Although her eyes were open, they resembled pools of stagnant water, empty and lost in the realms of trance.

Zwide repressed a shudder. Lately, he'd become convinced that his mother's head was beginning to resemble those she had collected so assiduously over the years. But there was no other way.

'I have need of your powers, Mother,' he said, choosing his words carefully. 'My enemies are closing in on me...'

Five

Dingiswayo and his council of war had gathered to discuss the forthcoming battle campaign. Beyond the camp, the river ran deep and silent. Reflected in its dark surface, brilliant stars hung like loops of diamonds in the night sky.

In deference to the rank and position of his superiors, Shaka, his newly-promoted and youngest commander, was seated well to the rear, listening quietly while opinions were put forward and discussed.

Finally, Dingiswayo looked across at him. A smile creased his open, generous face. 'What say you, Shaka of the Zulu? How do you say the coming battles should be fought?'

The answer was instant and unequivocal. '*Impi ebomvu,*' Shaka responded, 'a red war, a war to the finish. If Zwide and the Ndwandwe are to be conquered once and for all, it must be this way.'

An immediate buzz of dissent broke out. Shaka knew he was treading on dangerous ground, but had no intention of backing down or changing his opinion.

On one side there was the old guard, the experienced commanders who liked to fight their battles in the old, tried and trusted way, fighting from a distance with long throwing spears.

On the other, there was Dingiswayo, the kindly democrat, who sought only to teach lessons to ambitious and wayward rogues like Zwide, not destroy them. His way was to show mercy to the vanquished, then to entice them to come under the fiefdom of the Mthethwe with the minimum of confrontation and bloodshed.

For the moment, Shaka knew he was within his rights to propose what he just had. A democratic feature of these councils of war, introduced by Dingiswayo himself, allowed every member, irrespective of rank or seniority, the right to put forward their opinions, even if it meant disagreeing with the King himself.

Dingiswayo raised his hand to still the babble of voices. Gesturing to Shaka to continue, he added soberly, 'You know that I would prefer to be merciful, waging war merely to rebuke and not to destroy. It is my way.'

Shaka nodded respectfully but made no comment.

Dingiswayo sighed inaudibly, knowing full well that controversy would no doubt break out again by the time his youngest commander had finished what he had to say. But not even he was prepared for what came next.

'In future,' Shaka began, 'the army must be drawn up with a central head, a main body of men whose duty will be to face the enemy.'

He placed his clenched fists close to his chest to demonstrate. 'Close behind them will be a second row. If a warrior falls, then another will step forward to take his place.'

A rumble of curiosity came from his military elders and betters. To a man, their eyes fixed on Shaka's fists. His black eyes skewered those of Dingiswayo as he went on. 'On each side of the main body there will be half a regiment, thrown out like the encircling horns of the buffalo.'

His muscular arms snaked out and moved in a wide, curving semi-circle. 'Only the best warriors will be used in these positions,' he said softly, 'for they must be as fast and deadly as the striking mamba. Their aim is first to encircle, then crush the enemy.'

The long fringes of ox-hair knotted around his upper arms swayed in the firelight as his broad, calloused fingertips touched, closing the circle. In the deathly silence that followed, the gurgle and suck of the river could be clearly heard.

Veterans of many hard-fought battles, the king's military commanders had no difficulty imagining the aftermath of Shaka's brilliant manoeuvre-the silent battlefield, the war feathers of the dead and dying tossing in the wind, shields and weapons discarded, the cawing of crows settling to feast on the spilled entrails of the dead.

As Shaka repeated the mantra, his voice was steady, implacable in its certainty. 'First must be their capture, then the destruction of all. If we are to prevail against our enemies, this is how it has to be. There is no other way.'

Dingiswayo slowly traced a pattern on the ground with his point of his spear. The flames of the camp fires flickered fitfully in the breeze that rustled through the reeds, stirring ash and fanning the embers in a crackle of expanding wood.

The steady voice of his youngest commander continued, as resolute as before. 'It must also include the heirs and all the sons of the chiefs, no matter how young.'

The silence deepened. Many of the listeners bowed their heads as they sought to come to terms with the new and brutal philosophy being laid out for them.

Shaka spoke softly, as if to lessen the impact of his message. 'That way, there will be an end to the line and no future battles will have to be fought. Peace will follow.'

The man on the brink of great leadership looked across to where King Dingiswayo sat slumped by the fire, his greying head bent in studied contemplation of what he had just heard.

Yours is the way of compromise, was Shaka's silent message. Unfortunately, it only prolongs strife. *Impi ebomvu*, total war, this is my way.

After order had been restored, Shaka drew himself up to his full height and asked for permission to announce his next military proposal. An extremely thoughtful Dingiswayo nodded his consent, wondering what was coming next.

Clasping his hands behind his back, Shaka paced to and fro. His opening statement was just as bald and to the point as his previous edicts had been.

'Soldiers are not children,' he said. 'Men worthy of being called warriors do not need shoes. From now on they must do without.'

An indignant gasp followed. One of the senior commanders got up to protest, but Dingiswayo waved him down. Shaka went on.

'Warriors must be able to run and fight barefoot, to fly over stones like the wind and feel nothing of the pains of the flesh as they strive to reach the enemy. Their assegai must be at the enemy's throat before he knows it.'

To illustrate his next point, Shaka drew out his new weapon from where he'd concealed it earlier. Firelight glinted off the razor-sharp edges of the blade called Iklwa. In the half darkness, it looked just what it was, a silent, ruthless killer.

A growl of surprise came from the other commanders. The broad-bladed, stabbing *assegai* was like no other they had ever seen, but they knew at a glance, that it would be murderous in close combat.

Slowly, Shaka turned the weapon around, so that its potential could be fully realised. At the same time, his eyes were busy registering their reactions. Eventually, they came to rest on Dingiswayo's most senior commander, the man who'd been leading the most vociferous dissent against him.

In a flash, he crossed the intervening space. Totally unprepared, Dingiswayo's general found himself staring directly into the eyes of the man holding the deadly blade to his throat. Behind the glint of humour, the black eyes of the King's newest commander were ruthless and implacable.

No one dared to protest. A tiny bead of blood appeared on the general's dark skin. Swelling outward, the scarlet globule wavered in the firelight for a moment before trickling into the hollow at the base of the man's throat. Then, as swiftly as it had found its way to its target, the weapon was removed.

In the crushing silence that followed, Shaka released the man with a smile, put a friendly hand on his shoulder and courteously thanked him for his co-operation.

Before a word could be said, he had slipped back into his place at the rear of the assembly and reverted to being the disciplined young commander of the *izi-cwe* regiment.

Dingiswayo struggled to regain his equilibrium. He was fully aware of the fine path he would have to tread in any response he might make.

After all, this forceful young character had merely been carrying out a military demonstration. His opinion had been sought and he had replied. It was the accepted rule of *i-bandla*, the council of war, no matter what anyone thought of the outcome.

It came as no surprise when Shaka learned that the entire war council had voted solidly against all of the proposals he'd put forward. He merely smiled quietly to himself.

He had made his point. No one present was likely to forget either him; his military tactics, his philosophy of war – or his new weapon. Time was on his side, and time was on the move.

The following morning Dingiswayo and his regiments forded the river and entered Zwide's territory. Shaka had been put in charge of intelligence activities, for this was another area in which he excelled.

His scouts fanned out to determine the size of the Ndwandwe forces and their state of readiness. They infiltrated the enemy camps, mingled around their camp fires and eavesdropped on what was being said. Then they reported back.

Shaka also had in place a web of trusted spies, chosen from different tribes, who would pass back vital information that could be swiftly interpreted and acted upon.

By noon, he knew enough to allow him to urge Dingiswayo to attack immediately. Any delay would mean that Zwide would have a chance to fully mobilise his troops. This time, the council agreed unanimously to his suggestions.

Shaka's request to be allowed to lead the vanguard with his *izi-cwe* regiment, the youngest and the fastest, was also looked on with favour. On approaching the enemy forces, he planned that the oldest regiment, the Yengondlovu, would form the centre while the i-Nyakeni and the *izi-cwe* regiments would hold the right and left of the line.

Without the generals realising it, Shaka had formed the head, chest and horns of the 'buffalo' formation under the disguise of the manoeuvre approved by Dingiswayo, their supreme commander. During the coming battle, he would use it to devastating effect.

Dingiswayo's only orders, made personally to Shaka himself, were that on no account should Zwide be harmed if taken prisoner, and that the killing on the battlefield be held to the minimum required to bring the Ndwandwe to submission. No massacres would be allowed.

Due to the brilliance of Shaka's tactical moves, the Mthethwe army succeeded in breaking up the Ndwandwe's forces before they had a chance to group. The *izi-cwe* regiment displayed tireless energy as it wheeled and manoeuvred the enemy exactly into the positions Shaka directed, first breaking the Ndwandwe formations then striking their warriors down as they fled.

That day, he put into place another of his maxims: '*Pursue a fleeing enemy ruthlessly. But, if you decide not to kill him, be sure to put the fear of death into him instead.*'

On returning to headquarters, Shaka learned that Zwide had been taken prisoner and handed over to Dingiswayo. When the council of war met later that night, he found that some things had changed, while others had not.

What had altered was that the most senior commander, out of whose throat Shaka had skilfully extracted that single drop of blood, stood up to accord him full recognition for his outstanding contribution in the defeat of the Ndwandwe.

'You are indeed *Si-gi-di – greater than one thousand,*' the battle-scarred man said, 'I saw your plumed head in the thick of the battle, towering above all the others. You are *nkalakata,* huge in body, and great and fearless in spirit.'

His deep-set eyes twinkled roguishly below the intricate leopardskin head-dress. 'I regret my harsh words about your new ways. After today, I hope they will all listen to you.'

Dingiswayo cautiously opened the subject of Zwide. Everyone knew that he had no intentions of putting the Ndwandwe leader to death.Twice before he had pardoned him and let him go back to his people, unharmed. Why should this time be any different? But everyone knew to whom his questions were really being directed.

Wisely, Shaka did not attempt to enter into the discussion. Curbing his impatience, he bided his time. When the moment could no longer be avoided, Dingiswayo nodded for him to step forward.

'I know that my beliefs do not match yours, Nkosi,' Shaka said, coming directly to the point, 'but since you have asked for my opinion, I will give it to you.' He allowed his eyes to glance briefly around the council.

'Kill Zwide and all his heirs – every last one of them.' There was no mistaking his emphasis on the final words. 'And be sure to put his mother, Ntombazi, to the fire,' he added 'for she is *umtagati,* a witch. If you do not, Zwide will not forgive you for defeating him. He will never cease to be at your throat, while his mother -'

A babble of voices rose in protest. Shaka waited for a moment then, with his eyes fixed steadily on Dingiswayo, finished what he'd started to say.

'While his mother, the witch Ntombazi, will not rest until the head of Dingiswayo, *your* head, Nkosi, joins the skulls of those who opposed her son and now dwell among the spiders and rats in her hut of death.'

A stunned silence greeted his blistering comments. The elders were appalled by the arrogance of such a statement, delivered by the youngest and least experienced of them all.

They dared a quick glance in Dingiswayo's direction. To their surprise, they caught a twinkle of amusement in the eyes surveying his most junior commander.

Shaka stared at Dingiswayo over the leaping flames. What he had said, he meant. His spies had already brought him a list of the witch's previous victims. Some of them he had known personally. All of them had opposed Zwide at one time or another. He had no doubt at all that Zwide, if allowed to go free for a third time, would become so desperate to avenge his honour that he would be forced to seek his mother's help.

And that would only mean one thing. Dingiswayo would be in extreme danger of losing his head. The hostility and disbelief emanating from the rest of the council was of no concern to him. But he wasn't finished. He had more to say.

'Put the kraals and villages of the Ndwandwe to the fire, and wipe them from the face of the earth. Collect their women, children and cattle and bring them to live in the land of the Mthethwe. Their men, those who are still alive, will soon follow. And in due course, the Ndwandwe will become one with the people of Dingiswayo.'

A blazing log tumbled from the fire, sending showers of bright sparks into the night skies. It was as if no one else was present, just as it had been the first time they had come face to face: Dingiswayo, the wanderer, King of a mighty nation, gentle democrat and peacemaker, and Shaka, also the exiled son of a King, rising out of poverty and rejection to gain his rightful place. Both men were bound together by so much, and yet divided by an even greater gulf.

'Strike an enemy once and for all,' Shaka said softly. 'Or he will live to be at your throat time without number. If there must be war, and there is no other way, then let it be total.'

After that, Dingiswayo had no option but to be as true to his convictions as Shaka was to his. After levying a fine of two thousand cattle on Zwide, he held out the hand of conciliation and once again allowed him to go free.

Zwide seethed, raged, and ground his teeth as he relived yet another shattering humiliation at the hands of Dingiswayo. The man likened to a crocodile licked his wounds in fury. It was the final insult. Dingiswayo must be brought to his knees like the old bull elephant he was, and trampled into the dust.

Reluctantly, Zwide had to acknowledge that he knew of only one power capable of saving his reputation. Men and armies alone were not enough to bring down a man like Dingiswayo.

There was no other way. He would have to look into the dead eyes of his mother, Ntombazi, and once again plead for her help.

Six

A year later

There was great mourning in the royal kraal of esiKlebeni. Senzangakhona, the king, was dead. A burial pit had been prepared for him in the valley of Emkhosini beside the seven ancestors of the Zulus.

In keeping with Nguni tradition, he had been dressed in his regal finery and placed with his back to the wall of the tomb with his legs stretched out comfortably before him. Close to hand was his huge war-shield, knobkerries and spears; gourds of freshly-brewed beer to quench his thirst; cooking pots for the preparation of his meals and his carved head-rest and sleeping mat for comfort as he slept.

But that was not all that would go with him into the afterlife. The pit was a long enough, and deep enough, to allow the slayers, the dreaded *abatakati abakulu*, to carry out the cruel and barbaric rites demanded by tribal law.

The bound and ritually-broken bodies of Senzangankona's body servants would then be placed in the pit to keep him company, for it was not fitting for a king to travel alone into the valley of death.

The news of his demise spread quickly. Senzangakhona had been in decline for some time, too fond of the soft life, the smoking of hemp tobacco and the drinking of sorghum beer.

Dingiswayo was furious when he heard that Sigujana, the son of the dead king's eighth wife, Bibi, would become the future king, and not Shaka, the obvious choice.

'Why have I not been consulted on this matter?' he demanded, his usually benign face suffused with anger. 'It is my right, as the overlord of the Zulus. All major decisions require my approval, especially one as important as their future leadership.'

Pacing angrily to and fro, he snapped, 'Was it not obvious to anyone with half an eye that the eldest son has brought battle honours and much respect to the Mthethwe, while the other, his presumed heir, was a traitor who chose to stand with the enemy against us? Shaka is the oldest surviving son of the Great House, his legitimate claim impeccable, his capacity to rule beyond doubt.'

Of course, the most potent factor of all was also undeniable, and it was that King Dingiswayo, their overlord, was fully in favour of it.

Shaka's half-brother Ngwadi was also loyal to Shaka, and they had always been close. Doing what he thought was in the best interests of his elder brother he approached Sigujana and offered him a chance to stand aside in favour of Shaka.

But while bathing in a river, a fight had broken out between them and Sigujana was later found floating face-down in the water. Whether he had drowned by design, or by accident, no one knew.

Some said that Ngwadi had simply decided to murder Sigujana, first making sure that Shaka was well away from the scene at the time. Since no rumour of blame arose, or at least none that openly surfaced, the way to the supreme leadership of the house of Zulu lay open.

The early morning was full of mists and golden sunlight as people streamed down towards esiKlebeni from villages perched in the surrounding hills.

Men and boys bearing shields, spears, knobkerries, and sing-ing *izibonga* in praise of the new king led the way, leaving the women, children and the elderly to come on at their own pace. The air rang with their voices as they splashed through the broad, winding stream that lay between them and the royal kraal.

Rays of light struck the tops of the mopani trees, turning them to flame. The massive gates of esiKlebeni were pushed open and the people began to flood through. Soon the whole place was afire with rumour and speculation, a great, furtive buzzing as of bees among honey.

Senzangakhona's family waited uncertainly for the arrival of the new king and his entourage. Only then would they come forward to pay their respects, or accept whatever fate awaited them.

Some present that day were very keen to witness the demise of those who had done great wrongs to the man destined to be their king. Surely, he must desire to sweep them away as chaff before the wind?

As they waited, the sun began its long climb into the cloudless sky. An odd stillness began to descend on the vast throng. Even babies were quiet, drooping on their mothers' breasts like small brown puppies, drowsy and pacified.

A mile or two away, the royal procession wound its way to the top of the ridge that overlooked esiKlebeni. The eyes of the state-ly woman accompanied by a knot of young soldiers flicked ahead until she found the person she was looking for. He was easy to find, for he stood head and shoulders above most of the others.

Her full lips parted in a smile. There he was, silhouetted against the blue and gold of the morning sky, flanked by his friends, Mgobozi, Nqoboka and Mdlaka.

As Nandi walked on, the nipples of her full breasts rasped against the soft under-skin of the monkey pelt cape, the weight of the beads around her neck satisfyingly heavy. Although aware of the increased pounding of her heart, her thoughts, and her eyes, were riveted on the man looking out over the valley.

The tip of the tall, blue crane feather in his head dress rippled in the breeze. As he gestured towards something below, the sunlight gleamed on the creamy ox hair fringes knotted around his muscular upper arms.

Nandi's thoughts were bitter. When you look at the accursed place we left so long ago, what do you see, what do you remember?

During the years her son was growing up, they had never spoken of it. Perhaps they never would, but she knew in her heart what his unspoken words would be.

All of it, Mame, I remember everything... every cuff, every blow, every kick, every sneer. Not one of your tears, Mame, or any of my own has been forgotten. I remember everything.

The phantom words hung between them for a moment like a curl of smoke before he was swallowed up by the warriors pressing up behind. Then all she could see was the tip of the blue crane feather as his entourage set off down the hill on the final part of their journey.

Nandi turned to look for her daughter, Nomcoba. There she was, stepping lightly between her brother, Ngwadi, and the young soldiers chosen by Shaka to escort his family.

Glancing with pride at her daughter's lovely face, she noted the small pert breasts beneath the strands of colourful beads, the shapely feet and legs gleaming with dew from the long grass. The quick frown, the tiny scowl that passed across her face as something said by one of the young soldiers displeased her, did not escape her mother's notice. Yebo, you are beautiful, my daughter, but still a Senzangakhona with your sullen pride, so quick to anger -

A surge of amusement rose up in her. But then, I can hardly

blame your father for everything. I too have played my part in shaping who you are.

She shrugged her shoulders imperiously below the cape of monkey skins. I know I can be perverse at times, but then who wouldn't be, after the life I've had to lead? Some still talk of me as 'the vengeful she-devil Senzangakhona had to throw out of his house'!

Her lips parted in a smile, showing the gleam of white, even teeth. She was still a handsome woman, her figure as erect and shapely as it had always been, only the faintest touches of silver in her dark cap of hair. Smiling broadly now, she savoured the thought of how she was looking forward to seeing some of those malicious chatterers again – only this time they would live to eat their words.

Nandi breathed hard as she bent forward to accommodate the rise of the hill. Eh, she thought, conscious of her pounding heart, this body of mine is heavier than the last time I was here! Even carrying my child on my back, I was light on my feet, like a bird.

Her breath was sharp with anticipation. Only a few more paces then they would reach the summit. In her mind's eye she could already see what lay below.

The glint of sunlight on the stream that winds softly below the hill where esi Klebeni stands, the copse of shaded trees on the bend of the river. . .

Nandi, the woman about to become the Nkosikazi, the Queen Mother of the Zulus, squeezed her eyes shut with the sudden pain of memory. Then without warning, she found herself at the place where the hillside gave way to the cool reach of morning sky.

The place of great and painful memory was spread out before her, more vivid and breathtaking than she remembered it, as if the passing of time had removed the bitterness and left only the beauty.

A vista of rolling hills stretched into the distance, the river and its subsidiary streams glittering in the morning sun. The summer grass was green and lush with wild flowers, the rustle of feathery seed heads echoing like music all the way down into the valley.

She felt as if she were about to float away into the gilded morning, her limbs no longer heavy but light as air. Giddy with emotion, she caught her lower lip between her teeth. Slowly, she lifted her eyes to the hillside that lay a mile or two away on the other side of the river.

The royal kraal of esiKlebeni fitted into the landscape as naturally as if it had always been there, its thatches silvered and timeless below the morning sun. Even from here she could make out the high fences at the head of the kraal. The private places of the King, the places where she had once lived.

The jewel flash of a kingfisher's plumage and the gleam of the river below distracted her. Instinctively, her eyes flicked to the patch of dark trees at the river's bend. In spite of herself, her heart leaped.

Unbidden, images rushed past her defences. She had only been a girl, hot-headed and rebellious, caught up in the first physical passion of her life. Warm sunlight, cool water and sun-dappled shade and the hot, sweet smell of a young man's flesh…

Drops of sweat escaped from below the beaded strands around her brow. Aii, she thought, if it had been only once that we two broke the laws of *hlobonga*, nothing might have come of it, but alas, it was not to be.

Nandi shook her head. What had happened between her and the virile young Senzangakhona had been like a forest fire, hot, fiery, all consuming and short lived. First the pleasure and then the pain; there had been plenty of that, a lifetime's worth. Having flaunted the permitted traditional rituals, sexual consummation being taboo and forbidden among the unmarried, in their wrath the ancestors had demanded a very high price of both her and her unborn child.

Her lips tightened. She stared long and hard at the patch of dark trees. What might my life have been, if it were not for the sweetness and the damnation of those stolen moments?

I will never know, she thought. Nor do I care, for I feel the *amadhlozi* have finally forgiven me. This is the day I follow my son with pride, back to where it all began, to claim his rightful inheritance.

Straightening her shoulders, she gestured to her young escorts that it was time for them to complete the last part of the journey.

Then Nandi, the 'sweet thing' and her daughter Nomcoba, Shaka's blood sister, began to move down the hill, through the meadows of long grass and wild flowers, across the stream to where esiKlebeni and the people of the Zulu were waiting for them.

Minutes stretched into an hour and then into another. The sense of impending drama was muted, coiled like a sleeping cobra waiting to strike, rumours and gossip stilled, dissipated by the heat.

At last, a great shout went up from the sentries on the lookout platforms on either side of the gates. '*He comes, he comes... the great warrior Si-gi-di, greater than one thousand!*'

The family of the deceased King stirred uneasily. The moment of truth was at hand. Now they would have to greet the man who, in all probability, would prove to be their nemesis, their destroyer.

Hundreds of pairs of eyes were fixed on the open gates. A great wave of expectancy rippled through the crowds.

First to step through below the high arch was Ngomane, soon to be the chief minister of the tiny ten-mile-square Zulu state, followed by Mbiya, Shaka's step-father. Behind them was Mbikwana, the nephew and representative of King Dingiswayo, followed by Shaka's half-brother, Ndwadi, and the military commanders of Dingiswayo's army, their servants and aides.

A multitude of eyes followed them as they moved into the huge oval enclosure then turned swiftly to focus once more on the empty gates. Tension and expectation began to build anew.

A bustle of activity outside, then Nandi, the new Nkosikazi, the Queen Mother, stepped through the gates, with her Nomcoba, the daughter of the dead monarch, escorted by a cohort of young soldiers.

The former royal family, and those loyal to them, remembered her only too well, Nandi, the fiery mother of *i-tshaka, the beetle,* the woman who had been such a thorn in Senzangakhona's flesh.

Now she was back, returning to the royal kraal from which she had been evicted all those years ago. Still beautiful and haughty, she held her head high, gazing neither to left or right as she moved up through the great empty oval towards the brow of the hill, her eyes fixed on the group of people who were watching her with acute apprehension as she came towards them.

Some of them fidgeted uneasily, sweating in the heat, blisters of fear breaking through their carefully arranged poses. Barely acknowledging them, Nandi and her daughter moved into the shade of the only remaining fig tree, the other having been hit by lightning after the notorious *umutsha* ceremony all those years ago.

A hush fell on the waiting people. Where was he, where was the new King? Then, at last, just beyond the gates, a flash of snow-white plumes and a subdued clink of weapons.

A hint of suppressed fear winnowed through the crowds as Shaka's *indunas* stood aside, allowing them a glimpse of the man who would soon have the power of life and death over them.

It was followed by a long sigh, a rising wave of approval. They had expected nothing like this, nothing like the man standing before them.

This indeed was truly a warrior king. A single blue crane feather in the circlet of padded leopard skin around his brow reached a foot or two into the air, adding to his already impressive height. Bright red *igwala gwala* feathers completed the head dress and created a brilliant splash of colour against the dark sheen of his oiled skin.

His ox-hide shield was pure white with a single black blaze at the centre, denoting the highest calibre of warrior. In the other hand he carried the legendary short spear known as *Iklwa*.

A frisson of awe ran through his people when they saw it, for the legend of how the weapon came to be made and the reason behind its creation was well known.

Gleaming white fringes of ox-hair covered his muscular arms from elbow to wrist while similar tails, fastened just below the knee, reached to his ankles. The kilt of animal tails he wore was of leopard and blue-grey monkey tails while draped over his shoulders and chest was a collar of leopard-skin, the royal prerogative.

Flanking Shaka were his commanders, the friends of his youth and comrades-at-arms. Behind them stepped the massed ranks of Shaka's *izi-cwe* regiment, adding their unique ingredient to the colourful spectacle.

Once they were arranged, Ngomane, the man who had offered Nandi and her children refuge all those years ago, raised his long ceremonial spear. An expectant hush fell over the parade ground. His voice rang out.

'People of Zulu! Before you stands Shaka, son of kaSenzangakhona, descended from the great lord Zulu, the one who is your lawful chief, by right of birth and the law. I am the voice of the great Dingiswayo who is your overlord. It is his will that this man should now rule the Zulu.'

It was here, the moment of truth. 'Is there anyone here who will contest the rightness of this decision?'

The words rang out in the pulsing heat. All eyes were fixed on the man who stood waiting for an answer. His destiny lay before him, only moments away.

Out on the fringes of the crowd, a scowl was imprinted on the face of an overweight nineteen-year-old with bad teeth. Up to this moment, he had hoped to acquire the title of King of the Zulus for himself.

Had not he and this upstart shared the same father who now lay in his burial place in the Mpembeni Valley? Why should this hated outsider step into the place that was rightfully his?

His desire to shout aloud was like the sting of a viper, biting and gnawing at him. To keep his anger under control, he bit his lower lip until the blood trickled down his chin.

As the forceful voice of Ngomane reverberated through esiKlebeni inviting a challenger, any challenger, to step forward and contest Shaka's right to be king, the youth turned and pushed his way through the crowds, full of hatred for his step-brother.

Nandi's eyes glinted with unshed tears. As she looked slowly around, the familiar outlines of the royal kraal blurred.

Vultures, she thought. All they see when they look at me are the memories; the broken taboos, the swelling belly and the birth pains. What they will neither acknowledge nor understand is the humiliation of my life in the royal kraal which followed.

Her gaze turned to the remnants of the Senzangakhona dynasty, seeking the hateful presence among them, but not finding it. Of course, he is gone, buried in eMakhosini, never more to hurt us.

She thrust away thoughts of the long, bitter road her first-born had been forced to travel, the road they had walked down together through all the anguish and triumph, until at last this day of days had come.

'My son, at last, you are come home.'

Nandi's softly whispered words were spoken from the heart to the man on the threshold of his destiny. Of course, she knew they would not carry above the tumult of the waiting crowd, but then they weren't meant to. Shaka, her son, would hear them anyway.

As Ngomane thundered out his demand for Shaka's acceptance, he thought of the long ago day when he'd looked up to see the sixteen-year-old holding out the pelt of his first leopard kill in a mute but proud gesture of gratitude. Ever since then, he'd been his champion.

Poor harried boy, Ngomane thought, so desperately protective of your mother and sister in a world that didn't want you.

Then, since there was no response, no defiance of either tribal law or the will of their overlord, Dingiswayo, he uttered the final words. 'No one speaks. Then people of Zulu, salute your king!!'

With one voice, the people acknowledged their lord and master. '*Bayete, Nkosi! Hail, mighty Lord and King! Bayete! Bayete!!*

Dust rose from the ranks of Shaka's warriors as the *izi-cwe* regiments raised their right foot and stamped hard on the ground in unison and rattled their spears against their shields in one great, accompanying drumbeat of sound.

The blue crane feather tilted downwards as Shaka bowed his head in open salute. Nandi and her daughter had tears of pride and joy in their eyes. His brother Ndwadi looked first at his mother and his sister, Nomcoba, then at his brother Shaka.

The children of Senzangakhona had indeed come home.

The eyes of the youth at the edge of the crowd were fixed on his half-brother, Shaka. Reluctantly, he was forced to acknowledge the undeniable physical likeness that bound and yet separated them.

His eyes roamed over the sculpted, physical perfection of this supreme warrior, moving to the splendour of his ceremonial dress; the trappings of high military status, the plumed head dress and huge war shield. Here was the legendary Nodumehlezi, the one the soldiers spoke of with such awe, a hero of monumental stature who was favoured by the great overlord, King Dingiswayo.

Instinctively, his hand went to cover his three blackened front teeth, cringing at the thought of his own overweight body.

Even though he had sought support for his claim to become the legitimate successor, his dreams had come to nothing. Even his wily aunt, Mkabayi, had changed her allegiances and transferred them to Shaka at the last moment. It was too late to challenge her, even if he dared.

He looked on the face of his half-brother for one long, bitter moment before turning aside and pushing his way through the crowds. The youth's name was Dingane. And he would have to bridle his impatience and wait for another day before seeking his revenge.

Apart from Shaka's half-brother, Dingane, there were others who were less than happy that day. One of them was the sister of the dead king.

Mkabayi's life had been overshadowed by a strange darkness. She was the second of twin daughters born to Jama, Shaka's grandfather. Under tribal law, such a birth was considered a sign of ill omen. To allow her first-born sister to live, free from any curse, she should have suffered the usual fate of all second-born twins – to have her infant life snuffed out before it had even begun.

Jama, being a kindly man, had refused to comply with the old superstition. But in spite of her father's best efforts, Mkabayi bore the stigma all her life. Rejected and embittered, she had long since earned the title of *impika*, the wild cat.

On this day of rejoicing, Mkabayi kaJama's soul burned with resentment at the re-instatement of her former sister-in-law, the new Nkosikazi. Her black eyes bored into the woman while the bile in her throat threatened to choke her.

This upstart had once occupied an even lower status than she, Mkabayi, the reviled sister. Now, because Nandi had a son – no, two sons, though the second was of no consequence – not only had she returned to esiKlebeni in a blaze of reflected glory, but she also held the highest position of any woman in the land.

The sister of the dead king moaned in her heart for the waste of her life. No child for her... Would life ever give her a role to play other than to suffer the mocking hand the ancestors had laid on her at the moment of birth?

Cursing her moment of weakness, *she* drew a surreptious hand across her eyes and straightened her shoulders. Against her better judgment, she had let it be known that naturally, she supported the unfortunate son of her dead brother. What other course was open to her? The house of Zulu needed him as king, for the moment, at least.

She, Mkabayi, would bide her time. Revenge would have to wait till another day, but it would surely come. She would see to it.

The creature skulking in the shadows disliked the bright glare of the sunlight, for she preferred dark places.

The face that turned to follow the new king as he walked among his people was a bland mask of white daubed clay, frightening in its simplicity, the eyes dead pools of black. Dried inflated bladders and skins of snakes were woven into her matted hair and the stench emanating from her reeked of death and old evil.

Nobela was like no other woman in the kingdom. Infamous and greatly feared, she was the leader of those termed the 'witch finders' whose business it was to carry out the abominable trade of 'sniffing out' those accused of being wrongdoers and carriers of evil.

Wherever the signs of 'witchcraft' were said to be, there also would be Nobela and her group of hags, with their deadly, sharpened skewers at the ready, waiting and watching for signs of fear or weakness.

Her full white lips parted in a silent snarl, showing yellowed teeth, the tongue and inner mouth blood red in contrast. Nobela sniffed the air expectantly. She could already smell the odour of jealousy and the heat of secret desires.

The pitiful wretches couldn't help themselves. The only trouble was they lacked the courage to step up boldly and use the spear or the knife to rid themselves of those who stood in their way. The red-rimmed eyes snapped open, reflecting the depths of the contempt Nobela felt for those she considered her prey.

You prefer to cringe and sweat and lust in secret... You think the only way to achieve your puny desires is to turn to the dark powers, to use spells or poison or call down lightning. It is afterwards... O my covetous ones, my fearful ones... that Nobela and her sisters will come to claim you.

She faded back into the darkness, leaving only the threat of her unspoken words behind.

Even you, new king of the Zulus, are only a man... like all the others. I shall measure your courage, and test you to the limit. If our skewers of sharpened wood cannot reach you... maybe those of sorrow will.

The new order

The king of the Zulus was shrewd, intelligent and fully aware that his plans would take time to bear fruit. The tiny Zulu nation was in a precarious position, hemmed in by potential dangers both from within and without.

Although conscious that he must step carefully and bide his time, Shaka ultimately decided that undue reticence on his part would not serve any useful purpose. Besides, it was not in his nature to be unduly patient...

Within a month, the new king of the Zulus had created an army of around five hundred men. Those between thirty and forty years old were formed into a brigade called the *amaWombe*. According to tradition, men who were married wore the *isi coco* – the head ring woven into the natural hair as a mark of their marital status. Shaka allowed this group to keep both the head ring and the status, and housed them in the new military kraal of Belebe.

Under the new rules, all unmarried men between twenty-five and thirty wearing the traditional head rings of maturity lost both their head rings and their status. They were then banded together and re-named *izimPholo* – the bachelors' brigade. Hard on the heels of these changes certain other new edicts were introduced, some of which were to shock people to the core.

From now on, it was announced, men would not be allowed to marry until they reached mature years, and then only with the King's permission. A man's first duty was to the defence of his land, the conquering of his enemies and obedience to his King, although not necessarily in that order. According to their new ruler, wives, children and the needs of the flesh only detracted men from their duties and distilled their energies...

General anxiety on this point was quickly followed by a sigh of relief. Sexual contact would still be allowed from time to time, but only under the continuing strict rules of the Zulu constitution of *ama hlay endlela*, the fun of the roads, an eminently sensible arrangement where a certain amount of love play was permitted – providing no male seed found its way to where it shouldn't.

Sula izembe, the 'wiping of the axe'- the age-old right of the warrior who had killed in battle to take any woman or girl who crossed his path, would still stand. Wisely, the new king allowed these to remain.

The formation and training of the final regiment Shaka created would one day form the core of the future Zulu army. Gathering up all idle youths between the ages of eighteen and twenty-four, he set about forming this unruly element into a regiment called the *Fasimba*. In time, they would become the formidable Royal Guard of the future. He looked on these unformed, undisciplined ones with great affection.

'On these young, headstrong lions I will impose my will and shape them into a new breed of warrior.They will change the face of war in Zululand for all time...'

Shaka's regiments of 'virgin soldiers' would do just that – and more.

But that was not all. Boys from the age of eight upwards would also be marshalled for the general good of the fledgling nation.

When the army went into battle, they would be expected to follow on behind the main force, their duties being to tend the cattle and be responsible for the sleeping mats, head-rests and personal effects of the warriors. A warrior's duty was to wage war and to pit all his strength against his enemies on the field of battle, not to be burdened down by trivialities. The u-dibi boys would play an important part in seeing that this would be so.

Young women were also to be formed into regiments and placed under the stringent discipline of the new commanders he had chosen to organise and supervise them. They were also given the task of supervising the sexual habits of those under their command. Regular inspections as regards their virginity would become the order of the day.

When the identities of the commanders of the new military kraals were announced, the entire nation reeled in shock. With his customary disregard for convention, those who were chosen by Shaka to oversee the *amakhanda* with maximum efficiency and discipline were all women.

The first was his mother, Nandi, the foremost woman in the land and well known for her imperious nature and strong will. Next were Langaza and Mkabi, two of the dead king Senzangakona's widows.

Both were women of implacable resolve who had shown kindness to Shaka when he was a boy, even in the face of their husband's bitter disapproval. Now he was honouring them by giving them an important place in his new kingdom.

Last, there was Mkabayi, the dead king's sister, the ferocious one they called *impika*, the wild cat, the woman who continued to defy the ancient taboos of the ancestors by merely being alive.

When she was told of her appointment, she betrayed no flicker of surprise or any other emotion, merely stared blandly into the face of her new king, and said nothing.

In the process of creating a fighting force capable of defending the tiny kingdom, Shaka brought Ngonyama the Lion and a clutch of blacksmiths down to the royal kraal. Their important task was to make a supply of the new short, broad-bladed assegai, replicas of the original blade called Iklwa, the king's personal, deadly weapon. These were needed to equip the Fasimba, the youth brigade. Only this time, on his instructions, the powers of the occult would be dispensed with.

Once they were trained in its use, the Fasimba instructed the other regiments, and the surrounding hills rang to war cries and the clash of weaponry.

Meticulous attention to detail and sheer hard work were the hallmark of Shaka's success. Tireless, he asked nothing of his men that he did not do himself. As commander, he was always in the lead, driving them and himself in a relentless campaign that demanded exceptionally high standards of physical fitness.

Night marches became the order of the day. Weary men, already exhausted after the day's disciplines, were often wakened in the dead of night to run till they dropped; to ford rivers below the gaze of a pale sickle moon, terrified by thoughts of what might be lurking there – and still be able to fight at the end of it.

And always, always, up ahead there would be the relentless, invincible figure of Shaka, leading by example. They lost all excess flesh, marched, fought and died as one, in step to the beat of the man who led them.

Bravery, courage and loyalty were generously rewarded, while the slightest sign of cowardice or hesitation was ruthlessly stamped on, the punishment being instant death.

With his young lions as the core of his garrison, Shaka then turned his back on esi Klebeni and built a new capital on the banks of the Mhodi River.

He called his seat of power kwaBulawayo. But others called it 'the Place of Killing.'

Seven

The scales of justice

The breezes of early autumn stirred the glossy leaves of the giant fig tree. To the nervous onlookers gathered for the first day of the long-awaited judgment, Shaka seemed uncommonly at ease.

His skin gleamed with the slick of red ochre paste and oils. The regal collar of leopardskin and the sweeping plumes of the black widow bird which graced the circlet of leopard skin around his brow only served to add gravity to the sombre occasion.

His mother Nandi was seated on his right, sleek and plump in her new-found role of Nkosikazi, Queen of the Zulus. Wearing a long skirt of the finest animal tails, with rows of brilliantly coloured beads covering her breasts and an ankle-length cape of sumptuous samango monkey fur draped around her shoulders, she looked every inch a queen.

On the king's left was his half-brother, Ngwadi, his staunchest supporter. On either side of the immediate family was a group of hand-picked councillors, chiefs and representatives of the military many displaying what could only be described as extreme apprehension.

Occasionally, their eyes would flick to the group of men standing at the rear. They were the dreaded slayers, the men who traditionally carried out summary executions at a mere flick of the fingers.

Since this had long been a custom of the Nguni kings, no one present was left in any doubt that they would be called on to apply their skills in one way or another before long. The only burning questions were – just who would live and who would die before the day was out?

Drawn up behind the royal party, in a phalanx of oiled muscle and ceremonial dress, were members of the Fasimba regiment. They were Shaka's 'young lions' the errant youths he had gathered up and subjected to rigorous military training, and who were now fast becoming the elite of the Zulu army.

A sudden stir as the first of the prisoners was brought in. Nandi's dark eyes, so like those of her son, narrowed as she observed the man being forced to his knees before them. Her fingers began to play among the strings of beads curling like colourful snakes in her lap.

In his middle years, the indelible stamp of authority and air of command surrounding him was somewhat dissipated by his bedraggled state, and the presence of the burly guards manhandling him.

'*Bayete, Nkosi.*' The words spilled out from between his cracked lips. Nandi's watchful eyes noted the flare of resentment in his eyes as he was forced to comply with the royal salute.

The guards pushed him face down in the dust. Having delivered him safely to Shaka's feet, they squatted respectfully some yards away.

Today was judgment day and the man sprawling before Shaka was Mudli, brother to his father the late king, his uncle, in fact. He would be the first of many to be brought before the royal court, to answer charges and be weighed in the scales of the new king's justice.

How they would fall would depend largely on Nandi, for Shaka had placed his mother's experiences and memories above his own. The solemn duty of this court was, above all else, to avenge the sorrow and anguish she had suffered.

Shaka's voice was soft, almost gentle as he addressed the man who was a close blood relative. To many watching, it would seem as if he were courteously greeting a visitor or an emissary to his kingdom. Those close to him knew better.

'*Sakubona*, Mudli, brother of my father. Although I have no recollection of meeting you, I am told that we did, although a long time ago.'

The court held its breath. The man called Mudli raised his head and wiped a streak of dirt from his face, but said nothing.

'But let us not waste time with such foolishness,' the new king of the Zulus said, a thin hiss of steel running below the honey tones, 'for there is much we have to talk about.' In spite of the warmth of the morning sun, Nandi felt a chill run through her.

'I believe you were very good at creating names.' Shaka paused to let the significance of his words sink in. 'Is this not so, my uncle?'

There was no reply. Mudli's head sagged and he seemed to shrink in size. The king's voice purred, 'I would like you to explain to me how I received the name I am known by.'

Nandi froze. The fingers twining the strands of beads were stilled while old, bitter memories hovered in the sunlit morning. Still, Mudli said nothing.

'Let me refresh your memory, then. My name is Shaka, or as you so cleverly named me, '*i-tshaka*.' It means a lowly insect, I believe.'

The calm words whipped around the aristocratic Mudli like hornets. A hiss of indrawn breath emanated from the ranks of the former royal house, a mixture of old fear and present terror. The hawk-like eyes of Mkabayi, the second-born twin, froze the perpetrators into silence.

The man who was King leaned forward and looked deep into the prisoner's eyes. 'You named me *i-tshaka, spawn of a beetle*. It seems you had an unhealthy interest in the foul insects reputed to lodge in women's bellies.'

Nandi's involuntary moan reached Mudli's ears. He knew, in that moment, he was lost. As Shaka went on, his voice was icily correct, holding all the elements of a leopard biding its time until the kill, the final snap of the neck.

'Ah, you have no answer to give your king, then?'

Sweat trickled down the prisoner's back. The next question followed hard on the heels of the last.

'Now, tell me, uncle – why were you so cruel to my mother? Why did you inflict such grievous wounds on someone who had done you no harm?'

As an intended aside, but loud enough for everyone to hear, he spoke to Nandi, the words dripping one by one into the fearful hush.

'See, *umama*, he does not choose to answer.' He sighed. 'His silence must surely convict him.'

Mudli raised his head in a gesture of mute, impossible defence, the signs of age and strain etched into his face. His weary, beaten eyes looked into the impassive face of the man who was his judge.

'And now, one last question…why did you influence my father so hard against me? Why did you support Sigujana, yet fail to extend a welcome to me, the Commander of the army of your overlord, Dingiswayo?'

Mudli stared dumbly into the face of the man who held his life in the palm of his hand. Although he knew deep in his soul that he was flesh of his flesh, blood of his blood, in that searing moment of truth he found himself unable to summon up the face of the small boy he had so shamelessly spurned all these years ago.

With a supreme effort of will, his throat as dry as bone, he replied, 'I have nothing to say.'

The voice of his judge dropped to a whispered aside. 'Do you hear that, *umama*? Once again, he has nothing to say.'

Turning to the silent woman by his side, he thundered, 'Tell me, Ndlovukazi, Great She Elephant, Nkosikazi of the Zulus, how say you on this matter? Speak, so all can hear you.'

The damned-up rage of the years of suffering was about to break.

Mkabayi turned her head slowly to look at the woman who would either condemn her brother-in-law to death or create a solution for his pardon.

'He treated me badly on every occasion he could,' answered Nandi coldly, her dark eyes piercing those of the man before her. 'Truly, my son, he hated me deeply.'

And you, also… she could have added, but did not. Shaka already knew that. As she clasped her hands loosely in her lap, the great burden of the years began to lift from her.

Shaka got to his feet, towering over the assembled spectators, guilty and innocent alike, his face twisted in rage and sorrow.

'Mudli, brother of my father, you were no friend to my mother or me. Indeed, you kept your hatred for us alive over the years. Not once, not twice, but many times you betrayed us. For this you are condemned to die. And your death will not be an easy one.'

A moan broke out among the crowd, swiftly stifled. Above Shaka's head, a flash of bright feathers as a bird with scarlet plumage settled in the fig tree, its full throated song innocent in the midst of the deadly reckoning,

"*And your death shall not be easy…*" Mudli closed his eyes. There was no mistaking the implication behind the words. The scales of justice had tilted and fallen, although not in his favour.His mind cast about in desperation, seeking to escape the awful reality of what lay before him. *Not that death, any death but that…*

People looked uneasily at each other. It was very clear what kind of justice their new king believed in. Even Mudli's royal heritage and rank had not saved him. Nguni justice could indeed be terrible, and usually was. The method of execution typically reserved for sorcerers, witches and the worst criminals, including traitors, was indeed a fearful way to die.

Mudli moaned inwardly, his scrotum shrivelling into a tight knot. The sharp bamboo stakes would be ready at hand in the valley of execution. On the king's signal, they would be hammered into his rectum, perhaps piercing his bowel or intestines.

After that he would be hauled upright and left impaled until death by bleeding, thirst or internal rupture claimed him, or until scavenging animals and birds of prey ended his suffering – whichever came first.

Mudli's head jerked up, the tendons on his throat distended with stress. He tried to keep his voice steady as he addressed Shaka for the first time.

'I was a soldier and do not fear death, for I have often faced it on the field of battle. Nor do I dread pain…'

He tried to struggle, to rise to his feet, to stand upright like the soldier he was. Shaka frowned, but with a peremptory wave of his hand allowed him to get up. His uncle drew himself up to his full height. Painfully, with a great effort of will, he forced himself to look into the eyes of the man about to have him killed.

'For one of royal blood to die the death of a criminal would bring only shame to the royal house – not only to the one who is executed, but also to those of the same blood who ordered it to be carried out.'

No one dared to move. Nandi's gaze flew to Shaka. There was a quick flicker of triumph in the black eyes of Mkabayi. Truly, this brother of mine is a brave man, she thought, grudgingly. To speak out for a better death is the mark of one who is superior… but then he is a true Senzangakhona. His blood is not diluted, made sour by mating with an inferior!

'You have spoken well,' Shaka answered, dryly. 'I see you still have some respect for the royal line of Zulu, even though you are about to leave it.'

Mudli bowed his head in wry acknowledgement. Shaka continued, 'I said you would not die an easy death, but because I am also a warrior, a man of honour, as well as a king – '

The bird with the bright plumage paused in its singing and

fluffed out its feathers, a splash of vivid colour among the glossy leaves. Mudli waited, not daring to breathe.

The eyes of Shaka were victorious now, the ruthlessness in them belying the sadness that lay behind the memories of the cruelties inflicted on him as a child. Then he delivered his verdict.

'I shall allow you a soldier's death – but only to protect the honour of the people of the amaZulu, their King and his heirs, not for any other reason.'

Mudli's pent up breath eased out in a long sigh. He felt a fleeting pang of regret for such a fruitless end to his life.

An *induna* approached carrying a short-bladed spear, not unlike the king's legendary blade, Iklwa. Shaka's final words followed the man to where Mudli stood waiting to die, his back straight and shoulders thrown back.

"But I will not allow you to lie in Emkhosini, a place of honour, along with those of the same blood, your ancestors, and mine. After it is done, your body will be taken from here to a far-off place. There you will rot, your bones picked clean by scavengers.'

Mudli saw the waiting slayer's hand tighten on the shaft of the weapon. Quickly, he looked beyond him to the bird in the tree.

The spear plunged. One quick thrust up and under the ribs. He felt the cold heat of it withdraw before the next made him stagger, then crumple and fall to his knees.

As the blood spurted from his mouth, the last thing to register in the dying Mudli's brain was the startling likeness to his brother, the dead King, stamped on the face of the man on whom he had bestowed such a dishonourable name.

After the execution, Shaka's judgments came swiftly to a climax. Each accused person, whether male or female, were brought before him, one by one.

After all the evidence had been weighed, they had either a fine of cattle levied on them, been forgiven or were executed, as decreed by Nandi, for Shaka deferred to her in the final analysis.

After all, he had been very young when many of the offences were carried out.

The new king of the Zulus and his mother carried out their tasks with an outward impartiality that left the onlookers trembling and cowed.

Although justice was swift and no one deserving of death was spared, the families of those executed were neither harmed nor their cattle appropriated, as tradition demanded, but were left in peace to live out their lives with the remainder of their clan.

By the end of it all, the ritual slayers were exhausted; their hardwood clubs spattered with blood, tufts of hair, slivers of bone and grey brain matter.

As the impact of these events slowly passed, many realised perhaps the bloodletting had perhaps been necessary, sweeping away the old hurts and hatred so that the embryonic kingdom of the Zulus could begin to prosper.

One last act of justice remained. Soon after the execution of Mudli, Shaka and the Fasimba set out on a night march. Once they'd crossed the mountains, they entered the lands of the eLangeni.

Before dawn, Shaka and his warriors surrounded iNguga, the kraal of bitter memory, the place where he and his mother, a daughter of the clan, had suffered persecution and cruel treatment at the hands of the people said to be her own.

At first light, just as the horns of the cattle became visible through the early mists, Shaka and his *impis* swept down on the village. When the elderly chief of the eLangeni realised who it was, he surrendered in fear and trembling.

By the time the sun had risen, Shaka had singled out those who had inflicted misery on his family all those years ago, while his Fasimbi were scouring nearby villages for those he had commanded to be brought before him.

By mid-afternoon, they had all been judged and sentenced. There was no need for Nandi to be present on this occasion, for this was an acutely personal matter for Shaka, and one he wished to undertake alone.

As the shadows lengthened across the valley, each of the remembered ones had been impaled on sharpened stakes on a hillside beyond the village. Only the fact that he and his mother both carried the blood of the eLangeni in their veins prevented him from wiping out the entire clan.

This, as he explained to the terrified Chief, was an example of the high levels of justice he intended to set upon the land.

Shaka did not linger to gloat over the suffering of those he had chosen to die, only passed by once with a brief nod of recognition as if finally erasing them from his memory. However, he did stop briefly before one small group set apart from the others.

Looking deep into the eyes of Somnamuzi, their former leader, his fingers unconsciously touched the crescent-shaped scar on his cheek bone, a reminder of the wound left by a flying stone on a certain long-ago night.

'Hau, Somnamuzi, my old friend,' he said, 'I have returned to repay you, just as I said I would.'

The implications behind his words were lost on the young soldiers who flanked their commander on his slow parade past the condemned. Before leaving, Shaka ordered them to end their suffering. Placing piles of dried grass around the victims, they set them alight, the dense smoke bringing the dying men to a swift and merciful end.

After they'd topped the rise above the village, Shaka stopped and looked back at the kraal of iNguga. The dull red glare from the funeral pyres lit up the night sky, the smoke writhing up from them like the departing spirits of the dead. As he looked on it for the last time, his eyes were deadly and cold, his gaze utterly final.

As he turned away, growls of thunder spoke from the far-off horizons and lightning began to flicker in jagged bursts of frenetic energy.

Even the bold Fasimba shivered at the fury of this last and unexpected storm of the season. If they had looked closely at the man at their head they would have noticed that their Nkosi, Shaka, whose praise name was Nodumehlezi, Sitting Thunder, was smiling as he looked up into the dark skies.

And as the storm continued to rage in the heavens, the final act in the legend of Shaka and the eLangeni came to a close, far below.

Eight

In spite of the triumph of the early days, there was someone whose heart was tinged with sadness. Nandi had sat stoically through all the staged judgments and acts of retribution, betraying nothing of her inner feelings.

Her sorrows had begun on the night Shaka became king. After the feasting had died down, she had gone to bid him goodnight. With a tender smile on her face, she had stood watching him for a moment or two as he sat alone by the fire, staring into the flames.

It seemed to her that he still bore the aura of the long day's adulation. It curled around him like an unseen cloak of the finest materials, adding power to his impressive stature and brooding face.

Sensing her eyes on him, he looked up from the dancing flames. Nandi stepped forward, smiling, and stroked his head, feeling the curl of springy hair in the nape of his neck, his own unique mark.

'This is a day to end all days,' she said, 'but yet a wonderful beginning. In time, the sons of Shaka will lead the house of Zulu on to even greater things.'

His body went rigid, a frightening stillness below her fingers. A feeling of dread began to uncoil in the pit of her stomach, and her voice tapered away into silence.

The eyes raised to hers were dark and very steady in the fire-light, in them the hard glint of implacable resolution she knew so well. 'I will say this just once, Mame,' he said softly, 'so listen well. There will be no sons and heirs to spring from my loins...'

Her hands flew to her mouth. Unable to speak, she could only listen, appalled by what she read in her son's eyes. From a long distance away she heard him say, 'I will tolerate no son to plan and scheme behind my back. No bone of my bone, no flesh of my flesh will change from a smiling boy into a waiting assassin.'

'No, no!' Nandi burst out, falling to her knees beside him. 'Give me your sons and I will teach them a different way!'

Pushing her hands away, he stood up, towering over her as she crouched by the fire, her finery trailing in the dust and ashes. She rocked slowly from side to side, her arms wrapped round her body protectively.

Just when she thought she'd finished with her lifetime's portion of pain and sorrow and could look forward to being a grandmother in her mature years, her son's final words set the seal on a new kind of grief.

In one day, she had seen the culmination of more than she could ever have dreamed of. The crowning moment of her life had been when she'd returned to esiKlebeni with her son to claim their rightful positions.

Seeing him so strong and powerful, looking every inch a king, while those who had cause to fear them looked on with equal parts of dread and foreboding had been the sweetest of moments.

Now, her body shook in cold fear, not only for herself, but also for him. How could it be that in the space of one day she had fallen from the heights of joy to the depths of despair?

The flames cast ripples of amber light over his powerful body, the man's body honed into such lines of strength and grace that she could have wept from looking on its beauty.

'You are a warrior and a king, my son,' she cried out from the heart, 'but you are also a man of flesh and blood. If you remain alone, it will kill your heart. You need wives and children to grace your years and give you comfort.'

He rested his hand on her head for a moment and his voice was soft when he answered. 'Ay, Mame, I hear your words, but you will have to look to Nomcoba and Ngwadi for the joys you seek. The children of your children will not come from me, for all the reasons I have given you.'

His tone hardened. 'Among our people, it has always been so – son against father, brother against brother, father against son. I want no part of it. No son of mine will ever live to betray me.'

'One other thing you can also be sure of, Mame,' he added. 'I will see to it that no one will ever again cause you one moment of grief – not till the end of your days.'

There was such cold anger in him that Nandi bent her head to hide her tears. Unspoken words echoed in her head and reverberated through her soul. '*Yebo*, no one except you, my son.'

Part II

Nine

The hut of Nthabiseng, the *isangoma*, was perched on a grassy hillside. It overlooked a stream and was protected on three sides by natural outcrops of rock. There was no sign of life, only a wreath of blue smoke twining up from a hole in the thatch into the cold blue of the morning sky.

The rising sun sat low on the horizon, its slanting rays brassy but without warmth. Frozen dew lay white on the ground, undisturbed except for the delicate trails of small night animals, birds and the occasional snake. A single track of footsteps also led down to the stream, those of a young male stepping lightly on the balls of his feet.

Nthabiseng's apprentice, Langani, stood blowing on his hands to ease the numbing effects of the icy water. At his feet were the two large earthenware pots he would have to carry back up the hill, just as he had done every day for the past two years.

About eighteen years of age, he was tall and slim, his skin light-coloured and supple. Behind the direct look in his dark eyes lay an enquiring mind and astute intelligence. The most compelling thing about him, apart from his long, tapering hands and shapely feet, was the length of his hair.

According to his mother, Jubilele, even as a small child he had screamed like a demon and thrashed about if she tried to cut it to make him look like the other boys. In the end, she'd had no choice but to leave it alone.

Now he wore it braided into long plaits, some falling over his forehead, the rest coiled into a bundle at the nape of his neck or hanging loose around his shoulders.

His skin prickled with cold. Langani shrugged deeper into the folds of his monkey skin cloak and thrust his hands into his armpits to warm them. In a few moments, he would have to carry the heavy water pitchers back up the hill.

Nthabiseng, his demanding mentor, bathed every morning before beginning the lengthy rituals of prayer, dance, drumming and meditation in which Langani would also participate.

Afterwards, he would prepare the morning meal then set about cleaning the hut, sweeping the ground outside, watering the vegetable gardens and feeding the domestic animals. Then the main business of the day would begin, with village people coming to seek their advice and intercede with the ancestors on their behalf.

A booming female voice hailed him from above. Glancing up, he saw Nthabiseng standing at the door of the hut. A stout woman of indeterminate years, with a frosting of grey on her mop of peppercorn curls, she wore an unbecoming skirt with an old skin cloak thrown round her shoulders.

To casual eyes, she might resemble someone's grandmother, a woman past the first flush of youth with greying hair. But seeing her arrayed in her ceremonial dress transformed her into what she really was, a powerful diviner with outstanding skills in interpreting and dispensing the wisdom passed down to her by the ancestors.

'Would you like me to come down and begin the day's meditations by the cold, flowing waters, deprived of the warmth of my house?' she called out, wagging a stumpy finger at him. 'Perhaps if you stand there long enough the water jugs will fly up the hill on their own?'

The gruff voice held a trace of her usual humour, a trait fully appreciated by her eighteen-year-old apprentice. Never once had she resorted to bringing her clubbed stick down on his back or knuckles to punish him for an unwitting mistake or minor infringement of the rules. He'd heard rumours of former apprentices being punished by fire, starvation, or various other forms of subjugation during their apprenticeship.

Aiii, he thought, wincing as the flow of blood returned to his hands, she never seems to feel either the chill of winter or the heat of summer, not for her the weaknesses of ordinary flesh.

Quickly, he bent to pick up the water pitchers and made his way back up the hill to where she was waiting for him.

It was late afternoon before Langani found himself with some time on his hands. This he accepted as a reward for his diligence during the first two years of his apprenticeship.

During the first long, arduous year of training, Nthabiseng had been merciless. She had filled every minute of his waking hours with demands for water, wood for the fire, cleaning the dwelling inside and out, tending the gardens, memorising incantations, searching for herbs, praying, drumming and hours of intense meditation. Relentlessly, she had tried to force both his body and spirit into submission, using her stubby fingers to prod him awake in the middle of the night with yet more demands.

The second year had been much the same. Sometimes, it felt as if she were driving him towards either total submission to her will or to an explosion of frustrated rebellion, perhaps even the breaking of his spirit.

During this difficult and testing time, Langani had learned many things. By giving her his best, but not an inch more, by keeping his mouth closed and his thoughts under control, he was able to protect the precious kernel of inner calm and mask any youthful resentment regarding her attempts to dominate him so thoroughly.

To his surprise, at the end of the second year, Nthabiseng had taken him aside and told him how pleased she was with his progress. With her face still daubed with the traditional white clay of her calling, she had stared deep into his eyes for a long time before speaking.

'The path the *amadhlozi* have chosen for us, their servants, is a hard one. But you already know that. As a young boy, you suffered the deep spiritual anguish known as *ukutwasa*, as all who are chosen must do.'

He'd nodded, remembering the times he'd been driven frantic by dreams, voices and visions, fearing he was going mad, as had his gentle mother, Jubilele.

According to his grandmother, Cebile, who was a more pragmatic character, she had broken down and confessed that she been waiting for it to happen since he'd been a child.

Langani had run away more than once, trying to break free of the demons he was sure were playing tricks on him. In the end, it was his *ugogo*, his grandmother, who had saved him.

Cebile had appealed to the local *isangoma* to intercede, and protect him from *umnyama*, the mystical force of darkness she believed had been hovering around him since the day of the great storm of esiKlebeni some ten years earlier.

The adolescent Langani had refused to ask just what had happened to him on that day. In the end, around the age of fifteen, he had bowed to the inevitable and accepted the spiritual path the ancestors had chosen for him. After that, there was no turning back, no changing his destiny, no pining for the loss of things a young boy thought important – such as friends, stick fighting, or young girls.

After her initial compliment, Nthabiseng had gone on with her appraisal of him. 'In the beginning,' she said, 'I had grave doubts about your willingness to be obedient, but you showed great humility, submitting to all I have asked of you without reproach – or very little, anyway,' she added, with a flash of her customary humour.

Leaning forward, she had tapped him on the knee and with a twinkle in her eye, commented, 'Even though we are servants of the *amadhlozi*, their messengers and interpreters until the day death takes us – we are also of humankind, with all its weaknesses. We do not have to be perfect and without blemish, only to be true to who and what we are. Remember it well.'

Now half-way through his third year of apprenticeship, Langani relished the short periods of time he was free to call his own. They tended to be in the calm intervals of time between the fading of light into darkness and the first blush of dawn and the rising of the sun.

Often he would wake with his heart thumping, the threads of dreams still spinning through his conscious mind. He would lie there, rigid and sweating, while the fractured images spooled around him.

Afterwards, there was invariably a web of questions to be answered. Where do the images, the dreams, come from, and what do they mean? Are they from the ancestors, or from another source?

Gradually, he lost his instinctive fear of the unknown and accepted the 'waking dreams' for what they were – seemingly unrelated fragments of time or shadows of events, though whether from the past, present, or the future, he had no way of knowing.

But that was not all. Through no volition of his own, he sometimes found himself on another level, another plane, often flying through space and time, sometimes afraid, sometimes not, yet fully conscious of all manner of strange things around him. Reluctant to bring these experiences to Nthabiseng's attention, he said nothing. His instincts told him that these dreams, visions, or part-visions were not connected to his training or his services to the *amadhlozi*.

Take the eye, the 'magical' eye, for example.He had awakened a few days ago in the still calm hour before dawn to find it filling his vision.

An eye, a single human eye...

Langani knew it belonged to a living person because of the light of life in it, also the natural sweep of the eyelid as it opened and closed, and the way it blinked from time to time.

Although he could see nothing of the rest of the face, he sensed there was nothing to fear from whoever the eye belonged to. In short, it was not a manifestation of evil delivered by a sorcerer looking to torment him

The intriguing thing about the eye was that the coloured ring, the iris, was not all the same colour, in this case, dark brown. It looked as if a part of it had been removed by a very sharp knife and the rarest of jewels inserted neatly into it to form a glittering, swirling mass of gold and emerald green, flecked with darker, floating specks of both colours.

To Langani, this 'magical' eye was unique, mesmerising, and different from any human eye he had ever seen. Whether it belonged to a man or a woman he couldn't say, though he thought it likely to be male. There was a bold ferocity in its depths not usually found in the gentler gaze of a woman.

Who do you belong to? he would silently ask it. Have you come to me of your own will, or did someone send you?

The eye, of course, did not reply. But from time to time, Langani, the apprentice diviner, thought he could detect in it a fleeting echo of mischievous laughter.

Early one morning in the dead of winter, Langani turned over in his sleep and muttered a warning to someone he didn't know.

'*Jakot! Look out!*' Then he proceeded to ascend into a place where his dreaming spooled out like ribbons floating in the wind, twisting and turning, twisting and turning.

Outside, hoar frost sparkled on every blade of grass and outcrop of rock, while the icy waters of the stream continued to wend their way down to the sea through the silent, sleeping land of the Zulus.

The place where Langani found himself, however, was very different.

Ten

The air was full of the dust thrown up by the hooves of the long-horned cattle.

By nightfall, the eyes of the Xhosa raiders would be bloodshot and gritty. But darkness would also be their ally. They would be able to cross the river, holding on to the wide, curved horns of the steers while cajoling them with talk of the sweet pastures on the other side.

But for now the sun was still high, and it would be some hours before they could leave the clearing and make for the river. Sheltered in deep bush a mile or so away, it would be safe to light a small fire and eat some food, the first they'd had since the day before. The raiders were exhausted and the rest would give them much-needed stamina for the hard night that lay ahead.

Fifteen-year-old Jakot caught sight of his friend Majozi and laughed out loud, his teeth white against his dusty skin. Majozi gazed back at him, his mouth an open round O, the whites of his eyes luminous in his mud-caked face.

To Jakot, he resembled nothing more than an ancient earth spirit, a goblin sprinkled brown with dust, his mischievous eyes glowing like coals. He reminded him of the paintings he had once seen etched on the walls of a cave in the mountains.

Majozi's teeth flashed in a brilliant smile, cracking the caked mud. He waggled his fingers in his ears and pulled a face.

Ever since Jakot had run away from the Boers some years earlier, the bright-eyed, eternally curious Majozi had become his shadow, following him everywhere. He'd been about the same age as Majozi when he'd been captured during a cattle raid carried out across the Bushman River. Stoically, he had endured two long years of captivity and back-breaking work with little food and the occasional beating, while he watched and waited for the right moment to arrive.

When it came, he took it. One night, while the farmer and his friends were sitting around the fires carousing, he had slipped away into the darkness. Travelling by night and lying low during the day, living off the land as best he could, twelve-year-old Jakot had eventually found his way back to the river.

Crossing it under cover of darkness, he doggedly pushed on until he reached the kraal of his father, Chief Ndlambe, who had given him up for dead.

Now, still only fifteen years old, Jakot was considered a seasoned veteran of the running battles between the Xhosa and the Dutch farmers of Cape Colony – not simply because of his skills in cattle rustling, but because he could speak the guttural language of the Boers, which allowed him to eavesdrop on their conversations and report back their secrets.

Consequently, Jakot was all that ten-year-old Majozi aspired to. Already tall and handsome, the confident swagger in his walk had the young maidens and even some of the older women casting longing eyes in his direction.

Fearless and daring in the running fights with the enemy, able and skilled at most things, the boy longed to be just like him –

except, of course, for two other matters relating to Jakot, one bad, the other infinitely desirable.

The 'bad thing' was that Jakot suffered from the falling sickness. It made him fall to the ground with his eyes rolling back in his head, his teeth clenched and froth bubbling from his mouth. Majozi had seen this happen and it had terrified him, thinking that demons had possessed his friend.

The fact that Jakot was still alive – in spite of the deeply rooted tribal superstitions concerning such matters – was only one more example of his friend's great good luck.

The 'wonderful thing', on the other hand, was what had drawn Majozi's admiration to his hero in the first place – Jakot's 'golden' eye.

There had been nothing godlike about the boy who had crawled back into the village, half-starved and painfully thin after weeks on the run, but as far as Majozi was concerned, nothing could dim the glory of Jakot and his left eye.

What an eye! It was the talisman of a special person on whom the ancestors had already bestowed many gifts. A segment of about two thirds of the deep brown of the iris had been sliced out, as neatly as if by a sharp knife, and replaced with a tawny, gold section, full of swirling green and brown fragments.

To Majozi, it was part of the living eye of a lion, feral and implacable, an embedded jewel of gold fire in the eye of the youth already being hailed as a hero.

Without it, Jakot was impressive enough. With it, Majozi truly believed, nothing could ever go wrong for his friend.

Hermanus Rademeyer stood out head and shoulders above many other hard Dutchmen on the frontier, and Jakot knew all there was to know about him.

Rademeyer's code was very simple. The white man was king out here, as well as everywhere else; his was the rule of law, the right to take land, graze it, and settle on it. No one else counted, and no one who stood in his way would be tolerated.

He rode with his five sons at the head of the commando, burly, bearded silhouettes with slouched hats, black against the sky, men who could ride like the devil and shoot with deadly precision just as accurately from the back of a galloping horse as from any other position.

Hermanus himself could not easily meld into a group, any group. His six foot five of hard muscle, bone and enormous girth of back and shoulders saw to that. His jutting silver beard, long moustaches and roan stallion also helped to identify him, to make him stand out among the others.

It was because of all of these things that Jakot and Majozi were here on the southern bank of the river on a hot afternoon, waiting for night to come before slipping back across it with the cattle Rademeyer had stolen from them in the first place.

The diversion created the day before by the more experienced members of the Xhosa raiding party had been planned solely as a decoy, to draw the Rademeyers away from the farm long enough for the Xhosa cattle to be retrieved by Jakot and the others, eight of them in all. They had not killed the women, children and petrified servants, but had merely shut them up in one of the barns and barred the doors, before running off the livestock, which had been theirs, anyway.

After mercilessly pushing themselves and the cattle for all of yesterday and most of that day, they needed to rest before attempting to cross the river after dark. If things went to plan, the rest of the raiding party would be able to either catch up with them or ford the river on their own.

Jakot's stomach rumbled loudly. It seemed an age since he'd last eaten. The tantalising aroma of cooking meat, the drip of sizzling juices and spat of fat as it burst out of the skin made his mouth flood with saliva.

Majozi looked up with his usual cheeky grin and said, 'Eh, I hear your stomach complaining. Mine too! How long until we eat?'

Shielding his eyes, Jakot looked up at the sun. Three or four hours more, then it would start to slip slowly behind the tree-tops. 'Soon, I hope,' he replied, 'otherwise my bones will begin to show through my skin.'

He slid gratefully down beside Majozi and went about the serious business of checking the soles of his feet for thorns, pieces of grit, and burrowing jiggers.

The sunlight filtering through the leaves was pleasant. A gentle breeze stirred the topmost branches of the trees. He began to relax. Eyes closed, he turned to say something to Majozi. Getting no reply, he squinted round, half-expecting to find him asleep. Instead, he saw the unmistakable pallor of fear below the caked dust on the boy's face.

Looking around, Jakot's eyes bulged in disbelief. A man on horseback had just emerged from the bush and was picking his way into the sun-dappled clearing. Behind him were four or five others, menace staring out of their bearded faces, aggression in the set of the bodies below the sweat-stained clothes.

Boers! But how had they managed to find them? The leader's mount, a chestnut stallion, snickered gently and tossed its head, the jingle and clink of harness clear in the stillness.

On his feet now, Jakot yelled to Majozi. 'Run! Make for the bush!'

The clearing erupted into a bedlam of noise; the crack of rifle fire and bellowing of terrified cattle, curses and shouts of pain, the stink of cordite sharp in the air. Jakot darted a glance over his shoulder, expecting to see Majozi behind him.

Instead, he saw the massive bulk of the chestnut stallion rearing over the boy. The man on its back began to uncoil the fearsome rhino-hide whip, the *sjambok*. His laughter boomed out above the bedlam of bawling cattle and gunfire. 'Hey, little kaffir, how'd you like a tickle with this, then?'

Majozi was backed up against a tree, terror written large on his chubby face. Jakot feverishly cast around for something to use as a weapon. The only thing to hand was the length of springy sapling he'd used to herd the cattle. The only trouble was that it was on the ground, almost below the horse's hooves.

Before he could make a dive for it, another bearded rider burst out of the thicket, blood streaming from a gash on his arm and spattering the horse's flanks. Spotting Jakot, he yelled out in guttural Dutch, *'Vang hom, catch him! Maak gou, hurry!'*

Wheeling round, he deflected a spear-thrust with the barrel of his rifle then discharged the weapon into the face of the Xhosa who had tried to bring him down. Meantime, the man on the chestnut stallion turned sharply away from Majozi and cast a swift eye over Jakot. Deciding against the whip, he reached down to pull his rifle from the stock.

Jakot needed no urging. He dived under the horse's hoofs and made a grab for the sapling, his voice hoarse with fear.

'Run, Majozi! Now!' he yelled. 'The river, hide…wait for me there!'

He was so close to the flailing hooves he could smell the animal's pungent sweat and hear the creak of saddle leather. Grabbing the length of sapling, he rolled swiftly away. On his feet in seconds, he brought the springy lash down on the horse's rump in one stinging cut after another.

The animal screamed shrilly, and reared up on its hind legs, threatening to dislodge its rider, and collide with the second horse. Startled curses rang out as the men struggled to control their mounts.

'Move, Majozi! Go, go!! '

Behind them, the static crack of a whip cut through the air. Majozi sprinted for the dense bush. 'Don't look back, I'm behind you, little brother,' Jakot yelled.

The youngster raced away, his skinny legs pumping. Diving into the thick bush, he was quickly swallowed up by the summer greenery.

The tightly-plaited whip snaked out with a vicious snap, making Jakot flinch. Tobacco on the man's breath, a dark patch of sweat staining the front of the homespun shirt visible between the bandoliers slung across his chest.

'You like whips, boy?' The words were ground out from a throat parched by the dust of a long ride. 'I'll give you a taste of mine, kaffir, teach you not to strike my bleddy horse, man!'

In his haste to avoid the *sjambok*, Jakot almost backed into the rider who had come up behind him. He spun round, but not fast enough. A vicious blow from a rifle butt caught him on the shoulder. He crumpled to his knees, his right arm numb to the finger tips.

A brief flash of an assegai blade in the bright sunlight, a sucking smack of metal as it entered flesh and bone, then a strangled cry. The second rider slumped in the saddle, the trailing whip falling uselessly to the ground. One boot caught in the stirrup, the body was dragged along the ground by the terrified horse, the slack limbs jerking while blood spattered in a wide arc around it.

Then Jakot was on his feet and running, trying to protect his numbed arm and bruised shoulder, watery blood trickling out from between his fingers. He dodged away, looking neither to right nor left, his breath ragged.

Unarmed, it would be pointless to stay, to provide sport or a source of free labour for the Boers. Cattle could always be found again, even in *amabhuna* country. The main thing was to survive, to live and fight another day.

As he ran, his mind was racing. Their carefully laid plans had somehow gone wrong. These men were not Rademeyer and his sons, because they were miles away, following the Xhosa decoys. Somehow, this other group had appeared out of nowhere, like spirits on the wind.

Running, stumbling, shafts of fire shooting through his arm with every jolt, Jakot's heart was heavy with the thought of the Xhosa casualties. When he slammed into the taut strand of rope strung between two trees, it caught him unawares.

Slicing him straight across the throat, it threw him backwards, knocking the breath from him. He lay on the ground, choking, desperately trying to draw breath. Above him, there was triumph in the taunting voices.

'Well, boy, don't be running away from us now. Don't you want to come with? Ach, siss, man, you'll just love it, back on the farm with us!'

To avoid the vicious kick aimed at his ribs, he tried to roll to one side, but was hampered by his useless arm and the searing pain in his shoulder. Dazed, gasping to draw air into his lungs, resistance was useless. He was dragged upright and his wrists bound roughly together, the thin rope biting into his flesh. He clenched his teeth, determined not to show weakness.

'So, kaffir, it hurts, hey? Bleddy pity!'

A well-aimed kick in the buttocks thrust him bodily towards a small group of Xhosas captured during the raid. His heart sank when he saw Majozi and noticed the long scrape of raw flesh along the side of his jaw. The younger boy's face lit up when he saw Jakot, but fell when he saw his bound hands and the pain on his face.

The man on the chestnut mare rode into the clearing, prodding another captive ahead of him, the barrel of his rifle aimed at the back of the man's head.

Jakot saw it was Kalimba, the leader of their raiding party. He was also someone who had fallen foul of the Boers and consequently understood their language. He glanced at the livid red weals crisscrossing the chestnut's sleek brown haunch. Reacting to his smell, the animal snorted and pawed the ground, rolling its eyes.

'So, what have we here, gentlemen?'

The guttural voice was heavy with sarcasm. The rider dug the toe of his boot into Jakot's ribs, '*Meneers*, I believe we have a young man here who likes whips! Hey, boy?'

A titter of gruff laughter followed. The toe of the man's boot connected with Jacob's thigh, making him stagger. 'See what you did to my bleddy horse, you stinking black. Now you'll get a taste of what I promised you.'

Jakot closed his eyes, and steeled himself for the first cut of the whip. A sharp command rang out. The hand wielding the *sjambok* fell to the man's side.

'No time for that just now, *kerel,*' said a hard voice, hoarse with dust. 'The light's beginning to go – and we must take Vannie and Dirk back home. Poor bastards, we can't leave them out in the *bundu.*'

The gloved hand pulled at the reins, the horse's head turned and the man cantered back the way he'd come, his final words floating over his shoulder like deadly fireflies on the dusty sunlight slanting through the trees. 'Bring these 'gentlemen' along, or just get rid, one way or the other – but get a move on!'

The man on the chestnut stallion swung himself out of the saddle, his body stiff after hours of hard riding. Pulling out his rifle, he checked the firing pan.

Jakot felt his legs begin to buckle. Lack of food and water, pain and shock were beginning to take their toll on him. His eyes met those of Kalimba. In them, he saw confirmation of his own fears about how this was going to end.

In desperation, he caught Majozi's attention. Jakot shot a warning glance at the rider, then at the bush, desperately trying to alert him as to what he should do. The answering flicker of hope in the boy's eyes told him the message had been received and understood.

A few yards away, one or two of the Boers had been arguing, casting angry looks in their direction. Obviously, their fate was being decided. So far, they hadn't realised that he and Kalimba both understood Afrikaans.

The discussion ended abruptly when one of the Xhosas was dragged across the clearing, forced to his knees, and the barrel of a rifle held to his head. The click of the trigger was loud in the silence. Another click and another, followed by a stream of guttural oaths as the gun's mechanism failed to work. One of the young Xhosa boys fell to his knees, sobbing in terror.

Jakot called out in Afrikaans, desperation in his voice. '*Nie, meneer,* don't kill him! He's a good man, better he lives to work for you, *baas.*'

The unexpected experience of hearing his own language issue from the mouth of a cattle rustler stayed the gunman's hand.

'What the fok are you talkin', boy?' His face was plum coloured with rage. 'Get yourself over here!'

Jakot was propelled towards him by a shove in the back. He fixed his gaze somewhere beyond the man's shoulder, aware of the cocking of rifles behind him.

'So you speak the *taal*, eh?' the guttural voice said. 'In which case, you'll know enough about my people, my *volk*, to know what's going to happen next.'

This time the firearm's mechanism didn't fail. Two shots rang out, close together. Jakot felt the warm spatter of blood on his bare feet. He saw splinters of bone and blood spurting from the back of the man's head and the shuddering tremors of the body as it collapsed face down on the ground.

The red-faced farmer wiped spots of blood from his face. He grimaced, looked at the back of his hand then wiped it on the seat of his homespun trews. Grabbing Jakot by the arm, he shouted, '*Vertel die muntoes*, tell the natives…'

Before he had a chance to finish, there was the blur of a fast-moving body and the solid thwack of flesh on flesh. A hoarse cry burst from the man as Kalimba dealt him a swift, chopping blow across the throat, followed by a second, which crushed the Boer's windpipe.

Kalimba rose from the gurgling body with a triumphant cry, the dead man's rifle held high. A sudden movement to his right; sun glinting on a rifle barrel, Jakot shouted a warning, but it was too late.

Three shots, one after the other. They caught Kalimba full in the chest while he was still fumbling with the mechanism of the unfamiliar weapon. His knees buckled and he slid to the ground, his hands blindly trying to stem the flow of blood.

It was the end of any resistance. Kalimba and the other dead were left behind where they lay, while the bodies of the Boers were tied to their horses, ready for the long trek home.

Jakot, Majozi and the other Xhosas were led away, their hands tied in front of them. A tether rope was then attached to the saddle pummels and they were forced to jog along behind the horses. Overseeing the prisoners was the rider with the *sjambok*, while bringing up the rear were the dead men's horses with the blanketed bodies slung over the saddles.

As they stumbled away, Jakot became aware of the circling birds of prey, dark against the slowly sinking sun. Resolutely, he shut his mind against what he knew would follow. He ran on, sight and sound closed against everything around him, even to the whimpering of poor Majozi, who was finding it hard to keep up.

Jakot did not weep when he thought of his people who had been left behind for the predators. He did not cry out when the lash of the *sjambok* bit into the flesh on his back, laying it open to the bone. All that he silently prayed for was that the epilepsy, the 'falling sickness' would not come upon him now.

But when they cut the flayed body of Majozi from the rope attached to the rider's saddle horn, and left him behind, a small, crumpled heap on the *veldt*, only then did Jakot close his eyes and allow the tears to fall.

Eleven

Langani woke up with a gasp, struggling for breath, convinced he was drowning. His eyelids fluttered open. Unsure of where he was, he lay still for a few moments, his heart pumping against his ribs.

Gradually, familiar things began to float into view, bringing him back to a sense of perspective. He turned over on to his side, still breathing heavily. Judging by the chinks of grey light seeping in around the goatskin flap covering the doorway, it was still early, not yet sunrise.

A quick look told him Nthibesing was bundled up asleep in the far corner of the hut, snoring gently. With an effort, careful not to wake her, he rose from his sleeping mat and padded over to the doorway. Pulling back the goatskin flap, he crawled outside.

The cold morning air hit him with an icy sting, making him gasp and raising prickles of gooseflesh on his still warm skin. Ducking back inside, he hastily wrapped his tattered goatskin cloak around his shoulders and thrust his bare feet into a pair of ox-hide sandals.

The sky was a pale wintry blue with wisps of mist coiling around the tops of the surrounding hills. The tip of the sun had only just risen above the horizon. Golden shafts of light caught the crystals of hoar frost and made them sparkle.

Langani looked at the shimmering panorama before him and drew in a deep breath of smoky air. He smiled. At times like these, the world had no need of a sorcerer's magic.

A young black bird flew down on to a nearby rock, folded its wings and cocked a beady eye expectantly at him. 'Hey, little sister,' he said, 'it's not time for breakfast yet. Be patient, wait a while.'

As if on cue, the bird fluttered into the air and disappeared among the rocks. Later, it would wait to be fed crumbs of bread from their morning meal, as it always did.

Langani walked down to the stream, the stiff blades of grass crunching beneath his feet. Using a series of flat rocks as stepping stones, he waded out to mid-stream and stood there watching the water flow over the mossy green stones. The gurgle and glide of the rushing water cleared his mind and helped to focus his thoughts.

He had no way of knowing whether what he had just witnessed had come from the past or was rooted in the present. Somehow he did not think it was from the future. He doubted his powers were strong enough to allow him to project his spiritual energy forward, out of his own time.

One thing he was sure of, though – what had occurred had not taken place here, in his own land. The colour of the soil, the terrain and vegetation was different.

As for the people, their tribal markings and dress had been unfamiliar. Although he had understood what had happened, the actual words and inflection, although broadly rooted in the Nguni language, had sounded subtly different to his ear.

And then there were the *abelungu,* the white men. He shook his head.

Aiii! The weapons they'd carried, the noise and destruction... their clothing, so heavy and stiff, reeking of sweat, their feet encased in ugly wrappings. And as for the animals on whose backs they rode!

He clicked his tongue in amazement as he recalled the pungent animal sweat, the flying manes and rolling eyes as they'd risen up on their back legs, snickering in fear. Truly, the power and magic of the white men must be mighty if their pointing sticks could kill men from a distance.

Although he had heard of the existence of the *abelungu*, he had never seen them in the flesh, or had known anyone who had. Now that he had witnessed their cruelty at first hand, he was not sure he ever wanted to.

It was rumoured that Shaka's supplies of beads, trinkets and the other marvels were obtained by trading with them, but how or when such events occurred, it was impossible to say.

In any case, you did not ask too many questions concerning the comings and goings of the Zulu court, or who Shaka, Lord of the World, met or did not meet.

All he knew was that white men lived far to the south in the place where the land of Africa came to an end amidst the roaring of mighty waters – or so the elders said. Did this mean that what he had seen had taken place in the lands of the *abelungu*? He could think of no other explanation.

A trickle of ice-cold water lapped over his feet, a reminder of his present whereabouts. Langani shivered, stepped back on to the bank and shook the water from his sandals.

Now that he had narrowed down the location of what he had seen, he also realised something else. The youth called Jakot and his 'magic' eye were no longer fleeting images from the nether world of dreams, but as real as he was.

A flare of compassion welled up in him for the youth's pain and anguish. He had suffered much – not only for the bones laid bare on his back or the wounds on his wrists caused by the ropes lashing him to the saddle of the white man's horse – but also for the heartbreak of having to leave the body of his friend, abandoned, broken and pathetically alone.

Later on, just before the day's meditations began, it came to the young diviner, Langani, like a bolt of summer lightning.

What if Jakot Msimbithi was connected much nearer to home, to Zululand itself, perhaps? If not, why had he experienced what he had, and seen it in such detail?

But at this point in time, Langani was sure of only one thing. It was inevitable that he and the youth with the magical eye would meet again – if not in the flesh, then in that other place, the one between one world and another.

Twelve

A year or so after Shaka became king of the Zulus Dingiswayo was lured to his death by Ntombazi, Zwide's devil of a mother.

After the flesh was removed from his body, the bones were boiled in a pot then scattered to the four winds. Then exactly as Shaka had warned, his head joined the pyramid of skulls in the foul hut of the witch, Ntombazi.

It was a poor end for Dingiswayo, the man who was once called Godongwana, the wanderer. He had been a brave and honourable man who had tried to offer his enemies the olive branch of peace instead of imposing conquest, ruin and death on them.

In their joy at his downfall, both Zwide and his mother chose to ignore the fact that Shaka, now the Commander of the Mthethwe army, was not of the same forgiving nature as the dead king.

Also, he had a very long memory indeed concerning those who used the powers of witchcraft to fulfil their ambitions – especially when those plans might seem to threaten his own.

Shaka was in a sombre, brooding mood. His dire warnings to Dingiswayo had become reality. The more he thought about it, the more incensed he grew.

'Why didn't you listen to me when I warned you of the danger of humiliating Zwide for a third time?' he muttered. 'Even a *dassie* will turn and try to bite its tormentor if pushed too far. You ignored the fact that Zwide, the man his enemies liken to the crocodile, has a long snout, and very sharp teeth.'

He got up and paced the floor. After a time, his rage cooled. It was inevitable that Zwide, puffed up by the disposal of his arch enemy, would begin to turn his attentions elsewhere. And the commander of the Mthethwe army knew just where that would be.

Shaka continued his relentless pacing. At all costs, the tiny kingdom of the amaZulu must survive. It would be necessary for him to take steps to ensure that the Zulus would never again bow the knee to another overlord, not even one as charitable as Dingiswayo.

So, in one of the audacious moves for which he was famous, Shaka turned to Chief Patakwayo of the Qwabe, hoping to make him an ally in the coming struggles with Zwide.

When he was a boy, Patakwayo and the quick-tempered, obstinate youth had clashed on more than one occasion. Totally disregarding the fact that the young Shaka of old had become a powerful leader of men, the Qwabe leader received his overtures with some amusement.

The old insults concerning the size of Shaka's genitals were bandied about by the ill-advised, over-confident Patakwayo in much the same way as they had been all those years ago. Even the minute size of the Zulu army provoked ribald comments among his commanders.

Shaka, therefore, decided he had no option but to fight the Qwabe as well as Zwide and the Ndwandwe. And fight them the Zulus did, with such ferocity that their small, well-trained army routed Patakwayo's army and forced it into full retreat.

Afterwards, Patakwayo was found sitting on the ground with his head buried in his hands. In the same way as Dingiswayo had done with Zwide, Shaka contemptuously refused to harm him and allowed him to go home.

The following day, Patakwayo was found curled up in the same position, stone dead. *'In his great fear and dread of Shaka, his spirit had fled in the night'*- or so the rumours went.

Not only was the Zulu Nkosi stubborn and fearless, he was also a master of propaganda. As the story spread, it served to add to the growing belief that his power was deeply rooted in the other world, and that his cunning and prowess was superhuman, beyond that of ordinary men.

Just over a year after Dingiswayo's death, Shaka's ambitions had surpassed even those of his former patron. As his reputation grew, other small clans agreed to come under the command of the Zulus.

If they refused, they were annihilated, the survivors scattered to the four winds and their cattle appropriated. Finally, the former Mthethwe nation, which had been in danger of breaking up into small, warring clans, was brought under his influence.

Zululand was no longer small or insignificant. From its original area of only a hundred square miles, it had grown to more than five or six times that size.

'Impi ebomvu…a red war, a fight to the finish' had become the order of the day.

A year later, Zwide mounted what he believed would be the final defeat of the upstart Zulu, once Dingiswayo's protégé and now a serious thorn in his flesh. In the great battle of Gqokli Hill, Shaka and his *impis* faced the Ndwandwe for the battle that would decide matters once and for all.

Shaka, wily as ever, took up a position in wooded country, which favoured his disciplined, well-trained army. During a pitched battle that lasted for more than eight hours, they scattered the enemy and inflicted severe punishment on them.

Eventually, the Ndwandwe were close to collapse. Suffering from thirst and lack of food, delirious from the spells and magic charms slipped into their drinking water, their fitful sleep was haunted by the dark shapes of the audacious Zulus who flitted among them during the night, wailing like lost souls

The Ndwandwe, although convinced they were bewitched, put up a spirited last stand. The battle lasted for days, and casualties on both sides were heavy. At one point, Shaka himself became hemmed in and was in imminent danger of being slaughtered.

At the end of it, four of Zwide's sons lay among the dead, their sire running for his life, the Ndwandwe power fractured, if not for good, then for the foreseeable future.

The king of the Zulus emerged from the bloody conflict to find himself ruling a territory far larger than that of any other ruler in the history of south-east Africa.

In the safety of the Swazi mountains, Zwide had ample time to nurse his wounds and dwell on his fate. Nightly, his sleep was haunted by the bone-chilling sounds of Shaka's encircling warriors, while his waking hours were spent nursing his grievances.

The prophetic words of his mother, Ntombazi, returned many times to haunt him over the next few years.

'*There is another yet to beware, one who has neither the mercy nor the temperate heart of the mighty Dingiswayo, one who has not yet come into his own. Like the herds of buffalo, black on the plains, I see his great armies come...* '

Thirteen

After her son's defeat, Ntombazi came under the extremely close scrutiny of the King of the Zulus. Snarling like a cornered beast, she was forced to submit to those he'd ordered to bring her to justice.

The trial was held in the Place of Judgment situated in the centre of the former leader's stronghold. When Shaka swept in to sit in the chair once occupied by the ill-fated Zwide, a frisson of superstitious horror ran through the watching people.

His gaze swept round the crowded interior of the great hut, and the hubbub of chatter swiftly dwindled to a respectful hush. Understandably, it was tinged with a natural terror of the man who had just slaughtered their armies and disposed of their chief and four of his sons.

When Ntombazi was brought in under guard, a sibilant hiss rose from the watchers, every eye fixed on the woman who had been personally responsible for the deaths of so many. A glance at the implacable face of the Zulu king told them that her fatal mistake had been in turning her evil powers on Dingiswayo, the man who had helped him rise to power.

Below the grotesque mask of white clay, Ntombazi was still a handsome woman, amazingly youthful for her age. For what would undoubtedly be her last public appearance, she had dressed in the full regalia of her calling.

Holding a switch of gnu tails across her breasts, on her head was a macabre head-dress of feathers and animal tails, while the long, braided hair snaking over her shoulders was threaded with inflated goats' bladders. Every time she moved, the dry rattle of the animal bones, teeth and claws strung around her neck and wrists sent shivers through the crowd.

Nothing escaped Shaka's keen eye. She had what the Zulus called 'shadow'- character and personality to a marked degree. When he saw how she was secretly enjoying her powers of intimidation, his eyes narrowed in amusement.

Tension ran around the assembly. This would be no ordinary trial or judgment. It had all the hallmarks of a contest, a duel to the death.

Breathlessly, they waited for the battle to begin. Who would win? The warrior King was invincible on the field of battle, it was true, but how would he fare against the supernatural powers possessed by the witch, Ntombazi?

The young man tucked discreetly into a shadowy corner of the Place of Judgment had absolutely no doubt as to who would turn out to be the stronger of the two. Clad in a simple *umutsha* of unadorned leather, and with his long plaits bundled below the tattered goatskin cloak thrown around his shoulders against the morning chill, no one gave Langani a second glance.

The King of the Zulus' overt dislike of the occult was well-known – apart from the odd occasion when he'd seen fit to use such practices to his own advantage, Langani thought, dryly. Take the case of the short, flat-bladed sword called iKlwa, for instance.

Rumour had it that he had deliberately chosen to have the weapon ritually tempered and consecrated by the human fat delivered by one of the *inswelaboya,* the infamous secret society of murderers and procurers. It also added to the belief that the occult was the real source of Shaka's power and legendary skills in battle.

Langani thought it unlikely. For one thing, no one, no matter how powerful, would be allowed to publicly oppose the malignant forces, yet still avail himself of their protection, or their services. The dark forces of the spirit world were not that forgiving – or accommodating.

He glanced around the shadowy recesses of the Judgment Place. The expressions on some of the faces made him wonder what had drawn each of them there that day. Simple reasons mostly, he thought – personal revenge, the thirst for blood, a chance to witness the spectacle of the mighty Zulu King bring down one of the minions of darkness – or the other way around.

His own excuses for being there were more complex. The main reason, or so he told himself, was purely professional. In watching the trial of a notorious witch, he hoped to gain insight into the practices and beliefs of the sinister sisterhood to which Ntombazi belonged.

There were, of course, other deeper and more private reasons why nineteen-year-old Langani was secreted among the crowds that day. First of all, he wanted to see Shaka of the Zulus in the flesh. After all, who would not want to catch a glimpse of the legendary warrior king, the man who had risen in the firmament of Zululand like a shooting star?

His heart beat a little faster. Not long ago he had found out that his grand mother, Cebile, was dying. Knowing her days on earth were about to end, she had insisted on telling him what had happened on the day of the great storm of esiKlebeni, when he was just four years old.

With her usual wicked sense of humour, his grandmother had looked at him with a twinkle in her faded old eyes.

'It would be a great pity, would it not,' she said, 'to wait until I had become spirit and then have to use your services as *isangoma* to come back and let you know what I am about to tell you now?'

And they had laughed together, Langani holding her gnarled work-worn hands in his, she gazing fondly up at him. 'Do you remember the day of the great storm,' she asked, 'the one that blew away half of esiKlebeni?'

He had shaken his head. 'I was only a small boy, *ugogo*. And we have had many storms since then.'

She cackled softly. 'Well, that may be true, but let me tell you, it was a storm that your mother, among many others, will never forget.'

'So I have heard,' he replied, a little impatiently. 'Tell me, why has this great fear followed her for so long?'

'She was afraid you'd been bewitched,' Cebile answered, watching his face carefully. Langani's response had been one of incredulity.

'Bewitched? She thought that someone had put a curse on a four-year-old child?' he said. 'What made her think such a thing?'

'Because of your dancing and your laughing – and a few other small things like that,' his grandmother answered, with her usual tricky smile.

Seeing his confusion, she relented. 'Since I was never afraid of the matters that alarmed your mother so much, after she told me what had happened, I saw the future, your future, clearly. Even as a *toto*, and certainly before the great storm, I knew that the path in life you were destined to follow already lay there open and clear in front of you.'

Understanding began to dawn on him. How wise was this *ugogo* of his to have understood what his poor mother had not.

'Your hair, for one thing,' his grandmother went on, eyeing the coils of hair tumbling over his forehead. 'No ordinary child, especially a male child, screams like you did when we tried to cut it. I knew then you were not as the other children, but were destined for something else.'

Exhausted, she lay back for a moment or two to rest. Then, rallying her strength, she said, 'The truth, I promised you the truth, and that is what you shall have.'

Langani lifted her up to make it easier for her to breathe. Putting her mouth close to his ear, she whispered, 'Remember how you always liked to dance? Well, while dancing to the beat of the drums during the celebrations, somehow you slipped into a state of dreaming. It was only when the storm came and the drummers fled for their lives and the great drums had fallen silent that you came back to the world.'

'So my mother suspected someone had put a spell on me?' Langani said. Cebile nodded. '*Yebo*, but that wasn't all that happened that day.'

Langani found himself intrigued as to what might come next. 'You mentioned "laughing as well as dancing." Tell me, *ugogo*, what kind of child doesn't laugh and shake its body to music?'

He grinned and shook his head, sending the long plaits rippling snakelike down his back.

'Well, it was not so much the fact that you were laughing,' his grandmother said, rather sternly. 'It was when, and how, and with whom you chose to do it.'

Langani raised his eyebrows. Cebile sighed and coughed a little.

'Well, I will tell you. At the height of the storm, when every living soul in esiKlebeni was running in fear, where were you, at only four years of age?'

She paused to draw a rattling breath. 'Were you also terrified by the roaring of the thunder, the trembling of the ground and doom breaking out over your head? Were you burying your head in your mother's skirts and shrieking in fear like all the other small children?'

'*Cha!*' she'd said, answering her own question. 'Not you, Langani! You were clapping your hands in delight, greeting the fury of the heavens like an old friend. While everyone else was fleeing for their lives, you were like one possessed, dancing and laughing, your small body moving to a rhythm only you could hear – so you can see why your poor mother was frantic.'

'Because she thought someone had bewitched me?' Langani echoed, his eyes wide open in disbelief.

His grandmother clutched at his hand. 'She was mortally afraid for you. Surely you know what would have happened if people suspected you had been bewitched?'

He, of all people, was certainly aware of the penalties of being accused of consorting with the dark powers. Such was people's fear of the occult that even a four-year-old child would be shown no mercy if it came under suspicion. No wonder his mother had been fearful.

Langani stared hard at Cebile. 'But that's not all, is it?' he said. 'You have something else to tell me, *ugogo*?'

'It was because you were not alone, because of who she found you with,' his grandmother said, her eyes bright with the telling of her last secret. 'High up on his shoulders you were, both of you laughing like devils, challenging the gods, while the heavens rained down thunderbolts and the winds blew people away and sucked them up into the sky.'

Langani's brows shot up. 'Dancing, challenging the gods? So, tell me, who was I dancing with?'

Cebile rocked herself to and fro for a few moments. Then she opened her toothless mouth and cackled. 'Who else but the Nkosi Shaka himself! He was young then, of course, only a few years younger than you are now. It happened on the same day he refused to accept the *umutsha* from his father, the old king, kaSenzangakhona.'

Reaching out a trembling hand, she stroked his head, patting it just as she used to do when he was a child.

'A very dangerous friend to have, especially for a four-year-old *toto*, you must agree,' she crooned. 'On that very day, the day of your dancing, the King, his father, the royal court and the people of esiKlebeni were all blaming him for bringing the anger of the *amadhlozi* down on their heads.'

She rocked to and fro for a few moments, her mind going back to that fateful day.

'Eh,' she said at last, sighing, 'but they couldn't accuse him openly, because they were terrified of what he might do if he really got angry. Naturally, your poor mother was beside herself with the fear that he'd put a spell on you. After all, if people had found out, or even suspected that you had been with him, dancing while the storm devoured esiKlebeni, they would certainly have killed you.'

The young diviner had been stunned by his grandmother's revelations.

So, even as a small child, his life had had its mysteries. It was true he had never feared lightning and thunder – in fact he had always been excited by the sound and fury of the lightning storms, a regular occurrence in Zululand.

For the first time in his life, he began to wonder just why that should be. Was it because he sensed that the power of the heavens was greater than anything the world of man could command?

And when he had danced with the young Shaka as a child, was it because they had both been drawn by the sound and fury of the tempestuous storm, knowing they had nothing to fear, because they were somehow connected to that power – *or even part of it?*

His heart thumping in anticipation, Langani craned his neck in an attempt to see the man occupying the seat of Judgment. Because of the constantly shifting crowd, he had not yet had a chance to get a clear view of the King of the Zulus.

His grandmother's words echoed in his head. 'There you were, high up on his shoulders, the two of you laughing like devils. To your poor mother, it looked as if you were challenging the gods.'

A gap opened up in the press of people in front of him. Langani moved quickly. Slipping into the vacant space, he found himself looking directly at the Zulu King.

His eyes did not linger long on the brutally handsome features, the trim, bearded jawline or the strong neck rising from the massive shoulders, or even on the regal circlet of leopard skin around his brow or the bright flare of the scarlet *igwala gwala* feathers tucked into it. Instead, they travelled instinctively to the crescent-shaped scar high on his cheekbone.

A jolt of recognition hit him, one which spun him back through the years.

Yebo, now he remembered…

Ntombazi glared haughtily at Shaka, her eyes glittering with contempt. Although he had read out a list of the thirty or so chiefs whose skulls she had on display in her hut, he had deliberately omitted Dingiswayo or any of the murdered men personally known to him.

'Why did you have all those chiefs killed, first luring them to your village then slaughtering them?' he asked her.

'To gain power, just as you do, King of the Zulus.' A gasp rose from the listeners. Such arrogance from one about to die!

'Gaining power is one thing,' retorted Shaka, acidly ignoring her deliberate attempt to annoy him. 'But why abuse our ancient laws of hospitality to achieve it? It is against the good name of the Nguni people, an abomination of our customs.'

The smooth-lidded eyes surveyed him with loathing. 'Power goes to the head and is somewhat like capturing a red-hot coal, best seized quickly before the fingers are burned,' she said.

'Why did you cut off their heads and keep them as trophies?'

It was Shaka's turn to be coldly angry, although he already knew the answer to his question. 'According to our laws, this is yet another abomination. Only those who practise witchcraft resort to such infamy.'

There was a rustle of anticipation among the packed audience. The source of Ntombazi's evil powers was well known, but few were brave enough to challenge her, face to face, as the King of the Zulus was doing.

The prisoner drew herself erect and literally spat out her reply. 'As I have already said, I did it to gain their power, to make it flow to me – to take it as my own. If a mere chief can be above the laws pertaining to witchcraft, how much more so can I, the Queen of the Ndwandwe?'

A swift intake of breath came from the onlookers. Ntombazi wouldn't give in without a fight. Heads craned to see how Shaka had taken the slur of being called 'a mere chief' and her veiled accusation that he had also dabbled in the occult.

Although he was calm, his face impassive, those near him could see a tiny hammer of anger pulsing at his temple.

'Witchcraft may help the weak to believe in themselves,' he said, 'but it is useless against a stronger enemy, a better trained and skilful one with a clear head.'

The gauntlet had been thrown down. Swift as a viper, Ntombazi moved to pick it up. 'How then did we succeed in ensnaring the mighty Dingiswayo? Tell me that, King of the Zulus!'

The tongue flickering out of her mouth was a startling red against the chalky mask of her face. There was no mistaking the hiss of pure venom.

Shaka closed in on her. 'You are ill-advised to boast of that infamy, woman. The downfall of that good man was due to his generous heart and kind spirit. I warned him of it, time and again, but each time he forgave your arrant coward of a son and allowed him to go free.'

The glance she shot him was one of pure evil. Ruthlessly, he pressed home his advantage.

'My very words to him were that he could not beget gratitude and reason from either you or your son, any more than he could expect it from poisonous reptiles he had nursed back to health.'

His eyes narrowed. 'Why did you return evil for good?" 'To gain power,' Ntombazi snarled. 'What else? One more step on the way.'

'One more step?' cut in Shaka, feigning surprise, though secretly savouring the moment. 'On the way to what, may I ask?'

The merest flick of the gnu tail was her only response. Pretending to be puzzled, he waited for a moment, then added, 'Ah, yes! Of course! To remove all obstacles so that your son Zwide could sit where I now sit, as overlord of Dingiswayo's Mthethwe nation.'

A terrible silence fell. Ntombazi regarded him through eyes narrowed to slits. The animal hairs in the whisk in her hand trembled for a moment.

'Did you also have to desecrate Dingiswayo's body?' Shaka demanded, his latent rage terrible to see. 'Was not killing him enough for you?'

An obscene cackle broke out of the smooth, unlined face. A moan of fear rippled round the crowd. Hidden in the crowd, Langani's hands were slippery with sweat and he gripped them together tightly in an effort to stop them shaking.

'Yes to the first question,' was the hissing reply, 'a thousand times yes! And as for the second, King of the Zulus, the answer is no! Killing Dingiswayo was not enough. I needed to gain all the power that lived in him, good and bad, to add to that which I already have. So I had to take his head, and his liver, as I had done with all of the others.'

Some in the crowd began to wonder what manner of execution the King of the Zulus had in mind for her after such blatant statements. But they continued to watch and listen as Shaka led her remorselessly into the centre of the web he had prepared for her.

'And what of Mashobane and my friend Donda?' he said, with a face like stone. 'Did you not also invite them to a love dance and with treachery kill them and take their heads from their bodies?'

'Yes, yes, all of them!' shrieked Ntombazi, shaking in terrible glee. 'I took their heads, their livers, and other parts.' Drooling at the mouth, she mimed the grotesque action of eating, relishing what she pretended to stuff ravenously into her mouth.

'I needed the heads for the power they held, the skills, the knowledge, more power and yet more, all the heads could give me – until I had sucked them dry of all their knowledge and skills and the last vestiges of life itself.'

Shaka felt her eyes drill into his. Revulsion crawled down his spine like scurrying ants. Briefly, he wondered what ploy she would have used to bring his own skull to join the others. The lure of a beautiful woman, a challenge in battle, some great prize he couldn't resist – or by using a spell, or a curse?

With loathing, he dragged his eyes from hers. The temptation to kill her with his bare hands, to snap her neck like a twig there and then, was overwhelming. To repay her for the treacherous deaths suffered by Dingiswayo and the others, so that their spirits could fly free, their powers restored, would be true justice indeed.

Instead, the King of the Zulus, exercising massive control, merely clenched his fists and leaned forward. 'And where is all your power now?' he demanded. 'Tell me, Ntombazi!'

An eldritch screech issued from the beautiful, spoiled mouth. She turned to point first in the direction of her hut and then to her own head, the bones and animal claws around her neck and arms rattling and clicking with every movement.

Shivers of dread ran through the crowd. Langani's body went rigid at the sense of evil emanating from her, the whiff of its putrid breath almost overpowering.

Shaka stood up suddenly and towered over her. Just as it seemed as if he was about to seize her by the throat, he took a step back. His next question was put in a voice that sounded oddly casual.

'I have heard those who practise witchcraft make use of hyenas. Is this not so?'

'Indeed it is,' replied Ntombazi arrogantly, as if trying to instil fear into this upstart who dared to flaunt his authority over her. Everyone knew that *umthakati,* sorcerers, used them as familiars and rode on their backs through the dark night skies.

'And you have complete command over these beasts? They will obey you at all times?' His tone was measured, even reasonable.

'Completely!' boasted Ntombazi, her full lips parting to display her carmined tongue. 'I have absolute power over them, always. They dare not defy me.'

Shaka slowly sat down again, nodding his head sagely, as if in deep consideration of her case. When he raised his head, it was to look deep into the cunning black eyes watching him.

'That is good,' said Shaka, 'because you are now free to return to your hut, to the centre of your power. I have finished with you.'

A start of surprise rippled round the Judgment hall. Surely Shaka didn't mean to set her free, not after condemning herself out of her own mouth?

The mother of Zwide looked confused for a moment and blinked her eyes rapidly. A trickle of sweat ran down the cracked white mask and dripped off her chin.

'And what do you intend me to do there?' Her voice was a croak.

Shaka was reason itself as he answered, a smile lingering around his mouth. 'You may gaze on the heads of those whose lives and power you stole. And in case you are lonely, out of the goodness of my heart I have decided to provide you with a companion.'

She looked at him, her eyes narrowing in suspicion. Then a faint spark of hope crept into them. 'Zwide, you will return my son to me?'

Shaka rose to his feet, his smile changing to one of bitter amusement.

'Alas, no, but have no fear, Nkosikazi – your companion will prove to be even closer to you than your son was, and one you will approve of. And to show you how fair I can be, I assure you that no harm will come to you from any of my warriors. My own hand will also not be raised against you. '

Ntombazi stared into the face of the man who occupied the seat where her son had once dispensed his version of justice. What she saw there did not bode well for the future, her future.

The handsome face looking back at her was cruel and impassive below the mass of feathers in the head dress, its masculine lines marred only by the scar on the cheekbone. Too late, she realized that behind the smile and reasonable, almost affable words lay a dominating intelligence far more powerful than her own.

Puzzled and ill at ease, she knew that from that moment on she would only have her dignity, her burning hatred, and the skills of her craft to save her from the retribution she suspected was waiting for her.

Disgorged from the stifling heat of the huge hut and buffeted by the jostling mob eager to get a last glimpse of the witch, Langani caught a brief glimpse of Ntombazi being led away, spitting in fury. A shiver ran through him.

Vainly, he tried to extricate himself from the press of sweating bodies, but instead was carried along with them, closer to where the guards were wrestling to keep the crowd at bay. The boldest of the voyeurs surged forward, shouting and gesticulating, hatred spewing out of their mouths at the sight of the witch.

All around him, people were trying to push in the opposite direction, terrified of getting too close to the violence about to erupt.

In spite of her crimes and evil beliefs, the young diviner felt a moment's sympathy for the confused, broken woman. The cracked white mask and the obscenity of the smudged red mouth, which had once been so desirable, revealed a certain vulnerability about her that touched him briefly.

Suddenly, a black pain shot through him, as wounding as if he had been run through with a spear. In the dimming light that began to swirl around him, Langani could feel the shades gathering around her and knew that very soon Ntombazi would die.

Details of what he saw waiting for her seeped into his conscious mind. Squeezing his eyes shut, Langani made a vain attempt to block out the horrific images. Involuntarily, a whimper of dread was wrenched from him.

Ntombazi's body stiffened. Her matted, dishevelled head swung from side to side, seeking the source of the pain. People on all sides scattered, thinking she was about to spring free. As Langani swayed on his feet, trying to focus on what was happening, his long plaits, snake-like and distinctive, came loose and cascaded over his shoulders.

It took him a moment or two to realise that he was exposed to the full glare of the witch. Nostrils wide and flaring, Ntombazi put back her head and uttered a high-pitched screech of triumph, the sinews in her neck standing out like cords.

'*Bheka*! Look! See how the Lord Nkosi already goes back on his word! He has sent a madman to kill me!'

Her slits of eyes were black and calculating as they met those of Langani. As the truth of just who and what he was began to filter in on her, they widened to a fixed stare.

A high-pitched scream of fury issued from her smeared mouth. Tearing herself free from the guards, in a whirl of rancid skins, rattling bones and dried goats' bladders, she launched herself bodily at him, her talons reaching for his eyes.

Langani dodged back quickly. Those nearest to him scattered and backed away, yelling in terror and hampering the guards. The witch prepared to move in again, her fearful, matted head swaying from side to side like a cobra poised to strike.

An instant later, somewhere beyond his line of vision, there was a sudden shift of people moving aside, followed by the sharp rap of an authoritative voice demanding to know what was happening.

There was a rush of muscled bodies, a struggle, a brief, but futile scream of rage and then Ntombazi was gone, bundled away through the crowds with only a whiff of decay left behind on the dust-filled air.

Still dazed by the rapid turn of events, Langani became aware of a strong presence behind him. When he turned round, it was to find he was staring into the dark and watchful eyes of Shaka of the Zulus.

It was not long before Ntombazi found out how she would die. After the door of her hut was closed and barred from the outside, she stood blinking in the gloom, dazzled after the bright sunlight.

Gradually, things around her swam into focus. She began to make out familiar objects in the sunlight filtering through chinks in the walls and thatched roof, and smiled when she saw her pyramid of skulls glowing green and phosphorescent in the dusk, the eye sockets gaping and empty. They were like old friends, each one known intimately to her.

Ntombazi placed a hand on each side of her head and began to hum to herself, swaying from side to side, the gnu tail gently keeping time to the melody running through her brain.

You are all here inside my head… the mortal power of the King of the Zulus could not contain the Inkosikazi of the Ndwandwe for long. My power, together with that all the others I have harvested will soon set me free…

A strong animal smell, feral and pungent in the stifling heat of the afternoon began to filter into her consciousness. Her concentration broken, she frowned and peered into the shadows. A pair of glowing eyes stared back at her.

Her heart gave a lurch. For a brief moment, she was a mere woman of flesh and blood, afraid of the unknown lurking in the darkness. What was waiting in the shadows did not remain a secret for long. The outline of the companion Shaka had chosen for her came into focus.

Ntombazi drew in her breath sharply, and opened her mouth in a silent scream, sending spider cracks through the white clay mask. Her eyes were enormous black holes in the flaking mud, her gaping mouth and nostrils vivid slashes of carmine.

There was no mistaking the humped back of the huge male hyena, no mistaking the massive slavering jaws, the most powerful of any carnivore in the land.

She was no longer in any doubt of how it would all end. She could hold back the powerful scavenger for a time, maybe a long time, with her powers and the force of her will. In the beginning, it would not dare touch her, but without food, water and sleep, her strength would begin to diminish, leaving her weak and undefended.

The beast's ravenous hunger would sweep away its natural fear of her. In an unguarded moment, its jaws would tear out lumps of her living flesh to feed itself. Sinking to her knees in a rattle of bones and claws, she tore off the elaborate head dress of dried bladders and let it fall to the floor.

As she stared helplessly into the shadows to where her nemesis waited, pieces of dried clay began to crumble from her face, ravaging and distorting the beauty below.

She moaned in abject fear. Already she could imagine the agonizing crunch and grinding as its teeth closed on her feet and legs, the plumpness of her arms, her breasts, as it worried and shook her flesh loose. How long might she live, mauled and half-dead, with the smell of her blood thick in the air?

Now the cruel irony and genius of Shaka's terrible sentence became clear. With consummate skill, he had led her into his trap. He had given his word that neither he nor his guards would harm her. Of course, he had been true to his word, but what he had not told her was that the huge dog hyena would do it for him.

The gnu tail whisk in her hand trembled and twitched as she clung to the last, physical symbol of her power. As she hovered on the brink of madness, the last of her rational mind was able to see her end clearly.

All the spirit and courage of the fine men she had lured to their deaths would pass from her into the belly of the animal with which she and her kind were associated.

No, wait! She could see the final part of Shaka of the Zulus' diabolical plan unfold. Once her blood and flesh passed into the belly of the brute, it would be voided later on to the ground as foul-smelling pellets of dung.

Putting back her head, she screamed in hysterical terror, ranting and shouting, calling down the powers, calling for Zwide, her son, for all of her sons, the sinews and cords in her neck straining to breaking point.

Aiii, Ntombazi Queen of the Ndwandwe, mother of Kings, high priestess of sorcery. *Your final role is to be excreted through the anus of a dog hyena!*

After her vocal cords gave out, Ntombazi began to take comfort from

the belief that the lifetime practice of her profession would come to her rescue. She grew calmer and began to concoct a plan.

Taking one of the grinning-head skulls from the pile, she rolled it across the floor to where the glowing eyes of the hyena waited in the shadows.

'Now I will feed you, my baby,' she crooned. 'Eat well and take the strength from the bones of our enemies. Stronger and more terrible than ever, you and I shall ride the black night skies together, searching for my sons and gathering together the armies of the dead.'

Above the awful crunching sounds, the horrified guards could hear the muffled ravings of the woman inside.

'*I will feed you my own flesh, my sweetness... until we come again to rip the throat from this upstart Zulu who dares pit himself against us.*'

It took Ntombazi a long time to die, but by the time the dawn of the fourth day had broken in the east, her screaming had mercifully ended.

Fourteen

L angani had chosen an unlikely spot to create his sanctuary. It was a place no one was likely to stumble across unless they were a bird of prey or had the gift of flight.

The approach was guarded by a steep-sided rocky canyon covered in thick scrub, curving along its base a dried-up river bed. Although the water course had long since become over-grown, patches of the pebble-strewn path could still be seen to show where a river had once tumbled and gurgled its way down to the Indian Ocean.

Roughly two-thirds of the way up the mountain, no doubt created by a huge landslip aeons ago, an expanse of relatively flat ground stretched back into the hillside. Sheltered by the curve of the hill and shaded by trees, a thatched hut of generous propor-tions stood with its back against the mountain.

A few yards away, a small waterfall trickled down the rock face. Over the years, the constant flow of water had formed a small pool partly sheltered by an overhanging shelf of rock. Except for long dry spells, which were rare, the waterfall provided a continual source of drinking water and the pool was rarely empty.

Langani had planted a vegetable garden nearby. Already, green feathery shoots of corn had sprung up, along with the trailing vines of watermelons, beans and a variety of other vegetables.

Looking up from below, no one would ever guess that a human being actually lived up there, let alone one as young and resourceful as Langani, the diviner.

Clad only in a simple *umutsha*, with his long hair tied back off his face, the young diviner was sitting cross-legged near the edge of his territory, looking out over the vista of endless bush.

Outwardly, he seemed at peace. His eyes were closed and his hands were comfortably folded in his lap. Inwardly however, his mind was buzzing with the activity of a frenetic bee trapped in a fine mesh net.

It was at moments like these, with the end-of-day stillness wrapped around him and the soothing noise of the waterfall in the background, that he usually addressed matters that might be troubling him. Today, however, was very different.

Since Ntombazi's trial, Langani had found it hard to return to the exacting rituals of meditation and study that formed part of his everyday life. All too often, he found his mind wandering back to the trial itself, the judgment, and what had happened afterwards. Take the thorny questions of good and evil, for instance.

Ntombazi had once been a beautiful woman, and as she herself had pointed out, had also been a queen and a mother of princes. Why then had she opted to leave the world of sunlight and the warmth of family life to inhabit one of dark dreams and death?

Her penalty had been to suffer an ignominious death, far worse than any she had forced on her victims. In the end, she had perished, not by the hand of the King of the Zulus, but by a combination of her own destiny and the dark powers she had sought to control.

The young diviner sighed. Why some people chose the paths of evil and darkness of the soul, while others chose the way of goodness and service to their fellow man, was another of the questions to which he had no answers.

Seeking distraction, he glanced up at the evening sky. Above his head, streaks of high cirrus feathered the deepening blue, the horizon suffused with the vivid carmine and golds of the setting sun.

He sniffed the air, savouring the faint tang of wood smoke coming in on the breeze. The evening fires of the villages scattered through the bush would be beginning to crackle below cooking pots.

His stomach rumbled. Maize porridge and a stew made from vegetables and scraps of goat meat would be bubbling away in the pots, the appetising smells filling the air. Women would be bustling around, calling their children to come and eat –

A sharp pang of homesickness filled him. Although dedicated to the path he had chosen, Langani was still a young man with the fires of youth in his belly, someone used to the closeness of family life. His thoughts turned to his grandmother, Cebile. Sadly, she was not long for this world. Soon she would become spirit and join their ancestors.

In the far distance, the last glimmerings of sunlight glinted on the waters of the Umfolozi River, a poignant reminder of the ebb and flow of time.

I shall always be grateful to you for telling me those childhood secrets, *ugogo*, Langani thought. Sadness caught at him. Although you had no way of knowing Shaka and I were about to meet again, you couldn't have chosen a better time to tell me what I needed to know.

An uncanny thought struck him then. What if she'd already known that a meeting between himself and Shaka of the Zulus was imminent? Perhaps being so close to death had sharpened her perceptions and lifted the veil that separated the past, the present and the future.

An even more startling possibility reared up at him. Could it be he had inherited his spiritual affinities from his grandmother and that his powers, or at least part of them, had come directly from her? He pushed such thoughts aside. Not now, another time...

In retreat, his mind spun back to another thorny subject: that of his recent meeting – or perhaps confrontation would be a better word – with King Shaka of the Zulus.

Coming face to face with him so suddenly, he felt dwarfed by Shaka's height and powerful warrior's body. But if the man's physical presence was overwhelming, the sheer force of the inner power emanating from him was even more so.

Clad in a kilt of blue monkey tails, his broad torso was partially concealed by a magnificent collar of leopard skin and several necklaces of the beast's teeth. Apart from the black widow-bird plumes in his head dress, his only other adornment was a pair of heavy bronze bracelets on his upper arms. The black eyes raked over him were cool and guarded, missing nothing.

A stab of apprehension had run through the diviner. The rarity of a man with long hair, particularly a young one like himself, would certainly alert the warrior King. It would be patently obvious that he belonged to no army, no *amabutho*.

Apart from that, there was Shaka's dislike of any manifestation of the occult. Those using supernatural powers for their own ends, to subjugate and terrorise simple villagers into parting with their cattle or crops, or exercise their powers to spread evil, had good reason to fear this man. Langani fervently hoped that the Zulu king did not regard all diviners with hostility – only those given over to evil.

As Shaka's gaze lingered on him, a frown began to develop. His scrutiny deepened. After a few moments, he said 'Tell me, *mdodo*, haven't we met before? There is something familiar about you.'

Langani's heart leapt into his mouth. The speed and accuracy of Shaka's instincts was unnerving. While a part of him wanted to blurt out that he had been the four-year-old who had danced with him on the fateful day of the esiKlebeni storm, his instincts warned him that after the heightened tensions of the trial and his own potentially damaging brush with Ntombazi, it might be wiser to keep quiet.

The young Shaka of old was not the man of the present day: the waxing and waning of many moons and much killing and shedding of blood lay between that time of relative innocence and the present.

As for himself, he was no longer a child. He was a man now and his calling, by its very nature, had to remain secret from the man towering over him – for the moment, at least.

Summoning up his reserves, Langani drew his tattered cloak around himself and bent his head. In bowing to show deference to the Zulu King, he was also desperately trying to cover up any give-away signs that he was about to tell the biggest lie of his life.

'*Cha*, Nkosi,' he said, keeping his eyes firmly on the ground. 'I come from another country, another tribe, that of the iziYendane.'

The long hair of the Yendane warriors was a little known fact here in the south, except for Shaka, of course, who would most definitely know of the warriors famous for their skills in tracking and hunting, their ferocity in battle – and their long, intricately plaited hair.

Trickles of sweat running down his back, Langani blessed his good memory for remembering it. During the long silence that followed, he kept his head down and waited.

'Why did the witch Ntombazi fly at you?' Shaka asked. His voice was soft, almost purring, as he put the question. 'What made her break away from her guards and try to put out your eyes?'

Langani shook his head. 'Truly, Nkosi, I do not know. Perhaps she needed to strike out at someone, to show she still had power.'

Sweat began to drip off the end of his nose. What if someone remembered him crying out as he foresaw the brutal fate that awaited Ntombazi? And what if someone had noticed him reel and stumble, and his eyes roll back in his head with only the whites showing?

He waited in dread for the terrible cry of '*Abathakhati!* Sorcerer!' to ring out. Langani knew he was no sorcerer, or a person of evil intent, but how could he prove it to a yelling mob?

After a few excruciating moments, acutely aware of the crushing presence of the Zulu King only a few feet away, it slowly sank in that nothing was going to happen. No one called out, no one stepped forward.

Mercifully, he felt Shaka's interest in him begin to wane. It was followed by a movement as if he was turning away, distracted by something else. The tension began to lessen.

After a few moments, the young diviner dared raise his eyes. Relief washed over him. Apparently, the King had other matters to attend to, and was in consultation with one of the *indunas* who had escorted Ntombazi from the Judgment place. The man was clearly agitated, waving his hands about and talking rapidly.

Taking advantage of the fact that Shaka's back was turned to him, Langani darted a quick glance at the massive shoulders beneath the leopard skin collar.

Briefly, he tried to imagine his small, younger self being hoisted on to them by a youthful Shaka. He envisioned his small buttocks jigging up and down as the two of them danced and cavorted beneath the rolling thunder and flashes of jagged light, his childish screams of joy ringing out over the sounds of the destruction being wreaked on esiKlebeni.

In spite of himself, a smile lit up his face. It was still there when Shaka, having ended his consultation with the *induna*, turned round and looked straight at him. Langani froze.

Shaka's gaze fixed on the smile and stayed there. Then it moved to the snake-like coils of hair visible below the diviner's tattered cloak. A flicker of half-buried memory began to stir in the warrior King's eyes. Tiny hairs crawled along the nape of Langani's neck.

The puzzled frown re-appeared, creasing the broad brow below the leopard-skin circlet.

'Yendane or not, *mdodo*,' Shaka said, as he came a step closer. 'Are you sure we haven't met somewhere before?'

Since Langani had never believed in co-incidence, he acknowledged that his accidental brush with the enraged witch and his subsequent encounter with Shaka had not been mere chance.

If anything, it only fortified his conviction that the youth, Jakot, the one who had come to him so vividly in his dreams had not been a chance encounter either, but was somehow connected, if not directly to Shaka, then most certainly to Zululand itself.

It was also no coincidence that his spiritual powers had intensified of late. His dreams and trance states had become more vivid and longer lasting, his senses more alert and finely-tuned than before.

The brief, but terrible flashes of what had lain in wait for Ntombazi continued to haunt him, and for the first time he realized he had been able to see into the future.

Sober reality had followed this revelation. Was this how his life was going to be, his senses highly-pitched and honed to receive whatever was sent his way? Would he have the power to control it?

Behind him the gentle noise of the water trickling down from the rocky heights performed its usual magic. It calmed his spirit and allowed him to contemplate the future with some degree of equanimity.

After a while, he stood up, stretched his long legs then glanced at the horizon. Small pin-pricks of village fires were beginning to twinkle like fireflies in the vast expanse of bush, their presence comforting in the dying light.

Turning away from the darkening land, he used the last of the light to water his gardens. As he waited for the water to fill the gourds, his mind slipped back to the tenuous link that bound him to the Zulu warrior King.

According to his grandmother, he and the young Shaka had been the only people that day to have no fear of the awesome power being unleashed above their heads.

Langani corrected himself – no, not only were they not afraid, it appeared they'd both been exhilarated and energised by it: he, a small child cut adrift from his mother, and an adolescent Shaka who had just defied both tribal convention and his own powerful father, and won.

Since he had no reason to doubt his grandmother's words, what might it say about them both? As a youth, he had finally accepted his destiny and submitted to the will of his ancestors. Shaka's chosen path, on the other hand, was one of conquest and supremacy; not for him submission of the will to a greater power.

A wayward thought struck him. It was widely rumoured that Shaka's awesome strength of will came from the other world. Some said he had already demonstrated his ability to call on these powers, by summoning up great lightning storms similar to the one which had almost demolished esiKlebeni, the one where they had danced together.

Could the long-held rumours actually be true? Water slopping from the overflowing gourd on to his bare feet brought him back to reality. Hastily, he put the container down, berating himself for his short-sightedness.

Messenger of the *amadhlozi* he might well be, but exactly who was he to speculate about those on whom the gods had bestowed great power, or the mysterious reasons behind their doing so?

A breeze drifted up from below, soothing the sudden heat suffusing his body. Glancing up, he saw that the sky had darkened to a deep indigo. Komotsho, the evening star, hung motionless in the immensity of space. In the far reaches of the bush, the twinkling campfires reassured him that he was not alone

Langani's steps turned towards the hut he had built for himself. Tossing his sandals aside, he stepped on to the earthen floor, cool beneath his bare feet.

His home was spacious and well-planned. One part was set aside for sleeping and ordinary living, the other for his life as a practising *isangoma*, including the storage of exotic herbs, potions, and other sacred artefacts.

It smelled of newly-cut timbers and fresh thatch, the gleaming floor rendered solid and glass-like, the result of many hours of patient working. A broad grin split his face.

Several layers of cow dung mixed with water had to be mixed together into a thick porridge and applied in several layers before the durable effect could be achieved. Manhandling baskets of cow dung up through the bush tunnels hadn't been the easiest, or the sweetest smelling of tasks!

It had taken him a long time to build the hut. Bringing the materials up the hillside on his own had been a mammoth task. While erecting the stout central post and the roof timbers which would support the thatch, he had almost given in and gone to ask his brothers for help.

But, stubborn to the end, and determined to guard the privacy of this sanctuary at all costs, he had persevered through many days and nights of aching, torn muscles, blistered hands and cut fingers.

A soft clucking above his head made him glance up. His chickens had taken up their nightly positions on the heavy crossbeams. As he moved over to the small fire burning in the middle of the floor, the black rooster cocked a golden eye down at him. While he was preparing his supper, a feeling of unfinished business continued to nag at him. An answer regarding the source of Shaka's powers was still proving to be elusive.

He sighed in resignation. Maybe it always would. There were some things even the wisest of men were not permitted to know – though whether for their own good, or for mankind in general – who could say?

Fifteen

The glittering eye of the sun had only just cleared the horizon. A group of women, many with babies on their backs, were making their way towards the wind-sculpted trees fringing the beach. On catching tantalising glimpses of the Indian Ocean, the children ran shrieking down to the water, scattering seabirds as they went.

Their mothers and sisters would spend the morning scraping crystals of sea salt from the rocks. Once they had collected enough for their own needs, they would use what was left to barter for a goat, a chicken or two, or extra corn in villages further away from the coastline.

Further along the beach, a high outcrop of rocks jutted into the sea. It was dominated by a huge boulder of craggy proportions, its summit flattened by aeons of wind and weather. Legend said it had been a ball of gigantic proportions, the plaything of a giant, which he'd thrown away in a temper after losing a game.

An hour or so later, one of the women stood up and pressed a hand to the small of her back. Glancing idly down the beach, she stiffened.

Her shrill voice rang out to alert the others. The rest of the women stopped work, their eyes scanning the sands to see what she was shrieking about. A noisy chattering broke out.

Distorted images began to emerge from the heat haze. A tightly-packed group of men could be seen loping towards them at a steady pace, sunlight glinting off the tips of their spears. In the lead was a tall man with gleaming, oiled skin. Lithe and superbly fit, his head feathers and fringes of ox hair fluttered in the wind.

To the terrified women and children, he was a figure from their deepest nightmares. Who had not heard of the dreaded Nkosi of the Zulus and his warlike *impis?*

They took to their heels, their bare feet slapping on the wet sand. Clutching their precious bowls of salt, their babies bouncing up and down on their backs, they ran sobbing towards the comparative safety of the scrub. Small children were snatched up from the water's edge and borne off by their sisters, their little black heads bobbing and jiggling as they ran.

Sparing them only a cursory glance, the body of warriors continued to jog at a steady pace up the beach. A few minutes later, they disappeared into the wavering heat haze.

Shaka stood on top of the flat, lichen-covered rock reputed to have been the plaything of a giant and looked out over the sea, his eyes half-closed against the glare.

The air was full of the cries of wheeling seabirds and the dull boom of surf crashing on the beach. The ocean always gave him peace. There was something about its limitless energy, ever-changing colours and mood that brought him relaxation and a feeling of awe. Often he would slip away with a handful of close friends for a few days hunting and come down to the coast to spend a few hours alone, gazing at the ocean.

Shading his eyes, he looked out to where the sea met the sky. The invisible line, as always, seemed mysterious and unreachable.

How far is it to the other side of the great waters? And what would I find there? he thought – a land like my own, or one very different, belonging to another kind of people?

The sun beat down on his shoulder blades, its burn pleasant on his oiled skin. A surge of well-being washed over him.

Recent events had been very satisfying. The Ndwandwe had been dealt with – for the time being, at least. Zwide, the misbegotten son of a goat, was too far away to rally his demoralised army. In any case, with both his mother and four of his sons dead, it was unlikely he would have the stomach for another fight.

Shaka was under no illusions about the tenacious Ndwandwe and their current disarray after Zwide's trouncing. He had no doubt at all that they would try to rise again under a new leader, but for the moment, it signified a significant end to the recent spate of battles and the spilling of blood.

His mouth tilted in a smile. Perhaps he would release his warriors from the strict sexual restrictions he had imposed on them when he came to power. Courage and fortitude must always be rewarded.

The smile broadened. True, prizes of cattle were always highly acceptable, but to free his warriors from this particular stricture, even for a short time, would show them the regard with which their Nkosi held them.

His attention turned to his new settlement, the second kwaBulawayo. The first had become too small to deal with his burgeoning army and the large number of people living there. He was looking forward to laying aside the demands of war and conquest for a while in order to perfect certain aspects of it.

He would be able to oversee the breeding of his prized white cattle, and there were new songs to compose and dances to create. The festival of *Umkhosi, the first fruits* was not far away and kwaBulawayo must be completely finished in time for the celebrations.

The King of the Zulus slid down into a sitting position. Leaning back against the rock, he allowed its warmth to permeate his body.

Only one small matter remained, one that would have to be attended to before long – that of Nobela, the witch-seeker.

Recently, he had been brought news that she and her infamous crones had become active again among the small villages scattered throughout the hills. He frowned. A curse on those who use the occult to achieve their own ends, appropriating cattle and crops and leaving behind starving people and a trail of skewered corpses. A sharp barb of anger rose in him. Having so recently disposed of Ntombazi, I would have thought the sisterhood would shy away from testing my patience.

He thrust down the slow beat of rage. So be it. The hag will not find Shaka of the Zulus slow to respond. Challenge my authority if she dares, it will do her no good.

Then, having dealt with the matter, Shaka gave himself up to the sound of the rhythmic pounding of the sea against the shore. His head nodded on to his chest and soon even the shrill cries of the seabirds faded away.

Unknown to anyone, another factor had recently entered the tempestuous arena of Zululand. After the death of Dingiswayo, Shaka had fallen heir to the valuable trade monopoly with the Portuguese at Delagoa Bay.

Not long ago, a group of extremely nervous olive-skinned, bearded men had been escorted under close guard to kwaBulawayo, the King's new settlement on the banks of the uMthlatuzi River. Few saw them come and even fewer saw them go. What remained behind, under the close eye of the Nkosi, were treasures indeed.

Coils of colourful beads, both large and small, slithering like snakes from their wrappings, glass baubles, necklaces and rings for the fingers and ears and necks, small twinkling mirrors, piles of blankets, bales of cloth in bright patterns, ribbons, axes, metal pots and dishes.

And then there were the medicines, the most prized items of all. In exchange for the ivory tusks of the great *ndlovu*, potions for colds, flu and difficult stomachs, purges, mixtures for coughs, sore heads and every type of skin ailment, creams for the complexion and bottles of sugary, coloured water found their way into kwaBulawayo.

Accounts of the visit to Shaka's stronghold by the Portuguese traders would soon be added to the controversy surrounding the warrior king.

Rumours of his existence, his notoriety, and his growing power would be discussed – not only around the campfires in the vast hinterland of Portuguese territory – but in the port of Delagoa itself.

Because it was a prime destination for seafarers and traders using the important sea-trading routes between India, Goa, the Cape of Good Hope and Europe, it was inevitable that the fabulous tusks of ivory, the principal bartering tool between Shaka and the Portuguese would, in due course, attract the attention of more than one traveller to those exotic parts.

And that, in turn, would trigger a series if events that would, in time, add to the controversy already surrounding the Zulu kingdom and its powerful creator.

Part III

Sixteen

uKhuhlumba, the Barrier of Spears

Langani stopped to catch his breath. Scree and gravel with outcrops of rough, springy grass and rocky boulders dotted the steep incline up which he was clambering. Panting with exertion, he slipped the woven bag off his shoulder and sat down on to a boulder to rest for a while.

Craning his neck, he squinted up at the rocky heights above and was rewarded with a glimpse of snow-dusted peaks and golden shafts of spring sunlight framed against a splash of brilliant sky.

uKhahlamba, the Barrier of Spears. The range of towering crags and high mountain passes formed a backbone of basalt and sandstone which helped to create a defensive border between his homeland and the outside world.

For as far as the eye could see, the land was green and fertile, the valleys threaded with the sparkling waters of streams and torrents rushing and tumbling their way down to the Indian Ocean hundreds of miles away. The deep silence was broken only by the sighing of wind among the peaks and the plaintive cry of eagles as they soared on the currents of warm air rising up from below.

Langani lifted his face to the sun. A feeling of euphoria and lightheadedness flooded through him. The effects of fresh air, sun, and wide-open spaces combined with physical effort always made him feel as if he had drunk too much beer. Perhaps this is why I like high, remote places, he thought, smiling at the joke. The truth was that he rarely, if ever, touched the yeasty *tshwala* beer favoured by so many of his countrymen.

This was only the second time in his life he had travelled as far as the southerly mountains. A few months ago, he had been invited to join a select brotherhood of diviners who met secretly from time to time, usually in remote places, to meditate and advance their powers of divination.

What he had discovered there, quite by chance, had lured him back to the high mountains with almost indecent haste.

Langani hitched the bag over his shoulder and resumed his scramble up the rocky slope. Very soon now, he would be able see the overhanging lip of stone marking the cave he was looking for.

Although he had been flattered to have been singled out by the brotherhood for inclusion in their rites of passage, at first he had been wary of their motives. But, after carefully studying their actions and methods, he was satisfied as to their good intentions towards their fellow man. There had been no hint of dabbling in the less savoury aspects of the occult or experimenting with the more extreme forms of hallucinogenic potions to enhance their powers.

This time there would be no one to distract him. He was convinced that these mountains contained treasures and mysteries greater than he had ever imagined.

Half an hour later, Langani came abreast of the overhanging lip of rock marking the entrance to the cave. Sweating profusely, he was conscious of his heart thumping against his ribs, and not only because of the steep climb.

A ripple of excitement ran through him. There were many such caves here, places where the people of the San had lived for thousands of years. Sadly, the small hunters were fewer in number now.

Each year more of them retreated westward to seek sanctuary in the immense wilderness of the Kalahari. The reasons were many, the most serious being the ravages inflicted on them by belligerent tribes such as the Xhosa and the Zulu.

The bag bounced against Langani's back as he scrambled up the last few feet on to the ledge. Etched on the shaded rock face before him were some exquisite San paintings.

Langani stared in wonder at the delicate artistry. Briefly, he wondered about the tools the small people had used to create such vivid pictures of the world they had shared with the wild life of long ago.

Cautiously, he moved closer. In spite of his curiosity, he resisted the impulse to reach out and touch the colourful images. The unmistakable tingle running through his body warned him that he would be wise to avoid coming into direct contact with the ancient art of the San.

His sense of humour took over. Joking, he told himself he hadn't travelled all this way to fall down dead at the mouth of a San cave half-way up a mountain!

He had come prepared. In the bag, there was enough food to last a good few days, a pair of rubbing sticks to make a fire, and a rolled-up sleeping mat. The deerskin cloak and the blanket he had left behind during his last visit would keep him warm when night fell.

Turning away from the painted rock, he ducked his head below the overhanging lip of stone and entered the cave. Langani drew in a deep breath. He immediately recognised the odour; a mixture of dry, spicy earth and dried grass, a place that had not felt the trickle of water down its walls for a long time. His eyes searched the shadows and found the cloak and blanket where he had left them on his previous visit.

Above his head the sandstone ceiling was blackened and in-grained with smoke, indelible marks left by generations of crackling wood fires.

His gaze shifted into the further recesses of the cave. Though it was fairly deep, stretching well back into the living earth, there was enough natural daylight filtering in to create a welcoming glow.

Beneath his feet, the floor was warm and sandy. Apart from the scuffs and trails of small animals, lizards and the occasional rippling track of a snake, it looked as if it had just been newly swept. Langani smiled at the image that sprang to mind, that of a small San woman busy at work with her broom of twigs, making sure her home was tidy before her family left it for the last time.

His eyes were drawn to the circle of stones in the middle of the floor. He squatted down to examine them. Scattered among the crumbled earth and ash were half-burnt embers and pieces of charred wood. Brushing away a few small red spiders, he picked up one of the charred remnants and sniffed at it.

If he had hoped for a trace of woodsmoke, he would have been disappointed, for only the faintest ghost of the long-ago fire remained.

Langani straightened up. A further spur of rock sloped away into the shadows. It provided a natural, smooth-faced buttress, an ideal surface for the small, wiry San to re-create their world for future generations to marvel at.

A mixture of excitement and apprehension uncurled in his bel-ly. Instinctively, he folded his arms across his chest before moving closer to the rock face.

The vibrant colours used by the small artists ranged from charcoal to grey, bright red and scarlet toning down to browns, ochres, yellows and white. The lines and strokes were exquisite in detail. The San artists had captured not only the minute physical details of the beasts but also the spirit and energy of both animals and men.

Here was the power, strength and speed of the hunters, with their bows and poison-tipped arrows and spears, close by the breathtaking delicacy of tender muzzles and animal eyes, the soft white of their throats and bellies and flanks and the daintiness of their hooves. The use of colour was so subtle and precise that it gave warmth and flesh and lifelike contours to the red-brown rounded haunches of the eland dominating the scenes.

Langani inched closer until he was less than a hand's breadth away from the rock face. He peered more closely at the textures and the colours, still vivid and undimmed by the years.

On his previous visit to the mountains, he'd learned something of the San from one of the brotherhood who'd had dealings with the small people as a child. He and the San children had been friends, playing happily together and often sharing their food.

'I used to squat down and watch the women grinding their pastes of clay, burnt wood and ochre and even saw them mix in blood, their own and that of the eland, their spirit guides,' his brother *isangoma* had told him. 'Sometimes they would add the whites of birds' eggs and the dyes from roots and plants.'

The corners of the man's eyes had crinkled in sly humour when he'd added, 'Because I was just a child and easily overlooked, all I had to do was to sit quietly and listen to the chanting and drumming as they prepared to commit their images to the rock and communicate with the people of the spirit world.'

The deeper meaning behind the man's words had stayed with Langani ever since, and had whetted his appetite to discover more about the small people and their extraordinary powers.

Langani stiffened as he caught sight of a specific detail. Inching forward, he peered closely at the painted images.

No bows and arrows now, no herds of twin-horned impala and plump eland, no scenes of the San hunting to fill their bellies and those of their children. The small, black prancing figures were those of the San *shamans*, the equivalent of the medicine men and diviners of his own time and culture. He drew in a deep breath, excited, yet aware of a flutter of apprehension in the pit of his stomach.

The skilful artists of old had captured the blood spattering from the noses of the shamans as they went deep into trance states, their arms lengthened and bent backwards with excruciating pain as the transformation of their physical bodies into spirit took place. Here again were the plump eland, the sacred totem of the San, the animal spirits who were both their keepers and guides.

While his mind tried to interpret the disturbing images of human beings in a state of being transformed from one species to another, he frowned in concentration. As he looked on creatures that were half-human, half-animal, some with hooves, laid-back ears and hair sprouting from their bodies, the painted images began to waver before his eyes.

Without warning, Langani felt the cave spin around him. He yelled out in alarm, his voice echoing around the cave.

It was almost as if a giant hand had taken him bodily and whirled him around before setting him back on his feet again. Nausea gripped him and he almost lost his balance. Lurching forward, his hands instinctively shot out to stop himself from falling.

Straining every sinew and muscle, he froze, mere inches away from the rock face. He then found himself staring into the wondrously alive eyes of a female eland, its belly extended with the unborn, ready to give birth. The animal's eyes were soft, languid and deep brown, brimming with tears.

Sweat pouring off him, Langani slid down on to the sandy floor and put his head between his knees, gasping in distress. It was what he'd suspected, on his previous visit. The San *shamans* of old were not only very wise, they were also extremely powerful.

What they had created here – and he believed there were many such caves scattered throughout the stone towers of uKhahlamba, the Barrier of Spears – was more than just a record of their way of life and spiritual beliefs.

The daubs of ochres, blood, soot and dyes, which had been imprinted with great skill onto the rock faces of basalt and sandstone, told another, deeper story for those who had the eyes and the will to see. And he meant to stay until he found out what it was.

Exhaustion swept over him in a wave. Curling up on the sandy floor, he drew his knees up to his chest. Soothed by the warm sunlight filtering in from outside, he closed his eyes and fell asleep almost immediately.

By the time he woke, the light inside the cave had changed and the bright rays of mid-day had given way to the roseate glow of late afternoon. The colours of the paintings had also subtly altered. They seemed remote and mysterious, as if shielding their secrets from careless eyes.

Langani got to his feet, stretching and yawning. If he was to stay here for the next few nights, he would have to go in search of firewood, for he had no illusions that the cave would retain its warmth after the sun went down.

Luckily, he had thought ahead, and had left piles of dry wood along the way during his climb. Casting a glance around him, he became suddenly aware of the immense silence of the cave long abandoned by the people who had once lived here.

The glow and warmth of a fire tonight will be very welcome, he thought, with the merest of glances at the back wall where the images of the dancing shamans slumbered in the dimming light.

Beyond the entrance to the fire-lit cave, all was still, unearthly still, the outside world painted in shades of silver and black by the half-moon that had risen from behind the jagged basalt peaks.

Inside, there was only the peaceful spit and crackle of the flames and the dancing of firelight across the blackened ceiling. Langani sat by the fire, facing the wall, his skin gleaming in the firelight. His legs were crossed, his hands placed lightly on his knees. Wisps of aromatic smoke from the dried, sweet-smelling herbs rose into the air, suffusing the interior with their fragrance.

Tonight, he would not use the fragrant *imphepho* incense to induce a sense of relaxation before entering into the trance state he desired. He would also not require the roots of *lesedi* or the flesh of the potato-like *labateka* to induce the higher levels of concentration required for journeys into the spirit world. His instincts told him they would not be needed, not tonight, and not in the cave of the San.

He fixed his eyes on the images on the other side of the flames. How long had it been since a fire had burned here, in this cave – years, or even longer?

His lips moved in prayer and he began to rock to and fro. Gradually his eyes closed and the lines of his face began to relax. His body continued to move, back and forward, back and forward…

The fire burned brightly, throwing shards of light and warmth around the walls and ceiling, the wood crackling and spitting from time to time.

Langani was aware of them now, the shadowy figures moving around him. Small people, bright-eyed and inquisitive, their delicate features and slanting eyes full of light and life, their bodies small, light-boned but perfectly formed.

There was no fear of him, only a great and gentle curiosity, as light and bright and innocent as only people of their kind could have. He was conscious of whispering in the shadows, the giggle of a young girl, the short sharp cry of a baby, soothing murmurs of comfort.

Snatches of their lives spun like silk around him. He smelled the meat roasting over the fire and heard the crackle and spit of fat, the crunch of bones as they ate. *Fat is good… the eland is full of fat, the food of the spirit.*

And now he could see the story teller sitting across the fire from him and listen to the gentle click sounds as his bird-like voice began the tale:

A long, long time ago, we, the people of the San roamed these mountains. We were nomads then, wandering with the great herds and the turning of the seasons. Where the animals went, we followed, leaving no huts or tilled gardens to mark our presence.

Langani nodded in understanding, and continued to listen, while the fire crackled and leapt, adding its vibrancy to the lives that had once been lived out here, in this very cave.

All we left behind were our stories painted on the rock, the tales of our sacred animals and our journeys to the spirit world. These mountains once gave us shelter while the herds of animals supplied our food and added meaning to our lives.

The diviner drifted once more on the current which bore him away to places that had no boundaries, no beginning and no end. Floating and turning in space, he could not say when the great dance began, or how long it had been since it started; all he knew was that he no longer was an observer, an onlooker, but part of it.

This then was the great dance of the San. The insistent, rhythmic sound of women chanting and drumming was the momentum that drove the shamans, one by one, deeper into trance states.

Leaning with their heads forward, their arms stretched tortuously and painfully behind them, their noses spattered blood with the agony of being transformed into something else.

Langani started in alarm when he saw the bodies of the shamans beginning to change, to take on other forms: feet becoming hoofs, horns sprouting on heads that were rapidly altering and elongating, their human body hair turning into thick, shining reddish brown, their wiry thighs becoming muscular haunches.

Glimpsing the writhing shades of creatures he knew to be half-human, half-animal, he also recognised what he took to be the spirit people of the San, the long-dead ancestors of the living who had come to join with the shamans in their transfiguration and entry into the spirit world. The diviner's eyes were riveted on them.

Physically they appeared no different from their more recent descendants, but it was only when one of the elders, a man scarcely as high as Langani's rib cage, drifted close and looked up at him, that he realised how the eyes told a different story.

Ages old, and very wise, they were a repository of the secrets of San tribal life; of how their shamans had the power to alter the weather and create thunder and lightning storms; of the single stones and rocks on which they had left their ancient symbols and markings and how these were also sacred and pointers to the deep spiritual life they shared with the gentle herds of eland.

The ancient eyes looking out at him from beds of tiny wrinkles were as bright and alert as they had been in life. In them, Langani found not only a deep curiosity, but also a respectful acknowledgement of his calling. The smiling invitation in their depths was also unmistakable, as was the small hand that beckoned him.

Come, brother shaman, it said, *step into our spirit world, if you dare.*

As he stood up, Langani felt the warmth from the fire in the sandy floor beneath his feet. The fire was still burning brightly so he assumed he had not been in a state of dreaming for very long.

There was no sound in the cave, no echo of the chanting and drumming that had surrounded him a moment ago, only the lick and crackle of burning wood and the occasional stir of tumbling ash.

Facing him was the wall of rock, bright and alive with its colourful images. Langani stepped forward until he was only a hairsbreadth away from it. He looked for and found the kneeling mother eland preparing to give birth. Its eyes were soft, liquid and infinitely compassionate, drawing him in.

Solemnly, he opened his arms wide. Then he pressed the length of his body against the rock as if he were embracing a lover or a good friend. As his flesh came in contact with it, he heard his voice cry out. A jolt of powerful energy ran through him making his limbs jerk and twist in a parody of the dancing of the San shamans he'd witnessed only moments before.

He felt the hard cold of the rock press against his face and body for a brief moment. Then there was nothing, only lightness, a sense of flying and the air and wind and the rushing of torrents cascading down the side of the mountain.

In the cave, the fire still burned, its flames leaping and flickering as it created an inter-play of light and shadow across the walls and blackened ceiling. Outside, all was still. Only the occasional sound of a bird or night creature and the tinkling echo of the mountain streams disturbed the silence.

Flooding the world with pale silver light was the young moon, which had risen from behind the towering spires of basalt and sandstone to hang suspended in the dark blue of space.

The cave itself was empty. Only the woven bag and the crumpled deerskin cloak remained to tell of the human presence which had so recently occupied it.

Seventeen

angani's bare foot twitched. He stirred then shifted to relieve the pressure on his hip and right shoulder. Finding little relief, he groaned and turned over on to his back. His eyes blinked open. He found himself staring up into the smoke-streaked roof of the cave.

It took him a few moments to remember where he was. Instinctively, his eyes went to the San paintings. Nothing had changed. But then, he hadn't expected it to.

Sitting up, he ran a hand over his face. The stubble was thick, even luxuriant, with more than a day or two's growth. The ashes of the fire were cold to touch, the heat long gone from the circle of stones.

He shook his head. How long have I been lying here? In fact just *where* have I been for the past few days? A quick examination told him that apart from a few scratches, he had emerged largely unscathed from his experiences.

Suddenly hungry, he padded over to where he had left his food supplies. The once succulent ears of corn were wizened and dry, the water brackish. Gulping down a few mouthfuls of water, he rummaged in the bag for the strips of dried impala meat he'd brought with him. He sat down crossed-legged at the mouth of the cave, grateful for the life-giving warmth of the sun. Judging by the angle, it was late afternoon.

The panorama of forested hills and lush meadows stretching out before him had not changed either. But then he suspected that nothing much had altered for centuries – except for the absence of the nomadic people who had once lived and hunted there.

Deliberately, he refused to allow his thoughts to drift back to his recent experiences in the spirit world of the San. That would come later, once he was back in his sanctuary. Only then would he allow himself to draw on the knowledge he had gained from the shamans.

All he needed to comprehend, for the moment at least, was that his understanding and knowledge had increased tenfold.

Getting to his feet, he turned back into the cave. This time he had no hesitation in standing close to the paintings. Looking at them with fresh eyes, he realised there was so much he had missed during his earlier examinations. Here were the shamans, drawing out disease and evil and hurling it back into the spirit world, while over there, they were flying, yes, flying through the air like birds, freed from the restraints of earth and space.

Suddenly, it all became clearer. A surge of excitement and awe flooded through him.

The exquisite, whimsical paintings were not intended to be just a record of the nomads' earthbound lives and spiritual rituals. The rock face, though as solid as the mountain itself, also served as a portal between the material world and that of the spirit.

Which is both above and below us, he thought, the divide between the two so transparent at times as to be almost non-existent. But it was not for everyone to know that, far less to tamper with, or treat it without due care and respect.

Langani marvelled again at the skills of the small nomads who were as wise as the hills and almost as ancient. Realisation began to dawn in him. I must never be afraid to touch any part of these paintings again, he thought. My sojourn into the spirit world of the San was awe-inspiring, terrifying, yet humbling, but they will not allow me to pass through the portal for a second time. Nor will I need to…

The soft muzzle of the mother eland seemed to quiver in response as Langani reached out to touch its painted outline. When I left Nthabiseng, he thought, I foolishly assumed that that my apprenticeship was over. Now I see it has only just begun. How much I still have to learn.

One thing he already understood and accepted was that his spiritual journey and that of the San people were different, a subject too complex to unravel in such a short time.

Was it because he was Zulu and they were San, their spiritual development different because of their tribal backgrounds and way of life – or was there another reason which only the ancestors and the old gods knew about?

The San were an ancient people, perhaps even the first humans to inhabit the world. They built no huts, no grand dwellings, only moved with the seasons and the herds of animals, passing as easily and lightly through the plains, the desert sands and the high mountains as the wind itself, disturbing nothing, spoiling nothing, their footprints and paintings the only markers of their passing.

Langani had good reason to remember his own words. Later that night, under no volition of his own, he fell into a deep state of dreaming. This time the images had a strength, clarity and duration that astounded him.

It began when he caught a glimpse of Jakot, the young Xhosa rebel. Engulfed by the darkness and rot of a prison cell in Grahamstown, the main frontier town of the Colony, he was chained to the wall, beside him the spiritual leader of the Xhosa people known as Nxele.. Half-starved and filthy, the sheen of despair emanated from them like a black fog.

In a flash, the walls of the prison disappeared as if they had never been, only to be replaced by walls of a different kind.This time Jakot was chained to other black men in what appeared to be in the belly of a frightening beast that rode the waters at dizzying speed.

While the white men commanding it scurried to and fro, harnessing the monster's obedience to their will, its white wings flapped and beat the air with cracks and groans.

Langani's body twitched in shock. He struggled to interpret the images, his heart pumping wildly against his ribs. What manner of a beast was this? Had Jakot and the others been swallowed up by this monster?

Peering about the murky interior, he could see all was not well with the young Xhosa. He viewed the young man's thrashing body with alarm. The eyes were rolled back in the head so that only the whites were showing. Saliva, froth and blood from his bitten tongue flecked his drawn-back lips and the corners of his mouth. Sweat poured off his body, his muffled cries torn from the depths of his being.

Was he possessed by evil spirits, or by the terrible sickness of the mind that caused men to act like madmen? Langani did not know. In any case he could do nothing, only look on in horror.

A sudden beam of sunlight came flooding in from above, lighting up the pitiful images of those confined in the creature's belly. The diviner strained his eyes to see what was happening.

He saw a dark shape crouching over Jakot, a man of authority, judging by the orders he was issuing. The diviner tensed, wondering if the unfortunate young Xhosa was about to be killed. No, wait! The crouching figure was trying to straighten out Jakot's thrashing body and edge something between his tightly-clenched teeth.

The diviner nodded. Perhaps he was an *inyanga*, a man of medicine.

More light flooded in from above. It was followed by a scurrying of bodies and a clink of metal. He peered closer. Jakot's slumped body was being lifted by several of the dark figures and borne up from the stinking darkness into the glorious sunlight above. Langani caught a glimpse of the sparkling blue sea across which the white-winged creature was flying like the wind.

A gasp of astonishment was torn from him when he caught a glimpse of the man who had led the rescue of the stricken Xhosa. Clearly, he was a white man, one of the *abelungu*. So, not all were men of rage and cruelty, then...

Langani studied him with interest. Paler of skin than the others, tall, well-built with humour in the lines of his face and around his mouth, he seemed a man of some principle. The diviner's eyes were immediately drawn to his hair. As long and dark as night, it was threaded through with wide streaks of silver and drawn into a single plait at the nape of his neck.

'As distinctive a pelt as the spots on the leopard, or the tear marks on the face of the cheetah,' Langani murmured. 'I will certainly remember you.'

The image began to fade as did the background of sunlight and clean, fresh air, giving way to a world of swirling water, one of pale, translucent green. Before his startled eyes, he saw it close over Jakot's head. With him was another black man, also a prisoner, he assumed.

Bewildered, Langani looked around this silent new world. Water without end, here and there the quick silver dart of a fish, a trail of green weeds, drifting and turning in the currents. Deeper and deeper, spiralling downwards, he spotted the struggling, kicking bodies of Jakot and the other poor devil. He felt their lungs strain for air and tasted their fear as they tried to rise to the surface.

Up close, Jakot's face was distorted with the effort of staying alive. His eyes were wide open, staring. But even as the murky depths of the ocean sought to close them for ever, the magical segment in his left eye continued to glow, as fearless as that of a lion.

Just as it seemed the swirling current was about to drag him down, the Xhosa kicked out strongly and began to rise. Struggling, fighting and clawing his way up towards the light, Langani knew that Jakot Msimbithi had only two choices left. Learn how to resist the destructive power of the sea – or drown.

As his head broke the surface, Jakot drew in deep, gulping breaths of salty air. Coughing and spluttering, somehow he managed to tread water and stay afloat. Looking around, he could see no sign of his friend, only the troughs and peaks of the ocean rising and falling around him.

Shaking the water from his eyes, he kept on paddling. On the upward rise of the next swell, he caught a glimpse of a dark smudge on the horizon.

Land! His heart leapt. What if he could reach it? He would be free. But what if it was the prison island? Once inside, he would die.

He could see no sign of the ship, but that didn't mean it wasn't close by, with the crew ready to drag him aboard and deliver him to where King Jo-ji's men had decided he should spend the rest of his life.

After being accused of killing English soldiers, he had narrowly escaped being hanged. The alternative, however, had filled him with despair. The other prisoners' tales of the notorious penitentiary had reduced Jakot to a state of blind terror. To live in such a place would suck the soul from his body and reduce it to dust. Even the kindness of the ship's master, the man who had rescued him from the rat-infested darkness, had failed to lift his despondency.

Better to cast himself on the mercy of the ocean and the ancestors than to die slowly in chains. These had been his last thoughts before he'd plunged from the deck of the *Salisbury* into the sea.

As he'd leapt from the rail, holding hands with his friend Jonas, there had been only a brief moment's serenity on the way down before they were swallowed up by the roaring waters.

Jakot's thoughts spun to Jonas. What had happened to him? The last time he'd seen him was just as the sea closed over their heads, tearing their linked hands apart.

Praying that he was still alive, he wondered briefly how the ancestors decided that it was one man's destiny to die, and another's to live.

Galvanised by fear, his teeth chattering with cold, he spat out a mouthful of sea water and concentrated on staying afloat. Gradually, warmth spread through his body, and his arms and legs began to settle into a comfortable rhythm.

The next time he rose on the swell, Jakot turned towards the smudge of land on the horizon. Thrusting down his fears, he kicked out strongly and began to swim towards it.

It could well turn out to be Robben Island, but, on the other hand, could it not be somewhere better? Let the ancestors decide, he thought. Inexplicably, his spirits began to rise.

Then, pushing any further thought of either destiny or failure from his mind, Jakot Msimbithi began to swim for his life.

Beyond the San cave, the night was cool and quiet, the stars a blaze of light above the mountain peaks. Exhausted and drained by the prolonged effort of maintaining a trance state, Langani's eyes opened briefly, as if seeking the reassurance of his own time and place.

Recognising the patch of starlit sky beyond the mouth of the cave, they blinked once or twice before closing in a deep and natural sleep.

On the following morning, just as the sun was rising, Langani took a last, long look at the paintings etched on the shadowy back wall of the cave. Then turning away, he made his way to the mouth of the cave to begin the first part of his journey back down the mountainside.

Eighteen

In the valley of Nkwalini, the evening fires were burning brightly, for the night had turned cool. The storyteller eased himself down on the karosse, taking a little time to arrange his limbs into a more comfortable position, for he was full of age and his bones were stiff.

Around the rim of firelight, people were eagerly waiting for him to begin, for Zulus, young and old, loved listening to stories. At last the old man was ready. He uttered only one word.

'Nobela...' Everyone, from the oldest to the youngest, knew who she was. Nobela, the witch sniffer, was a creature from their deepest nightmares.

The storyteller began: 'It all started on the day Shaka came to esiKlebeni to be hailed as King of the Zulus. From the moment she set eyes on him, Nobela began to plot and scheme. Her plan was to destroy him because of his open contempt for those of the sisterhood. His dislike of them was well-known and was beginning to hamper her success among the people of the villages.'

'Gradually, she brought a number of unscrupulous diviners under her influence. Then Nobela decided to put the mighty Shaka to the test. And this is what happened...'

177

The people clustered round the fires waited in eager anticipation. Women hushed the babies at their breasts, while children bundled closer together like nests of small puppies.

'Shaka had just returned from a hunting trip,' the storyteller said, drawing deeply on his pipe. 'No sooner had he entered the gates of kwaBulawayo, than a messenger ran to tell him of the strange things that had been happening in his absence. As you know, evil omens come in many shapes and forms . . .'

Voices whispered in the firelight. '*Yebo*, a strange animal appearing in the kraal; lightning striking in the wrong place; the hooting of a horned owl... a calf born with two heads.'

The storyteller's eyes were narrow slits in the firelight, tobacco smoke wreathing round his head. 'When sorcery is suspected,' he said, 'women such as Nobela were sent for. Those responsible must be sniffed out by practitioners who are skilled in that particular art.'

From time immemorial, this was how it had always been. Tribal law gave Shaka no other choice. Nobela must be sent for.

'A few days later, kwaBulawayo, the first kwaBulawayo, that is, was packed full of people. The regiments and adult males formed a half-circle in the great oval enclosure while women, children and old people occupied the other half.

'As you all know, only the King is sacred, untouchable, and beyond the powers of such as Nobela. Everyone else was bound by time and long tradition to accepting the verdict of the "witch finders." So this was what happened...'

Shaka frowned. This situation was not to his liking. If he had his way, he would round up every last one of the peddlers of the occult and dispose of them like the vermin they were.

An eerie silence hung over the arena. A moment later, the calm was shattered. Several grotesque figures appeared and shambled into the open on all fours. A terrible moaning rose from the crowd when they saw them.

Their long, matted hair was entwined with the bladders of dead animals and flew around their white-daubed faces as they whirled and capered about. Swinging their hideous heads from side to side, they sniffed the air ominously.

The moans of the crowd grew louder. The leader turned to face Shaka, defiance in every line of her body, her minions forming a leering chorus behind her. Shaka regarded them with ill-disguised contempt. Nobela and he were old adversaries.

Her red-rimmed eyes glowed like coals in her chalk-white mask. Grinning monkey skulls and snake-heads rattled against the necklaces of hyena and jackal claws draped around her neck. Every part of her was on the move, the gnu tail in her hand keeping time as if it were still part of the living animal.

Shaka stared her down. Convention dictated that even a King had to give way to the powers of these particular diviners, for it was held that they alone possessed the skills to interpret the signs of witchcraft.

Her minions slithered into a circle around her. As the frenzy mounted, their eyes rolled in their sockets until only the whites were visible. With bloodcurdling shrieks, the four acolytes dropped to the ground and lay face down as if dead, resembling little more than heaps of torn rags and old animal skins.

Only Nobela was on her feet, her eyes riveted on Shaka. The ragged head with its insane arrangements of snake skins and twisted coils of hair was thrown back to sniff the wind. When she spoke, her voice was hoarse and sibilant, as if unused to uttering human words.

'There are those of evil in your presence, King of the Zulu. Nobela can smell them on the wind. They cannot hide from me. I will seek them out, no matter how high or low they might be.'

Her eyes flicked past him and moved to his councillors. They shrank back in horror. But she was only teasing, and did not linger on them for long. The true source of her interest lay elsewhere.

With a wild shriek, she jumped high into the air in a whirl of skirts and animal tails. A group of burly men, bearing clubs, seemed to materialise out of nowhere and stood with their arms folded, waiting for her orders.

The ritual slayers!

Nobela's clawed hands swooped out. 'Chant!' she screeched. 'Chant for Nobela, people of the amaZulu. *Bulala abathakhati*! Kill the wizards! Kill the witches!'

Darting, shambling and sniffing like dogs, the sisters went spinning down between the rows of terrified people. One moment they would be on all fours, sniffing round their feet and ankles, the next, probing delicately at people's ears, eyes and mouths.

All they had to do was to swish the gnu tail around the victim's face then strike them once with it. The waiting slayers would then pounce on them and drag them away to await execution.

Shaka's eyes searched for Nobela. Where was she now?

With a shock, he realised she was showing an uncommon interest in his commanders, Mgobozi, Nqoboka and Mdlaka. *She wouldn't dare . . .*

Her bird's nest head probed in and around the men, who held themselves stiffly erect, refusing to be drawn into the frenzied chanting. Shaka rose half-way out of his chair.

Not even the Mother of Fear herself should dare flaunt her power so blatantly. To accuse his most trusted commanders! It was an insult of the worst kind.

Coldly, he thrust his rage down and focused on the sinister flick of the gnu tail as it darted to and fro. As if on cue, the ghastly white mask turned in his direction. He fixed her with a baleful eye.

Distorted by the lust for power, hers was the face of a malignant presence. In that moment, he knew she was capable of anything, even of having his military commanders accused of sorcery, then executed. His hands clenched into fists.

Mdlaka, the bravest of men, commander of the Fasimba, the Royal Guard; Nqoboka and Mgobosi, the comrades of his youth and his dearest friends. They had been together since they were cadets in the service of King Dingiswayo.

He swallowed down the rage that threatened to bring him out of his chair. As King, he could flout the law and command that they be stopped from killing his commanders. At the same time, he knew that he would be deemed guilty of breaking the strong, tribal taboos of his people.

Nobela's carmined tongue shot out, sending a shower of spittle spraying around her. One of the councillors moaned in terror, and shrank away from her. She sprang forward until she was almost at the man's feet.

This course of action brought her dangerously close to Shaka, her chalk-white mask only inches away from where he was seated.

Swiftly, he rose from the chair. 'Seek not wizards among those close to me, Mother of Fear,' he hissed, staring into her savage black eyes, 'touch them at your peril!'

The rage on Nobela's face was frightening. 'Evil is always found close to those whom they seek to destroy,' she spat, 'that is the way of the *abathakhati*, Lord of the World!'

The sarcasm was clear and very pointed. Shaka leaned closer until his face was mere inches from hers. The desire to take her by the throat was overwhelming, but he forced himself to keep his voice steady and deliver his message with cool deliberation.

'Leave my commanders alone, old woman, otherwise you will find yourself in a hornet's nest of your own making.'

His look was ruthless in its intensity. The challenge had been thrown down. 'Step carefully, Nobela!'

She jumped back as if stung, her tongue flicking in and out of her mouth. Incandescent with rage, she spat into the dust at his feet before turning away, her eyes already seeking those she wanted.

Sidling up to Mgobozi, she fingered the bundle of pointed skewers concealed below the flaps of her leather skirts. Longer than a man's hand, the skewers were very strong, and as sharp as thorns.

Nobela began to croon, hovering over Shaka's commander like an angel of death. Her eyes moved to Mdlaka. *Flick, flick* went her tongue as the black eyes lingered on him. *Half of what they owned would come to her if she succeeded in accusing them…*

She turned to stare long and pitilessly at the man on the dais.

I-tshaka, you crawling insect, you have forgotten your place. You need a reminder of how weak you really are. Take care not to put your foot too close to the viper otherwise you will feel its fatal bite!

Nobela threw back her head and howled like a hyena. Her sisters knew that the time had come to close in on their prey, and spread out in a pincer movement. Just as Nobela began to make her final sweep, a command rang out.

'Ho, Mdlaka,' Shaka called out to his senior commander, 'bring me a company of my young lions, the Fasimba. I need them to guard me. It is not fitting for the king to be unprotected while there are wizards or witches about.'

As a man, Mdlaka and some fifty Fasimba rose to their feet and made their way towards him. Nobela's body twitched in fury. The king of the Zulus was clever. Since he was not openly contesting tribal law, there was little she could do. Before she had a chance to move, Shaka's voice rang out again.

'Mgobozi, Nqoboka. I need you near me. I fear the *abathakhati* will threaten me. Bring your regiments with you, so I can truly feel safe.'

Nobela snarled, and twitched the gnu tail. The eyes of her four sisters raked the crowd, willing them to remain under their control.

Shaka stood up, his voice drilling into her head. 'Now I see the true *abathakhati* before me, the sorcerers who seek to cause me mischief.'

Nobela was almost beside herself with rage. Shrieking like a demon, she began to spin round and round. Animal skulls swung and rattled as she moved, while her tails of matted hair flew around her face. The sign she made to her sisters on her right went unnoticed, as did a similar gesture to those on her left.

Without warning, she launched herself at Shaka's warriors, pushing and trampling a pathway through them, striking out with the gnu tail as she went. The men, most of them very young, instinctively moved aside to avoid the stench of old blood and stale urine.

If Mgobozi and Mdlaka had imagined themselves safe behind the screen of warriors, the witch-finder soon proved them wrong. Realising the danger they were in, they shot a desperate glance in Shaka's direction.

Only a few yards separated them. If only they could reach him, they could claim sanctuary, the right of any person falsely accused of witchcraft. But Nobela and the sisters were barring their way, teeth bared, hissing and spitting. The slayers were only a few yards away, waiting for their signal to pounce.

Shaka cursed below his breath. How cunning Nobela had been! In a few moments victory would be hers. His hands were tied; he could not be seen to be openly advising his friends. At all costs he must keep within the strict bounds of the tribal laws that formed the cornerstone of the nation.

Nobela, however, hadn't reckoned on the razor-sharp reflexes of Shaka's commanders, men used to hand-to-hand fighting on the field of battle.

Mgobozi drove his knee into the belly of the nearest slayer, tore the club from the man's nerveless fingers and brought it down first on his head and then on that of the nearest 'sister.' Both fell without a sound.

Blood poured down Mdlaka's face where the long nails of one of the hags had torn it open. Nqoboka, standing astride one of the slayers, dispatched the man then with one bound was at Mdlaka's side. In seconds, they had reached the dais, the others following close behind.

Shaka leapt to his feet, his voice rising above the bedlam. '*Sanctuary!*' he urged them. '*Do you claim sanctuary?*' 'Yebo, Nkosi!' came the reply. 'We claim sanctuary under the laws of the land!'

From beyond the screen of Fasimba who had closed ranks against her, Nobela could be heard howling like a demon. Shaka held up a hand for silence. After the clamour had died down, he allowed Nobela to come forward.

'Before I give the King's consent for sanctuary to these men,' he said, 'I will ask them one question. Are you agreeable, Mother of Fear?'

Nobela nodded reluctantly. Her eyes were wild and staring, the gnu tail trembling in her hand. Shaka addressed his commanders one by one.

First was Mgobozi. 'Why do you claim sanctuary?' Shaka asked, 'is it because you are afraid to die that you seek to hide behind your King?'

'*Cha!*' replied Mgobozi, shaking his head. 'Many times you have stood with us at the height of battle, Nkosi. You know we are no cowards.'

In each case, the answer from the others was the same. No one in the crowd could accuse any of them of being cowards. Shaka pretended to reflect and took his time before answering. 'What you say is true. I can find no fault with you.'

Turning first to the councillors, then to the regiments, he threw the matter open to the people crowded into the arena. 'What say you? Are these men cowards?'

The answer came back in a single, mighty shout, which echoed over the vast enclosure. 'Never!'

Deadly serious now, he looked each of his commanders straight in the eye. 'They say you are also guilty of witchcraft. Are you *abathakhati,* wizards, or have you ever summoned their powers for some secret reason of your own, now or at any other time?'

Their replies were immediate. 'We are warriors who stand or fall on the field of battle. We have used no secret powers to find courage, or for any other purpose.'

Before Nobela had even time to blink, Shaka announced, 'Then I give you sanctuary. There is no charge of sorcery to answer.'

Turning to face her, he raised his voice over the moaning of the injured slayers. 'You heard their words. I did not intervene. They asked for sanctuary, which was their right. Do you agree this was correct under the law?'

The chalk-white mask regarded him sullenly, the gnu tail stilled now. Shaka took her silence as agreement, and pressed on. 'Do you have anything to say?' Nobela shook her head, her black eyes narrowed in fury.

Shaka drew himself up and looked down at her from his great height, the scarlet *igwala gwala* feathers in his head-dress vivid in the sunlight.

'You have your sphere of rule, Mother of Fear, and I have mine. In future, see to it that you and your sisters prevail only against *true* wizards and the evils of sorcery.'

His eyes bored into hers, making his meaning absolutely clear. 'I, on the other hand, *will* set my hand against the enemies of the people and the forces who would seek to destroy us. The army and all the warriors and *indunas*, whatever their rank, belong to me and are beyond the reach of any other power.'

His meaning was absolutely clear. Nobela was in no doubt that he included her. 'Do you understand this?'

Reluctantly, she had no choice but to agree. He had chosen his words so well that even she would not have been able to insert the most pointed of her skewers between them in protest.

'Stay with the shades, then,' Shaka said, 'but seek only to rid the land of evil. No more.' He raised a hand to dismiss her then hesitated. Leaning forward, he lowered his voice. 'One more thing, Mother of Fear, in future, keep your nose out of hornets' nests.'

Nobela raised her cracked, white mask, and looked at him through bloodshot eyes full of loathing.Then he raised his voice and shouted out loud and strong so that everyone could hear him.

'*Indaba ipilele...* the matter is closed!'

As shouts of triumph filled the air, Nobela turned away, blinded by rage, her eyes hooded to cover her fury.

A loud hiss of relief came from the listeners around the fires. After a few moments, a voice asked the storyteller, 'Was that the end of Nobela, then? '

He shook his head, '*Cha*. Nobela was true to her nature. Time and again, Shaka and she butted heads. In the end, the inevitable happened.'

The listeners looked expectantly at him across the dying embers.

'Shaka brought her to destruction,' the old man said, 'just as he did to Ntombazi, the mother of Zwide – though no court was required, this time!'

The old eyes twinkled at them across the fire. With a dismissive stab of his knobbed forefinger, he pointed to the smoke spiralling up into the night sky.

'Not long afterwards, Shaka held her to account for all her evil doings. She and all her sisters were put to the fire. Their villages burned brightly high in the hills, and the flames devouring them could be seen from a long way away. Now Nobela is as the smoke that rises to the heavens – one moment here, the next, gone for ever.'

With the defeat of Nobela, and the sweeping away of much of the sinister occult which had terrorised the people, Zululand continued to enjoy a time of relative peace.

While the turbulent tribal lands around it continued to echo with the sounds of war and strife, the kingdom of Shaka seemed to be an oasis of tranquillity in a troubled land.

Nineteen

Langani stopped grinding the seeds and waved away the fly buzzing round his head. A trickle of sweat ran down his face. With a sigh of exasperation, he pushed the carved bowl to one side and sat back.

Although the long dry winter was far from over, the air was restless and crackling with stored heat, almost as if the rains were about to begin. For the past few days, he had been unusually tense and short-tempered. Probably due to lack of sleep, he thought, those damned owls keeping me awake night after night with their hooting and screeching.

At first he'd dismissed the idea that the hooting of owls was an omen of impending disaster. But, after being wakened several nights in a row by their mournful cries and finding his face bathed in a beam of moonlight slanting through the doorway, he was forced to admit that something was indeed afoot, though whether here or in the spirit world, he was not sure.

He turned his attention back to the wooden bowl in front of him. It was half-full of gritty, yellowish powder, a substance he intended to add to the watering of the seeds he'd planted at the time of the last full moon.

If my calculations are right, he thought, the crop will exceed all normal expectations. The beans, corn and pumpkins should grow large enough and sweet enough to feed me for a whole season. A mischievous grin lit up his face. Some *isangoma* magic for my personal use from time to time – is that such a bad thing?

Just then, a sudden but noticeable change of atmosphere intruded into his thoughts. His smile faded. It was barely noon, yet in the space of a few minutes everything seemed to have grown much darker. Glancing around, he became aware of strange shadows shifting and moving in the far reaches of the hut.

A rustle of feathers above his head made him look up. The cockerel and a few of the speckled chickens had fluttered up on to the crossbeams and appeared to be settling down as if it was nightfall and not the middle of the day.

But why was it so dark? Where had the light gone? Rising to his feet, Langani padded over to the doorway and went outside. The sky had turned an ominous shade of grey. The heavens had a look of brooding discontent about them, the sun eclipsed beneath their sullen scowl. The air was dead, lifeless, yet filled with the same restless hum of energy he'd noticed from time to time over the last few days.

It was quiet, eerily so. Silence lay over everything; the birds had stopped singing and even the restless cricking of cicadas had stilled. The trickle of the waterfall could barely be heard, its melodious tinkling strangely muffled by the pall of silence.

He made his way over to the rocky edge of his territory and stood looking out, his arms folded across his chest. Miles of dusty bush stretched as far as the darkened horizon, the small villages in its depths hidden from sight.

Cocking his head to one side, he listened carefully. No birdsong, no rustle of wind among the leaves; even the cheerful crick-crick of insects was muted. Such a silence felt alien and deeply hostile.

Langani sniffed the air. When people spoke of an animal's ability to smell fear, they were only half-right, he thought. Most humans could too, although some were more alert to this than others. It was what he could sense now, a thin, diaphanous spiral of unease, growing and expanding. But whose fear was it? Not his own, for nothing had happened of late to cause him to be afraid or apprehensive.

Out on the edge of the world, lightning began to flicker in sporadic bursts, tiny spider-cracks of light barely visible to the naked eye. He watched as their delicate traces of filigree quicksilver flickered, probing the sullen skies.

Without warning, twin tongues of forked blue fire streaked down from the crown of the heavens and ran to earth in the distance. Langani shivered.

Usually, he welcomed storms and found them exhilarating company. Some would say he even had an affinity with them. But not today, today was different. In spite of the sporadic lightning, all was silent, no rumble or clap of thunder, the voice of the gods muted.

Langani stared into the distance trying to piece together the reasons for such strange happenings. The gods were angry; that was clear. He could sense their sullen rage in the strange weather patterns, the unseasonal heat and silent lightning, the storm without thunder. It might also explain why the owls had been behaving so strangely over the past few nights.

But why? That was the question. He stared out into the silent void. A thin grey veil of mist was beginning to creep towards him across the bush. The more he looked at it, the more he sensed something oddly malevolent in its silent swirling and the speed with which it was travelling.

It had been no ordinary day. Still hardly half-way through, yet so dark, silent and abnormally quiet, the frenetic display of unseasonal lightning and the fear in the air giving it an eerie, foreboding quality.

He turned away. There was nothing more to be gained by tempting fate. Sooner or later, he would find out what it was all about. He usually did.

With a final glance over his shoulder at the encroaching mist, he made his way back to the warmth and shelter of his home and drew down the goatskin flap across the doorway to shut it out.

Next morning, it was as if nothing out of the ordinary had happened. He had slept soundly all night without being disturbed. For once, the owls were silent. When he stepped outside just after first light, everything seemed to be as usual.

The dawn chorus was in full-throated song, the sky rose-coloured and streaked with carmine and gold. A breeze rose up from the old river bed below and stirred the tendrils of his hair. He drew in a deep breath of air. It was fresh and untainted, the greyness and yesterday's lurking sense of fear totally dissipated.

It was with a lighter heart that he turned away to begin his morning routine of meditation and prayer.

Several hours later, after he had finished the day's work, Langani slid down into the shade by the waterfall and placed his back against the rock. Closing his eyes, he let the cool air from the pool flow over him. The water trickling down from the depths of the mountain formed a soothing background in the afternoon heat.

He yawned widely, his jaws cracking. The long hours of prayers and meditation he'd immersed himself in since first light had been tiring. The effects of the previous day must have drained the strength from him more than he'd realised. Closing his eyes, he allowed his thoughts to drift.

A little while later, a faint whirring sound caught his attention. Drowsily, he opened an eye to investigate. A dragonfly with wings shimmering like iridescent spun-silk was hovering and darting over the water in the rocky pool.

As it dipped and swayed over the water beneath the over-hanging shelf of rock, his eyes followed the flashes of colour in the insect's fragile wings. Its jewelled eyes glowed, almost as if it was admiring its reflection in the water.

Out of the corner of his eye, Langani saw a second dragonfly appear out of nowhere. It was followed by another and then one more. Intrigued by the cluster of exotic insects, he sat up and moved closer so he could get a better look at them.

The kaleidoscope of brilliant colours held his eyes, drawing him ever deeper into their whirling dance. The effect on him was almost hypnotic. As his body began to relax, his eyes grow heavy.

Then something struck him as odd. Blinking, he tried to focus on the swirling movement of the water and not on the dragonflies themselves.

Was it moving in the usual direction… or did it seem to be travelling the other way round? Are my eyes playing tricks on me?

He blinked hard a few times then looked again. This time the water appeared to be flowing normally. I must have been mistaken, he thought, perhaps because I'm tired, my eyes lacked focus.

It was then he saw some specks of material, small leaves, or pieces of twig being swept along on the gently swirling water. Nothing strange about that, he thought, only a few scraps of leaves blown in by the breeze. The only thing was, they seemed to be moving faster than the actual current – almost as if they were riding the ripples of water, using them to further their progress around the pool.

But then he noticed something else – something that clearly did not belong to mere wind-blown scraps of leaf. He leaned over to get a better look, his long plaits almost touching the surface of the water.

At the heart of each of the specks of floating debris, he spotted what appeared to be a miniscule dot of glowing light. Intrigued, he leaned even closer, his eyes following their bobbing progress. Each shining spark was composed of matter, *live* matter, it would seem. His curiosity quickened.

How many were there? He began to count. Two, three, no…four, perhaps five at most, each of them stronger and more vibrant than the lesser sparks bobbing about in their wake.

A movement above his head made him glance up. A small sunbeam seemed to be dancing and spinning around the light-dappled roof of the rocky overhang above the pool – almost as if it was competing with those below.

A smile tugged at the corners of the diviner's mouth. Instinctively, he reached out to touch it, but it danced out of reach, quivered briefly, then spun away again, a small bright orb glowing among the other ripples of reflected sunlight.

After watching it for a few moments, the diviner bent his head to concentrate on the rock pool itself. Leaning down, he selected one of the curious specks of floating debris and began to observe it closely.

His eyes moved with it, drifted with it, ebbed and flowed with it. Closer still, and he saw the spark at the heart of it expand gently, then contract, glow more brightly for a few seconds, then dim, before beginning the cycle again.

There was a certain familiarity about the pulsing movement which eluded him for a moment. Glancing over at the others, he saw the same small movement being repeated at their core. A moment's further blankness of mind – and then it came to him.

Langani sprang back as if stung. *Could it be – surely not!* He ran a hand over his face in disbelief then looked again. A heartbeat! His scalp contracted with the enormity of what his instincts were telling him.

Was it possible that each speck of material, whether a fragment of twig, leaf or grass, represented the earthly shell of a human being? If that were true, then it would mean that the glowing spark embedded in each could only be construed as proof of life; in other words, the existence of a soul, eternal and indestructible…

Shocked, his rational mind reeled with the nature of the assumption. Was this the reason for all the strange happenings of the last few days, a preparation for what he was seeing here?

Langani looked down at the bright, bobbing sparks of light then up to the dappled overhang where the orb continued in its merry dance among the ripples of reflected light. Although he expected no answer from it, he whispered, 'Who are you, and what do you want from me?' Closing his eyes, he let his mind drift.

Images, thoughts, some fragmented and disparate, others clear and definite began to flit through his mind. Snatches of the Xhosa, Jakot; the bearded farmers with their fearsome weapons that could spit fire; Nxele, the prophet, in the belly of the creature with the white wings; the *abelungu* with streaks of silver in his hair and human compassion in his heart...

Langani drew a short, sharp breath of exhaustion and sank back against the rock, his mind in a whirl. Gradually, the trickle of water in the background filtered into his consciousness. Water! It seemed to be the connecting motif for so much of late, spinning, flowing around the pool in ever-quickening spirals, shining, unfettered and free, yet following the dictate of the mighty elements that ruled the earth.

More images flooded into his mind...and he saw again the ocean reaching up for Jakot; the struggle and the darkness in its depths, choking, drowning; the wailing of dead souls... *and oh, what kind of a place is this?* Jakot's anguish and his failure to escape the island prison; sea mists and the crying of seals; a great city and a flat-topped mountain rising out of the place where the land met the sea at the last part of Africa – *is this where the world ends?*

Langani shivered, although it was hot in the shadow of the rocks.

The rushing of mighty waters came again, and in it he saw the handful of specks with the bright spark of their souls moving silently with the currents – not of their own volition, but propelled by the winds that were accountable to no one. Although he was aware of other unseen forces directing them in the paths they had to follow, these were forces he did not recognise, or even begin to understand.

He struggled on to his knees and peered down into the water. 'Who are you?' Langani whispered to the sparks of pulsing light.

They gave no sign they had heard him and merely continued on their way.

His eyes flicked upwards to where the golden orb of light pursued its impish way across the sunlit, dappled roof. As he watched it dance and spin, he smiled, 'And who and what are you, my little friend?'

Again, he expected no reply; it was enough that he had addressed it directly. Because the presence of the playful sunbeam lifted his mood, he stayed there for a long time, basking in its peaceful light. After a while, his eyes closed and he drifted into sleep.

When he woke, he saw that the sun was sinking, the long blue shadows creeping in across the bush. A restless clucking reminded him that the chickens were waiting to be fed.

He stood up and looked down at the swirling water and the tiny sparks of light for a moment longer before turning away and leaving them to the falling dusk.

Later that night, Langani turned his attention to one of his few personal possessions. He glanced sideways at the hand-carved drum that served as a small table. A beautifully-crafted pouch made of tawny lion-skin lay on its tightly-stretched top.

His brother Sobuza, his elder by five years, had been involved in cornering a rogue male lion which had been terrorising their village, killing cattle and goats and lying in wait along the bush paths for a child or old person to pass by. The men of the village had gathered, determined to trap and kill the marauding beast.

During its capture, Langani's sixteen-year-old brother had received deep scratches on his thigh. The poison from the dirt ingrained in the animal's claws had spread through his body, and though the *inyanga* had tried every *muthi* known to him, in the end the spirit of the slain lion had claimed Sobuza's life. Afterwards, the beast's pelt had been handed over to his mother, Jubilele, as a gesture of mutual sorrow and reparation.

When Langani completed his apprenticeship, his mentor, Nabiseng, had presented him with a pouch of sacred bones which had been passed down through generations of diviners, those of her own blood.

Aged and smooth with years of use, the bones were dark of colour and quite fragile. Langani had looked on them with reverence and awe, almost afraid to touch them.

'Treat them with care,' Nabiseng had advised him, 'for they hold great wisdom and power. When it is time for you to pass into the world of spirit, as we all must do, your wisdom will be added to them before being handed over to another of our kind.'

Langani had been in no doubt at all where he would keep the sacred bones. Where better than in the pouch made from the hide of the beast that had taken his brother's life? The strength of the lion and the guiding spirit of Sobuza would help him when he needed them most.

Tomorrow, before first light, he would daub his face and body with ochre and white chalk and place sweet-smelling herbs and sacred relics in a circle round him in the shade of the trees. He would smooth and flatten out a patch of earth and make the bones ready. As the first rays of the rising sun spilled over the horizon, he would first pray for guidance then he would cast the bones.

If he was right, and the glowing sparks were indeed the souls of men, he needed to know who they were and why they had appeared to him. The patterns in which the bones fell would be very revealing and would tell him much.

A pale crescent moon had risen and its silvery light illuminated the earthly place the young diviner had chosen for his sanctuary. His bare feet made no sound as he moved towards the tinkling waters.

The surface of the rock pool was quiet, the waters still moving, though not as strongly as before. The floating specks were still there; their glowing sparks tamped down, pulsing intermittently. Above his head, the darting globe of light was resting, seemingly asleep, a tiny pulse beating faintly at its core. A smile creased the diviner's face.

The golden orb would pose no threat either to him or to the world at large. Deep in his soul, he knew this to be true, for did he not also like to dance?

Although it was late, his eyes slipped back to the pool of water, reluctant to leave its mysteries. He stared long and hard at the flecks of light moving to the tune of the unseen forces stirring the waters.

There was no doubt in his mind they were connected to the incipient warnings he had received the day before; no doubt either that they were somehow connected to the Xhosa, Jakot, the man with the 'magic' eye and then Shaka himself.

How, or why, he did not know. Like all else of late, it would come to him when the time was right. But even as he turned away, he knew that it would not be too long before he learned more about the shadowy figures whose eyes were fixed on Zululand.

Twenty

The Maphuta River, Mozambique

Slowly, the man called Henry Fynn drifted out of the sweat-drenched fires of the fever threatening to consume him. The demons hovering around him were female, he was sure of it. The touch of the hands on his naked body was delicate, sensuous, with an identifiable musk in the air, strongly feminine and smoky.

Firmly and inexorably, he was being pressed down into the ground. Thinking that the dark, whispering shapes were trying to bury him alive, a hoarse cry of terror escaped him. He writhed madly, trying to flee both the dreams and the reality. Rough grit and soil brushed against his bare chest, the smell of damp earth and pungent leaf mould strong in his nostrils

Wait! What was wrong with his arms? Realising they were bound tightly against his body, Fynn arched his back in an effort to slow his descent into the ground, bellowing in rage and fear. The effort set off a spasm of feeble coughing, making his heart race and increasing the relentless pounding at the base of his

197

skull. Moaning, he spewed up a dribble of bile. As the sour smell filled his nostrils, his nose wrinkled in disgust.

Acrid smoke drifted into his eyes. He could feel the savage heart of the smouldering fire only a hair's breadth away. Scrabbling frantically at the sides of the tomb, his screams were high and full of terror, his mind brimming over with images of the Pit and the burning damnation that awaited all sinners.

He was a child again, kneeling by his mother's side, mesmerised by the blue, drifting coils of incense smoke and the fear of what might be lurking in the shadows beyond the flickering candles.

Oh, God, I repent of all my sins, I truly do. Save me from the Pit! Holy Mother, forgive us now, and at the hour of our death...

Babbling incoherently, Fynn threw himself from side to side of his earthy cell. Something was being wrapped around his head. He smelled the smokiness of the fibres, felt them rasp and catch at his beard.

Holy Mother! The covering of the face in death was a service he had often performed at Christ's Hospital when he was laying out the wasted bodies of London's poor.

Fynn screamed once more, a high, bleating sound that rebounded off the sides of the hole in the ground. Slowly, he began to drift away again into the place where the present and the past were one and the same.

The rough hands left him cocooned like a chrysalis with only his head free of the smouldering pit. Their final touches, however, were muted by something approaching tenderness, while their whispering rose and fell in soothing cadences around him.

A wave of loneliness washed over him. Mewling weakly like a lost child, he croaked out a feeble appeal to his tormentors not to desert him.

Abruptly, a new danger caught him up and tossed him about like a broken straw. As he shivered and burned, twisting and turning, dreamlike fragments of the last few years returned to haunt him.

Fynn was back once more with the sights, sounds and smells of this ferocious and magnificent country reeling through his brain in fitful images. Only now he was part of the night, flying upwards into the darkness along with the showers of sparks, at one with the black skies and pounding rhythms of the great tawny beast of a land.

Superimposed over and above it all were the faces of Africa, dark and mysterious as if carved from polished ebony, as implacable and powerful as the forces which held them all in their sinuous, unbreakable grasp.

He'd been barely fifteen when he'd fled the damp and cold of England to join the rest of his family who had been living at the Cape of Good Hope for a year or so. Determined to prove himself, he spent the next few years on the dusty reaches of the Colony's frontier, a territory as hard and unremitting as the struggle of both black and white to survive each other's savagery.

To Fynn, they represented an incredible mixture of new experiences, periods of uncertainty and boredom, heavily laced with moments of sheer, blind terror.

By the time he was seventeen, he was indistinguishable from any other frontier adventurer of his age. The African sun and the precariousness of existence on the frontier had burned any surplus fat from his body and honed his instinct for self-survival.

He wore the slouched, wide-brimmed hat of the Boer and had abandoned his leather boots for a pair of *veldtschoen*. Sporting a trimmed beard and moustaches, his shoulder-length brown hair was sun-streaked and tied back at the nape of his neck with a strip of ox-hide.

An expert marksman, he was able to drop a running animal with a clean shot to the heart at more than fifty paces, and he could ride and shoot from the saddle as well as any Dutchman.

The African tribesmen and their way of life fascinated him. Studying their hunting and tracking skills, their intimate knowledge of the land and the teeming wildlife they shared it with, he spent weeks in the bush hunting with his coterie of native followers.

As time went by, he was able to converse fluently in more than one native language. The medical skills he had picked up during his time as a surgeon's assistant at Christ's Hospital in London stood him in good stead, and he could frequently be found discussing the properties of various herbs and *muthi* with the *izinyanga*, the healers and medicine men.

What could only be termed as his 'rite of passage' came quickly and out of the blue – as is the way with most things in Africa.

One minute he was skirting a river bank keeping a wary eye out for basking crocodiles, the next he found himself facing an extremely irate black buffalo charging out from among the reed beds. Incensed by the intrusion into its territory, it pawed the ground, its beetling brows and curled horns lowered to charge.

The red spark in the animal's eyes shrivelled Fynn to the soul. He didn't need to recall the camp-fire tales to know he was facing one of the most dangerous animals in Africa.

His knees turned to water and his fingers became thick, clumsy stumps, unable to function. He fumbled with the rifle, trying to cock it. During several heart-stopping moments, the world stood still. Body and mind paralysed, one clear thought drummed through his brain.

One shot, Fynn. It's all you're going get… one good body-shot, so Holy Mary, do it right!

Later, spattered with blood and with the whoops of his jubilant hunters ringing in his ears, he stared down at the massive horns and muscled body of the dead buffalo. His eyes travelled to the carmine froth around the animal's mouth and nostrils then to the jagged hole where the ball had gone through its throat, severing a main artery.

Thank God I was able to stand my ground, didn't turn tail and run, or worse still, piss myself, he thought wryly. Not that I'd have been able to go very far, since my bloody legs seem to have stopped working!

Not long afterwards, he was to pass through another rite of passage, this time of a very different kind. On a moonless night, against a background of low growling thunder and forked lightning flickering on the horizon, he lost his virginity to an unseen, nameless African girl who came on silent feet to where he lay rolled in his blanket on the outer rim of the firelight.

Waking out of his sleep to find her slipping in beside him, he was never able to decide who had instigated what and with whom. It was over quickly; a tumble of oiled naked skin, slippery body fluids and hot flesh, his seed spilling out onto the hard ground.

A moment later, she was gone, disappearing as silently as she'd come, a shadow in the night, her parting gift a sharp bite to his ear lobe. All that was left to remind him of the experience were the faint traces of oil from her body, the salty taste of sex, and the blood trickling from his punctured ear.

At night, sitting round the fire, gun close at hand, watching the sparks fly up into the darkness like golden bees, Fynn would smoke his pipe and listen to the murmur of African voices around him and thank whatever Fates involved themselves in the affairs of men that he was where he wanted to be, under the brilliant stars on the limitless African plains.

A year or so later, a day of terror arrived for the tiny settlement of Grahamstown. Ten thousand half-naked Xhosa swarmed across the river and besieged the town. The attack sent shock-waves through the territory, and British troops had to be deployed to bring it to an end.

Fynn decided that it might be a good time to retrace his steps. On his return to Cape Town, one of the first people he called on was Harry Nourse, a young man with whom he'd struck up a friendship on the frontier. The Nourse family were merchants and ran a trading company that also had shipping interests.

As luck would have it, they were about to embark on a two-vessel expedition to Portuguese East Africa to seek out new trading opportunities. One of Harry's cousins had recently been appointed supercargo on one of the vessels. There was, however, a similar vacancy on the sloop *Jane.*

With ill-concealed relief, Fynn hastily signed up and went aboard. It seemed that fate was casting him with uncanny precision, back in the direction from which he'd just come, only much further north this time.

The alleyways and back streets of London Town would not reclaim him yet. With any luck they never would.

Three days after his curative experiences in the fever pit, Fynn regained consciousness, weak and shaky but still alive. Afraid to move his head in case it fell off his shoulders, he squinted gingerly at the patch of light beyond the low doorway.

From nearby came the steady, rhythmic thump of corn being pounded, a woman's groan of effort and a cockerel crowing its head off. Out of the corner of his eye he caught a slight movement in the deeper recesses of the hut.

Cautiously swivelling his head round, he became aware of a row of faces watching him intently from the shadows. The man, he guessed, was the *inyanga,* a tribal medicine man. The flamboyant arrangement of animal skins, necklaces of teeth and bones, quills and birds' feathers adorning his body marked him out as a man of learning and skill.

Crouching behind him in silent deference were four women. So he'd been right all along about the hands on his body and the musky woman smell.

Sudden understanding rushed in on him. Of course! The pit they'd lowered him into had been a *fever* pit, not the gateway to Hell! Their intention had been to sweat the sickness and infection out of him, to break the fever before it broke him.

Fynn knuckled the sleep from his eyes and stared back at them. Two of the women had an exotic look about them. Their thin aquiline noses, high slanting cheekbones, the skin that was several golden tones lighter and lips that were less fleshy than those of their companions, spoke of northern blood strains, probably Semitic.

He stared at them, intrigued. Sultry, dark-skinned Africa with more than a touch of Queen Cleopatra thrown in, aristocratic almost; their hair set in corn-crake rows of intricate patterns close to their heads, their skin oiled and supple.

His hazel eyes dropped below the faces and ranged over four pairs of naked breasts. The youngest of the women, a girl with hair teased out in stiff spirals around her head, put her hand over her mouth and giggled. Above the hand, her dark eyes were anything but shy.

The sound of a sharp slap followed, as the medicine man's hand came in contact with her bare arm in a stinging reprimand.

Immediate contrition followed, all of it Fynn's. Babbling in fragments of English and the native languages he had picked up along the frontiers of the Fish and Keiskama Rivers of Cape Colony, he thanked them profusely and sincerely, first for saving his life, and then in apology for letting his eyes wander.

The medicine man showed his tacit understanding of the sentiments by momentarily displaying his brown, stained teeth in an upward curl of the lip and a darting nod of his feathered head. Indicating a tall earthenware pitcher by the doorway, he motioned for it to be brought to Fynn.

While one of the women supported his head, another held it to his lips and bade him drink. The water ran in sweet rills down his parched throat, spilling out of the corners of his mouth and trickling into the folds of his neck.

After he had slaked his thirst, his head was lowered gently back on to the woven sleeping mat, and in no time at all he had dozed off again.

When next he opened his eyes, it was to find another face swimming into view. A white one, this time, with pasty skin the hue of curdled cream and a beard streaked with grey. A pair of slate blue eyes peered anxiously down at him.

Fynn, struggling to keep his eyes in focus, squinted up at the man kneeling beside him. Ragged clothes, pepper and salt hair dragged back into a tarry pigtail, a gold ring in one ear. He stared at the tattooed red and blue dragon twitching on the man's weather-beaten arm, his mind ticking over slowly, like a rundown clock.

In God's name, who was he? His heart leapt painfully as hard reality came flooding back.

Oh, yes, it wasTompkins, one of the seamen with whom he'd set out along the Maphuta River on foot, after the captain of the *Charlotte* had refused to go any further because of the dangerous sandbanks. The sudden image of a bearded, red face glaring angrily at him rushed in on him.

Bloody hopeless to think of going any further, man. Get grounded here, an' it'll be a bloody long walk back to the Cape, I can tell ye!

Fynn groaned. Now he remembered. Apart from himself, Tompkins was the only one who'd survived their ill-fated sortie up-river. The two others were dead, as was one of the native trackers.

In the end, neither he nor Tompkins had the strength or will left to scrape a hole in the ground and bury them, so they'd had no choice but to abandon the crumpled bodies of their shipmates. Shortly afterwards, they themselves succumbed to the virulent fever.

Fynn shuddered and passed a trembling hand over his face. Tompkins gripped his shoulder in clumsy sympathy. 'Gawd, it's good to see your peepers open, mate,' he said, relief in his voice. 'Thought you'd gone an' left me on me lonesome here.'

Fynn shook his head. After wiping away the tears of helplessness and regret with the back of his hand, he looked earnestly into Tompkins' face.

The whites of the seaman's eyes were yellow and bloodshot, still with a haunted look in their depths. The ragged canvas trews and blue tattered shirt hung on him, the flesh stripped away from his rangy frame by the ravages of fever.

Shooting a fearful glance in the direction of the squatting medicine man and his acolytes, the seaman hissed: 'No bad joss on these buggers, mate. Saved our bacon they did, but no way I'd want to overstay me welcome, if yer see what I mean.'

Fynn nodded weakly, his strength and concentration ebbing away. Vaguely he heard Tompkins' voice. It seemed to be coming from a long way away.

'First light tomorrow,' it said, 'I'll make me way back to the brig. These fella-me-lads have guides laid on for me. But I'll be back, mate, no fear. Just gotta let the cap'n know we're still in the land o' the living, like, else he'll up anchor an' leave without us.' The pressure of a hand on his shoulder and then the world faded away.

The next time Fynn opened his eyes, he was alone. Tompkins was no longer there, nor was the medicine man and his helpers. Apart from the earthenware pitchers and a pair of rolled-up sleeping mats, the hut was empty.

It was late afternoon. The air was hot and somnolent. Women's voices murmured in peaceful gossip from a hut across the way and even the noisy bands of children were quiet.

Fynn eased himself on to his elbow then sat up. From a purely clinical point of view, it was pretty obvious that his recent experiences had stripped most of the flesh from his body. His breeches and shirt hung loosely on his stocky frame, the stout cloth tattered and shredded. Heat and damp played the devil with clothing, rotted the very fibres as quick as Jack, the tailor's seams falling apart in no time.

But they were all he had. His pack had rolled away somewhere on the last few frantic miles when he'd spent more time crawling on his hands and knees than walking upright. His lips twitched in a smile. So, Henry, my lad, it'll be a light load on the way back to the *Charlotte*, then . . .

Noticing his hands, the smile faded. They looked like ancient claws; the nails broken and rimmed with dirt, the skin yellow and waxy, stretched tightly over bone and sinew. Wryly, he also noted the tremors running through them. *Not much use with the scalpel, then.* Ironic, really, just how little help any of his so-called medical experience had been when the fever struck him down without warning.

'Thank God for the medicine man and the healers who saved my life,' he muttered. 'If I've learned nothing else during my time in Africa, it's that this continent's not for the faint-hearted. Only the strong, the bloody-minded or the totally mad have a hope of surviving it. For me to turn and run from anything it can throw at me is not an option. Not now, not ever.'

A grin spread across his gaunt face. ' I'll be damned if London town will ever see me again.'

By the time he managed to totter unsteadily from the hut, the first evening stars were beginning to twinkle in the rapidly darkening sky. The crackle and spit of flames and smell of wood smoke announced that preparations for the evening meal were underway.

A faint smell of rotting vegetation and a waft of cool, watery air drifted in. River's not far away, he surmised.

For the last couple of nights, Fynn had been well enough to join the men around the fire after supper. On both occasions, the village *inyanga* was a salutary presence on the fringe of the tribesmen crowding around to peer at the strange *umlungu* who had come among them.

That night was no exception. A little later on, it was to the man who had saved his life that Fynn directed his faltering soliloquy. The small touch of human courtesy was all he had to give him in return.

Using a mixture of native tongues, he began to relate how he had come to be in their midst. Every time he looked up it was to meet the *inyanga's* dark, unfathomable eyes watching him across the leaping flames. In them, Fynn found a deep intelligence which intrigued him.

Sitting cross-legged on a tattered zebra-skin karosse, the man's ebony face was impassive in the firelight, gleaming with the sheen of perspiration, the feathers of his head dress stirring gently in the warm air.

'How did I come to be here?' Fynn spread his hands and shrugged his shoulders in the universal gesture of uncertainty. Looking round the circle of curious brown faces, he directed a crooked smile at them. 'You may well ask, my friends!'

Picking up a stick, he cleared a space on the dusty ground with the palm of his hand. On it, he scrawled an X to represent the village, a waving line for the River Maputha, gesticulating in the general direction of the unseen river.

'Here, my friends, is where we are now.'

A murmur of interest rose around the fire. Heads jostled to get a better look at what the white man was drawing in the dust. He broke off to scrawl a long, rough shape of the African coastline, another X to denote the Cape

Pointing to it, he said, 'And here's where I started off. In between then and now, there's a damn great amount of water, and a hellish long story to tell you.'

The whole wild escapade into the swamps had begun with Fynn's visit to the office of Luis da Silva Pereira, the Governor of Delagoa, for outsiders required his permission to go up-river, or deeper into Portuguese territory.

In spite of the high risk of fever, Fynn intended to travel among the villages and make contact with their headmen regarding future trade. With his knack for languages and his easy ways with native people, he would show Nourse and Company that he could be a great asset in setting up contacts on their behalf, if not his own.

As soon as he stepped into the Governor's office, however, all thoughts of why he had come flew from his mind. The magnificent elephant tusks stacked against one wall dominated the room – and literally took his breath away.

Even though Fynn stood at almost six feet, he felt dwarfed by their size. Graceful, curved and thicker than a man's thigh at their widest point, the tusks symbolised the splendour of the great herds that roamed the plains and bushland of Africa.

Reluctantly he tore his eyes away, conscious of the trembling in his knees. Almost stammering, Fynn dared to ask His Excellency about where they'd come from.

A disdainful shrug of the shoulders dismissed his queries. Wisely, Fynn did not pursue the subject, but bolted from the office as if he was on fire, questions burning a hole in his brain.

Where had the ivory come from? And who were the links in the chain between their source and the Governor at Delagoa Bay?

'Delagoa Bay,' said Fynn, looking round at the faces gazing at him across the flames, 'now there's a place.' Glancing quizzically across at the man wearing the feathered head-dress, he asked, 'Don't suppose you've ever been there, have you?'

The *inyanga* shook his head. Fynn stared at him for a moment, nonplussed by the man's response. Bloody amazing, he thought, I must be doing something right. Either that or the man's a damn fine linguist. Understands every word I'm sayin'.

'Their fort's a disaster,' he went on. 'A few cannon shells would bring the whole lot down. And, talking of cannon, the eight or ten pieces they had on show were solid with rust. The crew joked about it – saying they'd rather be outside the damn place rather than inside it, if it got attacked. More danger of being hit on the head with a lump of masonry than blown apart by a cannonball!'

A smile flickered across the *inyanga's* face. Fynn looked at him again, hard. Surely, he couldn't have understood what I was saying – not all of it, anyway? Glancing round the circle of faces, he noted the interest they were showing in his rambling discourse. Clearly, they seemed to be enjoying it.

'It was then I saw slaves for the first time,' he said, watching closely for any signs of reaction among them. 'Poor devils in manacles and leg-irons, chained to the walls.'

Idly, Fynn wondered if the tribe in whose bosom he was currently ensconced were also involved in the selling of strangers or those taken in battle. Most likely, he thought, so it's just as well there ain't a market for stray, down-at-heel white men!

After bolting from the Governor's office, Fynn had set about trying to find the likely source of such fine pieces of ivory. When he learned of the strict regulations governing the acquisition of ivory and gold throughout the Portuguese territories, his heart sank.

'No matter,' Fynn said to the circle of attentive tribesmen. 'For a bottle or two of grog, I wheedled some more information out of a young officer. Mind you, what I did hear wasn't exactly encouraging.

'The ivory...' Fynn had pressed him. *'Where does the ivory come from? How can I make contact with the traders?'*

Waving vaguely towards the south, the Portuguese lieutenant had crossed himself, mumbling that he hoped he would never be called on to fight the notorious warrior tribe whose lands lay there. Though few had ever seen them in the flesh, apparently the ferocious reputation of the amaZulu was legend.

Before the young lieutenant lapsed into a drunken sleep, there was one more thing Fynn managed to extract from him. Apparently, the superb tusks came from the personal hunting grounds of the warrior king himself.

Aha, he thought. So the tusks must come to Delagoa through a series of intermediaries, probably both native and Portuguese. If I could find my own way south, of course, I might be able to make contact . . .

A day or two later, he jumped aboard the brig *Charlotte* as it was leaving on an expedition up-river. Five days and forty miles later, the captain refused to go any further for fear of the vessel becoming trapped on the deeply silted river course.

Fuming with impatience, Fynn took on some native guides, acquired a dug-out canoe, and with three of the sailors, Tompkins, Will Jones and a man called Peterkin, set out south in what he hoped was the general direction of amaZulu territory.

'I'll wait four or five days, an' no longer,' Captain Barnham had snarled at Fynn's departing back. 'That's all I'll give 'ee. Not back by then, up comes the anchor and I haul out, leavin' your sorry arses to rot in this godforsaken hell-hole.'

After paddling up-river for some miles, Fynn struck off into one of the tributaries, hoping it would lead them south. As the canoe swept silently through dark, mangrove swamps wreathed in trailing mosses, creepers and lianas, the air was so thick with insects that he had to take off his under-drawers and wrap them round his head to protect himself.

In his burning desire to work his way south and get back with-in the allotted five days, Fynn ignored many of the lessons he'd learned during his frontier experiences. Against the advice of the guides, he persuaded the others to leave the canoe and go ahead on foot. Using bush trails and taking his bearings from the sun, he led them all in a risky and merciless drive south.

At each new camp-fire, Fynn made no bones about his interest in the whereabouts of the amaZulu. What he failed to notice, however, was the patent fear the mere mention of the Zulus aroused among his hosts.

But it was only when he uttered the name of the warrior king himself that Fynn's single-minded absorption with the ivory came to an abrupt halt.

As the name 'Shaka of the Zulus' came rolling carelessly off his tongue, a loud crack of exploding twigs brought moans of fear from the huddled listeners. They glanced fearfully at the strange white man who had dared to speak the name of the dreaded Zulu king aloud.

Shaka, sibilant like a snake, a deadly viper...Lord of all wars since time began.

Next day, their guides chose the easiest way out. They simply melted away into the bush, leaving Fynn and his party high and dry. Now they had no way of travelling further.

In any case, there was no time left, the captain of the brig would only wait so long. Cursing voluminously in every dialect he could think of, Fynn had no choice but to try to re-trace his steps through the maze of jungle paths, and at top speed.

It was then the fever struck. Jones succumbed to it very quickly, then Peterkin. Both were dead within a day. By this time, Tompkins and he were so ill they had no choice but to leave the bodies of their shipmates where they lay.

Crawling and stumbling, sweating and rambling, round and round in a circle, hopelessly confused, they tried unsuccessfully to find the way back to the brig, while the whining mosquitoes hovered around them in clouds.

'And that, my friends, is all Fynn has to tell you,' he said softly, looking round the dark faces burnished by the leaping flames.

Smiling, he stood up and bowed across the fire to where the *inyanga* sat cross-legged in the firelight. Smoke from his long, slender pipe wreathed up around his head, the quills, feathers and necklaces of animal bones exotic and ageless in the smoky night.

Henry Fynn's hazel eyes crinkled up in a smile of deep gratitude.

'And there, by the grace of God, were you, my friend...you, with your bloody great hole in the ground and your covey of witches. God bless you, *baba*.'

During the return voyage to the Cape, Fynn thought of nothing but the magnificent tusks. What each might weigh he had no idea, but at a conservative guess, perhaps a hundred and forty, two hundred pounds, or even more.

As he sat cleaning his gun on the open deck, Fynn's spirits began to rise. After the initial disappointment of discovering the stringency of Portuguese regulations, he had begun to realise that far from being bad news, several aspects of it might conceivably prove to be a godsend. Whistling an off-beat tune, he sifted for ways around the unpalatable parts.

The amaZulu lived a few hundred miles south of the Portuguese. A trader with enough nerve to reach Zulu territory would be well beyond the rigid rules of the Portuguese.

His bearded reflection grinned ruefully back at him from the polished barrel of the gun. Wasn't that what he had just tried to do? And look where it had got him! If it hadn't been for the fever-breaking properties of a steaming hole in the ground and the expertise of a native medicine man, he'd be a pile of rotting bones back where he'd fallen –

He muttered a prayer below his breath and crossed himself. The luck of the Irish had surely been with him that day. A moment later, his cocky optimism returned. To hell with the suspicious Portuguese bastards! He, Henry Francis Fynn, also known as *Mbuyasi, the finch*, would find his own way to the ivory.

With any luck, the swarthy Europeans would find to their cost that their supplies of ivory had dwindled away to a trickle as it was diverted elsewhere.

The night before the *Charlotte* was due to dock at Algoa, Fynn stood at the rail looking out over the darkened Indian Ocean. Somewhere on the forbidding coastline lay the kingdom of the amaZulu, and the man who held the key to what he desired. The ivory was what he had been searching for; a superb trading opportunity.

Cautiously, he examined his motives. Was it only for the money the tusks interested him? Or was it for the challenge, the colossal risks he'd be taking on trying to enter the territory of the most deadly tribe of warriors in southern Africa?

The thought of that great swathe of land lying out there waiting to be explored made the back of his neck tingle. I suppose some would call me a reckless adventurer, he told himself – or even a bloody fool!

Anyway, even if I did get my hands on a fortune, what would I do with it – go back to London and live the high life? The thought of returning to the great sprawl of a city – any city, if it came to that, jumped below his skin like a burrowing beetle.

Even a modicum of prosperity would mean he could live out the rest of his life without fear of being forced to go back with his tail between his legs. The knowledge that Africa had spat him out like an unwelcome pip stuck in its throat would haunt him to his last breath.

His grip tightened on the teak rail. As far as he was concerned, only one thing remained. And that was to find a way to the lands of the amaZulu, even though the vast kingdom belonged to a man whose name created rampant terror in everyone who heard it.

Shaka of the amaZulu…

Fynn drew in a deep breath. 'King Shaka,' he said to the black night sky and the singing stars above his head. 'You, my friend, are the one I must seek out. Then all else will follow, I'm sure of it.'

Langani's eyes snapped open. His heart thumped against his ribs and his mouth was as dry as the inside of an empty gourd.

Drained of energy, he slumped sideways, panting for breath and groped for the earthenware pot of water by the doorway. Seizing it with trembling hands, he gulped down a few mouthfuls of tepid water then tipped the rest of it over his head, gasping as it ran down his face and neck.

Conflicting emotions surged through him. Hearing the name of Shaka spouting from the stranger's mouth as if it were commonplace had taken him aback and completely unnerved him.

He had observed Jakot Msimbithi during various stages in his life; first as a young boy, then a youth, and finally as a grown man, a rebel, a prisoner, swimming for his life in a desperate bid to escape the white men's justice. All of it had taken place in the land that lay to the south, and all of it had been unrelated to the land of his birth, the land of the Zulu, Shaka's land.

But now, this bearded man, this *abelungu*, had somehow discovered not only the existence of the Nkosi, but also the riches that lay in Zululand.

His arrogance had stung Langani to the core. Even though the young man, Fynn, had heard of the great power and fighting skills of Shaka's *impis*, he still imagined he could breach the land of the Zulus with impunity and hunt the great *ndlovu* for the riches they would bring him.

Did the misguided upstart not understand that only Shaka of the Zulus was allowed to hunt the great beasts?

His anger cooled quickly. The man known as Fynn was, after all, only one man – but who knew if there were others out there with the same thought in mind?

Langani did not believe in coincidence. His instincts told him it had not been by chance the waters in the rock pool had begun to swirl and move of their own accord. The powers that lay beneath the earth often found their own ways of communicating with the living.

He drew in his breath sharply. And it had not been by accident that he had been on hand to realise the significance of the pulsing lights. And then there was the orb of light dancing its way along the dappled roof of the overhanging rock. What did it mean – and why was it separate from the others?

There might be other men out there, apart from Jakot and the bearded young *abelungu*, who had an overwhelming interest in the land of the Zulus. The idea that strangers might bring harm to his native land, and to Shaka of the Zulus, his comrade of the storm, filled him with dread, and not a little anger.

From now on, he must be vigilant and watch for the signs and portents which would reveal more of who they were, and what they intended to do.

Twenty-one

As the small fifty-ton supply ship *Julia* sped in close to the shore, the heavy seas tossed the small vessel about like a child's paper boat.

Braced against the rise and fall of the deck, Lieutenant Francis Farewell raised the glass to scan the shore for the third time in as many minutes. He swore softly below his breath. The glass only confirmed what the compass and sextant had already indicated.

'Damn and blast,' he muttered. Only unbroken coastline running as far north as the eye could see – no high, wooded bluff as they had been led to believe, nothing but dense bush and long beaches with glittering curves of surf pounding the shore.

It wasn't that he didn't trust Captain Garrett's judgment. When the experienced master mariner said it was most likely they'd swept past the headland in the night, Farewell knew he was probably right. It was just that old habits died hard.

The rigid discipline and training of His Majesty's Royal Navy stayed embedded until death parted body from soul – so it was to be expected that a war-decorated hero like Francis Farewell would believe implicitly in his own judgment, and no one else's.

At fourteen, Farewell had joined his first ship, the frigate HMS *Amphion*. Serving as midshipman under the audacious Captain William Hoste, a protégé of Admiral Nelson, his teenage years had been spent on active service during the Napoleanic wars.

At eighteen, he had been wounded at the battle of Lissa then promoted to Lieutenant on the thirty-eight gun warship HMS *Bacchante*. By the time he was twenty-one, he had been in sole charge of an island in the Adriatic and subsequently mentioned in the Naval Chronicle for gallant conduct.

In 1815, the battle of Waterloo brought the long, drawn-out war against Bonaparte to an end. By the time he was twenty-four, Francis Farewell, like hundreds of others, was left with no choice but to take leave from the Royal Navy on half-pay.

Now in his early thirties, he still carried himself with the flair and innate sense of command that had served him well during his naval days. His tall, spare figure had retained all the elegance of the old Napoleonic era.

His critics muttered behind his back that even when preparing to board an enemy ship, Francis George Farewell looked as if he were about to go to a ball. If his fair hair, blue eyes and refined good looks did not exactly aid his cause in the popularity stakes, then neither did the gold-rimmed monocle he sported in his right eye.

Those who knew him better silently acknowledged that appearances could be deceptive. There was little of the fop about Francis Farewell. The monocle was no mere affectation. It was to compensate for the weakness of an eye damaged by a splinter thrown up off the deck of the warship *Bacchante* while under heavy enemy fire.

Farewell was fully aware of public opinion, but cared not a jot for it. He went his own way, and on occasion played to the gallery for his own secret amusement.

He sighed in exasperation and handed the glass back to Joe Powell, the bo'sun. Dour, and not given to small talk, Powell was an experienced seaman from the old days on the *Amphion* and the *Bacchante* and had been mentioned in dispatches several times for his daring gunboat actions.

Their paths had crossed again last year on the Cape to Rio de Janeiro, St. Helena run. When Farewell had briefly outlined his plan to find a suitable harbour on the Natal coast to establish a daring commercial enterprise he had in mind, Joe Powell had just nodded his head, but not before Farewell had detected the flare of excitement in the bosun's keen blue eyes.

After the banal, lacklustre years of peace, a chance of action and adventure proved a heady, revitalising brew to men who had drunk so deeply of danger in time of war. To pit one's skills against the elements, the determination to win through at any cost, face any danger – well, the old familiar surge of excitement had risen up in him again, as keen as ever.

Farewell glanced sideways at Powell's impassive profile. It looked as if it had been carved from mahogany, seasoned by countless encounters with the elements, and just as durable.

If the man ever got really excited or panicked, he mused, it would be best to raise anchor and run like hell, because the Devil himself would only be an inch or so behind.

'Damn, damn the storm, Powell,' he said aloud, frowning. 'It looks as if we missed the place during the night – if the bloody headland was ever there in the first place, that is! Scallion might have got it wrong, you know.'

The bo'sun's profile didn't alter, either to agree or disagree. The blue and red snake tattooed on his weather-beaten forearm, the only sign of frivolity about his person, twitched slightly in response. The only visible change, if one knew him as well as

Farewell did, was the imperceptible lift of a grizzled eyebrow and the slight whitening of the knuckles on the ship's rail.

Scallion, the merchant trader who'd parted Farewell from a few bottles of best Cape brandy in exchange for an old map had not exactly found favour with the taciturn seaman.

Farewell refrained from further comment. It had been well over a century since British and Dutch slavers had last used the bay, apparently. It was just possible the bearings he'd been given were wrong.

He turned away from the rail to address the first mate. 'No sign of the headland yet, Thompson. Captain Garrett was right. Best we carry on, keep a weather eye open. Sea's running too high to get in any closer.'

Thompson, a bull of a man with a red face and hair bleached white by the sun, cupped a hand over an ear to catch his words before nodding in surly agreement.

Powell scanned the horizon, hoping to catch sight of the brig *Salisbury,* the *Julia's* sister ship. The larger and less manoeuvrable vessel had been left with no choice but to veer sharply out to sea to avoid being caught in the treacherous currents or driven on to the rocks by the gale-force winds.

The look-out perched in the platform above the swaying deck called down to show he was fully alert. The crew were bone-tired, trying to steal snatches of fitful sleep as and when they could.

Sea birds soared around the topsails of the *Julia* and were tossed around like streamers of tattered rags. A pair of curved dolphin fins broke the surface and raced alongside the scudding ship, forging ahead then criss-crossing in front of the bows in games of play. Some of the crew came to the starboard rail to watch them.

Farewell smiled. The antics of the dolphins lifted his spirits, eased his frustration. They also reminded him that he was in the place where he was happiest, a stout deck beneath his feet and the thrill of action before him.

For the past two months he and his partner, Lieutenant James King, had assaulted the deadly Wild Coast, launching one daring sortie after another. Stretching their navigational skills to the limit, they tried time and again to find an inlet, a cove, or an open river mouth so they could scramble ashore and begin to explore the hinterland.

So far, all the mouths of the rivers had been blind; either silted up by sandbanks or protected by dangerous reefs. Their hopes of finding the two-hundred-year-old harbour were fading fast.

Powell handed the glass back to Farewell and shook his head. The horizon was empty, the curved bowl of the sky hazing away into infinity. The *Salisbury* might be just out of sight below the curve of the horizon, or equally, miles out at sea, blown off course by the storm that had raged for the past few days.

Lieutenant King had stay aboard the larger vessel while the more agile *Julia* took the risk of running in closer to land in an effort to spot the headland. Given the weather difficulties, King, as the only officer capable of handling the ship in a storm had no choice but to remain on the *Salisbury* for the safety of both crew and vessel.

Farewell grinned at the thought of the kindly but mercurial Lieutenant pacing the quarter-deck raging against fate – as if having sole command of a large ship in a storm could be looked on as playing a secondary role.

As if reading his thoughts, Joe Powell turned a weather-beaten face in his direction. 'Mayhap the Cap'n will have had his heels cooled a mite by last night's blow,' he said, with a chuckle.

The bo'sun was fond of the spirited man from Nova Scotia. James King had also served on the *Bacchante* while in American waters during the latter part of the Napoleonic wars; another shared common bond.

Farewell put his head back and laughed. 'I doubt that, Powell. What he really needs is to loosen his stays and have a good tot or two of grog!'

The comment brought another grin from the bo'sun. King was, by upbringing, a Presbyterian and a strict teetotaller. His bluenose of a mother back in Nova Scotia had instilled her own strict views in him since the day he'd drawn his first breath. It was also suspected that she kept tight control of the purse strings even though her son had a full partnership in the family business.

'Nova Scotia wasn't named New Scotland for nothing,' James King himself had remarked more than once, with a wry grin. 'Old habits die hard. My mother is just as canny as the rest of the breed.'

Since he had also been at somewhat of a loose end since the war ended, he had jumped at the chance of joining fortunes with Farewell. Eventually, he had persuaded his mother to help him finance his share of the proposed costs of the joint enterprise.

Lieutenant Farewell gazed through the glass with hungry eyes. Shimmering in the heat haze, the land lay balanced in perfect symmetry between sky and sea.

'There it is,' he said, exasperation in his voice.' So near and yet so damned far, might as well be on the moon, Mr Powell.'

'All the better then, sir, when we finally find a way in, the prize'll taste sweeter then, always does.' Powell's brogue was unmistakably that of Devon, as solid and rich as the cream for which it was famous.

As if in response, the school of dolphins leaped clean out of the water delighting in the contest between themselves and the scudding ship.

Farewell put down the glass and glanced sideways at him, a glint of humour in his eyes. 'I have your word on that, Powell, for certain?' He added, laughing, 'I'll remind you of that next time we're hanging arse over elbow in the longboat, bound for the bottom of the ocean!'

Powell nodded, his shrewd grey eyes twinkling in a rare show of humour.

'Aye, cap'n, but I reckon it'll take more than a middlin' piece of wind and water to sink three good men and true from the old *Bacchante.*'

As Farewell watched the coastline slip by, it seemed to glow in the morning light like the emerald to which he'd compared it the first time he had set eyes on it.

It was over a year and a half since he'd been here last. Homeward bound from Goa and en route to England, he had been commanding his own frigate, the *Fame*.

During the frequent voyages Farewell made between India and the Cape, he had never sailed that close to the Wild Coast before. Its unpredictable storms had resulted in many shipwrecks over the years and seafarers wisely gave it a wide berth, preferring to view the treacherous coast as a mere brown smudge on the skyline, if at all.

However, due to unaccustomed off-shore winds and calm seas, he had taken the unprecedented risk of allowing the *Fame* to venture closer.

Tantalising glimpses of misty rolling hills and palm-fringed bays had attracted the attention of both passengers and crew alike and the starboard rail had been crowded with people admiring the landscape slipping by.

Small black and white birds could be seen trotting along the water's edge. The sight of a herd of elephants emerging from the bush had brought gasps of amazement from those watching, especially the ladies.

It had also been close enough for Farewell to focus the glass on a thin curl of smoke rising lazily in the distance. To his keen eye, it seemed to hang in the air like a tantalising question mark, drawing him in to discover its secrets.

With such an unexpected clear view of the mysterious coastline, the vague plan that had been formulating in his mind during the voyage south from Delagoa, began to turn into something very different – an idea that would turn into near-obsession and alter the course of his life for ever.

When he'd caught a glimpse of the magnificent tusks stored in a filthy cell below the Portuguese fort at Delagoa Bay, Farewell had been impressed by their sheer quality and size. He had also been greatly intrigued by the ease with which the Portuguese had seemingly acquired them.

After some discreet questioning and larding of palms, Farewell had managed to winkle out some of the facts. It hadn't been easy, considering how jealously the Portuguese protected their lucrative trade in ivory and slaves from outsiders, especially the British.

'Frankly,' as he said to James King later, 'I don't see why the Portuguese should assume they should be the sole beneficiaries of trading in such booty. Give me one good reason why they should continue to monopolise such a lucrative market?'

Apparently, so he found out, the Portuguese carried on the trade with a native tribe whose lands lay to the south of their territory. Supplies of ivory tended to be rather erratic, due to the fierce warfare intermittently raging throughout the south-east of the continent.

One of the root causes of the trouble, apart from drought, so it was rumoured, could be laid at the door of this same tribe. They were warlike and aggressive, superbly fit and able to run tirelessly, mile after mile, covering long distances with frightening ease. These ferocious people were known as the amaZulu. At their head stood a man, an awesome warrior king, his most terrible majesty, Shaka.

Secretly, the Portuguese feared that, if left uncurbed, his power and influence might eventually threaten Delagoa itself. The idea of a tribe of savages being able to disrupt their lucrative trade in gold, ivory, hides, precious hardwoods and slaves, was not something that appealed to them.

The only problem was that this tribe, or rather their King, had the dubious distinction of being the actual source of the fabulous ivory, a commodity they were reluctant to relinquish.

Farewell's legendary approach to the tackling of serious difficulties took a dent on hearing this. But, being a pragmatist, and also an astute businessman, he had quickly brushed these details aside. Every man had a price. And he was sure this native ruler was no exception. The trick was to find out what it was – and then offer it to him.

As Farewell continued to stare at the mysterious coastline, it was as if a lightning bolt had snaked across the divide between him and the silent magic of the mysterious land beyond the starboard rail.

Here was a prize for the taking. Not only was this a land of forests, mountain peaks and rolling hills a paradise of rich timber and good farming land, it was also a source of that other, more dangerous commodity. Superb quality ivory…

He would make contact with the tribal king and convince him that Farewell and Company would be more beneficial to deal with than the Portuguese. There would be no need to maintain the time-consuming process of trading through a system of intermediaries, delayed by distance and acts of war.

What he had in mind would be mutually advantageous to both British and amaZulu alike. Farewell and Company would be able to supply all their needs by way of the harbour he would construct at some suitable point on the coast.

Twenty-two

Unable to sleep, Langani turned over on to his back and stared up into the darkness. All was quiet and still, only the scritch-scratch of lizards stalking the long-legged spiders and insects in the thatch.

The hut was hot and airless, the faint acrid smell of charred logs and smoky thatch adding to the odours of the herbs, roots and esoteric materials stored for use in his rituals. Langani rose off his sleeping mat and padded over to the doorway. One of the speckled hens clucked sleepily from the rafters before settling down again.

Outside, the air was cool and the sky clear with thin drifts of cloud passing across the face of a silvered half-moon. Beyond the edge of his territory stretched miles of darkened bush, a limitless expanse of pale night sky above it.

Alert to every sound, he listened carefully, half-expecting to detect something which might be preventing him from sleeping. The rumbling grunt of foraging animals, interspersed with intermittent squeals, drifted up from somewhere among the tangled scrub below. Warthogs, he thought, thinking of the tufts of wiry hair left snagged on bushes and thorns in the tunnels.

Apart from the odd snake or rock rabbit, nothing predatory had ever braved the bush-covered steep gradient to threaten his safety, or at least, had never emerged from the winding animal burrows to show itself.

Langani knew he should wait until the sun rose, but his youthful impatience over-rode caution. As if by instinct, he made his way towards the sound of trickling water. Even lying awake, unable to sleep, it had remained a siren sound in the night, enticing him back to explore its mysteries.

The half-moon sailed out from behind the drifts of cloud and illuminated the world with its pale light. Langani moved forward cautiously.

A stray moonbeam glinted on the rock face and turned the rivulets of water to molten silver. When he bent down and looked into the pool, he saw that the water was dark and still. As his eyes grew accustomed to the light, however, he saw something that made his heart leap.

Before, there had been four or five steadily pulsing lights with smaller dots bobbing about in their wake. Now, there were only three. As if sensing his presence, one of them flickered and the glow grew fainter.

Yebo, the diviner whispered, I know who you are because I have already seen you. A fleeting image of the man with the pale hair and blue eyes came back to him.

You have the look of the wolf about you, Langani thought, but you are also a warrior, someone who has seen much during the sea battles of your people. Brave too, a leader of men.

He narrowed his eyes and stared hard at the faint pulsing light. It is because of you, others will search for a way into Zululand, for you are the leader, the one that will find the way here.

The diviner looked at the water for a long time, striving to look below the surface and probe its depths. Slowly, the moon slid behind the curve of the mountain and the pre-dawn darkness crept in to cloak the rocky pool and its mysteries.

Langani sank back on his heels. It is what I feared. There are others besides the young *abelungu*, Fynn, who have seen the riches of Zululand and covet them. But what of the man with the hair like night, streaked with silver, the one who showed kindness to the Xhosa, Jakot? Are you also part of this?

Leaning forward, he dipped his fingers into the water and trailed them gently around the edge of the pool. Gradually, the image of the man he had been searching for swirled to the surface.

Ah, he thought, probing beyond the stranger's outward appearance and demeanour, you are close to the sea hunter and share his ambitions, another warrior, wise to the ways of the sea, and also skilful.

He stared at the throbbing sparks of light for a few moments longer. Then his eyes travelled to the overhanging shelf of rock above his head. The small orb was resting there as before, its glowing heart pulsing peacefully.

Something about the clarity and purity of the light emanating from it struck a chord in the young diviner. Innocence, he thought, wondering why he hadn't realised it before. There's innocence here…

Langani started back in surprise. Could it be a child? Only the souls of the very young shine with such a clear light, he thought, shaking his head in wonder.

As if in response, the gently pulsing globe glowed more brightly for an instant, like a new star being born in the heavens, before subsiding once more.The diviner stared at it, suddenly at a loss for any coherent explanation. *A child! But what does a child have to do with any of this?*

He sat there for a few moments, lost in thought. A small breath of wind stirred the air, bringing with it the smell of earth and fresh growth. Even before the strident crowing of the black cockerel ruptured the silence, he knew that the night was over. As if on cue, the last of the darkness gave way to the approaching dawn and the twinkling stars began to fade in the lightening sky.

Langani sat there for a long time, watching the small orb at rest on the roof of the cave and saw it stir and tremble with the coming of the new day.

Then he rose to his feet and walked back through the early birdsong to begin his meditations.

Twenty-three

The man on the look-out platform near the *Julia's* topsails sang out: 'Ship ahead! Nor' nor' east to starboard!'

All hands rushed to the rail, shading their eyes against the noonday sun. It was bound to be the *Salisbury*, for it was unlikely another merchantman would be striking a course so close to the temperamental coastline without good reason.

A ragged cheer went up. The *Salisbury* it was, limping a little, minus some rigging and a sail or two torn and flapping, but apart from that, appearing none the worse after the storm.

'She's ridden it well,' Farewell commented, with a surge of affection for the sturdy vessel. Using the glass, he ran a professional eye over her, scanning the spread of the topsails and tangle of ropes and rigging, noting the damage caused by the bad weather.

The *Salisbury* had carried him far – from the Cape of Good Hope across the southern Atlantic, sailing with the trade winds to Rio de Janeiro before returning to Cape Town via St Helena.

It was also where his association with the former Royal Naval Lieutenant from Nova Scotia, James Saunders King, had really begun.

The sun began to slip down towards the distant mountains in an oily sheen of red and bronze. Up on the mastheads by the royals, the flags of the *Salisbury* fluttered in the off-shore breeze.

Lieutenant King, standing at the port rail, lifted his head and sniffed the wind. There it was; the faint, but unmistakable, spicy aroma of land. Three-quarters of a mile or so off the port bow, silhouetted against an expanse of rose-tinted evening sky, lay the land in question. He stared hard at it, his dark brows drawn together in a quizzical frown.

The last months had been devilish hard, both on officers and crew alike. The constant bombardment of the impenetrable coastline had taken its toll, both on their dwindling resources of food and water as well as their reserves of perseverance and stamina.

A faint movement caught King's eye. Turning his head, he caught sight of the interpreter Commander Owen had so generously handed back to them after the British Navy's failed survey.

The young Xhosa moved across the deck with innate grace, his wide, splayed feet making no sound on the stout oak deck. Sensing he was under scrutiny, he turned to offer James King a gleam of white, even teeth and a hand lifted in respectful salute.

King returned the gesture then resumed his contemplation of the silent land off the port bow. The Xhosa's brief appearance, however, had brought certain memories back into focus.

Two years earlier, while master of the *Helicon*, King had undertaken the transportation of two hundred or so felons from Grahamstown to Robben Island, the notorious penitentiary situated in the bay overlooked by the city of Cape Town. Although it was not the kind of commission King would have willingly sought, the coffers were running low, and funds were urgently needed to complete the survey of the south-east coast they'd undertaken on behalf of the Admiralty.

Reluctantly, he'd agreed. And that was when it had all started.

A day or two out from Algoa Bay, a terrible hullabaloo had broken out below decks. A seaman had come tearing along the deck.

'Cap'n, cap'n, best you come quick!' he yelled. 'All hell be let loose below. Kaffirs sayin' the Devil's got inta some poor bastard, intent on breakin' him loose an' murderin' the lot of 'em. Jest listen to 'em shriekin' – they think their number's up an' no mistake!'

The scenes that greeted King as the hold covers were hauled open were appalling. The stench rising from the depths was a mixture of abject terror and the human waste of two hundred manacled prisoners. Hysterical screaming filled the darkness. The whites of hundreds of pairs of eyes shone in the gloom as they scanned the patch of blue sky visible beyond the hatches, desperate for light, fresh air and a breath of freedom.

Accompanied by a burly Master at Arms and a few sailors, King clambered down into the hold. Frantically scrabbling over rows of chained men, literally feeling their way through the murky darkness, they finally stumbled on the thrashing, bucking figure said to be in the throes of demonic possession.

'Dear Christ! No wonder, they thought the Devil was at work here,' King muttered, trying not to retch. 'Poor bastards must've thought they'd been swallowed up by a monster when they were taken aboard and put in irons down here.' A bolt of shame hit him. 'And God forgive me, I'm the man who put them there.'

He looked down at the victim's contorted face and emaciated body. The prisoner was young, in his early twenties, he guessed. Teeth bared in a rictus of distress, his eyes were rolled back in his head with only the whites showing. As he thrashed from side to side, saliva and bloody froth from his bitten tongue splattered in an arc around him. Blood seeping from a gash on his scalp had trickled into his eyes reducing his face to a fearsome mask of gore.

King had seen this particular condition before, during his wartime service. 'No evil spirits here,' he shouted to the burly Master at Arms who'd come aboard with the prisoners at Algoa Bay. 'Epileptic seizure, a severe one, I fear. Here, hold his arms and legs while I try to straighten him out.'

James King prised the victim's jaws apart, and even though the tongue was already badly bitten, thrust his sheathed knife between the man's clenched teeth to prevent further damage. Desperately, he and the Master at Arms hung on to the thrashing body.

Gradually, the paroxysms began to die down and the dead-white eyes fluttered weakly and opened. After the man had recovered sufficiently, King stood up and pushed his sheathed knife back into his waistband.

'Strike his chains. And see to it he's brought up on deck, lively like. No rough stuff, mind. The poor devil's suffered enough.'

Wails of despair came from the men chained on either side of the prisoner. King said, gruffly. 'Aye, and bring those two as well. A spell of good sea air should set them right.'

Afterwards, King had allowed the Xhosa to stay on deck, free of shackles and leg irons, along with those who had been chained next to him. 'After all, where can they go except over the side?' he had remarked to his first officer. 'It's either the sharks or the currents, not much of a choice, I'd have thought.'

But that was precisely what the young Xhosa prisoner did. Nearing the end of the voyage, the vessel had sailed into Table Bay. And there, looming out of the fog, were the stark contours of Robben Island, a grim reminder of the *Helicon's* mission.

Jakot had stood frozen by the rail, watching the island come closer. Then, with only a moment's pause, he had swung himself over the rail and leapt into the sea. And he had not gone alone. One of the other prisoners who had been brought up from the hold had also jumped with him, holding hands as they went down.

The shout of 'Man overboard!' went up. The crew rushed to the rail. Long minutes passed with no sign of either of the prisoners. Then at last, shouting erupted along the deck. A bobbing head had been sighted in the churn of the ship's wake.

King, on being brought the news by the bo'sun, knew in his bones which of the prisoners it was likely to be. He shook his head, ruefully. 'What did I say about the Xhosa not having any choices? Seems I was wrong, dead wrong about that. '

Glancing at the forbidding sprawl of the island penitentiary, he muttered, 'Perhaps he's made the right one, though.' Joining his men at the rail, he focused the ship's glass on the rapidly receding black dot bobbing about on the swell.

As the *Helicon* responded to his commands and began to head for the main harbour at Cape Town, it was with some satisfaction he looked through the glass, and saw that the Xhosa not only seemed to be still afloat, but was actually striking out towards the shore, well away from the city.

Although by rights he should have lowered a longboat in pursuit of the Crown's missing prisoners, King had already decided to do no such thing

For one thing, the sympathies of a crew, any crew, irrespective of race, creed or colour, were invariably in favour of the underdog. In the case of daring underdogs like the young Xhosa, a man who refused to accept what the law of the land had in store for him, the tacit support would be double fold.

In his heart of hearts, the captain of the *Helicon* sided with his crew.

Having survived years of rotting in jail, been plucked from the hold of a ship during an epileptic seizure and then choosing a slender chance of survival rather than spend the rest of what would, in all likelihood, be a short, but brutal life on Robben Island, as far as James King was concerned, the man called Jakot had earned a chance of freedom.

The next day, while the pitiful wretches were being brought up from the hold and handed over to the authorities, the officer in charge of the detail had come up to him. 'The skellum you lost overboard, *meneer*? We picked him up along the shore. Hiding under an upturned boat he was, sleeping off his swim.'

He grinned crookedly. 'We gave him a few more lashes to add to the ones 'e has already on 'is good-for-nothing black hide. The other one gone over the side? Well, he wasn't so lucky – sharks or rip tides musta got 'im. No sign of 'im, no great loss.'

King felt an odd pang of regret. He'd got to know the young Xhosa reasonably well and had been impressed by his quick wit and skill with languages. He had also learned a great deal about his people's long-running battles with the Boer farmers.

Putting two and two together, the source of the vicious scars and weals on the Xhosa's back and wrists was all too clear. King silently cursed the knowledge and the tragic illustration of man's inhumanity to man.

But that was not the last he heard of the lone survivor, Jakot Msimbithi. A year or so later, King and Farewell happened to be in Cape Town at the same time as a British exploratory fleet. Invited aboard the flag ship to meet the fleet Commander, they learned that he was planning to make a full survey of the coastline between Algoa Bay and Portuguese territory on behalf of the Admiralty.

During the evening, Commander Owen had mentioned a need to take on interpreters, since the work of the survey would involve going ashore and making contact with local tribesmen

The young Xhosa incarcerated on Robben Island immediately sprang into King's mind. 'A bit of a daring character,' he'd intimated, 'but clever, resourceful – and damn good with languages. He speaks passable English, also the Dutch lingo.'

On the strength of James King's recommendation, Owen had negotiated with the Cape Governor for the release of Jakot Msimbithi.

After giving the matter some thought, and realising the benefits of accommodating the Admiralty, Sir Charles gave his consent. Not only did he offer the Xhosa a chance of employment, but providing he served His Majesty's Navy to the best of his abilities and conducted himself satisfactorily, he also hinted that there might be a pardon at the end of it.

Unable to believe his good fortune, Jakot readily agreed. Also released with him was Fire, one of the men brought up with him from the hold of the *Helicon*. Luckily, he had chosen not to jump overboard with him on that fateful day.

So that was how Jakot Msimbithi, runaway slave, cattle rustler, political spy, enemy of the Crown and ex-inmate of Robben Island came to be on the payroll of King George's Royal Navy.

A few months later, however, the British expedition came to grief. Bad weather and the deaths of over seventy sailors due to the virulent fevers raging along the coasts brought the mission to an untimely halt. Consequently, Commander Owen had no longer any need for interpreters and handed back the handsome, but wily young Xhosa to the captain of the *Salisbury*.

Who, of course, just happened to be Lieutenant King, the man who had saved his life, not once, but twice. It seemed that Jakot's 'great good fortune' was still holding.

The jolly boat belonging to the *Julia* swung out on its davits and was slowly lowered into the sea. After clambering down the side on a rope ladder and stepping into the boat, Farewell made his way forward and sat down midships. Powell took up his place at the stern, while a couple of seamen fitted the oars into the rowlocks.

The gentle splash of the oars provided a backdrop to the early evening calm. From somewhere below decks, the wheezing notes of a concertina, the thin piping of a tin whistle and a snatch of song drifted across the water.

As Farewell scrambled on to the deck of the *Salisbury*, he caught a whiff of fresh cologne. Looking up, he observed the captain of the vessel leaning over the rail, offering a hand to help him aboard.

King's deep blue eyes twinkled in good humour as his partner stepped aboard, unaided. Farewell shot him a quick glance. His partner's skin was darkly tanned against the crisp whiteness of a clean shirt, his mass of black hair with its distinctive broad streaks of silver still wet from his recent ablutions.

Farewell had little doubt that very soon the formal dark blue jacket would be discarded, slung carelessly over the back of a chair. It was one of the things that set them apart.

The colonial contingents of His Majesty's Royal Navy were not noted for being the same sticklers for dress rules and naval etiquette as those of the native-born English, he thought, stiffly. Unconsciously, he patted the collar of his jacket into place and made sure the black velvet ribbon of his monocle was safely attached to the lapel.

'What say you then, Frank?' queried the Canadian. Even in the dying light, Farewell could see his eyes were red-rimmed and bloodshot from the strain of the last few days. 'I expect you'll be in need of a dram or two after that little blow!' Clapping a hand casually on Farewell's shoulder, he led him below to the Master's cabin.

It was part of the good-natured banter that flowed between them, the customary topics about which men of their age and class usually conversed; ships, action, times and tides, and last but not least, the fair sex.

Mind you, the subject of women had undergone a radical change since Farewell's marriage the year before to the former Elizabeth Schmidt of Cape Town.

After a brief courtship of only two months, Francis Farewell had married the flaxen-haired young woman he had first seen silhouetted in the light of an oil lamp as she came down the stairs of her step-father's guest house in Cape Town.

As if in slow motion, he had watched this vision of loveliness move towards him, her blue eyes full of concern while he'd stood dripping water on the doorstep. His thoughts had been confused, to say the least.

Was it only a few hours since he'd stood at the rail of the *Fame* watching the lights of Cape Town dwindle into the darkness in the full belief that his next port of call would be Southampton and a spell of home leave?

Less than an hour later, the *Fame* had run aground on the rocks off Sea Point, due to a gross miscalculation on the part of the first officer. Farewell, ship's owner or not, found himself swimming for his life in the icy waters of the Atlantic.

As he stood shivering on the doorstep, watching the blonde young woman in a blue dress flit towards him in the lamplight, Farewell knew with a queer jolt of the heart, that during the space of only a few hours, the whole course of his life had changed irrevocably and forever. Africa, the quest for the ivory, and the young fair-haired woman approaching him were now his destiny.

Later, in the early hours of the morning, Farewell found himself sitting at the dining table of the former widow Schmidt. Dressed in borrowed clothes, and painfully aware of just how unkempt he must look to the ravishing Elizabeth, he stared across the table at her step-father.

About sixty years of age, rotund, red-faced and somewhat bad tempered, Johann Lodewyk Petersen presented himself as a formidable critic as he listened somewhat sceptically to Farewell's account of what had transpired during the voyage between Calcutta and the Cape.

Taking a perfunctory sip or two of brandy, Petersen deigned to nod his head as he listened to the bedraggled stranger's description of Delagoa Bay – until he came to the part where the rusty iron door of the Portuguese treasury had swung open to reveal the man-high ivory tusks stacked inside – then he suddenly began to show a great deal of interest.

By the time Farewell got round to casually mentioning the estimated figures of what each tusk might bring on the open market, the fine Dutch cigar had slipped from Petersen's fingers, scattering ash and burning tobacco on the widow Schmidt's damask supper cloth.

It lay there smouldering until Lieutenant Francis Farewell, so recently plucked from the ocean and with the smell of the sea still on him, politely rescued it.

Without a word, but acutely aware that he now had the upper hand, he handed the smouldering cigar back to the speechless merchant, before picking up from where he'd left off and setting out his plan for success.

Two months later, the prosperous, calculating and extremely quick-tempered Petersen became his father-in-law.

After catching up on their reports, Farewell and King went on deck to stretch their legs and get some air.

King had relaxed his strict rules concerning alcohol and had a brandy goblet with an inch or so of fiery 'Cape smoke' in his hand. They stood shoulder to shoulder at the rail, savouring the evening calm, the aroma of good Dutch cigars wreathing about their heads.

The eye of the sun slowly slipped down behind the distant hills. Rays of gold and scarlet flared into the sky in a last defiant act of surrender. The two men stood in companionable silence, watching the sun disappear, leaving only the afterglow behind.

King muttered appreciatively, discarded the butt of his cigar and yawned widely. He was about to turn away and head below when Farewell grabbed his arm.

'Look over there, James,' he said, peering into the distance. 'About halfway between the shore and the hills, what do you reckon that is?'

King rubbed his aching eyes and peered into the gathering dusk. Farewell shouted for Powell to bring the glass. Even though it was getting dark, he wanted to get a closer look at what had caught his eye.

A tiny thread of flames appeared to be running along the folds of the rolling hills in the background. Visible even with the naked eye, their vivid tongues of gold sucked at the contours of the high ground.

Farewell took the glass from Powell, put it to his good eye and began to scan the horizon. 'What in hell is it, James? Bush fires, or what?'

'Well, it could be. It's the end of the dry season; everything's like tinder.'

Taking the glass from Farewell, he steadied himself against the rail and focused it on the flickering lights. Tiny spurts of orange and red flame leaped into the foreground and he could almost hear the crackle of the flames and smell the smoke.

Farewell was reluctant to concede that he might be wrong. 'You might well be right. It probably is just natives, burning off the grass before the new season.'

King continued to stare. The capillaries of liquid gold, running in tiny threads high up in the hills, could clearly be seen. He was about to make a comment when he saw something that brought the telescope sharply back up to his eye.

'Look along to the left, Frank, lower down, about thirty degrees south. What do you make of that? At first I thought it was just another fire. Only it doesn't move or change. It looks like a group of small lights, spaced out – and static.'

Farewell stared at the clusters of light, pinpricks in the vast night. They formed a circle or as near one as dammit, a steady and unchanging ring of twinkling flames. Diamond pin-points of fire, sparks of light, making up a larger jewel -

'Good God, I think I know what it is! Of course, it all fits.'

Slowly, he brought the glass down and leaned against the rail, staring into the darkness. 'What you see out there, my friend, is, most probably, an army camping for the night.'

'An army?' repeated King, his eyes watering from strain. 'I take it you mean the Zulus?'

'Indeed I do. There's nobody else it could be. Shaka Zulu is *the* power, the *only* power for hundreds of miles in any direction, north, south, east or west of here.'

He gestured towards the miniature filaments of flames forking up the hillsides. 'My God, James, just think how near they are.'

As they watched, the tiny lines of fire began to peter out, while the sparkling diadem made up of individual points of fire continued to pulse in the looming darkness.

The men stood at the rail, unwilling to go below, their eyes fixed on the distant pinpoints of lights. King was stiff and weary, the effects of the last days heavy on him now, but there was just one thing he needed to know before going below for some well-earned rest.

'Francis,' he said, thoughtfully, 'just how great a force would you say these camp fires represent?'

Farewell went on looking through the glass. After a long moment, he said, 'There's no way to be sure, but I'd make a conservative estimate of a few thousand, at least.' Suddenly, there was chill in the night air. A keen little wind had inexplicably risen off the ocean.

Before the two men went below, they looked out to where the land lay curled in the dark like a silent, predatory beast, the expanse of twinkling campfires a huge and watchful eye in the gathering night.

Twenty-four

Langani was breathing heavily as he crawled up through the last few yards of scrub. Dragging the heavy baskets of supplies after him, he dug his heels in and scrambled up on to the rocky edge of his territory. Once he'd safely deposited the baskets on solid ground, he took a good look around.

Everything seemed much as he'd left it. The vegetable gardens were a riot of greenery; the vines of beans, pumpkin and water melon a virtual jungle of trailing tentacles. The tall spikes of growing corn and flourishing yams were testament to his good sense in building a series of water channels to run from the waterfall to the gardens.

A loud clucking made him look up. Racing towards him, squawking as they came, were his chickens, mostly of the red-feathered variety, but with an occasional white or speckled one thrown in.

The sound of Langani's laughter bounced off the rocky hillsides as they came clucking, fussing and pecking around his feet.

'It's good to be home,' he said aloud, 'even if only a handful of chickens are here to welcome me!' Picking up the heavy baskets, he walked towards the hut, scattering chickens as he went.

There was no sadness or regret in him for the life choices he had made, either in his profession or for where he'd chosen to live. With its wide panorama of vast skies and endless miles of bush, it was the kind of place in which most people would never contemplate setting up home. But then, Langani hardly fell into the category of 'most people.'

An *isangoma* of exceptional skills, with a high degree of intelligence and innate mysticism, by their very nature his gifts had tended to set him apart. As his powers of divination increased, so did his need for lengthy periods of solitude.

But, because he was also young and by no means monastic or lacking the need for human companionship, he frequently left his 'eyrie' and went out among the people, to see to their spiritual needs. After all, this was what his training as an *isangoma* demanded of him. Also there was his mother, Jubilele, and the rest of his family to visit.

This time, he had been away for over a month, ministering to the people living in small, remote villages perched in the foothills of the high lands to the west and north.

He had also attended another meeting of the cabal of diviners to which he belonged. Like the previous gathering, it had taken place in a secret location, a remote valley reputed to be where elephants went to die.

It was indeed true, for Langani had seen for himself the great mounds of whitened bones, skulls and curved tusks lying scattered in the grass.

Many lay entwined as if the dying beasts had come to seek out the bones of their loved ones and then lain down beside them to die, often with their trunks curled around the bones of their ancestors.

The most senior member of the cabal had chosen it. He'd said with a smile, 'What better place for us, we secretive people of the spirit, than to gather in this valley with the gentle ghosts of the patient *ndlovu* around us. If it is a sacred place for them, so must it be for us.'

Now Langani was back, tired, but satisfied, his duties over for the time being.

During his time away, he had tried to push to the back of his mind the series of events concerning the mysterious activities surrounding the rock pool below the waterfall and the *abelungu*, the men of the sea.

But if he were truthful, sometimes he wanted nothing more than to return to his sanctuary and the mysteries being revealed to him in the swirling waters – and in particular, the brief but tantalising glimpses of the childlike, dancing orb that had so amused and entranced him.

Above the strident shirring of cicadas, the gentle trickling of water made its presence felt. Langani felt a quiver of anticipation.

Unbidden, an image of the gently moving waters and the pulsing glow of the human souls on its surface came to him, as sharp and clear as if he were actually standing there looking down at them.

Resolutely, he pushed it away. First, he needed some time to himself; time to restore order to the place he called home, to rest and pray, and to put all he had learned in the valley of the great *ndlovu* to good use.

Only then, with a mind that was clear and restored to tranquillity, would he steel himself to look deep into the waters once more.

Twenty-five

St.Lucia Zululand

Thoughts concerning the mysterious fires returned to haunt Farewell moments before he was catapulted head first out of the ship's boat and into the sea.

Caught between the brilliant blue of the tropical sky and the towering wall of green water which had suddenly reared up out of the sea bed, the men in the *Salisbury's* longboat were powerless to save themselves.

The last thing Farewell remembered seeing was a strip of brilliant white sand and high dunes fringed with tall palms, enticingly close. After that, the wall of solid water sucked both light and the air away from him. The roar of the water and the thunder of surf pounding on the shore receded until there was only the smell of ozone and the frightening silence in the funnel of water enclosing him.

He kicked out blindly, his eyes still open. Then he was falling, tumbling over and over into a world of opaque green laced with foam and trailing seaweed. A stab of excruciating pain hit him just below the ribs. Dammit, he thought, I must have hit the side of the boat when I went over…

Above his head he could see ripples of sunlight playing on the surface of the water. He tried to strike out upwards, but his clothes were waterlogged and heavy, hampering his movements, the pain in his side excruciating. All he had the strength to do was to try to resist the downward pull of the current.

Air threaded out of his mouth in a thin stream of bubbles. The temptation to drag great gulps of air into his lungs became overpowering. The roaring in his ears was at thunder pitch and he swallowed hard to relieve the agonising pressure. In a last desperate attempt to save himself, he allowed his body to go limp, praying that the air trapped in his clothes and body would be enough to carry him back up to the surface.

His head drooped on to his chest, his hair floating in a swirling cloud around his face. The face of his wife Elizabeth appeared behind his closed eyelids. She was smiling. All was calm and quiet and the thundering in his ears receded.

Farewell felt a jolt of great sadness run through him as he thought of her. *Poor Elizabeth, only a year married.*

Suddenly, something bumped into him hard and seized him by the shoulder and neck in a vicelike grip. Instinctively, his eyes snapped open and he tried to swivel his head round to see what had him. The shape was black and very strong.

He fought to loosen its grip, but it bore him upwards, defying his attempts to break free. The eyes close to his were tinged with red, the mouth stretched over a set of white teeth. The grip tightened further, so that he was clamped closely to its rubbery flesh and borne upwards along with it.

Farewell's head broke the surface. He dragged a mixture of air and salt water into his lungs in great whoops. Daggers of sunlight refracted off the creamy surf, dazzling him and making his eyes smart.

Realising he was still in the grip of whatever had seized him, he struck out blindly at the dark shape, yelling in terror. A ringing slap was delivered to the side of his face, stunning him. A voice hissed in his ear, *'Be calm! Let go of me!'*

Strong hands forced him over on to his back. A shaft of dazzling sunlight struck him between the eyes, blinding him. A muscular brown arm snaked round his neck and shoulders and began to pull him through the water.

They came ashore in a welter of trailing seaweed, pebbles and sea shells and deposited onto the wet sand where they lay panting like stranded fish. Farewell felt himself seized below the arms then dragged up the short stretch of wet beach and dumped unceremoniously face down on hot, dry sand.

His head was forced to one side and his rescuer began to press down rhythmically between his shoulder blades. Farewell retched weakly, dribbles of salt water and saliva trickling out of his mouth. Never had clean salt-laden air tasted so good...

A searing chill of shock hit him, raising shivers deep inside. He stuttered his thanks through clenched teeth, unsure of whether his mumblings made any sense to the man crouching over him.

Silhouetted against the brilliant sky, the tones of his skin were accentuated by the contrast between dark flesh and the shining blue of the heavens. Sea-water clung in beads to the tightly-wrapped acorns of his short woolly hair and ran in rivulets down his body, dripping onto the sand. Thick strands of twisted beads around his neck were plastered against him in hues of startling blues and reds.

The eyes observing him coolly were of such a deep brown as to be almost black, the whites shot through with streaks of red from the salt water.

Farewell stared at the astonishing sliver in the man's left eye, as if he had never seen it before. Jakot, the interpreter! Every time he came face to face with the Xhosa, the curious wedge of colour lodged in the iris of the man's eye never failed to intrigue him.

.Splintered planks of wood, coils of rope and smashed oars were all that remained of the *Julia's* longboat. Fears for the safety of the other men leapt into Farewell's mind, pushing all else aside. A sickening lurch of his stomach sent his head pounding. Joe Powell, the bo'sun, had been in the longboat with him -

Desperately, he tried to speak, to move his chilled lips. They refused to form the words he needed to say. All he could do was look pleadingly into Jakot's face and gesture seawards before coughing up further dribbles of sea-water. *Powell? The others...*

The interpreter swivelled slowly round on his heels then stood up and looked out beyond the turbulent surf, shielding his eyes from the glare.

Farewell found himself staring up at the man's muscular back. Narrow ridges of pink scar tissue ran from shoulder to buttocks, cruelly criss-crossing the fine brown skin. They had clearly been made by a whip, and a vicious one at that.

He was not unfamiliar with the effects of what a lash could do to a man's flesh. Until very recently it had been one of the staple punishments meted out in His Majesty King George's Royal Navy. The lead-tipped cat-o'-nine-tails had been infamous for over three centuries of British naval history.

Farewell felt a stir of revulsion at the sight of the puckered, abused flesh. Old, bitter memories of his naval days began to surface. Pushing them away, he turned over and spread-eagled himself on the hot dry sand and dug his fingers into it as if he would never let go.

Gradually, the rhythmic roar of the pounding surf lulled him into a doze. He could hear the rattling of small stones and the hiss of sea water as the tide ebbed and flowed, in and out.

Soon, even the imperious squawking of the circling sea birds began to fade and he drifted into a deep sleep.

Wakening some time later, he flopped over on to his back, groaning and stiff. His clothes were caked with sand and plastered to him in stiff folds, his lips cracked and encrusted with salt. Struggling to sit up, he looked round for the man who had rescued him.

The wide curved beach was empty except for the scattered debris littering the waterline; the sand where Jakot had dragged him up the beach still marked with deep grooves.

Only one set of clear footprints led back down to the water's edge, but of Jakot Msimbithi, his rescuer, there was no sign.

James King stood at the rail of the *Salisbury*, his face twisted in concern. He looked as if he hadn't slept for days, his eyes red-streaked with the strain of staring at sun-hazed seas and bright sunlight for too long.

In spite of the dangerously high seas, he had made a further desperate attempt to rescue the men by launching a second longboat. But, due to the worsening of the weather, it had also foundered. The would-be rescuers were thrown into the water and were now added to the list of those unaccounted for.

The situation was dire. No one knew that better than he. At that stage, there had been only one boat left: a small jollyboat. He'd had no choice but to launch it.

From the heaving deck of the *Salisbury*, King had followed the boat's progress through the glass. Gamely, it tried to struggle into position so that it could ride shoreward on the crest of the breakers.

He had watched it disappear into a deep trough of water. But incredibly, there it was, rearing up on to the crest, its oars clear of the water. Once or twice, it looked as if it was going to succeed.

Then loud groans broke out along the deck. The remaining crew could only stand and watch as it plunged helplessly down into the next trough following on behind.

One moment the boat was there, its oars flailing, the stick-figures of the crew frail against the immensity and power of the ocean, the next she was gone, the men spilling out like marionettes.

Some of the watchers on the shore strode up and down the beach in agitation while others waded out into the surf as far as they could. Like many seamen, very few of them could swim.

All they could do was to stand by and watch helplessly while the last of the *Salisbury's* boats was pounded to matchwood by the raging surf.

A cry from Joe Powell alerted the survivors to something in the water. He raced down the beach, pointing seawards. The dark head of a lone swimmer was heading for the men struggling in the water.

Slowly but surely, the swimmer began to make headway, pushing out strongly against the current. As he was caught up on one of the crests, his dark, gleaming skin and muscular body stood out against the foam-laced water.

Powell shouted. 'It's Jakot, the Xhosa lad! By larrikins, look at him go!'

Ragged cheers broke out as the sailors shouted him on. Anxious eyes swung between the heads bobbing in the water and the swimmer. The distance was closing.

Then disaster struck. They could only look on in horror as a sinister black fin circled one of the men lucky enough to have been washed into calmer waters. He disappeared in an instant and failed to surface again.

Only a few yards away, a second man was desperately trying to reach the shore. Men waded out to try to help, but before they could reach him, he was pulled under, in water that only reached the top of his thighs.

Powell's face was grim below its steely composure. All eyes were now on the men who still had a chance. But, wait, it looked as if something else was happening out there...

Two flailing bodies were joined in what seemed to be mortal combat. It seemed to be the Xhosa and another man. The interpreter had him by the scruff of the neck, trying to manhandle him towards the safety of the shore. Incredibly, he seemed to be resisting Jakot's attempts to save him. The watchers saw him angrily lash out, aiming blows at his rescuer.

It was clear they were locked in some kind of personal battle, their angry shouts snatched away by the wind and the roaring of the sea.

With a final heave, Jakot landed the man on to the sands of St Lucia with as much grace as if he were a fish on a line. When the crew rushed forward to help them, they realised the man whose life he had saved was the surly red-faced Alex Thompson, the mate of the *Salisbury*.

No word of thanks came from his lips; only oaths and streams of abuse.

'Fockin' black,' he sputtered, retching up sea water. He swung a fist weakly at the man who had rescued him. 'Get yer bleedin' hands off me – else I'll see you swing! Get yer sent back to fockin' Robben Island, best place for kaffirs!'

When Powell next looked up, Jakot had gone. Already in the water, he was heading back out through the surf, his body rising and falling in the mountainous swell.

King feverishly paced the deck of the *Salisbury*, concern for his crew visible in the deep grooves etched on his face. Not knowing how many had survived the loss of the first boat, let alone the second, worried him deeply. All he knew was that any survivors were stranded on the beach, the others either drowned, or taken by sharks.

Farewell was lucky enough to have been rescued during the initial sortie made by the longboat before it foundered on the second attempt. He'd admitted he owed his life to the interpreter, Jakot, but had no idea what had happened to him. He had simply disappeared.

The footprints leading back down to the water's edge told their own story. Whether the man was still alive, or what had become of any of the others, Farewell had no way of knowing. It was possible he and the other two men picked up were the only survivors.

King paced the deck distractedly, the silver streaks in his dark hair standing out vividly in the half-light. His shirt, jacket and trousers were dripping wet, soaked by spray and sweat.

God damn the sea, he thought savagely. If Thompson was lost, and God forbid, the dependable and experienced Joe Powell as well, it would mean that only he and Farewell would be capable of taking command of the *Salisbury* and running her with any degree of safety.

Captain Garrett, in the smaller supply ship *Julia*, could be depended on to provide stalwart support, but if the worst came to the worst, the remaining crew was the barest possible complement with which they could hope to get safely to port, any port.

To add to their problems, only one ship's boat remained, and it belonged to the *Julia*. If any further attempt to rescue survivors was to be made, the small boat would be crucial. But if anything happened to that, not only would the survivors ashore have to be abandoned, but both vessels, the *Julia* and the *Salisbury* would be left without a safety fall-back.

King stripped off his sodden jacket and threw it across the cabin in frustration. He couldn't risk grounding the *Salisbury* by taking her closer in-shore. Even if he did, it was unlikely any of the survivors would be able to swim out and climb aboard, not only because of the high seas and the risk of shark-attack, but also because, like most seamen, they'd never learned to swim.

As he began to write up the incidents in the ship's log, King knew that a decision had to be taken, and very soon.

As officer in charge, he had little choice in the matter. The survival of the *Salisbury* and the remaining crew was paramount. There was nothing else for it; they would have to leave the survivors behind for the moment and head south to Algoa Bay. There they could pick up fresh supplies, new longboats and extra crew before returning to search for the lost crew.

The only other alternative was to wait out the ferocious storms pounding the coast before risking the remaining boat while heading in dangerously close to shore.

He shook his head wearily. With only one boat remaining, it would be madness to risk it. Added to which, it would only waste time. The deadline for completion of the survey for the Admiralty was looming, and if they failed to comply with it, all their plans would have to be abandoned.

Reluctantly, he gave the order to lift the anchors and head out to sea. Once a safe distance away from the coast, they would change course and head south with all speed.

That night, in the warmth of his cabin, with the wind keening and thrumming through the rigging, James King thought of the tiny figures he'd picked out through the telescope. If the black dots he'd counted were the sum total of the crew who had survived the foundering of three of the ship's boats, it meant that many of the crew were lost.

The thought haunted him. Even those who had chosen the sea as their livelihood were never immune to the fear of being drowned and lost forever with no known resting place.

King paced up and down the cabin floor with his hands clasped behind his back. The ways of the sea, and of the Almighty himself, for that matter, were unfathomable.

He sighed, and glanced at the Captain's log spread open on the table. In it were the names of the crew who had signed on for the expedition to complete the survey of the infamous Wild Coast.

Who had survived, and who had not? The captain of the *Salisbury* resumed his pacing. Reluctantly, he was forced to admit that, for the moment, there was nothing more he could do.

Later that night, he went on his knees and prayed to his Maker for the survivors and their safe delivery from the deprivations he feared lay before them.

He also prayed that a kind and merciful God would protect them from the ferocious *amaZulu* whose campfires he and Farewell had seen twinkling in the darkness only a few days earlier.

Twenty-six

Langani woke long before dawn while the world was still dark. Today, he would look into the waters gathered in the hollow of the rock. Although he had been looking forward to this moment, apart from the initial surge of excitement, there was also a feeling of reluctance, as if something was holding him back.

Am I laying too much store on what I think I'll find there? he asked himself. Or is it perhaps I'm afraid my own interpretations will be proved wrong?

The more logical side of him argued: What, you fear being proved wrong, *isangoma?* Perhaps you think you are no longer capable of error? If the glowing sparks of light are no longer there, how will this prove that they were ever connected to the men you believe are linked to Zululand?

He shook his head, doubt warring with certainty. You've been away for some time, his inner voice insisted. Perhaps the glowing sparks are just a natural occurrence, their existence brief and your interpretation of them too fanciful?

The bird with the black feathers and bright eyes fluttered on to the branches of a tree close by. As it cocked its head to one side and fixed him with a penetrating look, his brief period of self-doubt melted away.

But, is not that the task of diviners – to interpret signs and wonders wherever they may be found? I am not afraid of being wrong, only of being proved *right* – and that one day Zululand will find itself in grave danger.

He looked over to where the waterfall came splashing down from above. Inexplicable forces are at work here, and I mean to follow their course and listen to what they tell me, for I can do no other.

Even though there had been no rain for a while, the flow of water welling up from the spring's hidden source had slowed only slightly. The cascade of cool water trickling down the rock face was as crystal clear and sparkling as the last time he had stood there, gourd in hand, waiting for it to fill.

Langani cupped his hands and let the water run into them. As he drank deeply, the cold filled his mouth and made his teeth tingle. Kneeling down, he dipped his head below the overhang of rock.

The water looked cool and inviting. Its surface was calm and untroubled with only the merest hint of a current moving somewhere in the depths.

His eyes travelled round the sunken pool. No trace of floating debris or small winking lights. It was as if they'd never been… except, that is, for the sweet, tender glow on the overhanging, lichen-spotted roof.

A sense of relief washed over him. The orb! It was was still there, glowing steadily in the early dawn light.

So he'd been right, after all. The last time he'd seen the flecks of natural matter floating on the surface, the small bobbing lights had all expired, or were about to, their mission complete. Each one had represented a major player in the game: Jakot, Henry Fynn, Farewell and James King. And they had all been made known to him, each with their own tale waiting to unfold.

But not you… Langani smiled as he watched the glowing orb dance among the other ripples of light. *A child!* Am I right in thinking you are a child?

The orb stilled. A trembling movement ran through it, as though it was listening. He shook his head in disbelief. No sooner had he solved one thing, than another piece of the riddle raised its head.

If this was true, and the orb did represent a child – what role was there for a small human being among the tangled webs of ambition, greed and lust for power that he'd recently witnessed?

What place for a child in the unfolding tale of a warrior King who was ruthless and powerful in the extreme, driven by his obsessions as much as all the *abelungu* put together? He needed to know...

The orb was motionless, its lightness of movement held in check. Langani leaned forward and stirred the waters. Suddenly, they grew cold and his fingers numb. Soon he ceased to feel them at all. Looking deep into the pool, he saw it change, first by colour then by the cold air rising from it.

Its smell, too, was different, salty and reeking with the tang of ozone and drifting seaweed. There were dark seething masses of it, lurking somewhere below, a danger for unwary feet, and in particular, the small, unsteady feet of a toddling child.

Dark, cold and forbidding, it was water unlike any Langani had ever seen before. The wind blew around him, chilling him to the bone. He shivered, his skin rising in prickles of gooseflesh.

As he darted glances around him, his thoughts were fused into only one question. *What kind of place is this?*

The parapets of stone were patently a shelter for the vessels bobbing about on the water, sailing craft he recognised as being similar, though many times smaller than those of the *abelungu*. Many were large, with three or four masts, their sails no longer flapping and full of wind, but at rest, rolled up close to the spars. There were other, smaller boats, some with no sails at all.

His eyes watered in the cold wind blowing off the sea. Clearly, he was in an alien land. Its smell was different, even the patches of blue in the skies were colder and more remote than those he was used to. Beyond the stone parapets he caught glimpses of a grey, forbidding sea with storm-tossed clouds above it. He became conscious of noises, a great deal of hammering, metal on metal, like smiths beating out spear-heads, voices shouting over the din, although he could see no one.

Something made him look sharply to his left. It was then he saw him. A child, a boy, of perhaps three years of age, with hair of an astonishing colour, his little cheeks red with cold as he toddled along the quayside. A sense of impending danger caught at the diviner.

The child appeared to be walking towards the edge of one of the stone parapets. Below it, lay waters dark and dangerous. Too close…

Langani's heart was in his mouth. Unaware of the danger, the child was laughing as he moved nearer to the edge and leaned over, intrigued as to what might be below.

He thought of himself at the same age, with no fear of the storm and the lightning, as Cebile, his *igugu* had described. Perhaps this child was the same, not aware of the danger lurking in the dark, treacherous waters.

The sound of the sea was loud in Langani's ears now, a malevolent sucking and gurgling. He cast a frantic gaze around. *Where was the boy's mother? Why was no one looking after him?*

One spring morning, the red-haired three-year-old known as Charlie noticed that the garden gate had been left open, either by accident, or blown ajar by a gust of wind.

He smiled hugely, his blue eyes crinkling up with the thought of the unknown lying out there beyond the boundaries of his familiar world. He pushed the gate open and squeezed out.

After that it was easy. It being still early in the day, and a Monday as well, the fishing fleet had sailed and both the streets and the harbour were quiet.

Following some deep instinct or drawn by the squalling of the circling herring gulls and the restless roar of the sea, the boy found his way down to the harbour.

The small figure, clad in blue jacket and trews, his red hair blown about by the wind coming in off the firth, toddled on, unnoticed by anyone. The coopers hammering out their fishing barrels or the girls and women gutting the silver herring and packing the fish in layers of coarse salt were in another part of the harbour.

Charlie's sturdy little legs led him unerringly down on to the pier itself. The massive iron rings used for mooring boats lay embedded in the solid, yet uneven stone slabs, a trap for unwary little feet.

The slap, slap and sucking sound coming from somewhere below aroused his curiosity and drew him closer to the edge of the pier.

Prattling away to himself, he squatted down in his stout little leather boots to get a closer look, his cheeks reddened by the sea wind. His eyes spotted an iron handrail, which led on to a set of iron bars set into the concrete. It appeared to lead down to where the water was restlessly moving below, stirring the fronds of seaweed and making slapping and sucking noises.

Edging a little closer, he put out a chubby hand to touch the top bar. His curiosity was aroused. Where did it go, that little stairway? And what would be at the end of it? He bent forward to peer over the edge...

To his delight, something interesting began to rise up the iron rungs of the ladder. First to appear was the top of a seaman's woolly tam pulled down over a thatch of iron gray hair. It was followed by a pair of startled, far-seeing blue eyes topped by a pair of sweeping eyebrows that were grey, almost white, to match the man's hair.

Currently, they were raised in a mixture of alarm and astonishment at seeing three-year-old Charlie perched precariously at the edge of the pier, looking down at him, his red hair blowing about his face. One slip...

'Och, my fine lad, just you wait till Sandy comes up alongside,' he heard a gruff voice say. 'Where in the world has a wee body like you come from?'

Charlie obligingly stepped back from the edge and watched as the man clambered up the iron rungs with the ease of long practice.

The three-year-old beamed in delight and took a good look at his new friend. He was quite old, but he had a kind face, weatherbeaten by years of exposure to the sun and rough winds of Scotland's coasts. Clad in sea boots, hand-knitted thick stockings, and the heavy black and white flecked seaman's hand-knitted garment known as a *ganzie*, he was immediately recognisable and familiar.

After tying the mooring rope of the small boat to one of the rings bolted on to the pier, the fisherman stretched out a hand calloused by four or more decades of hard toil. The boy reached out and took it, laughing up at him as he did so.

'You come with Sandy, young lad,' the man said. 'We'll first ha'e a wee walk around the pier to see the boats, and then we'll find out who belongs you and take ye hame.'

Langani pulled back from the rock pool, relief rushing over him. Dizzy with emotion, he thought of what he had just seen: the old man and the small boy turning their backs on the stone walls, moored boats and dangerous sea and walking away, the *toto's* chubby hand clutched in the work-worn hand of his mentor, for that would be the role the man would play, far into the boy's life.

The diviner's final doubts had disappeared, tossed aside by what he had witnessed in the country of chill winds and grey seas. They were replaced by a gamut of conflicting emotions; a mixture of overwhelming relief, incredulity and a feeling of deep personal satisfaction.

What he had just achieved went far beyond his wildest expectations. This time, he had transcended both space and time in equal measures. But with the knowledge came more than a little fear.

Exhausted, Langani crawled into the shade and was soon asleep, soothed by the sound of the water trickling down the rock.

The first thing he noticed when he next opened his eyes was that the golden orb had moved down from its playground on the roof and was now hovering above the surface of the water, its small, throbbing heartbeat as full of life and joy as ever.

He smiled at it, an open human smile of recognition and greeting. '*Yebo*, I know now who you are, little one. You belong to the sea people in a far-off land – but what you have to do with the land of the Zulus, its warrior King or the other players in the game, I really have no idea!'

Twenty-seven

W hen they saw the line of flickering torches coming along the beach towards them, the survivors from the *Salisbury* scattered back into the undergrowth.

As he crouched behind a clump of bushes, the bo'sun, Joe Powell, was painfully aware of how defenceless they were, how vulnerable to attack. Their sea-boots and waistbands would yield up a few knives and the odd chiv, but that was about all. He noticed one or two of the sailors glancing over their shoulders, uneasy about the night sounds emanating from the dense bush.

The off-shore wind stirred the thick scrub and rustled through the undergrowth. The sea glowed milky and luminescent in the starlight. The boom of the surf had faded to a low rumble, the dense bush muffling the sound.

Thompson irritably fanned away a whining mosquito. Powell's voice hissed a warning to the crew to spread out among the stunted trees and scrub.

'Keep your heads down. Try not to show your arse-white faces, they'll stand out like moons in the dark. Dead give-away, mates, so keep 'em down.'

Powell pressed a hefty cudgel into Thompson's hand. Surly bastard he might well be, but if it came down to it, he'd give as good as he got. He glimpsed the gleam of the mate's bared teeth in the darkness and heard the low growl of approval.

The string of torches was close now, almost level with where they were hiding. Powell counted a dozen or more dark shapes. With a sinking feeling, he saw the torchlight glint on spear blades.

The flames smoked and flickered in the night breeze. Dark bodies milled about, then gathered into a knot. Illuminated by the sputtering light of the grass torches, the group stood out clearly against the milky blue phosphorescence of the sea.

Joe Powell tried to assess how many were there. Nine or ten at least, if you included the leader, who was crouched on one knee, studying the tracks in the sand.

Behind him he heard a hiss of in-drawn breath and the soft smack of a cudgel being weighed in the palm of a hand. 'Hold your water, man!' Powell hissed. 'We've lost enough good men today, Mr Thompson, no need to lose more. Unless need's must, o' course.'

No sooner were the words out of his mouth, than the leader stood up, turned in their direction and raised his torch higher. In its flickering glare, the bo'sun knew he was looking straight at them. The hair on the back of his neck prickled. His muscles tensed, ready to spring into action.

The natives came towards them in a soft slurring of sand, lights bobbing up and down. A few steps nearer and the light from the torches threw a set of fierce black faces into sharp relief. The spears were viewed with a tangible stiffening of bodies and muttered oaths as fists tightened on cudgels, a slick of sound as knives were drawn.

Only a few yards separated them now. Tensions rose. Then from the depths of the thicket there was a loud snort of relief followed by a cackle of nervous laughter.

'God's bodkins!' croaked the voice of Able Seaman Sims from behind the first mate's shoulder. 'Blow me down if it ain't Jakot! By all that's sainted, it's himself, for sure!'

Thompson swore and smacked the cudgel down in his palm with a vicious crack. The disgust in his voice was patent. 'An' here's me thinkin' the blackamoor had been eaten by sharks, an' good riddance to his scurvy black hide, I sez.'

Powell released his pent-up breath and lowered the cudgel. The group of natives surrounded them, jabbering and chattering in excitement. It was clear they'd never seen white men before.

Jakot raised his torch, peering at each of them in turn. In the flickering light, he seemed taller, part of the shifting, ever-changing shadows, his dark skin glistening with sweat.

Standing more than a head taller than the stocky Thompson, his glance flicked over the mate's sullen face before turning away, dismissing him. It was Powell he addressed in his curious, idiosyncratic English.

'Here is Jakot. I take you first for food and beer, then sleep!'

His face creased in good humour as he rubbed his flat, muscled stomach in a gesture that was instantly understood by mariners and natives alike.

The atmosphere changed in the twinkling of an eye. The laughter of overwhelming relief broke out among the survivors of the *Salisbury's* longboats.

The bedraggled sailors were led through tortuous bush paths for a mile or so inland until they reached a cluster of villages. Later, exhausted by the sobering events of the day and the gratifying effects of food and beer on their empty bellies, they were only too glad to collapse on to the sleeping mats in the hut whose previous occupants had been unceremoniously cleared out to make room for them.

It was only then Joe Powell remembered that no one had uttered a word of thanks to Jakot, not only for rescuing more than one of the *Salisbury's* crew from the raging seas, but also for arranging food and shelter for them in the village of Madaka, the headman.

Some weeks later, in the darkest hour of the night, the Xhosa rose up from where he'd been pretending to be asleep by the fire. Gathering up a woven bag containing some food, a few pieces of clothing and a rolled-up blanket, he crept softly away.

He intended to pass through the night like a shadow, without sound or trace. By sunrise, he would be well on the way to where he really wanted to be. It was how it had always been; first as a mere boy, running from the *amabhuna* back to his people, then again, doing the same thing, when he'd been older.

The huts around him were like large beehives, their inhabitants buzzing gently in sleep, the stillness disturbed only by the occasional whimper of a dreaming infant or cattle moving about in the pens.

Jakot gave a wide berth to the hut housing the white men. In his mind's eye, he could see all eight of them hunched in sleep. He thought briefly of the red face of the angry one, Thompson, and supposed that even in sleep it would be scowling. Silently, he threw a curse in his direction.

The man was the main reason why he had to steal away like a thief in the night. Saving the man's life after the boats had capsized had earned him only blows, oaths and accusations that Jakot's intention had been to drown him, not to save him. But that was not all.

Thompson had threatened to have him returned to Robben Island at the first opportunity, threats which had chilled the Xhosa to the bone. Puzzled, Jakot shook his head. Why does the man hate me so? What have I ever done to him?

Late yesterday afternoon, the hunters from Madaka's village had brought information that had forced Jakot to decide to disappear, and quickly. When the fluttering white sails of a ship had been spotted close to shore, Jakot's spirits had taken a nosedive.

Calm weather must have brought King and Farewell back to search for their missing crew. The sailors would have to be told that rescue was at hand. But how could he go back on board with them?

What if the red-faced Thompson carried out his threats and accused him of trying to drown him? By then, it would be too late; there would be no way for him to escape, except to jump back into the sea. Who would speak the truth for him? What if no one did? Then there would be no pardon as promised by the Governor at the Cape, only the return to the island prison with the cold, the fog, and the mournful barking of its many seals.

He shook his head. There was no trusting the word of the white men. He had to go, before the crew found out about the ship that had come looking for them.

Jakot glanced up at the night sky. Wisps of cloud drifted across the crescent moon and a sprinkling of mist drizzled on his upturned face. The air was cool, smelling of damp earth mixed with the faint aroma of roast meat and the acrid tang of the cooking fires. He drew in a few deep breaths and allowed his rapid heartbeat to slow down.

Ay, ay, he thought, always I am running from the white men, first the *amabhuna*, the Boers, and now the people of King Jo-ji...

Carefully, he skirted the cattle pen. A pair of wide, sweeping horns clattered against the thick wooden stakes. The curious beast lurched over and amicably snuffled the palisade, its eyes luminous in the dusky light, its breath rising steamily into the cool night air.

Jakot whispered a few soft words below his breath. They were not directed at the cow, but to the *umnumzane*, the spirit of the former head of the household who had been buried in a sitting position inside the enclosure, as was the custom.

His eyes instinctively went to a spot below the wide spread of the buffalo thorn tree. The ancestor would have been placed in cool shade to make sure his spirit remained a benevolent one. Facing the most important dwelling in the village, the grandmother's house, his spirit would continue to guard the interests of the clan.

'You, or your people, have nothing to fear from me, O powerful One,' Jakot breathed, 'I owe them a debt for their kindness.'

Soft wings fluttered high up among the spiked branches of the thorn tree. Jakot felt the hair stir along the back of his neck. He whispered urgently,

'I must move like a thief in the night so the *abelungu* can not take me back to the prison. Then I should surely die.'

The night air stirred in a gentle sigh. He became aware of a pattering sound, as if the feet of a tiny animal were scampering among the dusty cowpats. Sudden heat rushed through Jakot's body. His heart thudded against his ribs.

The gentle eyes of the black and white speckled cows regarded him kindly as they peered out between the stout branches of *tamboti* wood, their mouths placidly chewing. The crescent moon appeared from behind its veil and a pure white light filtered down into the kraal.

Out of the corner of his eye, he caught sight of a pale blur high up in the thorn tree, and glanced away quickly, not daring to look directly at it.

'If I do not flee, the red-faced one will lie and say that I tried to drown him. They will not believe the word of a Xhosa, but will send me back to the place of stone where the souls of lost men cry out,' he whispered hoarsely. 'Better to fly like the wind and try to find a place in the land of the Zulu King.'

The sliver of moon disappeared behind a ridge of cloud and the world suddenly went dark. The silence seemed deeper than it had been a few moments ago. Jakot bent his head in supplication, his heart pounding.

Something pale swooped out of the tree and brushed the top of his head. Startled, he ducked and stayed down, crouching, until he was sure it had gone. He stood up, breathing hard. As he did so, rain began to patter softly on the dusty ground in fat, dark spots. A cool breath of wind followed.

Jakot Msimbithi smiled, then hefted the small pack on to his shoulder and moved silently away.

The dug-out canoe slid silently through the marshy waters of the wetlands as Jakot paddled carefully and slowly as he'd been instructed. Madaka had explained how to find a way through the mangrove swamps and intricate waterways that lay between the village and where he wanted to go.

The ship wrecked sailors had come ashore at the southern-most end of an immense wilderness, an intertwined mosaic of rivers, lakes and saltwater pans, criss-crossed by reed, sedge and mangrove swamps, and populated by many kinds of wildlife.

If we had landed further to the south, Jakot thought, I wouldn't have been able to find a village like Madaka's. We would have had to stay on the beach, or been forced to go inland to find fresh water and probably perished in such a place as this.

In spite of the winnow of cool air created by the steady motion of the canoe, he was sweating profusely, and his hands were slippery on the paddle. I hope some of my good fortune is still with me, he prayed.

The deep, almost unearthly silence beyond the chatter of insects and frogs was at the root of Jakot's apprehension. What might be hiding in such a silence?

The heat and humidity heightened the swirl and sucking sounds of the water. The flash of the jewelled eyes and glowing bodies of fireflies were reflected in the liquid darkness below the overhanging fever trees. The rank smell of mud and decay added to the sinister atmosphere. Clouds of insects hovering over the surface reluctantly let him through, closing behind him after the silent passage of the canoe.

He had never been in such a place before. His natural habitat was the rolling plains and hills of the Xhosa lands, with wide, sweeping skies above his head, a place where a man could look out to the horizon, spy an enemy or predator approaching, or feel the earth tremble as a storm approached.

He shivered in spite of the heat. Not here, though. This place is dangerous, the water washing away any scent of danger. Maybe I should have listened to the old man and waited until sunrise.

But it was too late to turn back. Dipping the paddle deeper, he forced the canoe to surge ahead.

Sea cows and crocodiles, sometimes even sharks, lurked in the swamps, Madaka had told him. Any of them were capable of over-turning a canoe, pitching even an experienced boatman into the water and dragging him down. Deadly snakes whose bite meant delirium and eventual death also haunted the mangrove swamps.

'By day, it is bad enough,' the headman had said. 'But by night, *dadwetu!* Clearly a man needs to be fleeing from devils if he wishes to go there in the dark!'

From the haunted look on Jakot's face, it was clear to Madaka that there were indeed devils pursuing the Xhosa, forces so power-ful and vindictive that he would risk his life in the swamps trying to avoid them.

As he paddled, Jakot's thoughts kept time with the strokes. He was bewildered, no longer sure of anything. Had he not been good to the white men, doing their work on the ship, saving them from the sea?

Stark memories of the penal colony on Robben Island returned to haunt him. *Never will I go back there...*

Senses jangling, he swivelled around to scan the darkness. Dark ripples of oily water lapped against the side of the canoe. He caught sight of slanted yellow eyes glinting in the starlight, luminous evil above a scaly snout.

His scalp contracted in horror. Both the jaws of the reptile and those of the penal settlement of Cape Colony seemed to be clos-ing in on him.

Arms moving like pistons, the power and thrust of his strong shoulders made the canoe fairly skim through the water. Grimly, he concentrated on avoiding the tangle of mangrove roots lurking below the surface.

The high piercing scream, when it came, jarred deep down in-side him. Distracted, he lost his thread of concentration, and failed to notice the submerged sand bank ahead. The rough wooden craft juddered to a halt. Its nose dug into the sand at an upward angle almost catapulting him into the murky water.

Behind him in the darkness, he could hear a frantic splashing and churning, the squeaks of an animal in terrible pain. Jakot dragged himself up from the bottom of the boat and peered into the gloom.

A small grey monkey, gripped between the jaws of a crocodile, its mouth and eyes frozen wide open in a rictus of fear, slowly sank below the surface in a froth of bloodstained fur and bubbles. To his horror, he saw a small baby clinging to its mother's back.

Jakot stared in horrified fascination as the yellow eyes and ridged snout disappeared with its prey below the brown waters. Looking at the oily swirl, he shivered in spite of the humidity and paddled furiously away.

A few hours later, the first streaks of red and amber light began to soar up from beyond the high dunes fringing the beaches of St Lucia.

Jakot eased back and let the canoe drift. Surely, he was far away enough now. The white men would never find him, even if they had a mind to.

Strange how he credited them with greater powers than perhaps they had. He knew the sailors he'd left behind had no weapons apart from a knife or two, but he still feared that they had the power to seek him out.

Very soon, Madaka and the hunters would escort them back to the beaches, perhaps light a fire to attract the attention of the ship. King and Farewell would send a boat to pick them up. Then they would disappear out of his life forever, along with the murderous Thompson.

Ay, but they were difficult people, these *abelungu,* as full of twists as the black mamba. A man could never be sure where they would rear their heads next. The only exception was Kingi, of course, the man who had saved his life and brought him up into the sunlight, and helped him to find a way out of the prison.

The craft bumped gently into the shore. Jakot snapped out of his reverie and looked around. Ahead he could see sweet meadows fringed with forests. Beyond that, were distant green and rolling hills that rose as sweet and soft as the breasts of Nozipho, the girl he had left behind in the village of his youth, in the far-away lands of his Xhosa people.

The soft contours of the high ground stretching away into the distance made his heart race. That was where the next, and infinitely more dangerous part of his journey, would lie.

Dragging the dug-out from the water, he propped it up under a tree, so rainwater wouldn't collect inside and cause it to rot. One of Madaka's men would eventually find it, or he might still have to fall back on it to escape if his plan didn't work out.

He turned to look back the way he had come, back to where the Madaka's village lay. Beyond that was the never-ending ocean, and beyond that his homeland, lost in time.

Jakot groaned, knowing only too well the futility of his situation. In the place he called home, in the village of his father, Nozipho would be at the stream with the other maidens by now, laughing as they filled their patterned clay jars with water, ready for the morning chores.

His heart stirred again, in a lonely echo of what might have been. The country of the laughing girls of his youth, the courting and the conquests, the loving times, lay as dead as his hopes of ever returning.

Wrenching his eyes away from the shining water trails, he turned and resolutely faced the meadows and the high, rounded folds of the green hills beyond.

It was no time to be weak. Now was the time for action, time to strike out for the next stage of his plan, his only hope of survival.

He had been sceptical at first when he'd heard the whispers about the warrior King who had conquered most of the lands between the Portuguese territory and the frontier lands of the Cape.

But, after only a few days in Madaka's village, his disbelief had rapidly evaporated.

The fear in the eyes of Madaka had been real, and there was no mistaking the ripple of nervous agitation that ran like wildfire around the village fires at the mention of the dreaded name, Shaka.

When Jakot asked how large the kingdom of the Zulu king was, Madaka indicated its span with the tip of his spear. It traced the entire heavens, from horizon to horizon, north to south, east to west.

The hairs on his arms and the back of his neck had tingled in apprehension. Very quickly, he realised that the village must be either within the kingdom of Shaka, or very close to it, hence the agitation of the villagers.

But after some consideration, his quick wits had already seen a new opportunity open up, a way to escape from the white men.

I have things of value to impart to Shaka, the Zulu king, he thought. Only Jakot has seen with his own eyes the soldiers of King Jo-Ji in their red coats with their buttons of shining brass. I alone have heard the thunder of their weapons and seen how they can kill a man, even an elephant, from far off.

Jakot thought back to the first of the soldiers he had killed, a golden-haired boy no older than himself. The young soldier had fallen to his knees clutching the shaft of the spear embedded in the breast of his handsome red tunic, the dark spread of his life-blood beginning to seep through the scarlet cloth.

As the youthful face closed down in death, the Xhosa had stared down at him in mingled pity and wonder. The force of the fatal blow had knocked off his white helmet and the sun glimmered on hair that shone like gold. The boy had whimpered and clutched his hand in mute appeal as he began to die.

Not only have I seen them, he said to himself, but I have fought them, killed one or two up close, and eye to eye. I have heard their cannons thunder, and have seen the magical place of Cape Town, with its great buildings, watched their ships speed like the wind over the great waters, with their bellies full of the riches of the earth. Only Jakot has sailed in these vessels and lived to tell of it...

A bold smile caught at the corners of his mouth. The Jakot of old, the handsome Xhosa who had as many lives as a cat, began to emerge.

First, he said to himself, I have to find the people of the amaZulu. Then, if they let me live, I will ask them to take me to their Nkosi, Shaka.

He thought hard for a moment or two then added, with more than a flare of his old self. Then, if Shaka of the Zulus will let me live, I will say to him, 'Nkosi, beware the cleverness of the white men!"

Jakot threw his head back and laughed, causing a few pied crows to flutter up, cawing in alarm. He knew in his heart there was no way he could foresee what Shaka might, or might not, allow him to do. But there was no way back, not to the village of Madaka, for nothing lay beyond it. Nor could he return to his Xhosa lands and his past life. It was too far away, impossible to reach, except with the greatest of good fortune, of course.

For Jakot Msimbithi, cattle thief, Xhosa warrior, ex-felon and interpreter to King George's Navy, it was time to begin a new chapter in life. In spite of all the dangers and setbacks he had faced, he was still alive, by the grace of the ancestors.

The chubby face of the twelve-year-old boy who had been his friend so long ago floated into his mind, as clear as day, grinning mischievously, with only the whites of his eyes and his teeth showing in his dust-caked face.

Majoze, my friend, he thought – Majoze, who had to be left behind on the veldt for the scavengers and predators. The scars on his back began to throb. Majoze's spirit would remain with him always.

Jakot began to walk towards the distant green hills, his eyes resolutely fixed ahead. As they grew closer, he could see the wind sighing and rippling through the grass, singing its song of things to come.

In spite of everything, he thought, I have learned much from the white men, things I can turn to my advantage. *Yebo*, I have much to tell the man who is King of the Zulus. The old, confident smile lit up Jakot's face.

There were battles still to be fought, worlds and cattle and women still to be won. With a spring in his step, he moved on, ever closer to whatever the future held for him.

Twenty-eight

Langani pushed aside the overhanging branches and looked out over the wide expanse of shimmering silver and blue water dozing in the afternoon sunshine. The deep silence was broken only by the occasional cry of wheeling sea birds and the rhythmic splashing of waves against the sandy shore below.

'eThekwini...' the diviner whispered, looking at the wild and beautiful bay spread out before him. 'This is the place the *abelungu* seek, I'm sure of it. Otherwise I would not have seen it in the throwing of the bones and been led here to it.'

It had taken him many days to find it. First, he had travelled from his eyrie on the mountain all the way down to the coast. Then after crossing the Umgheni River, he had followed an old elephant road that had wound up to the top of a ridge. As soon as he'd seen the lagoon and its islands spread out below, he knew he had found what he was looking for.

On the far side, a ridge of misty hills rose out of the haze. A number of guano-spattered islands were scattered within the sheltering arms of the lagoon. Some were large, some small, but all of them sported bird colonies, their rocky surfaces teeming with flocks of flamingos, ibis, storks and a multitude of assorted sea birds preening their feathers in the sunshine.

Shading his eyes, he looked out to where a long narrow spit of sand and the forested headland he was standing on seemed to meet in the distance. Although he could not see the hard-packed tongues of silt and sandbanks which formed a barrier against the entrance to the bay, he knew they were there.

The guardians of eThekwini, he thought, with a shiver. But will they be enough to prevent the *abelungu* from finding their way here?

He was enough of a pragmatist to accept that the men he had seen during his trance states would not simply drift away into the morning mists like phantoms. Even if they failed once or twice to find the entrance to the bay, he knew they would try and try again, until they succeeded.

He stared, unseeing, into the sunlit distance. Time was growing short. Soon, they would come. The Xhosa, Jakot, was already making his way towards the King of the Zulus.

In spite of the day's warmth, a shiver ran down Langani's spine. Jakot was young and foolhardy, but he also had great, enduring courage. The diviner was in no doubt about his will to survive.

What did concern him, however, was Shaka himself. How would the unpredictable King of the Zulus deal with someone who not only had the temerity to enter his territory, but was also Xhosa, a warrior nation similar to that of the Zulus? Would he regard him as an enemy, an intruder – or as an ally?

Langani shuddered. Whatever the headstrong young man might have heard about Shaka of the Zulus, he had simply no idea what he was capable of. Messengers bringing unwelcome news to the royal court frequently suffered an ignominious fate.

A sigh of cool air wafted up from the lagoon and stirred the branches of the pine trees. To the young diviner's ears, the gentle soughing was like the sighing of lost souls.

Involuntarily, Langani sent up a silent plea for Jakot Msimbithi. After so many skirmishes with death, the young man with the magical eye had surely earned another chance to live.

The warm brush of an animal body against his legs made him look down. The delicate face of a young female cheetah looked up at him, its keen black eyes seeming to express concern for his well-being. He surveyed the distinctive tear marks running from eye to muzzle, the long rangy legs and high-backed rump.

One day a few months ago, the animal had simply stepped out of the bush and onto the path in front of him. It had stared at him with curiosity, its long tail twitching.

Fully expecting a hostile mother and the rest of the litter to appear out of the long grass at any moment, Langani had not sought to approach it or make any sudden moves. After a while, he had simply backed away, still keeping a cautious eye on it. To his surprise, it had padded after him, stopping when he stopped, moving on when he did. Nothing seemed to deter it.

On reaching the foot of the ravine leading up to his sanctuary, he'd shot it a last look before plunging into the animal tunnels that wound up through the dense scrub to the lip of ground where his home stood. When he reached the top, he was amazed to find the young animal already there, waiting for him.

Once it saw him appear, it padded over to the rock pool, crouched down and began to drink. Afterwards, it settled down in the shade, and continued to watch his every move through lazy, half-closed eyes.

'Where have you come from? And what do you want from me?' During the first few days of their curious domestic arrangement, Langani put the same questions to it many times. Naturally, he received no answer.

As he soon found out, it was old enough to hunt for itself. Apart from giving it any left-over scraps of food, he didn't even have to feed it. The first time it disappeared, it was gone for almost two days. When it returned, its muzzle stiff with dried gore, Langani viewed it with a cautious eye.

Cheetahs were, after all, predators. Should he be more concerned about it? And what would happen when he went about his duties in the villages? Would it still insist on following him?

After a few weeks had passed and it still showed no signs of leaving, he asked it another question. 'Who sent you?'

The graceful creature with the fuzz of adolescence still on its rapidly maturing body had merely yawned and continued to observe him with its usual sphinx-like scrutiny.

In the end, Langani had no choice but to accept its watchful, though affectionate presence, as he had done with so many other inexplicable factors in his life.

By late afternoon, the weather had changed. White-topped breakers began to pound in from the ocean to break in fountains of spray on the rocks at the foot of the headland.

The colours altered from deep blue and shimmering green to shades of gold, grey and black, the crimson stain of the setting sun daubing the palette of colours with brilliant artistry.

This was only the second time in his life that Langani had been so close to the ocean. As he walked along the sands, with the long cloak billowing out around his tall frame, his eyes were riveted on the crests of the breakers rolling in against the rocks. Certainty welled up in him.

Yebo, he thought. This is where the white men will try to enter the land of the Zulus. In his mind's eye, he could see the white wings of the *abelungu's* vessel coming within sight of the high, wooded bluff marking the entrance to the bay of iThekwini.

As he walked on, his eyes were constantly drawn to the restless pounding of the ocean. It struck him just how large a part the sea had played in the lives of the men who had come to him during his times of dreaming.

First, there had been Jakot, a Xhosa from the wide, rolling

lands to the south. Langani shook his head in amazement at the twists and turns of the man's life, many of which seemed, of late, to involve the great waters and those who sailed it. This included the one Jakot called iKingi, the *abelungu* who had saved him, not once, but twice.

Next, there was the raging storm off the coast of Zululand, the one which had crushed the boats of the white men and thrown them into the raging waves. Once again, Jakot and the sea had won the day. It had allowed him not only to survive, but to save other lives, among them Farewell, the leader – and also a man who hated him. Afterwards, it had left him free to find his way to kwaBulawayo, the heart of Shaka's kingdom.

And now, because of all these things, and because he did not believe in co-incidence, Langani realised the significance of the important part that the ocean had already played in their lives.

The wind pulled at his hair and tugged at his cloak. Seabirds rode the currents of air, dipping down to touch the water before soaring upward again. An image of himself sitting peacefully by the trickling waterfall flashed into his mind. With it came the memory of the dragonflies, with their iridescent wings and jewel-like eyes hovering over the surface of the water that had come from deep inside the mountain.

Water, the life-giving source, he thought. Without it, every-thing would die, man, beast and all living things. Water, whether fresh or salt, had been the great connecting factor between them all, from Jakot, the men of the sea, the one called Fynn, and also –

Langani's lips curved in a smile as he watched the wind ruffle the young cheetah's fur. The small, playful globe of light jinking around the roof of the rock pool had intrigued and beguiled him with its innocence.

And its influence had been strong enough to lead him far be-yond his own shores to where another ocean, another sea, had threatened the life of a small boy with hair the colour of fire. The link between them all was undeniable, a pointer to the future, and to what was yet to come.

The diviner drew in a deep breath of salty air. The *abelungu* would not be easily deterred from trying to find a way to enter Zululand. Another thought struck him. Even if the great waters brought them here, might they not also carry them away again, once they'd found what they were looking for? A flare of hope rose in him.

A moment later, doubts clouded his mind. Farewell, the man with the cold blue eyes – what he desired above all else was more, much more than the others, for it was the land itself he wanted to possess.

The diviner thought briefly of other men who had come a long time ago to the bay of eThekwini with the same thought in mind; to own the land and steal the people who lived there.

But where were they now? Apart from a few stone pillars that had once formed part of a jetty, they were gone, no trace of them left. Might not the same happen to Farewell and the others, in time?

As he walked along the shore, the wind pulled at him, reminding him of its strength. Air, unseen, and with no visible shape or dimensions, was another force to be reckoned with, he thought. If the *abelungu* belonged to the oceans of the world, what might men like himself and even the mighty Shaka rightfully claim as theirs?

The answer came to him in a flash. *Earth – it had to be the earth.* Equally powerful, it was rich and full of treasures, both above and below ground. It was also what supported life, from the lowliest insect to the most powerful of beasts and men. Without it, there would be no kingdoms, no mountains, no rivers, and no oceans, either.

The diviner smiled as the wind loosened his hair from its braids, making it streamed out around his head. Mankind came from dust and then returned to it, he reminded himself. Fish belong to the sea, as do the great creatures of the deep – while men do not.

His eyes returned to where the grey-green breakers were rolling in and swirling over the lethal tongues of silt and banks of sand blocking the entrance to the lagoon.

'Guardians of eThekwini,' he said, 'do your work well, I pray you.'

Reaching down, he stroked the young cheetah's head. Celiwe, he'd called her. After discovering it was female, he had named her Celiwe, after a tribal Queen of long ago.

'And we shall also be here,' he said, 'two more guardians of eThekwini.'

Wrapping his cloak around him, he turned his back on the sea and headed back the way he'd come. After he'd walked a few yards, his bare foot came up against something hard. Looking down, he saw that he'd stepped on some shells half-buried in the sand. Something about their colour and shape intrigued him. Bending down, he prised them out of the sand and held them up to the light.

There were six of them, ranging in size from the largest, which was half the size of his fist, to the smallest, no bigger than his fingernail, a miniature replica of its larger brothers. He blew grains of sand away from its tiny ear and examined it more closely.

The inside was pale pink coated with the delicate sheen of pearl while the outside was a speckled brown, full of twirls, twists, and curious, fluted ridges.

Langani, being a stranger to sea shores and what could be found there, was intrigued by the shells, especially the smallest one.

'A good omen, a gift from the sea,' he murmured, pleased with his find.

Slipping them into the pocket of his cloak, he thought of the child with the cloud of wonderful hair in his far-off land, and wondered whether he too collected shells from the sands of his homeland.

Leaving the shore, he followed the winding paths leading up through the trees to the headland. As he walked, he thought of the questions that still remained. Now he knew of the *abelungu's* plans, should he meet with Shaka of the Zulus, reveal who he was, and warn him of his suspicions – or bide his time until there was something more to report?

The second question was, if not problematic, then certainly more intriguing. Just who was the small *abelungu* child represented by the lively orb playing in the dappled sunlight on the roof of the overhanging rock?

That he belonged to the people of the sea was clear. The man who had risen out of the sea to save him was not known to Langani, nor, he suspected, would he ever be. All that he knew of him was that he was a story teller and that he had a kind heart.

As for the *toto*, the small boy with the hair like flame and the eyes as blue as the sky, Langani knew for sure that he too, unlikely as it may seem, was destined to play a part in the events destined to unfold in Zululand.

On reaching the top of the headland, the diviner paused for a moment and looked out over the bay to the place where the ocean and the sky met. It was lost in sea haze and drifting spray.

Like time itself, Langani mused, its mysteries hidden. We mortals can only stand and wait.

Twenty-nine

An iron-hard foot caught Jakot in the small of the back and knocked him face down on the ground. As he lay there, winded, all he could hear, apart from the thrumming in his ears, was the rustle of leaves, the relentless crick-crick of cicadas in the noon-day heat and the painful rasping of his own breath.

Beyond his limited range of vision lay the formidable presence of the man he'd seen reclining on a pile of rolled-up reed mats in the shade of a tree. As he was being manhandled into submission, Jakot had received only a split-second impression of the huge, near-naked figure and the terrifying stillness emanating from it, but it had been enough to terrify him.

His thoughts were erratic and feverish. Is this where my great, good luck finally runs out? Will Shaka listen to what I have to tell him, or will he have me killed before I have a chance to open my mouth?

After leaving the wetlands, he had struck out in a southerly direction away from the coast. His freedom had been short-lived. Two days later, a group of armed Zulus had sprung out at him from a stand of high elephant grass and overpowered him before he even had a chance to call out.

Though not exactly a novice when it came to moving silently through unknown territory, Jakot had neither seen, heard, nor sensed the approach of the silent group of men who had overpowered him in a matter of seconds and held a blade to his throat. For some time after that, his life had hung in the balance.

It was only after he'd insisted over and over again until he was hoarse, that he had news of great importance for Shaka, their king, that the Zulus had reluctantly removed their short-bladed assegai from his throat.

On being interrogated further, he had managed to gasp out just enough of his story to be believable. 'Strange men with pale skins like the underbelly of a fish are about to set foot in your land,' he'd said. 'Their great *umkumbes* with white wings, which can fly over the sea like the wind, are already on their way.'

For a moment, the pendulum of his life had swung this way and that. Then came the moment when he could tell by their expressions and the way one of them waved a hand in the direction of the coast and rattled out a string of words, that at least he had a fighting chance of staying alive.

At one time or another, the man in question must have caught sight of a ship in full sail as it skirted the coast on its way north to Delagoa or south to the Cape.

The brief intercession bought Jakot time to think. When he was able to get to the part about the white men's weapons, the ones that spat fire and could kill from a distance, he knew his chances of staying alive had increased dramatically. The stillness of his captors' bodies and the intensity of the fierce eyes fixed on him told him so.

He had held his breath and prayed. Would these warriors really take the chance of killing a man on his way to bring such important news to their King, the man they feared above all else?

In response, they had hauled him to his feet and given him something to eat and drink. The following morning, they'd set off south taking him with them.

Jakot had breathed a sigh of relief. For the moment, he was safe, but the true test would come when they eventually reached kwaBulawayo, the place where he would come face to face with the mighty Shaka himself.

The man observing him was inscrutable, his features as bland as if carved from the rich, dark wood of the *mkhula* tree below which he was sheltering. The eyes, chips of obsidian in the bright sunlight, reflected no hostility, only curiosity.

Jakot had barely time to register these facts before he was commanded to crawl on all fours to the foot of the dais. A ringing slap to the side of his head was accompanied by a reminder that his eyes remain lowered, it being forbidden to look directly into the face of the Lord of the World.

Too late, he thought, I've already had a glimpse of it. Even though his head was down, he could feel the gaze of the black eyes pierce his flesh, his very soul. He bore the intense scrutiny with as much fortitude as he could, conscious of the trembling running through his body.

A deep voice spoke from above his head. It told him to stand up then slowly turn round so he was facing away from the pile of rolled-up reed mats. After a long silence, the same pleasantly modulated voice spoke again.

'The wounds on your body – how did you get them? Who did this?'

Jakot found he had no difficulty understanding what was being said, the Zulu language having an affinity with that of the Xhosa. From a mouth that could barely gather a slick of saliva, he croaked, 'The *amabhuna*, the Boers – a tribe of the *abelungu* who live in the lands to the south.'

'For what reason?'

'After they'd held me for a long time, I escaped. Not once, but twice,' Jakot replied.

Should he have been so truthful, admitting that he had been taken prisoner, not only once, but on several occasions? Would the Zulu ruler take it as a sign of weakness, dishonour, and believe it better to die in battle than be taken alive? And would he get a chance to explain that he had been only an unarmed boy when the Boers had jumped on him?

A movement behind him instinctively made him flinch. His scrotum shrivelled in anticipation of a blow to the head or body. Instead, there was only a touch of a hand, surprisingly gentle as it traced the jagged weals inflicted on him by the lash of the rhino-hide whip known as the *sjambok.*

The voice spoke again. 'These *amabhuna* you speak of – which weapon did they use to do this?'

Jakot stumbled over the words, his voice breaking as he tried to describe the dreaded whip that was used equally on beasts of the fields and humans alike. 'It is made from the skin of the rhino,' he explained. 'Once it has been dried to hardness in the sun and oil put on it.'

A long silence followed. Jakot wondered wildly for a moment if the King of the Zulus had lost interest in him. His knees began to shake with the strain of his ordeal.

Behind him, the Zulu King rapped out an order. Jakot caught a glimpse of his captors moving towards him, their hard eyes raking him up and down, and steeled himself for the worst.

This time, there was a profound change in his treatment as he was ushered out of the square and down the slope towards the living quarters. A surge of relief went through him. At least, I'm still alive, he thought. Shaka let me live – *for now,* his natural caution added.

When a bowl of food was thrust into his hands and a pitcher of water placed by him, he knew one thing for sure. His bid to stay alive was not yet over.

A week or two later and Jakot still remained unscathed, though wary. Although he had been allowed to talk, sleep, eat, and talk some more, he remained painfully aware that his life still hung in the balance.

Either the *amadhlozi* will decide my fate, he thought, shrugging his shoulders, or the Zulu king will take matters into his own hands. He did not have long to wait. Shortly afterwards, late one night, he was called to attend Shaka in his private quarters.

After days of holding court, listening to his subject's discontent with their lot in life, discussing current military affairs, or heeding advice from his councillors, the Zulu monarch needed to find some light-hearted distractions to while away the night hours.

And who better to amuse him than the young Xhosa who had fled from the *abelungu* in a desperate bid to find sanctuary within the gates of kwaBulawayo?

He had been about to retire for the night when Shaka's messenger appeared. The sight of him had induced a feeling of helplessness in his legs, and he had almost stopped breathing.

'Come with me, Xhosa,' the man had instructed him, curtly. 'Be quick, the Nkosi must not be kept waiting.' Stumbling through the darkness with only the sound of the man's padding footsteps and a faint glimmer of light ahead, Jakot's mind had been in a ferment of suspense.

When the massive bee-hive structure loomed out of the darkness, the impact of its vast, shrouded bulk brought fresh bouts of sweat. The ring of torches flanking the Great Hut served to add to its mystery, the flickering oily lights creating the illusion of movement, of it being a living, breathing entity.

Only Shaka of the Zulus could command such a dwelling to live in, he thought, for it chills the soul with its power.

His eyes were riveted on the high, arched doorway. From within, a glow of soft light moved and flickered like the tongues of many snakes. When they reached the threshold, a rapid whispered command and a shove in the back forced Jakot to his knees.

'Head down! No eyes!' came the hissed warning. Startled, Jakot received only a brief image of the man he was forbidden to look at; a dark silhouette, framed against the suffused light of burning tapers and small oil lamps, the body massive, powerful.

They waited, kneeling, on the threshold. Moments slipped by. There was no sound from within. Only the ceaseless whine of insects and the chirping of cicadas in the cooling night air, a reminder of the lateness of the hour.

'*Woza.* Come.' The single word was sufficient. The messenger began to shuffle forward on his knees. Digging Jakot in the ribs, he issued the usual muttered threat. 'Head down! No eyes!

As he crawled on all fours across the floor towards the shadowy outline of the man in the carved chair, Jakot was stiff with fear, his heart pumping.

Are these my last moments? Perhaps Shaka chooses darkness to rid himself of the unwanted, the troublesome?

A moment later, and the voice spoke again, issuing a brief command. 'Only the Xhosa...'

Feet scuffling, his escort retreated back the way he'd come, careful not to turn his back on the monarch. Jakot, breathing hard, sweat trickling into his eyes, began to resume his slow crawl forward.

The floor was cool, its surface highly polished and smelling faintly of sweet grass. Not daring to lift his eyes, Jakot concentrated only on the foot or so directly in front of him, before moving forward carefully, slowly.

At last he was told to stop and sit up. With his legs crossed, he waited, still careful to keep his eyes fixed on the floor. A long silence followed, a sense of deep quiet in which Jakot was painfully aware of intense scrutiny.

'Now, Xhosa,' the deep voice demanded. 'Tell me what you know of the *abelungu* who live in the lands beyond the Rivers Mthatha and Mzimvubu. I need to know all their ways.'

And so it began. Unable to believe his good luck, Jakot vowed to use this golden opportunity to his best advantage. For many nights after that, he would be called forth to provide company for the great Shaka.

Once there, he would amuse him with all the powers at his

disposal, spinning tales of the foibles, cunning and dangers of the white men; the magical things they had created; and the wonders and terrors of the great city that lay far to the south where the land came to an end and the mighty oceans began.

'Aiii,' he would say, 'the *abelungu* are doubly cunning, as the snake and hyena put together.' At this point, he would tap his forehead knowingly.

After waiting for a few moments, he would add, 'One must be careful, always watchful, for they can move as fast as the wind on their horses, these animals they have trained to do their bidding. Truly, Nkosi, these men ride on their backs, and bid them pull strange carriages with people inside. They help farmers in their fields and do many other things. Some of their soldiers also use these creatures to ride into battle.'

And he would shake his head, whetting Shaka's appetite for more, before allowing himself to be drawn into the Zulu king's most favoured topic of all – that of the mighty British Army. This needed no carefully-rehearsed performance, for was not Jakot himself a living witness to the destructive power of the white man's soldiers and their fearful weapons?

Shaka never tired of hearing of the scarlet coats and gleaming buttons of the white warriors, of how they drilled and marched, and wheeled in formation.

Jakot would sigh, 'I am even afraid to remember the noise of the battles, Nkosi. The firing of their weapons is greater than the loudest thunder in the heavens, sharper and more deadly than the crack of lightning, the shooting sticks that brought fire to the flesh of my people.'

Rolling his eyes, he would clutch his head and sway to and fro. 'I have seen warriors fall to the ground, dead, or with a leg, an arm or another part of their body destroyed. And this was without the white man even touching them, or being close. Such is the power of their long sticks that shoot fire.'

Very soon, he came to understand how astute a mind Shaka had, especially when it came to warfare, any man's warfare.

'How fast do they run?' he would demand, 'do their *indunas* go into battle with them, or stand on a hill and direct them how to trap the enemy?'

'You say they can kill from a distance, with no need to see the faces of the enemy – but, if the enemy slips through his defences and is at his throat, what then will the *abelungu* warrior do? Does he stand and fight – or does he run away like a cringing village dog?'

Jakot was canny enough not to divulge *everything* he knew of this interesting topic. He intended to stick to his carefully thought-out plan. Not unsurprisingly, it was based on primarily staying alive, becoming indispensable to Shaka, and making a niche for himself in the kingdom of the People of the Heavens.

Once ensconced, he believed that not even the white men, including the dog, Thompson, would be able to remove him from his place of safety in the court of Shaka of the Zulus.

So, after Shaka gave him the praise name *Hlamblamanzi, the swimmer,* and promoted him to stand guard outside his quarters at night, Jakot knew he could begin to breathe a little easier.

Even so, there was still more to be done. Determined to raise his standing in Shaka's eyes still further, he bided his time until the perfect opportunity arose.

The morning dawned bright and fair. The hot, rainy season was almost over and the air was cool as it drifted up from the south.

Shaka was holding an important *indaba* and the square was crowded with his chiefs, ministers, councillors and their attendants. He sat resplendent on his dais below the giant tree, frowning a little from time to time as he raised various points with his ministers.

Dressed for the occasion, he appeared in fine fettle as he listened to the petitions brought to him for consideration.

A rogue male lion, too old to hunt, had been stalking cattle and lying in wait for the occasional child or elderly person in the village a few miles away; someone was stealing cattle; a woman had been accused of casting a spell on her brother's wife – and several more land disputes.

From the rear of the crowd, Jakot watched Shaka intently. Every nuance of expression was noted, as was every smile, every frown. Soon, he began to notice that they fell into a distinct pattern.

Anything touching on the military, cattle or matters of state always held his attention, while the more mundane issues dealing with wives, wayward daughters or quarrels over land, saw the light of interest replaced by a bland expression of indifference or boredom.

Thus armed, Jakot waited for an appropriate moment, one where he saw the shutters of disinterest lower in Shaka's eyes. Then, gathering himself together for what he intended to be the most convincing performance of his life, he put his head back and let out an eldritch, piercing shriek.

'Eeeeee! eeeee!!... ay...ay… ayaaaaa!!

It penetrated to the furthest corners of the square and stopped people in their tracks. Eyes darted from this way to that, searching for the source of the terrible screaming.

Leaping out of the crowd, howling as if a pack of demons were at his heels, he hurled himself towards Shaka, manhandling people out of the way. The cape covering the terrible weals crisscrossing his back was torn aside, revealing his scars.

Horrified ministers, chiefs and servants alike scattered in every direction, thinking him possessed. None of them were armed because it was forbidden to bear weapons in the presence of Shaka.

If ever the Xhosa had been tempted to act out a part to save his life, this was the perfect opportunity. Here was the ultimate charade; his audience the highest in the land, his illustrious patron the feared and volatile King of the Zulus.

Rolling around on the dusty ground, foaming at the mouth, biting, scratching, spitting and screeching in fury, Jakot pretended to be a witch who had taken on the shape of an *impika*, a wild cat who sought to do Shaka harm.

One moment, he was a maddened wild beast, the next he was playing the brave Xhosa who had survived the cruel ocean to seek out Shaka to warn him of the wiles and dangers of the fearsome white men whose skin was the colour of fish bellies.

With his captive audience looking on, he pretended to beat the evil spirit to the ground, rolled with it in the dust, and eventually, after a long and bloody struggle, managed to pound it to death with his bare hands. Afterwards, exhausted but victorious, he revealed the long, weeping scratches inflicted on him by the claws of the spirit cat...

After an appropriate period, he sat up and raised his eyes with what he hoped was a suitable degree of humility. Daring a glance in Shaka's direction, his heart shrivelled in his breast.

Unbelievably, the King of the Zulus was sitting in exactly the same position as before. Nothing had changed, except that the dark eyes shrewdly observing him had a cold glimmer of amusement in their depths.

The icy brilliance of that long look shattered Jakot's hopes. He sank to his knees, squeezed his eyes shut, and prayed for a quick death. His famous luck had run out at last...

To his surprise, he heard Shaka laugh out loud above his bowed head, an explosion of genuine, unrestrained humour which made his knees shake.

Incredibly, he later rewarded him with a dozen cattle, a fine piece of land and several baskets of seed corn. Looking Jakot straight in the eye, he'd said, 'Thank you for facing so many dangers to tell me such interesting things about King George and his people.'

The eyebrows had quirked slightly above his direct gaze as he'd added, 'Also, I am grateful for your bravery in vanquishing both the *impika* and the witch that sought to harm me.'

Later, after he was out of sight, and his heart had started to beat again, Jakot fell to his knees and thanked his ancestors for allowing the incredible luck of Jakot Msimbithi to continue.

But even as he went on his way whistling, the memory of the mocking intelligence in the eyes of Shaka Zulu stayed with him.

He had the uncomfortable feeling that they had pinned him with as much compassion as a spider would a fly struggling in its web.

Thirty

T he news of the imminent arrival of the white men was delivered to Langani by a messenger. When the bird with the
shiny black feathers fluttered down on to the branch of a
lightning blasted tree and cocked a yellow eye at him, the diviner
knew what it had come to tell him. The ships of the *abelungu* were
coming, just as he knew they would be.

Wasting no time, the diviner went into his hut and reached for
the lion skin bag holding the sacred bones, precious relics and
other essentials of his calling. On the way out, he gathered up his
monkey skin cloak and slipped his feet into a well-worn pair of
ox-hide sandals.

As he made his way across to the edge of his territory, the bird
watched him leave, but did not try to follow him. The young
cheetah needed no urging. Silently, it fell into step behind him, its
small, rounded ears twitching as it padded after him, the long,
banded tail swinging gently.

Within a few minutes, diviner and animal were swallowed up by
the labyrinth of tunnels that snaked down the precipitous slopes
towards the dried-up river bed and the wider world beyond.

Aboard the *Julia*, Francis Farewell screwed the monocle into his eye and glared at the mass of ridged banks of sand rearing up in front of them. They reminded him of giant lizards he had once seen in India, their skin wrinkled and creased with age.

The mate, Thompson, growled out an indecipherable comment. 'What did you just say?' Farewell asked, without removing his eyes from the malignant mass of greyish sand pitted with the debris collected over the years. Thompson aimed a gobbet of spit over the side.

'What yer needs to shift 'im is a barrel or two o' gun-powder. Quick as yer like, then we'd be in.'

Farewell's head swivelled round, the early morning sun glinting off the gold rim of his eye-glass. 'You might well be right,' he replied. 'In my opinion, though, it would take a lot more than a couple of barrels to blast that amount of hard-packed grit to kingdom come. Best we get the longboat out and do a spot of reconnaissance first, to see if we can't find a way in without wasting the powder.'

After another month of failing to locate a landing place that looked even remotely accessible, tempers aboard the *Salisbury* and *Julia* were frayed.

Even after picking up the survivors from the beaches of St Lucia and with the extra manpower they'd taken aboard at Algoa, the crew were often forced to work double watches, with only short spells of sleep in between, while the work of the survey went on.

The deadline for its completion was almost upon them. It would do their future plans no favours with the Admiralty in London if it was late. But the real source of King and Farewell's frustration came from their apparent failure to find a trace of the promised bay.

All they had to go on was Scallion's rough, scrawled chart, the sketchy outline of a headland, a narrow tapering point of land and a dubious location of 29 degrees 55 South by 30 degrees 41 East.

This time, it looked as if things would turn out to be no different. Both ships lay at anchor inshore, close to what looked like a river mouth. They had been drawn to it by the sudden appearance of what they had hoped was the mysterious but elusive headland they had been looking for.

The crew, men and officers alike, stared in mounting frustration as yet another series of grey, stone-pitted sandbanks reared up in front of them, blocking their progress. Francis Farewell snapped out an order.

'Best we get the longboat out and do a spot of reconnaissance first. See if we can find a way in without wasting valuable gunpowder.'

Joe Powell, being within earshot, lost no time in shouting out orders for one of the longboats to be made ready, and seamen to stand by, ready for a sortie.

Up on the headland, in a clearing screened by a dense stand of trees, a figure sat cross-legged on a goatskin karosse. The face, a mask of white daubed clay, belonged to a young man. The features were smooth and unlined, relaxed and at peace.

In one hand he held a beautifully-crafted bag made from the cured skin of a male lion, and in the other a small beaded pouch, lovingly created by his grandmother.

Anyone familiar with the practices of diviners would immediately notice the absence of the more usual artefacts, such as the dried animal bladders, teeth, bones and claws of animals and other relics considered essential to their calling.

This was because Langani was very different from others of his kind. He was no ordinary *isangoma*, but one of high intelligence and skills, a true man of magic.

Laid out before him were the sacred bones entrusted to him by a long line of long-dead diviners. Wisps of smoke rose lazily from the smouldering twists of *impepho*, *lesedi* and the *labateka* root placed around him to clarify his mind.

His eyelids flickered then opened, the narrow pinpoints of his pupils contracting as they adjusted to the sunlight. Carefully, he placed the lion skin bag and the beaded pouch to one side and stood up.

Beneath the cloak he was almost naked, his lithe, muscular body daubed with white clay and the secret markings of the brotherhood to which he belonged.

As he walked over to the edge of the clearing and parted the overhanging branches, the amber eyes of the cheetah followed his every move.

Beyond the rocky point of the headland, two ships with furled sails lay at anchor, swaying on the tide. Langani stared at them for a long time, a look of profound resignation on his face.

Then, cupping his hands together, he started to breathe into them, muttering incantations as he did so. Sweat trickled down his face and his body became tense with effort.

After a time, he opened his fingers and allowed what was within them to fly off into the wide expanse of air and water beyond the headland. After it was done, he stood with his eyes closed and his lips moving in prayer. Long moments passed.

The cheetah in the shadows stretched lazily then rose to her feet. She raised her head to sniff the air, the long, banded tail twitching gently.

A gentle sigh began to rustle through the pine trees and stir among the branches. Ripples began to spread across the lagoon and move outwards, raising whitecaps as they went.

The diviner's near-naked body was as taut as a tightly-drawn bowstring. The cheetah pressed closer to him, baring her teeth and snapping at the gusts of wind beginning to spiral around them.

The sky, which had been a peerless blue, had turned into a battleground of billowing clouds. Grey and ominous, they began to roll in from the ocean towards the headland, driven by the ever-rising wind.

Aboard the *Julia*, James King stared at the rising seas in disbelief. His bearded face showed signs of the exhaustion and irritation they were all feeling.

'What in hell's happened to the day, Farewell?' he demanded, raising his voice above the booming of the sea. 'This damn coast – one minute the sky's as blue as a robin's egg, the next a full force storm seems to be blowing up!'

Farewell spread his feet apart and braced himself against the rise and fall of the deck. 'We've seen all this before, James. In case you've forgotten, that's why it's called the Wild Coast.'

'God damn it,' King exploded, the wind plucking at his water-stained blue jacket. 'We've been chasing our tails over this head-land for months, only to find it as elusive as a hoor's innocence. First, we missed it during the night, next we sailed past it in a gale, then just when we think we've found it, what happens – another bloody storm starts to rise!'

The squall had come up out of nowhere, threatening to blow them all to kingdom come. There had been no time to even lower the longboats.

'Well, at least this time we've managed to keep our boats and crew, which is something, I guess,' King retorted sarcastically.

Farewell made a grab at the rail to steady himself against the wildly pitching deck. 'I wouldn't speak so soon,' he said, blinking against the spray. 'This time round, King old boy, I fear it might be even worse. We're in real trouble.'

Once again, the larger vessel, *Salisbury*, had been left with little choice but to pull up anchor and speed back out to sea. Having little or no sail power to fall back on, the smaller brig, *Julia*, had not been so fortunate.

By chance, both King and Farewell happened to be aboard at the same time. They had decided to leave the larger vessel in the capable hands of an experienced officer taken on board at Algoa Bay and use the smaller, more manoeuvrable vessel to investigate the river mouth.

Unfortunately, the *Julia* was now in a disastrously unstable situation. Even the second and third anchors thrown out were failing to hold her, and only seemed to be delaying the inevitable.

King squinted round at Farewell, his eyes half-closed against the drenching spray, his face grey and resigned below the tan. Francis Farewell surveyed the scene with mounting unease.

Mountainous seas were breaking against what little they could see of the shore, while the tearing winds were whipping up a maelstrom of green water, terrifying to behold.

The sturdy frame of the *Julia* strained against the cables, her timbers groaning and creaking in protest. In spite of their precautions, it was clear the little ship was being driven closer to the jagged line of rocks at the base of the headland. And there was little they could do about it.

Farewell shouted out above the roaring of the ocean. 'We have to make a run for it, it's our only chance.'

He pointed through the driving rain in the general direction of the blind river mouth they had noticed the day before. Although they hadn't had time to fully investigate, it had looked as if there might even be a narrow channel capable of allowing a small vessel through, if the tide was right.

Beyond the ship's rail, the world was grey, visibility so poor the opening could barely be seen. Very soon they would not even have the luxury of having a choice as to what they might, or might not, do to try to save the ship – and their own lives. As if to remind them of the extreme urgency, the *Julia* bucked, heaved, and inched ever closer to the rocks.

James King cast an experienced eye over the narrowing distance. He rarely swore. This time, he made an exception to the rule.

The massive bulk of the headland reared up through the spray, dominating the frail brig. It was so close he could smell the earthy smell of dense woodland. Wiping his face, he boomed out, 'You're right, we have to head her in, and pray like buggery we make it.'

An ominous barrier of sand banks loomed through the slanting rain. Surf creamed and swirled evilly over the tongues of sand visible below the surface.

Farewell repressed a shudder. Icy fear spread beneath his sodden clothes. 'God help us all,' he muttered.

Garrett, the captain of the *Julia*, hailed them, the wind whipping and slapping at his ancient, gold-braided jacket. The experienced master mariner presented a stalwart, reassuring figure, in full command of the vessel, if not of the elements. He jutted his silver-bearded chin in their direction.

'Gentlemen, I take it we are in agreement about our course of action?'

It was not a query, but a statement. As master of the vessel, the final decision would be his, but Garrett knew that both officers were veterans of many a storm and tight piece of action, both during wartime and out of it.

Both men nodded their agreement. The topsails were set with frantic speed, the vessel brought round to face into the gaping maw of turbulent waters.

King put his weight behind the wheel to help Captain Garrett keep on course. In such high rolling seas and cross-currents, losing control of the wheel and the rudder even for a few seconds could prove fatal.

Suddenly, one of the anchors lost hold and the second cable chain snapped clean through. The *Julia* was driven forward like the frail, desperate little craft she was.

Completely at the mercy of the tides and winds, she headed for the treacherous barriers of sand she must cross if she were to have even a faint chance of surviving.

Farewell tried to think of his wife, Elizabeth, but her face refused to come to mind. The Halsteads, father and son, stared white-faced at the towering walls of water, while Henry Ogle, the young Yorkshireman who had come aboard with them at Algoa Bay, was as pale as death, his knuckles white as he desperately hung on to the companionway rail.

A swift pang of regret hit him. None of these poor devils, frontier farmers, immigrants straight out from the depths of ruralEngland, could ever have imagined a scenario like the one in which they now found themselves.

Their urgent need for work had been the deciding factor in their signing on as temporary crew to allow the Admiralty survey to be completed. What might have looked like a way out of their predicament on the quayside at Algoa Bay could well turn out to have been the worst decision of their lives.

The *Julia* was caught up in a whirling vortex of surf and spray and tossed about like a child's toy. She struck a sand bank with a judder and spun off-course. There was no time even to pray. Every man-jack aboard clung to what he could and held on for dear life.

Someone screamed and cursed above the keening and howling of the wind. Farewell frowned at the blasphemies then braced himself for the next onslaught.

A towering wall of water hit the vessel broadsides. It streamed over the rails hissing like a live thing and scoured the decks of anything not tied down. The ship was carried up and up on a terrifying ride until it was tilted at a precarious angle, disaster mere seconds away.

A long shudder and a groan went through the little brig. Garret and King were spread-eagled across the wheel, desperately trying to keep her steady. Farewell closed his eyes and hung on to the capstan. He tried desperately to pray, but his mind was unable to form coherent words.

But somehow, *somehow*, the brave and battered *Julia* went soaring up and over, before plunging down once more into a valley with translucent green walls, a place of dim light and muffled noise.

By some miracle, she staggered upright before lurching on to the crest of the next wave then crashing down into the troughs once more. A shuddering grinding noise brought Farewell's heart into his mouth.

'Sandbanks scraping the keel,' he muttered, his teeth chattering with cold.

The brutal rocks were only yards away now. They were so close he could see their barnacle-encrusted surfaces and tangles of seaweed whipping about like the tentacles of a demented octopus. Gouts of spray jetted into the air before falling back with a dull boom, the iodine smell of ozone strong in the air.

All Farewell could do was to hold on. Desperately, he tried not to think of the sound the planks of the hull would make as they were staved in, the judder and rush as water poured into her hold, dragging them down.

He had lost sight of King and Garrett, although he knew they would never let go of the wheel, not until the bitter end. What a way for it all to end, he thought, savagely. Does fortune ever make fools of us all?

Hauling himself stubbornly upright, he hung on to the rail, determined to die, if he must, on his feet, looking the devil mistress, the sea, straight in the eye. But then, against all the odds, he felt the *Julia* rise and fly as smoothly as if she were on velvet, speeding and skimming, on and on, like a dancer performing a *glissade*.

The long, grey swell of sandbanks on either side of the frail vessel showed their ghastly pale bellies, ribbed by years of surging waters. The high bluff loomed out of the mist and driving rain, frightening in its proximity. Voices yelled out in fear, while others cursed.

Farewell's heart thundered in his chest. Out of the corner of his eye, he saw the blur of faces around him turn to stone by the sight of the lethal tongues of silt and the high, forested bluff looming over them, perilously close now.

More scraping and grinding along the keel, then, oh glory be... the little ship went up and over, riding the crest of each long, rolling breaker, running into the river mouth at speed, as sure and true as a homing pigeon.

Soaked to the skin, his hair plastered to his skull, King prised his stiff fingers off the wheel and raised a shaking hand in formal salute to Captain Garrett.

'By God, we've done it, Garrett! A close thing – and I doubt the *Julia* will need the barnacles scraped off her backside for a few years to come!'

He slapped the captain on the back, his voice gruff with emotion. 'That was as pretty a piece of steering as I've ever seen. And what luck, what great good luck, that this little beauty had the guts to fly up and over.'

There but for the grace of God and Captain Garrett, King thought, as he turned to search for his partner, we'd be finished, lost without trace, vessel and all.

His eyes searched for Farewell. He was standing by the rail, unmoving, his body rigid. Considering their narrow escape, he seemed strangely detached as he stared at the forest-clad mass looming above the *Julia*.

King noticed the pulse beating erratically on his partner's clenched jaw. Blinking his eyes several times in rapid succession, Farewell straightened the shoulders below the sodden blue jacket.

'Take a look at what lies off the port bow and tell me what you see, James,' he said. King crossed the deck, his feet squelching in his sea boots, Powell close behind him. One look told him all he needed to know. His voice cracked with excitement.

'My God, man, I do believe this is what we've been looking for. We've actually found it!'

The scrawled writing on the rough, water-stained map they'd inherited had described in detail what they were now looking at. King quoted from memory. *"A low sandy spit running in... about two, three miles long and stretching back to ever and aye. Almost directly opposite is a tall, wooded headland...*

He stared around him in sheer disbelief Not only had they averted total disaster, it appeared that they had, quite by accident, discovered what they had been looking for, the only safe mooring place of any substance between Portuguese territory and Algoa Bay.

After months of backbreaking work, fatal accidents, storms, men lost at sea and many deprivations, it seemed they had found their way into the promised river mouth.

But the miracle was not yet over. One moment they were sailing through a narrow channel between the high, forested bluff and the long spit of land, the next they found themselves afloat on calm, untroubled waters.

But this...this was no river mouth.

King could hardly believe his eyes. For once he was speechless. The men crowded the rails. A wide, beautiful lagoon was opening out before them, its waters as calm as a millpond.

It was another world. Here there were no raging winds, only gentle breezes playing over shimmering waters. The turbulence and roar of the angry surf and towering waves beyond the mass of sand banks was muted and distant now.

The *Julia* glided slowly into the bay. Silent now, the men stood at the rails. Overcome by the moment, some blinked away tears. After the battering of the storm and steeling themselves for destruction, words were totally inadequate to express their feelings.

Guarded by the wooded bluff on one side and the long spit of sand on the other, the bay was surrounded by gently rising hills, the white, sandy beaches ahead fringed by tropical vegetation.

A deep, almost uncanny silence lay over the wild, tangled beauty. A shaft of sullen sunlight broke through the scattered clouds and bathed the headland in sunlight.

The image of the *Julia* was mirrored on the water, the ripples bending her reflection so it seemed she was part of the magical quality of this living paradise.

Young Tom Halstead, a lad in his early teens, went to stand at the rail, his sallow, rather moonlike face flushed with excitement. Henry Ogle, the stocky eighteen-year-old Yorkshireman, playfully poked him in the ribs.

'What do ye think on that, Tom? Better than Grahamstown, eh? A pox on that dusty hole.'

A rocky island stood off their port bow. As they slid past it, pink flamingoes could be seen preening their feathers on the guano-spattered rocks, while flocks of pelicans, herons, egrets and a multitude of sea birds were displayed against their natural habitat of water, rocks and sand.

With a rustling of wings and a long sigh like that of a rising wind, a flock of flamingoes suddenly rose into the air. Once they were clear of the water, they folded their ungainly legs with surprising agility and grace then swept in a wide circle out and over the *Julia*, their wings beating in unison.

King could feel the emotions running the length of the deck. No one had really said much since being swept over the bar. The sea-faring fraternity were usually silent when faced with displays of emotion.

Schooled to hardship, sudden storms and 'acts of God' their lot was to accept the loss of both men and ships during the span of their working lives. Living with the constant reality of death had made them tight-lipped and stoic.

Now the charge of collective, unspoken feelings running among the sailors brought a lump to King's throat. 'I'm bloody proud of you all,' he muttered. 'Good men and true… '

A crooked smile lit up his face, '…except when you're roaring drunk, in the grip of rum, or fighting over women, of course.'

Just then, a voice broke into song, removing the immediate need for words. Henry Ogle, the young immigrant farmer from Yorkshire turned survivor, began to sing in a fine tenor voice.

King, the more emotional of the officers present, blinked rapidly several times in succession.

The loud screeching of a troupe of baboons came from the shore. The grunting of hippos sunbathing on a nearby island answered them. It was as if a spell had been broken. Amid much coughing and clearing of throats, Powell moved to Farewell's side and spoke quietly.

'Well, Mr Farewell sir, what was it old Joe said about bein' all the sweeter, for the waiting?'

Francis Farewell nodded absently. Removing his monocle, he cleaned it with a handkerchief pulled from the pocket of his salt-stained jacket. His mind was already racing, occupied with details and the outlining of plans for the next stage of the expedition.

Swivelling the eye-glass into his eye, he executed a slow turn around the deck. Taking in the wide sweep of the bay from north to south, east to west, he measured and calculated as he went. This was what had beckoned to him from across the rail of the ill-fated *Fame*; this was what had led him to abandon his business in India and take an abrupt and different turning in life.

What he saw before him was more, much more than he had ever anticipated. Not only had they found a wide river mouth, he had been handed a much greater prize, a bay large enough for a whole naval fleet – several fleets, if necessary, to find safe anchorage.

In spite of the overlying birdsong and the grunting of hippos sunbathing on the sand banks, the silence was profound. Not only was this a wide, natural harbour, fresh-water streams were there in abundance, also good timber for felling, and, he was sure, an abundance of game in the hinterland.

Farewell drew in a deep breath of satisfaction. All the necessary commodities were in place, and its potential was staggering. Straightening his shoulders, he clasped his hands behind his back and began to pace the deck.

Here it was; theirs for the taking. Initially, Farewell and Company would establish a base and then make contact with the Zulu king, Shaka. They would be the sole company to arrange trade terms with him regarding the superb tusks of ivory. But that was not all.

There would also be subsidiary products such as animal hides, timber and sisal, not to mention the inevitable commerce that usually sprang up with the establishment of a new colony.

The ivory, along with the other by-products, would provide so lucrative a market that investors from far and wide would fight with one another for the privilege of doing business with them.

As if in a dream, Francis Farewell heard the order for the anchor to be dropped and the cable run out. The ship's boat creaked in the davits as it swung out and was lowered into the water.

From long habit, his fingers moved automatically to his eye-glass. He removed it, polished it, before placing it carefully in his breast pocket.

Who knows just how grateful the Crown might be to someone enterprising enough to raise the British flag over the country Vasco da Gama had once christened Natal, in honour of Christ's birthday?

Only time would tell.

Up on the headland, Langani watched the party of white men step out of the small boat and on to the soil of Zululand. His eyes were fixed on the figures of the two men in the lead.

Even though they were some distance away, he identified the taller of the two as Farewell, the other as Kingi, the man who had saved Jakot's life and helped free him from Robben Island.

Yebo, I know who you are, he thought, staring at him, for have I not seen you before, several times? The streaks of silver in your hair mark you out, just as I knew they would.

Langani was exhausted, his eyes red-rimmed and weary. Deep grooves of fatigue were carved from his nose to his chin, and the white chalk-like daubings on his face and body were streaked with sweat and effort.

He sighed, a deep sound of regret and weariness. 'I was not strong enough to stop you entering my land,' he said aloud, 'because I am only a man, and not a god. But I am glad I did not allow the ocean to take you and your vessel, as I well could have. It is not my way to crush and kill, even though I do not like the reasons you have come here.'

He looked down at the figures spilling out of the small boat. Then he added, 'Be warned, though, there are other ways to stop you besides killing you.'

The diviner allowed the screen of leaves to fall back into place, blotting out the sight of the ship lying at anchor in the bay of iThekwini.

The men of the sea would not stay long. Not this time. But they would be back – of that he was sure.

Part IV

Thirty-one

May 1824. Cape Town

A white drift of cloud spiralled over the flat-topped massif dominating the city. Within moments, the legendary 'tablecloth' had rolled down to cloak the rocky buttresses and lower slopes of the mountain with swirling banks of mist.

The tall youth stepping briskly along the waterfront glanced up at the cloud-covered heights of Table Mountain. A frown crossed his broad, sun-tanned face when he noticed the golden light change to grey.

'I hope this isn't a warning from the old gods for me not to try to go north again,' he muttered, resisting the temptation to cross himself. Some things die hard, even with a reprobate like me, he thought.

It had been the best part of a year since Henry Fynn had returned to Cape Town after his adventures on the River Maphuta. Unfortunately, his plans to finance a foray into Zululand had moved forward not one jot. Every avenue to find work, or a way north, seemed closed to him.

Having heard that his old friend, Harry Nourse was back in town, he was on his his way to the Company's offices on the waterfront, hoping beyond hope that the answer he was looking for might conceivably be within his grasp.

Before entering the imposing doorway marked 'Nourse and Sons, Shipping Merchants,' he surreptitiously rubbed the toes of his shabby boots against his trouser legs and ran a hand through his mop of brown hair

Pausing for a moment with his hand on the polished brass door knob, he put up a silent prayer. 'Come up trumps, Harry old boy, there's a lad,' he breathed.

Turning the knob, he opened the door and stepped inside.

Ten minutes later, an impatient Fynn was pacing the well-polished parquet floor, his hands clasped behind his back. His friend Harry peered at him over his gold-rimmed spectacles, 'Sorry, Fynn old boy.'

Fynn let out a sigh of exasperation and batted the apology away.

'What else can I tell you?'Harry Nourse repeated.' Trade's poor just now. The usual storms, onset of winter, you know how it is. Vessels need caulking, the rudders and steering overhauled, sheets and cordage replaced, before we can even think of another voyage. The Wild Coast's no place to be with leaking seams and rudder off the true, I can tell you.'

Thrusting his fists into his trouser pockets, Fynn exhaled sharply, 'I know, old friend. It's just that I'm looking to find a way north again – and pretty damn quick, at that.'

Harry looked up from the ledger. Carefully, he removed his glasses and pinched the bridge of his bony nose between thumb and forefinger. 'You're hiding something, Fynn.' he said, peering myopically at him. 'Why don't you just spit it out, save us both time and energy?'

Watching the tell-tale flush spread across Fynn's face, his eyebrows lifted a few notches higher. 'Must be something damn interesting up there to get you so fizzed up.'

The corners of his mouth quirked in a sly grin as he crowed, 'It's a woman! Don't tell me Cupid's arrows have stung you, Fynn! If so, it's damn bad luck the lady in question lives up there, while you, dear boy, happen to be almost permanently confined to the Cape!'

Fynn slapped his hand against his forehead in exasperation. 'Don't be bloody daft, Nourse. If it'd just been a woman, I'd have stayed up there a mite longer and worked my passage back after the notion had worn off.'

Harry stood up and flexed his bony fingers. The joints cracked alarmingly. A full head and a half shorter than Fynn, he had to restrain himself from standing on tip-toe to look him squarely in the eye. 'So if it's not a woman, what is it then? What are ye scheming this time, Henry, me old Cockney sparrow?'

Fynn gazed down at him speculatively. Harry was only a couple of years older than he was. But with a father who was the owner of the Nourse Company, his financially secure future was a far cry from his own prospects.

Surely, a good trading opportunity would be of interest to an astute businessman like Nourse Senior, he thought. Should I take a chance and tell Harry what I have in mind?

A moment later, he found himself spilling it all out, his discovery of the magnificent ivory, his futile searching for the amaZulu, the fever pit, the possibilities, his hopes and dreams...

After he'd finished, he paused to draw breath. Glancing over in Harry's direction, his heart sank. The junior Nourse had the look of a stunned rabbit about him. A drop of sweat trickled down his forehead and disappeared into the pristine, starched collar of his sober business suit.

Fynn eyed him impatiently. 'Well, what d' you think? Might your father be interested in such a scheme? I've no money, of course, but I'm willing to pitch in with what skills I've got.'

Harry, having at last regained the use of his vocal cords, croaked, 'Which are, of course? Remind me?' Fynn picked up the broad-nibbed pen Harry had laid down, and examined the tip for a moment.

'Well,' he replied, squaring his shoulders. 'I learned a lot in my years on the frontier. Rub along with the natives all right, can track with the best of them, days and nights on end, do a spot o' night hunting as well, can ride like the wind and live off the land if needs be.'

Shooting a quizzical look at the unimpressed Harry, he pushed his credentials to the limit. 'I've picked up a few of the native lingos, can handle firearms, shoot straight standing up or from the saddle, oh, yes, and I've a fair knowledge of native medicines. I can also lay out a corpse, splint a broken leg or arm, stitch up a wound, deliver a baby, treat scabies, ringworm, and the pox... '

Stopping only to draw a ragged breath, he roared out, 'So what the hell else d'ye want, ye ink-stained little fart?'

Harry Nourse subsided into his high-backed leather chair like a suddenly deflating balloon. He swallowed quickly, then said, 'All in all, Fynn, you're a pretty handy fellow to have at hand. Nobody's denying that. But, as far as I can see, there's only one thing wrong with your thinking.'

Fynn blinked rapidly, his mind racing as he back-tracked, looking for a chink in his plan. Before he could open his mouth, Harry said, 'Fynn old boy, you've been out in the *bundu* for too long. Jesus, man – are you out of your mind? There's plenty of trade to be had here in the Colony. Why risk your neck up there in unexplored territory? All you'll get for your pains is probably a spear in the back, or worse.'

Fynn gazed at him, thunderstruck.

Harry rose out of the chair. 'Don't be an arse, Fynn, stick to the Colony. I ask you – who in hell's going to spend good money chasing after some native chief's elephant tusks – and this man's not just any old native chief, if I've heard you correctly. These Zulu fellas, I'd steer a wide berth clear of them if I were you. Bloody madness, if you ask me!'

With Nourse's sarcastic parting shot and his own colourful response ringing in his ears, Fynn bolted out of the door of the shipping office and almost cannoned into a tall, fair-haired man striding along the cobbled quayside.

Fynn found his elbow held fast in a steely grip. A voice said, 'Stand fast there, lad! Where's the fire?'

Momentarily distracted by the gleam of the gold monocle in the man's eye, and the faint aroma of bay rum, the apology froze on Fynn's lips. The eye-glass looks familiar, he thought. Where in hell have I seen it before?

Recovering his wits, Fynn mumbled hasty apologies. The hand gripping his elbow loosened its hold, only to steer him out of the path of a dray horse pulling a cart laden with barrels. A rich aroma of leaked red wine lingered on the air as it swerved round them.

Fynn's eyes took in the tall man's neatly-trimmed beard and moustaches, the dark blue naval jacket, polished brass buttons and leather boots. A quick flash of memory restored what he'd been searching for.

Of course! About a year ago, HMS *Leven*, the flagship belonging to a fleet of Royal Navy warships had been berthed at Cape Town. A party had been arranged to welcome its Commander, Captain Owen and a contingent of British officers. Fynn had managed to wangle an invitation, through Harry Nourse.

Looking at the fair-haired man more closely, he was sure he'd been introduced to him on that occasion. *But his name – what was it, again?*

As if on cue, the tall man supplied it. Regarding Fynn quizzically through the eye-glass, he said. 'My name's Farewell. Lieutenant Francis Farewell.'

His pale blue eyes scanned Fynn's face. 'Haven't we met before? I seem to remember you from somewhere.'

This time it was Fynn who supplied the information. 'Last year, February, I think it was, at a party aboard HMS *Leven*. Just before I left for Delagoa.'

A spark of interest flared in Farewell's eyes. 'Delagoa, eh? What were you doing up there, if I might make so bold?'

'I took on a berth as supercargo,' Fynn explained, 'but my real interest was in seeking out trading opportunities,' he added bluntly, pressing his lips into a tight line. Nourse's attempt to throw cold water on his ideas still rankled.

'And did you find what you were looking for?' Fynn sensed the question was not quite as casual as it seemed. He snorted, a sour knot of resentment rising in his throat. 'Well, just let's say that "finding" is one thing, "carrying out" is quite another,' he retorted.

The pale blue eyes roved over him, taking in his frayed trousers and shabby but presentable brown leather boots.

'Quite,' replied Lieutenant Farewell, thoughtfully. He seemed to have made up his mind about something, for he touched Fynn lightly on the shoulder.

'Look,' he said, amiably. 'My ship, the *Salisbury,* is lying just along the quayside. It's where I'm headed now. If you've time to spare, I think it might be to your advantage, Henry Fynn, if we had a little heart-to-heart about Delagoa and trading opportunities.'

It was almost sundown by the time Fynn eventually trooped back down the gangplank of the *Salisbury.* Waiting until he was clear of the vessel, the nineteen-year-old took an exuberant leap into the air, scattering seabirds and sending them squawking skyward.

'Yes! Yes!' he hissed, punching the air with his fist. Always a believer in the guiding hand of fate, Henry Fynn needed no further convincing.

From failure to success in the space of an hour or two! From the reactions of Harry, the hidebound, junior scion of the Nourse Trading Company to a full-blown offer of a contract by a man who had been there, seen what he had seen, and shared both the enthusiasm and the sense of adventure that were essential ingredients of the whole affair.

Fuelled by half a bottle of best claret and a substantial quantity of Cape 'smoke,' Fynn's excitement bubbled up again as he pondered on the steely determination of the man he had just met.

Lieutenant Francis George Farewell RN – an authentic English naval hero, a man of substance, good breeding and experience. Wounded in action, he'd been mentioned in dispatches for gallantry during the Napoleonic wars. This was no indecisive soul, craving only a desk and a safe billet. Here was a man, who, like himself, had laid eyes on the superb ivory tusks while en route to the Cape.

Fynn slanted a glance up at the shrouded bulk of the flat-topped mountain. The molten ball of the setting sun was sinking slowly beyond the western horizon, the shadows changing to hues of grey and black. All over the town twinkling lights sparkled like tiny fireflies in the dusk.

What a day it had turned out to be!

Fynn's heart gave another lurch, and he had difficulty controlling himself from turning cart-wheels along the quayside. Whistling loudly as he went, he considered stepping into one of the nearby alehouses to toast his good fortune with another glass or two of Cape 'smoke.' Already done that, he thought, grinning. Any more, an' I swear I'll take wings an' fly.

After discussing terms and shaking hands on it, Farewell had opened a bottle of best claret to toast the venture.

Fynn was to be overall manager of the project, seeing to the practical aspects; hiring workers, erecting suitable accommodation, responsible for supplies of food and the general running of the settlement Farewell intended to establish. And where was this settlement to be?

Farewell had thrown his head back and roared with laughter, 'Zululand, of course! Where in the hell else do you think it would be?'

Tears of merriment glinted in his eyes. 'Oh, didn't I tell you, Henry? When we were completing the survey of the coastline, we came across the ideal place to start our venture. You'll see what I mean when we get there.'

When Farewell went on to describe how a series of unrelated happenings had totally changed the course of his life, Fynn had absolutely no difficulty in believing him.

'The decision as to whether I should remain in Africa or return to England was taken out of my hands,' Francis Farewell had said ruefully, looking at Fynn over his glass of claret.

'And it cost me a good ship. Before we were even out of sight of Cape Town, a storm blew up, and the bloody vessel was driven on to the rocks at Sea Point. I was one of the few survivors. After spending hours clinging to the rocks, a fishing-smack came by, and brought me ashore.'

Fynn's mind was spinning, and not only with the effects of the claret. And he'd thought he was the one Fate had in its clutches!

In his case, it had been a buff-coloured one-way ticket to Africa, paid for by his father; a routine visit to an official's office in Portuguese East Africa, followed by an indeterminate period dangling between one world and the next in the fever pit of a befeathered medicine man.

Farewell went on: 'I arrived dripping wet and wrapped in blankets, on the doorstep of one Johann Lodewyk Petersen, the owner of a hotel near the Adderley Street Gardens.'

He raised his glass in mocking salute. 'Once again, Lady Luck took a hand in my affairs – for the third time in one night, I may say.' Farewell laughed.

'Two months later, I married Elizabeth, Petersen's step-daughter. After a bit of humming and hawing, the old man's extremely keen on investing, though he insists on seeing Zululand for himself first. A few other investors will be making the trip with me.'

He had also thrown in his lot with Lieutenant James Saunders King, also former British Navy, from Nova Scotia, whom he had met while on a trip to South America to raise funds for the venture. King, who was now his partner, was currently in England, consulting with the Admiralty and trying to raise funds.

For Fynn, it all suddenly clicked into place. James King was the tall, sun-tanned officer with the deep blue eyes he'd noticed deep in conversation with the said Captain Owen who'd been about to conduct a survey of the coast between Algoa Bay and Portuguese territory.

Two things about the man had stood out in Fynn's mind. The first had been the streak of prematurely silver hair sweeping back off the man's brow, in sharp contrast to the rest of his jet black hair. The second had been his accent, the Yankee drawl that tended to break through at times.

Fynn closed his eyes. He knew, deep in his bones, that the trading adventure he was about to set out on would prove to be no ordinary run-of- the-mill scheme.

Although Farewell and King had been drawn here from different parts of the globe, one from India, the other from North America, the one thing they all had in common was their desire to play their part in the great, life-changing adventure that was about to begin.

But why did he have the uncanny feeling that more than their fortunes would change because of it? Once the door to Zululand was open it might be almost impossible to close it again...

Thirty-two

Shaka and his military commanders stood on the banks of the Tugela River and watched as the *impis* began to cross to the other side, wending their way around the debris brought down by earlier floods: bleached skeletons of dead trees and bushes and the odd hut, with here and there the dull gleam of animal bones among the detritus.

The sky was blue and crystal clear, the air cold even though the sun was almost directly overhead. Even with their battle decorations pared to a minimum, Shaka's warriors were impressive, deadly-looking and very fit

Wave after wave of his elite regiments poured across the river, invincible and unstoppable, the water reaching only to waist level.

Holding their weapons and rolled up-shields above their heads, the regiments moved on and over; the Zimazane and the Kwenkwe, the Kwembu, Fosisaq, Folozi, the Dabankulu and many others advancing in waves of gleaming black flesh, whooping, yelling and singing as they came. Adding to the din were the raucous cries and shrill whistling of the *udibi* boys as they urged the bawling, long-horned cattle into the water.

Shaka viewed his troops with a critical eye. Long enough in the sweet pastures, he thought, now it is time to meet the challenges of the battlefield again.

This would be the first major campaign where he would not be fighting alongside them in the thick of battle. His commanders Mgobozi and Mdlaka were more than capable of taking command and leading them against Faku and the amaPondo.

He looked across the river and then beyond to where the long white beaches met the horizon. A pang of regret hit him. By rights, he should be going with them, leading his warriors and rejoicing with them at the moment of victory – but other matters had become increasingly important.

What the Xhosa, Hlambamanzi, had told him about the people of King George had given him much to think about. And he needed time for that – time to consider, to plan ahead.

For the last few months, his warriors had been restless, straining against prolonged inactivity. Long night marches and bouts of hard training only went part of the way in curbing their dissatisfaction. The lack of battles to fight, with no victors' bounties of raided cattle to sweeten life, tended to make soldiers lazy, drunken, and prone to in-fighting. The coming campaign would take them further south than they had ever ranged before, possibly to the Mzimkulu River or even as far south as the umZimvubu.

Shaka glanced skyward. Tonight there would be a full moon, the best time for launching a new campaign. It might take three full moons or even more to accomplish victory over the amaPondo and return. The journey alone would undoubtedly be long, hard and through difficult territory-but he had no doubt that the campaign would be successful

Faku, the amaPondo chief, must submit to Zulu authority.

He, Shaka, would brook no refusal, no matter how far away the lands of the amaPondo lay, no matter how many battles the *impis* would have to fight -or how far Faku and his army might run.

Thirty-three

Fynn felt his hands tremble as they gripped the rail of the *Julia*. He could hardly believe they were here at last, with Zululand in sight, and preparing to step ashore.

Shimmering in the early heat haze, the coast lay balanced in perfect symmetry between sky and sea, the white sands and lush vegetation in vivid contrast to the indigo and turquoise of the Indian Ocean.

His eyes swept the foreground until he found what he was looking for. There it was, just as Farewell had described it, a tall, wooded headland rising out of the sea to port. A wave of excitement uncurled in his belly.

The bluff marked the entrance to the narrow channel Farewell and James King had accidentally discovered the year before. During a storm, the *Julia* had been swept in over the deadly sandbanks guarding the entrance, and only by the skills of the captain and the sheerest fluke, had both vessel and crew survived.

'Thank God, the weather's clear and the sea is fairly calm today,'

Fynn said, watching the surf surge against the rocks at the foot of the headland.

'Looks innocent enough, don't it?' said a voice at his shoulder. 'But don't 'ee be fooled by it or anything else on this damn coast. The weather can shift in the time it takes a rat to scuttle up on deck.'

The broad Yorkshire accent was unmistakable. Fynn turned round, a smile on his face.

A dark-haired, ruddy-faced lad about his own age, Henry Ogle was one of the men he'd chosen to go ashore with him as part of the advance party. The others were Otto, a Prussian engineer, and a silent Frenchman, known only as Dupres.

'Heard about the rough passage you had last time round,' Fynn said, 'same vessel, wasn't it?'

Ogle nodded and whistled through his teeth. 'My stars, but that was a ride and a half! But we made it, thanks to the Almighty an' Cap'n Garrett.' He darted a nervous glance seawards. 'I hope to God we get through safely this time.'

Twenty-year-old Ogle had already survived the hardships and dangers of life on the Cape frontier, much as Fynn had. His family had been among the four thousand or so settlers brought out from England by Sir Charles Somerset. After his father died, his mother and the rest of the family had retreated south to the safety of the Cape.

The *Julia* slowed to a virtual crawl. Her bows carved silently through the water as she made her way towards the narrow channel. The helmsman in the bows began to call out the draught of water below the keel, first in fathoms and then in feet.

Fynn peered over the rail. Below the surface of the rippling green water, he could make out the outline of the sand banks beneath. Ribbed and greyish in colour, the result of centuries of silt washed down from the surrounding hills, they reminded him of the monstrous sleeping beasts of childhood nightmares.

Gradually, the Julia forged ahead and began to pick up speed. A grunt of relief came from Henry Ogle. 'Safe through, thank God,' he muttered.

Otto and Dupres came forward to join them at the rail. The plan was for the four of them to go ashore, unload the supplies, tools and necessities from the *Julia* and make a start on the construction of suitable living quarters before Farewell and his investors arrived in a few weeks.

The German, Otto, let out a gasp of amazement. 'Mein Gott!'

Fynn's head swivelled round. He stared about him. A wide and beautiful lagoon was opening out before them. Its waters were as calm as a millpond, only a light breeze ruffling the surface. The roar of the surf beyond the fearsome barriers of sand seemed muted and distant.

Guarded by the high forested bluff on one side, and a long, narrow spit of sand on the other, the bay was surrounded by gently rising hills, smooth and green against the vivid blues of the lagoon.

'Quite a sight, ain't it?' Ogle muttered, 'a slice of paradise and no mistake.'

Captain Garrett, a stocky, grey-haired man in his fifties, handed over the wheel to the mate then pulled out his tobacco pouch and pipe. Slipping the stem of the pipe into his mouth, he said, 'Well, Fynn me lad. Here we are, then. Some berth, eh?'

Fynn could only nod in agreement. The lagoon was so wide he could make no useful guess as to its actual size. At least a few miles across, he thought, amazed. You could hide whole fleets of ships in here, by God!

He watched the verdant shore come closer. This must been even more than Farewell had hoped and dreamed of during the long months of back-breaking effort trying to find a toehold on the dangerous coast. It was also what had sent his partner scurrying off to London to raise funds for the venture.

He thought about what the coming days and weeks would bring. According to Farewell's instructions, they would first establish a base and then try to make contact with the Zulu king, Shaka.

Farewell's ambitious plan was to own the company that would be on direct trading terms with the monarch. Handling not only the export of the ivory, it would also control their price at auction as well as earning a substantial commission on the sale.

Although Farewell had not referred directly to any of the risks incurred in breaching Zulu territory, Henry Fynn hadn't forgotten the terror he'd seen in the eyes of the poor devils around the campfires not so far north of here, at the mere mention of the warrior king's name.

Careful not to be seen as setting himself up as an expert on African matters and risk scuppering his chances of future employment, Fynn had, just once, posed a mild question on the subject to the ex-Naval war hero who was his employer.

'What do you reckon our chances are of getting an opportunity to trade with this chief, Shaka?' He'd almost added '... *before we're speared to death,*' but had refrained from doing so.

Wisely, as it turned out, because the former lieutenant had obviously given no heed whatsoever to the rumours he'd heard concerning the reputation of the Zulu warrior king.

'Excellent, Fynn, our chances are excellent,' he'd rapped out, his blue eyes daring the more experienced Fynn to disagree with him.

'I've had plenty of dealings with natives in India,' he said, squaring his shoulders. 'Most of these chaps respect authority. Act accordingly. Show no weakness, that's the best way forward.'

Fynn wisely said nothing, though his heart sank somewhat at such cavalier sentiments.

His honest answer could well have been, 'With all due respect, sir, you could get us killed with thoughts like that! Natives, the Zulus might well be-but I can tell you now- they don't keep their brains in their arse, nor their fighting spirit!'

But again, he was silent. Why start an argument before they'd even started? Time would tell which of them was right.

As he stood looking out over the spectacular vista of hills and lagoon, Fynn's mind raced ahead, leapfrogging into the future.

Besides ivory, other subsidiary products no doubt would be found here; hides, valuable timber and hardwoods, sisal -

He drew in a sharp breath. My God, it could be such a lucrative market! Pity young Harry back in Cape Town didn't have the wits to listen to what I'd been trying to tell him.

Now he realised why Farewell had been so insistent that he order such large quantities of trade goods, everything from mirrors, beads, lengths of brightly coloured cloth, blankets, to patent medicines and trinkets of every sort.

Fynn was jerked out of his reverie by Captain Garrett bellowing out the order for the anchor to be dropped and the cables run out. A rumbling and clatter of rusty chains followed.

Shortly afterwards, the creak of the davits announced the lowering of the ship's boat. A couple of sailors shinned down to take charge of it before bringing himself, Ogle, Otto and Dupres ashore. Also going with them would be Michael Jantyi and Frederick, two native interpreters.

Captain Garrett directed a stream of tobacco juice over the side then squinted up at the sun.

'A good few hours of daylight left, still time for you to have a nose around, Fynn, before bedding down for the night. We'll stand off-shore after dark, then swing by at first light an' start ferrying ashore your supplies. With any luck, we'll be able to catch the noon tide, be on our way back by then.'

As he lowered himself into the longboat, Fynn cast a quick glance at the waiting shoreline.

Fynn old lad, he said to himself, here and now, this is where it all begins. What started in Delagoa goes on from here.

He lay awake for a long time that night with his hands behind his head, looking up at the stars and listening to the soft wash of the lagoon. He could just make out the dark bulk of the *Julia* gently swinging at anchor, a thin wash of green phosphorous rippling around her bows.

Choosing a sheltered hollow, they had pitched a tent, lit a fire and eaten the food they'd brought with them. Then, wrapped in blankets, they had settled down for the night, Ogle and the others sharing the tent, Fynn preferring to sleep below the stars.

Firelight played over the closed tent, and a gentle snoring issued from one of the dark shapes inside. Ogle, probably. An owl hooted eerily somewhere in the dense tangle of undergrowth. As if in answer, jackals and wild dogs began to howl beneath the sliver of the crescent moon suspended above the forested headland.

Fynn was restless, still not ready for sleep. Idly, he began to speculate on just how long he might expect his employment to last. Involuntarily, he grinned.

Although the stated plan had been to establish the whole project within six months, by the amount of trade goods Farewell had insisted on ferrying northwards, Fynn was positive that a much longer stay was high on the lieutenant's agenda.

Suits me fine, he thought, yawning widely. The terms of my agreement are that I'm in for a handsome percentage of profits at the end of six months. If Farewell wants to extend it for a further six, or for as many six months stints as he likes, why then, Henry Fynn will be pleased to go along with it.

Pulling the blanket over his head, he fell asleep almost immediately, well-pleased with his future prospects.

Around midnight, loud cracks of thunder split the skies. The heavens opened up. Pellets of ice-cold rain began to bounce off the ground. Within minutes, the hollow was awash with water.

'God Almighty!' swore Ogle, struggling to disentangle himself from his blankets and exit the tent. Fynn opened one eye. 'What the hell's this?' he muttered, bleary eyed.

'Rain, ye bloody fool,' yelled Ogle, trying to gather up his belongings. He launched a kick or two at the blanketed humps that were Dupres and Otto.

'*Raus*, ya dozy bastards!'

Fynn yelled out for Michael Jantyi and Frederick. 'Move your arses! Grab what you can and move to higher ground, before we're swept into the bloody lagoon!'

No sooner were the words out of his mouth than a flood of icy brown water poured down on them.

'The bastard stream's broken its banks,' he shouted through the hissing downpour. Otto and Dupres were awake, looking like half-drowned rats.

'Take what you can and make for higher ground,' he urged them. 'Keep Michael and Frederick in your sights, and make damn sure they come back down here to help you with the rest. Don't let them slope off!'

Fynn had the foresight to start rescuing what was left of the fire. Using his bare hands, he tried to scoop up as many burning branches as he could and chased after the others, yelling at Ogle to follow suit.

'If we can keep the wood dry, at least we'll have heat and light. I've a feeling we're going to need both!'

Luckily, Frederick had found a reasonably sheltered place on higher ground. In the lee of thick clumps of bamboo, it gave them some protection from the wind and slanting needles of rain.

'At least the bloody water will run downhill this time,' growled Ogle as he tried to coax the fire alight.

Eventually, they managed to huddle round the pitiful flames, keeping close to one another for shared warmth. Sleep was impossible. Hunched in their soaking blankets, they tried to keep the fire going by feeding in the dwindling remnants of dry firewood.

It was then they heard it. A maniacal howling and cackling in the darkness, a sound that made their knees turn to water. '*Mein Gott! Was ist das?*' Otto muttered, the rain dripping off the end of his nose.

Fynn's head jerked up. Peering into the murk, he saw animal eyes, gleaming in the dark, hump-backed shapes with sloping shoulders, circling ever nearer. His mouth suddenly went dry.

Hyenas! There was no mistaking the snuffling noises and the bursts of high-pitched yelping which sounded like the crazed laughter of the criminally insane. Judging by the racket, there were legions of them out there.

Fynn wiped the water from his eyes and cursed his short-sightedness in not bringing firearms ashore with them. He, of all people, should have known better. Now, all they had to defend themselves with was what they had to hand.

Throwing off his sodden blanket, he grabbed a smouldering branch from the fire. 'Don't let the bastards get behind you,' he shouted, manhandling Dupres into place behind him. 'Stand back to back an' try to fight 'em off! It's the only chance we've got. But protect your backs, for God's sake!'

Yelling and shouting like banshees, they stood their ground around the sullen fire, lashing out at the predators when they got too close.

Suddenly, Ogle gave a great bellow of rage and leapt out of the circle of firelight. 'Dammit, ye great brute!' he roared. 'Get your ugly snout away from there or I'll ram this burning stick up your arse!'

Unbelievably, one of the slavering brutes had managed to thrust its snout into one of his bags and was rooting about in it. Jerking and tugging at a pair of black leather trousers, the beast was in the throes of trying to drag them out.

In spite of the seriousness of the situation, a grin split Fynn's smoke-blackened features. Ogle had paid a fortune for the trousers in Cape Town and hardly stopped talking about them. As the hyena prepared to slink away with them clamped firmly in its slavering jaws, Ogle thrashed it across the snout with a burning stick.

'No, ye don't,' Ogle shouted, making a grab for his trousers. 'Let 'em be! There's sixty Dutch dollars in the pocket... and ye're not having either me trewsers or me money! Over my dead body, ye're not!'

The spotted hyena and Ogle were now pitched in a frenzied battle of tug of war, the hyena digging its toes in, Ogle equally determined not to let go.

Fynn let loose a bellow of laughter at the incongruous sight of man and predator fighting over a pair of trousers. Suddenly, there was a loud ripping sound, audible even over the hiss of falling rain. The trouser seams had given way!

Abruptly, the hyena, trousers and Ogle parted company. The hyena ran in one direction, one leg of the garment gripped in its jaws, while Ogle, marginally the victor, lay flat on his back clutching what was left of them. Luckily, he was able to salvage an untouched, though slightly damp, sixty-dollar note.

German Otto didn't have his troubles to seek, either. Seeing his belongings spilling out of his knapsack on to the rain-soaked ground, he knelt down to stuff them back inside. While he was squatting down, one of the hyenas darted in and grabbed him by the foot.

'*Mein toag!* My toe!' he screamed, leaping to his feet and hopping around in agony while trying to batter at the beast's head.

The normally silent Dupres, who hadn't uttered a word throughout the whole proceedings, suddenly launched into the fray.

Brandishing his blazing weapon like a sabre, shouting and cursing in indecipherable French, he slashed and parried his way through the slavering beasts, scattering the hyenas and inflicting whatever injuries he could on them until Otto's foot was freed.

After order had been restored, the men resumed their positions around the fire. Hunched back to back for safety, blankets draped round their shoulders, coughing and red-eyed from the drifting smoke, they prepared to wait out the rest of the night.

The rain continued to slant down from the skies, while the thunder continued to rumble and crack. The glinting eyes still circled, though more wary now. The men dozed intermittently until the first streaks of light began to creep in over the lagoon.

Thirty-four

Sunrise found them dishevelled, stinking of sweat and wood smoke, their eyes red-rimmed from lack of sleep and the effects of peering through drifting smoke.

Stiff as a boot, every bone in his body aching, Fynn woke to find himself still clutching a charred branch. Tossing it aside, he bent to rinse his mouth out with a handful of brackish rainwater from a fold in the tent's canvas. He yawned, groaning as he tried to flex his cramped muscles.

The overnight rain had disappeared as quickly as it had come. The sun was just clearing the horizon, a ball of fire rising out of a hazy ocean, bringing with it the promise of warmth.

Fynn filled his lungs with clean, fresh air. A surge of relief ran through him. They'd survived the first night in Zululand, unscathed – or almost.

Behind him, someone stirred and groaned. He turned to find a bedraggled Ogle crawling towards him on his hands and knees.

'Jesus, Fynn,' he moaned. 'D'you have to be up and about so damn early?' Fynn stirred the torn shirt covering Ogle's ribs with the toe of his boot.

'Up an' at 'em, Ogle old fruit,' he said, grinning down at him. 'We've got a hell of a lot to get through today. There's no way those sons o' bitches are going to catch us out another night, I tell you. They've got to learn just who's master around here.'

Ogle got to his feet and staggered off towards the beach, his bladder fit to burst. Undoing his flies, he relieved himself in the lee of a tall palm jutting over the water. As the stream of urine hit the sea, he sighed in relief. A moment later, he happened to glance idly down the beach. It was then he spotted a line of footprints in the shimmering sands, several sets of footprints to be precise.

'Fresh, too, by the looks of them,' he muttered, hastily doing up his trousers. 'Now, who in the hell are 'ee, lads – friend or foe?'

Alerting the others to the fact they'd had company, he demanded of Fynn, 'What d'you reckon? Would they be Zulus, them warlike lot you been tellin' us about, or jest a handful o' peace-lovin' natives passin' by?'

Fynn surveyed Ogle through watering, red-rimmed eyes.

'Ogle, if you're still breathing and talking through the hole you call a gob, and you ain't spread out with a spear between your ribs, then I reckon your guess is as good as mine.'

He snorted. 'In any case, even if they were the 'warlike lot', what d' you suggest we fight 'em with? We're clean out of burning branches!'

The rest of the day was spent in frantic activity. Supplies, tools and all the accoutrements for setting up camp were unloaded from the *Julia* and piled up on the sands clear of the waterline.

That included a plentiful supply of the powder, shot and firearms Fynn had omitted to bring along the day before. Thoughtfully, Fynn added a few stout billyclubs and assorted hammers and pickaxes to their personal supplies.

Ogle squinted down at the growing armoury. Raising an eyebrow, he remarked, 'Ain't takin' any chances, are you, me old mate?

We run out o' powder and shot, an' we still got a few surprises up our sleeves, eh? I like your way o' thinking.'

With help from Garret and the crew, they ferried boxes, chests and packages off the beach to the spot they'd chosen for their camp.

After setting out on a brief reconnaissance of the area, Fynn had opted for a spot a half-mile or so distant, near enough to a source of good drinking water, but far enough away to be in no danger of being flooded.

Set in a natural clearing, the site was protected from the night winds by stands of trees and thick bamboos and hidden from anyone passing casually by along the shore.

By mid-day it was hot, the sun blazing down from a cloudless sky. The four men cast off their shirts and worked stripped to the waist. Their first priority was their personal security. After the previous night's running battle with hyenas, nobody wanted to repeat the experience.

First, they constructed a stockade of stout bamboo stakes reinforced with woven lianas and plastered mud. Inside the crude fences, they erected tarpaulin tents until sturdier, more permanent accommodation could be built. Brushwood and piles of firewood were stacked high for cooking fires and night-time protection. Top priority, of course, was given to the storage and protection of their muskets, flints and powder.

At the end of the day's gruelling work, Fynn gestured to a pile of freshly-sharpened bamboo stakes.

'Just in case,' he said, with a grin. 'Don't want to waste our powder and shot unless we have to. Who knows what else might come lookin' for us in the night?' The irony of his statement was not lost on his companions.

It was Michael, one of the interpreters, who next reported signs of life. Squatting in the sand, he held up first five fingers, than another three.

A sizeable group, thought Fynn, eight to our six. He wondered briefly how good the two interpreters or Otto and Dupres would be in an all-out scrap. Just Ogle an' me, then...

Other reports followed; the turn of a heel in a muddy patch of ground, several deeply indented toe marks in the sand. Alert to every sound, they went calmly about their work. Firearms were placed discreetly at hand, ready to be snatched up at a moment's notice.

There were other signs, too, that told them they were not alone: the rustle of bushes when there was no wind; whispers, scuffling and a trigger hair's awareness of a presence nearby.

On their third day, things came to a head. One minute they were hard at work, storing the last of the supply boxes, the next Fynn let out a yell, dropped his end of the box, and took off down the beach.

A group of naked black figures burst out of the thickets and sprinted away, with Fynn racing at full pelt after them.

Head back, bare feet slapping on the wet sand, his arms and legs pumping, Fynn was slowly gaining on the last of the fleeing pack. His quarry was an older man, his wiry body and thin, stick-like legs straining with the effort of trying to escape the white devil *abelungu* pursuing him.

The others scattered in different directions and disappeared into the tangled undergrowth. A look of sheer terror was stamped on the little man's wizened face as Fynn gained on him.

Fynn threw himself forward. Catching the man round the middle, he brought him down on the sand in a flying tackle. Turning him over on to his back, he sat astride his chest, and kept him pinned down. Then, shushing him like he would a child, he began to speak to his petrified victim in every dialect and tribal tongue he knew, in an attempt to find common ground.

Fynn's linguistic skills eventually paid off. Five minutes later, he got off the man's chest and gestured for him to sit up. They then moved off into the shade and sat cross-legged, deep in conversation.

The wiry old man pointed up the beach, indicating some-where distant. Shaking his head, his hands fluttered helplessly as he tried to explain something. Half an hour later, keeping a firm hand on the little man's shoulder, Fynn strolled back down the beach.

Giving him a re-assuring little nudge towards the others he said, 'This here's Mahamba. Skinny little devil, ain't he?'

The corners of Mahamba's mouth lifted in a nervous grin, displaying his few remaining teeth. Unblinking, he scanned each strange white face in turn.

His most suspicious stares, however, were reserved for the interpreters. Their yellowish skins and slanting eyes seemed to unleash a strange kind of hostility in him, much as a dog would eye up an intruder while deciding whether to merely bare its teeth or leap for the throat.

Ogle commented on the man's wizened limbs, caved-in belly and the many scars and cicatrices criss-crossing the leathery body.

'He's from the amaTuli, the tribe who live around the bay,' Fynn explained. 'Poor devils, they're terrified of their own shadows. Lost all their cattle and crops to the Zulus, now they're reduced to keeping out of sight and scratching a living by fishing, petrified in case they come back.'

Fynn chuckled. 'He must have thought his last moment had come when a *silwane* got him, fair and square. Just so you know, that's what they think white men are – *silwane*, white sea-slugs. It's what all the yellin' was about, thought I was going to drag him off into the sea. After a bit, he quietened down and we managed to winkle out the lingo an' get the drift of things.'

'Sea slugs, you say?' sniffed Ogle, feigning offence. The German looked blankly from one to the other, not understanding, while the Dane kept his usual silence.

Ogle looked up and said quietly, 'What else did he tell you, Fynn?'

Fynn's gaze was impenetrable as he met Ogle's. 'I take it you mean the Zulus – and their king, in particular?'

'Who else?' retorted the man from Yorkshire. 'We might be sittin' in a nest o' vipers for all we know, an' not realise it till we wake up an' find our throats slit from ear to ear. What did 'ee have to say on the subject of that there king?'

Fynn shot him a keen look. 'Not much, since he's never set eyes on him. To them, Shaka is part god, part devil, somebody to be avoided at all costs.' All I could get out of Mahamba was that the Zulus lived to the north, by his reckoning about ten or fifteen days' trek. That could be anything up to a hundred, maybe a hundred an' fifty miles away.'

'Thanks be to the good God,' the Dane broke in, breaking his self-imposed code of silence

'Amen to that,' added Ogle, nodding his thatch of black hair.

Next day, after recruiting some of the amaTuli to help with the construction of decent-sized huts, Fynn set out with Mahamba and the interpreters to explore a section of the coast beyond the bay. Striking out north, they kept to the sands to avoid any predators that might be lurking in the dense thickets fringing the beach.

Keeping the high rolling breakers of the Indian Ocean on his right, Fynn strode out in good humour, whistling as he went. Mahamba pattered along beside him, while Jantyi Michael and Frederick brought up the rear, carrying food, water and cooking utensils.

'At least, on the sands, with a long beach like this, a man can see what's comin' from a good way off,' Fynn said aloud, and to no one in particular.

The only trouble with his statement was that in the end, it didn't turn out to be quite like that.

After an hour or two, they came to a wide river mouth fringed with dense mangrove swamps and tangled vegetation. The rains must have petered out earlier, because the water levels were low.

Sluggish streams of brackish water swirled round submerged

roots and the whitened, skeletal remains of uprooted trees and matted vegetation. Among the tangle of debris were the remnants of huts swept away by floods and the yellowing rib cages and horns of drowned animals.

Mahamba gestured towards a spot about a hundred yards upstream. Several scaly crocodiles lay sunbathing on the mud flats. Keeping a wary eye on the reptiles, Fynn asked, 'What is the name of this river, *baba?*'

'It is called Umgheni.'

A mile or so further on, Fynn took off his hat and mopped his brow. Glancing up, he saw that the sun was climbing towards noon. 'Time to brew up some coffee, I reckon,' he directed at Michael. 'Bit of a sit-down wouldn't come amiss.'

Pointing to a hollow in the sand dunes, he said. 'Best to light the fire back there, *mdodo*, out of the wind.'

Fynn took his pipe and tobacco from the pouch around his neck. After finding a spot on the dunes, he sat down. Once the tricky operation of trying to get his pipe going was accomplished, he inhaled deeply, the burr of the tobacco a welcome taste at the back of his throat.

Shortly afterwards, the aroma of brewing coffee began to waft towards him. This is the life, he thought, preparing to lie back on the warm sand. Idly, he glanced down the beach, back the way they'd come. What he saw made his blood freeze in his veins, and for a split second, he thought his heart had stopped beating.

A great body of men was advancing down the beach towards him, a virtual river of black bodies which seemed to ebb and flow, changing shape as it came.

The pipe slipped from his nerveless fingers in a shower of sparks and burning flecks of tobacco. The wind caught them up and scattered them across the sands.

Transfixed, Fynn stared at the long, winding columns of armed men. Here and there, he could make out the glint of spears and the toss of streaming war-feathers. The closer they came, the more terrifying they were.

Shading his eyes, he squinted down the length of the curved beach. Frantically, he searched for the end of the column – only to find there didn't seem to be one.

Their sheer physical presence was frightening enough, but it was the sound emanating from the terrifying entity that made Fynn's hair literally stand on end. It was like an earthy, growling purr issuing from the throat of a single, great beast. 'Holy Mary, Mother of God,' Fynn whispered. 'It's Shaka's army…an' I think they're singing!'

Superstitious fear clutched at him. Hurriedly, he retrieved his pipe and tobacco and stuffed them back into the pouch.

Just then, Michael, closely followed by Frederick and Mahamba, chattering and laughing, appeared from the hollow in the dunes, carrying a pot of coffee and several tin cups.

On catching sight of Fynn's rigid body, their eyes looked beyond him to the beach. A strangled cry issued from Michael Jantyi. The pot of boiling coffee dropped from his hands, the tin mugs clinking as they rolled away in the sand. The smell of hot coffee hit Fynn's nostrils. Mahamba began to whimper in distress. The three natives looked as if they were about to bolt.

'Don't you bloody well run, you bastards,' Fynn hissed from the corner of his mouth. 'Stand your ground!'

Against a background of vivid blue sea and sky, the mass of black bodies came on and on, spears bristling like the spines in a porcupine's back, their head-feathers tossing in the wind. The army of the Zulus, flowing back for as far as the eye could see, looking as if they could march for all of eternity.

Nearer still, and Fynn could hear the clink of their weapons and the shuffle and slap of their bare feet on the wet sand. Fynn and his men stood like petrified stone, unable to move, mesmerised by what was advancing up the beach towards them.

A loud hissing as if from a thousand bees told him they'd been spotted. The front ranks stopped dead in their tracks. Shouted commands echoed back down the column and were in turn passed further down the line. The long snake of Shaka's army began to slow down and then come to a halt.

For a brief space of time, there was a deep, thunderstruck silence, broken only by the crash of the surf, the cries of the wheeling sea birds and the shuffle of bare feet on the wet sand.

A trickle of sweat ran down Fynn's face. Feeling as vulnerable as a butterfly pinned to a collector's board, he restrained the impulse to wipe it away. Beside him, Michael's body trembled uncontrollably, as if with a fever.

Oh God, Fynn thought, his heart thumping wildly. What about Ogle and the others?

One of the Zulu leaders stepped forward. Tall and well built, he stood easily on the dry sand a few yards away, his bare feet slightly apart, a short spear held loosely by his side. His black eyes flickered briefly over the light-skinned men from the Cape then came to rest on Henry Fynn.

Fynn straightened up and slowly removed his hat. The warrior leader took a few steps closer. Frederick moaned in his throat and mumbled something in his own language.

The wind from the sea stirred the black and white ostrich plumes in the warrior's head dress. Below the circlet of leopard skin, his face was impassive, his eyes watchful. Sweat oiled the dark skin, distorting the streaks of war paint daubed on his cheeks and forehead.

Half-healed scars were clearly visible below the leopard skin cape and the profusion of animal claw and tooth necklaces around his neck, more angry wounds on the shoulder and a deep slash on his upper arm. Flies buzzed round the drops of blood oozing from it, delicately touching and probing.

Fynn's eyes travelled briefly over the warrior's ox-hide shield. It was almost pure white, with only a few tufts of black hair to mar its purity. Spatters and gobbets of blood turned to dull rust were dried hard into it, mute testimony to battles fought and won.

The *induna's* second-in-command slipped like a shadow into place beside him. From below the feathered head dress, piercing eyes with undisguised hostility in them raked over the strangers, while the long fringes of animal hair around the man's upper arms ruffled in the hot wind coming off the sea.

Fynn decided to take the initiative. To do nothing might be taken as a sign of submission, capitulation. Gripping Frederick by the elbow, he propelled him forward. 'Listen to me, man,' he hissed in his ear,'for God's sake, just do as I tell you. Never mind your whimpering, that'll only get us killed.'

His fingers dug into Frederick's elbow and squeezed it hard to make his point. 'We've travelled from a distant land to meet your king. We have many important things to tell Shaka of the Zulus. We need you to take us to him.'

A strangled croaking came from Michael Jantyi, the second interpreter, at this dangerous new move. Mahamba of the amaTuli seemed to have shrivelled into himself, resembling nothing more than a wizened old turtle, his eyes unblinking, rigid with fear.

Fynn repeated the same message over and again, keeping his eyes firmly on the leading warrior, trying to gauge what his reactions might be, as he desperately willed Frederick to convey his words accurately.

The odour of the *induna's* sweat, the animal fats and oils on his skin tinged with the unmistakable coppery taint of blood, assailed Fynn's nostrils. The eyes that surveyed him were bloodshot, the pupils narrowed to pinpoints against the glare of sunlight.

Fynn plastered a smile to his face, hoping beyond hope that the universal sign of goodwill also prevailed in the land of the Zulus.

With a hint of impatience, the leader raised his muscled forearm and drew his hand across his throat.

Fynn stared helplessly at the cracked nail on the man's thumb, the strength leaving his knees. Is this how it's going to end, he thought, with the blade of an assegai across the throat, my life-blood pumping on to the sands?

A flurry of movement nearby was followed by a strangled yell of fear. The interpreters, closely followed by the amaTuli, had taken to their heels and were hot-footing it across the sand, their legs pumping madly as they headed for the bush.

He flinched, expecting to hear the thrum of spears going past his head and the dull thud of blades entering flesh. He tensed, waiting for it.

Nothing happened. Only the scuffling of departing feet in the sand and the frantic rasping of breath as his men fled. A gobbet of spit from the Zulu *induna's* mouth hit the sand behind them in mute contempt.

Now he was alone on the beach, facing the battle-scarred leaders of the twenty-thousand-strong Zulu army. He stared into the *induna's* face, the pounding of his heart threatening to cut off his breath. Oddly enough, he was no longer afraid. If all else fails, Fynn, he told himself, just try and see each setback as another opportunity…

And so he went on repeating that he wished to meet Shaka, their King, and that it was very important that he be taken to him. He said the same thing over and over again; first in English, then in every tribal dialect and tongue he could think of.

The *induna's* black eyes bored into his. Once again, he drew his thumb across his throat. This time, however, his eyes were fixed on something around Fynn's neck. Instinctively, his hand went to his throat.

A wave of relief swamped him. He had totally misinterpreted the man's gesture! Instead of a precursor to cutting his throat, the *induna's* sole interest had been in the strings of beads he was wearing.

Hastily, Fynn's eyes searched for the pouch he'd dropped in the sand. Retrieving it, he frantically rummaged about inside. Dragging out strings of beads, he held a handful out to the *induna*. In an instant, everything changed.

The fearsome, war-painted faces split into smiles of delight. After accepting the beads graciously, the two leaders draped them round their necks and took turns in admiring each other.

Fynn's equilibrium returned. The look on their faces when they heard their King's name hadn't escaped Fynn. The shock of hearing it from the lips of the *abelungu*, the white man, had been absolute. Much discussion and nodding of feathered heads took place before the more senior of the *indunas* turned back to him.

By the man's gestures, Fynn took it they wanted him to wait, to stay where he was. Their body, hand and eye signals made two things very clear.

The first was that they had many days' march ahead of them. Fynn nodded, shrewdly realising that this fitted in with what Mahamba had said about the likely whereabouts of the Zulu warrior king. The second part of the message was equally clear.

Wait here, do not follow us. First we must report to our king. You will be sent for.

The *indunas* returned to the head of the column, the soft sand kicking up from their heels. Their shouted orders were once more passed back down the column and slowly the long, winding snake of men began to filter up the beach and dwindle away into the heat haze.

Fynn sat watching them until the shadows lengthened across the sands and the sun began to slide down behind the horizon in a blaze of gold and scarlet. And still there was no end to the long columns of Shaka's returning army.

Not being one to miss an opportunity for new experiences, Henry Fynn had already decided what his next move would be.

In no way could it ever have been construed, either by sign or word, that Shaka's *indunas* had issued an invitation for him to follow them. On the contrary, all their orders to remain where he was had been forceful, adamant and very clear.

But, in the end, Henry Fynn did exactly the opposite. '*A walk on the wild side…*' was a less than accurate description of what he was about to do.

Setting out to trail thousands of Shaka's battle-hardened and armed Zulus was either the act of a total simpleton – or an adventurer with more guts than brains.

Even Fynn himself would have been hard put to choose into which category he fell at that particular moment in time.

Thirty-five

Flynn crouched below a clump of scrub and stared thoughtfully into the rapidly descending twilight.

Strange thing, he said to himself, though the sight of the Zulu army swarming up the beach put the fear of God into me, by the time they'd passed on, some of it had turned into respect for their discipline.

Having said that, he had a shrewd suspicion that what had probably saved his life during those long, petrifying moments out on the exposed sand dunes had not been down to sheer luck, or the personal magnanimity of Shaka's *indunas*, but his own dogged persistence in demanding to be taken to their king.

Shaka, it appeared, was the magic name that opened doors, stopped a spear, or drove people to run for the hills in terror.

What happened afterwards proved equally fortuitous. Keeping well to the rear of the long snake of returning warriors, he had pressed on alone and out of sight, guided only by the clouds of dust marking their progress.

Now, taking a well-earned break before deciding where he would spend the night, he gave a passing thought to Mahamba and the interpreters.

Damn their black hides, he thought, trying not to laugh. By now they're most likely back at the bay, no doubt spreading the word that I'm lying dead among the dunes with my throat slashed.

To his great surprise, however, he found the trio skulking along behind him, waiting for a chance to slip back into his good graces.

Not only had the rather shamefaced threesome managed to retrieve the coffee kettle and tin cups, but they also had his travelling bag, inside which were blankets, a small silk pillow, sea biscuits, rice and a small medicine chest containing several scalpels and some medicines.

Next morning, he sent Mahamba back to the bay to check that the others were still alive. If so, they were to be alerted as to where Fynn was and what was happening. A few miles further on, they stopped at a small village.

When the occupants of the small cluster of huts saw the rumpled, bearded figure of a strange white man with two yellow-skinned natives with slanting eyes skulking behind him, terrified screaming broke out.

'God save us,' muttered Fynn, frantically pulling handfuls of beads from his bag and scattering them about as if he was feeding wild fowl. He gestured for the servants to pull back and wait until things had calmed down.   ,

After a bit, the headman emerged to investigate the strings of colourful beads. In no time at all, there were smiles all round, and gestures of invitation. A cow was slaughtered and the interpreters set about skinning the carcase in preparation for the midday meal.

Some time later, a commotion at the gate made Fynn look up from where he was conversing with the headman. A stew of red dust heralded the arrival of another stream of warriors.

'And still his army comes,' Fynn muttered.

The terrified village women took to their heels and with much screaming, bleating of goats and cackling of alarmed chickens, scattered into the bush with the children.

The Zulu *induna*, a tall, wide-shouldered man with greying hair, stalked in through the gate. Immediately, a group of soldiers headed off to where Michael and Frederick, bloodied to the elbows, were busy skinning the cow.

Shouting and yelling, they relieved them of their knives and pushed them aside. Fynn shot the two a warning glance and shook his head. Not that he expected either of the bold boys to partake in a bout of fisticuffs with the Zulus, but then – you could never tell.

The *induna* and the headman were locked in excited discussion waving their hands about and throwing sidelong looks in his direction. Fynn could hear the words '*Shaka*' '*abelungu*' and '*indaba*' being bandied about. Clearly, news travelled fast.

The flow of language stopped abruptly. The *induna* threw out an order to the soldiers indicating that the butchered cow was to be handed over to Fynn.

'Oho! ' he muttered with some amusement, 'so he's got the message that this *abelungu's* got the mark of Shaka on his forehead.'

Fynn intervened, suggesting that the meat be cut up, and shared out among everyone. After receiving their share, the column moved off, heading north.

Later that night, Siyingila, the headman, advised Fynn that it would be best for him to remain where he was, because he had just dispatched runners to inform Shaka that a white man had arrived in his village.

'Soon,' he motioned, 'soon, the Nkosi will send for you.'

It was at this point that Fynn learned that the Zulu regiments were returning from hostilities in the lands of the amaPondo, a considerable distance away, down the Wild Coast. Their chief was called Faku, and he was an enemy of Shaka.

Three days later, a party of around thirty natives arrived. Their leader, a good-natured, pot-bellied man of about sixty years of age, introduced himself as Mbikwana and presented Fynn with a gift of oxen.

After launching into a long speech in honour of the great Shaka, relating his greatness and his valiant deeds as a warrior, he went on to intimate that he was Shaka's uncle, and had brought Fynn the oxen so he would not be hungry in the land of his nephew, so great a King. After some verbal parrying, he added that he had also been sent by the Nkosi to ask why Fynn wanted to meet him.

'No point in hiding my light,' muttered Fynn. He went on to explain that he and a party of white men had come to pay their respects to the King of the Zulus, about whom they had heard much, and to trade with him for the ivory tusks of the great *ndlovu*.

During the exchange, Fynn was acutely aware of the skilful, almost cunning tactics Mbikwana had used while questioning him regarding his intentions.

Since Fynn had been completely truthful with the answers he gave, he knew that the chief was too observant an interrogator not to have been carefully watching his demeanour – and his eyes.

Much later, he found out that Mbikwana had also been given orders to kill him, if he suspected him of foul play, or of not being who he claimed to be.

Shaka's uncle then went on to suggest that Fynn should accompany him to his kraal and wait there, for it was far more comfortable and nearer to Shaka's country.

So, on that basis, and having little choice in the matter, Fynn agreed to go with him next day.

Two days passed without incident. On the third, however, something happened that was destined to set a precedent for the future.

It would also earn twenty-year-old Henry Fynn the dubious title of *'the one who raises the dead.'*

Thirty-six

Fynn was jolted out of his mid-afternoon doze by the sound of shrill ululating and the voices of squabbling women. He groaned, tipped his hat back and swivelled a bleary eye in the general direction of the fracas.

At first, all he could see were the backs of several pairs of sturdy legs and the ample flesh of rounded buttocks. They belonged to a bevy of village women who seemed to be dragging something along the ground.

An old man with greying peppercorn hair was darting around trying to stop them, his voice reedy and frail. Fynn stood up to get a better look at what was going on.

On catching sight of him, no matter that he was a total stranger and of a completely different skin colour, the old man came rushing up to him, wringing his hands and gesturing wildly.

Fynn screwed up his eyes against the hot sunlight and tried to see what the women were trying to manoeuvre towards the open gates. The object seemed to be about four feet long and was wrapped in a bundle of threadbare animal pelts.

The old man's rheumy eyes were wild and distressed; the plea for help in them unmistakable. His bony fingers clutched at Fynn, urging him to do something.

Fynn was about to shake his head, when a sudden movement caught his eye. A frail, wizened hand was poking out from among the rancid skins. The hair stirred on the back of his neck. What in God's name was in there?

'Here, wait up!' he shouted, his long legs covering the distance in a few strides. 'What's going on here?'

The old man pushed his way past the sweating women, grabbed the protruding hand and held on to it. A buxom female with pendulous breasts and stiff, spiked hair spat a string of angry words at him and pushed him away hard, so that he tottered and fell.

'Enough!' Fynn shouted, angry now, as he hoisted the old man back on his feet. Just then Mbikwana appeared. His eyes flicked over the scene. He put a placatory hand on Fynn's shoulder, indicating that the matter was of no importance.

A weak moan issued from the bundle of pelts. Fynn brushed away the chief's restraining hand and pushed past the women who promptly dropped the bundle and scattered.

Hunkering down, Fynn carefully unravelled the layers of animal skins. A waft of stale sweat and urine hit his nostrils. An old woman, frail and obviously suffering, was curled inside, her head lodged in an awkward position. Sweat beaded her forehead and ran in rivulets down her neck.

Mbikwana peered over Fynn's shoulder. The sneer of contempt on his face was clear enough as he glanced down at the old woman. A rapid flow of words followed.

By this time, Fynn's ear for language was reasonably well-attuned to the local dialect. Added to which, the age and condition of the woman and the way the women had been dragging her towards the open gate of the kraal told him all he needed to know.

He had seen it before up on the Cape frontier. The disposal of those too old, ill, or incapable of looking after themselves, had been the same. And the age-old remedy? Drag them out beyond the village and let the scavengers deal with them. This was especially true if times were hard, the rains had failed or tribal warfare was raging. The survival of the tribe was everything.

One night was usually all it took, thought Fynn, as he bent over her. Just a few scraps of torn flesh and clothing left by the time the sun rose.

Although very fevered, the woman's colour looked reasonable, her breathing not as thready as he would have expected. Standing up, he looked around for the old man. Mindful of protocol, he'd refrained from actually touching her. He knew enough about tribal taboos to act cautiously, especially around women, young or old.

The old man's eyes were full of tears. His trembling, heavily-veined hands fluttered over his wife's comatose body. Mbikwana made an aggressive move towards him, but Fynn shot him a long, hard look. Taking a determined a step forward, he effectively put himself between them.

'Dammit!' he muttered below his breath. 'Why do I always seem to be in the right place at the wrong time – or is it the other way round?'

Another few minutes of hand-wringing from the distraught husband and Fynn capitulated. First, he made gestures asking the man for permission to examine his wife. The grey peppercorn head nodded furiously. Fynn sent Frederick to fetch his medicine chest.

'God knows what I've got to give her,' he said after Frederick came running with the box, 'if only we were nearer the bay and I could get at the stuff we brought with us.'

After she was carried back to the hut, Fynn hunkered down beside the old lady to make an examination. Inquisitive heads appeared over his shoulder and breathed heavily down his neck as he took her wrist and felt for a pulse. Snorts of laughter, tongue clicking and shaking of heads followed every step of the procedure.

Mbikwana shook his head. 'Why are you bothering with this old dog?' he asked, 'she is already dead, gone to the *amadhlozi*.'

Fynn said nothing and went about his business. Adding a little water to what medicine he had, he lifted her head and trickled some into her mouth, stroking her throat to encourage her to swallow. This again produced raucous spitting noises in the background.

Finally, he made some warm camomile tea, propped her up and persuaded her to take a few sips. The women were then instructed to bathe her fever-wracked body and settle her comfortably. After covering her with one of his blankets, Fynn withdrew.

Not trusting anyone except the husband, he advised the old man to stay by his wife during the night. Frederick would sleep in the adjoining hut and would come for him if there was any more trouble.

Next day, there was a little improvement in the woman's condition. By sundown, she had opened her eyes and asked for something to drink. A few days later, she had more or less recovered, and was up and about.

Overnight, Fynn was elevated to the position of near-deity, a man of magic. Mbikwana being Shaka's uncle, the news of this magical *inyanga,* who could bring the dead back to life, lost no time in reaching the ears of the Zulu king.

A few days later, a party of Zulus arrived, bringing Fynn gifts from Shaka. Apart from the half dozen head of cattle, oxen and milk cows for his immediate needs, there were also two large elephant tusks, almost exact replicas of those he had seen in Delagoa and the spur which had lured him to Zululand in the first place.

There was also a message. It said that Shaka was much pleased that Fynn had come such a long way to visit him. He would not be able to see him until his army had rested as they had been away for a long time, but instructed him to wait at eThekwini until he was sent for.

'Hey,' Fynn muttered, 'how does he know where I started out from? I never mentioned it to either Mbikwana or Siyingila.'

The small incident would be the first of many reminders that very little escaped the notice of Shaka of the Zulus. His informers and far-ranging web of spies saw to that.

A short time afterwards Mahamba returned in a state of great excitement, and produced a sealed letter from the canvas bag looped around his neck.

It was from a Captain Collison of the sloop *Antelope*. It informed him that he had delivered Farewell and a party of over thirty people safely to the bay. Since he'd urgent business to attend to back at the Cape, he would be leaving on the next available tide.

The *Julia*, apparently, had been purchased by Mr Farewell and would remain at the bay.

Thirty-seven

Fifty or so yards off-shore, the small brig swung gently at her moorings on water the colour and texture of pale blue shot-silk. Boxes and packages of differing weights and sizes littered the sands. Sailors from the *Julia* and a group of amaTuli were busy portering them down the beach towards the camp site.

Fynn, dripping sweat and sea water after the tricky manoeuvre of transferring several nervous horses from the deck of the brig safely on to dry land, swept off his hat and mopped his brow. He looked across to where Farewell was standing by watching the unloading of the cargo.

'The *Antelope*? It didn't stay long, then?'

Farewell shook his head. 'Captain Collison had to get back to the Cape, urgent business to attend to.' He shot a proprietory glance at the gently swaying brig. 'We'll have to depend on the *Julia* from now on. I bought her for a good price before leaving the Cape – at least, Farewell and Company did.'

Something in the overly confident tone of his voice sparked a perverse response in Fynn. He surveyed the tall ex-naval lieutenant through eyes half-closed against the glare.

Ever since he'd returned to the bay and found Farewell waiting for him with his coterie of would-be investors, something about the predatory gleam in the man's eyes as he'd boasted how easily Farewell and Company had already established itself in the land of the Zulus, had irritated Fynn.

And since warning signals were something Henry Fynn paid close attention to, he treated the latest as being no different from any other kind. His well-honed instincts told him that Lieutenant Francis Farewell, ex-naval war hero or not, was a man to be watched.

The revelation came as a bit of a shock to the twenty-year-old Fynn. Only a few months earlier, he had hailed the man as a saviour and the epitome of English *savoir faire*.

His eyes moved to the ridge of hills on the far side of the lagoon. Beyond it, lay the way north. And that was where they were bound, as soon as the message came from Shaka.

Oddly enough, it was not the ruthless king of the Zulus or his warlike *impis* who were responsible for the unease currently disturbing Henry Fynn. Instead, it was the flare of raw, burning ambition and overweening arrogance staring out of the eyes of Francis Farewell.

As far as he was concerned, a man who pursued his goals with such blind persistence and total disregard for the very real dangers involved could well turn out to be not an asset, but a man with all the dependency of a half-cocked gun.

That night, sitting around the fires, Fynn studied the new arrivals. Foremost and virtually inescapable was the stout, bombastic figure of Johann Lodewyk Petersen, Farewell's father-in-law.

A man of about sixty, his manner was abrupt and frequently bordering on the choleric. With a face plum red and heavily jowled, the silver-trimmed beard, mutton-chop whiskers and bushy eyebrows gave him the look of a hound about to spring at your throat, given half a chance.

Broad-shouldered and stocky, he was clad in a tweed jacket and a pair of knee-length woollen knickerbockers, the sort mostly worn by gentlemen going duck-shooting on their country estates.

Fynn viewed him with some trepidation. Currently, he was holding forth in angry bursts of guttural Afrikaans interspersed with English on the biting habits of the insects currently bedevilling him.

Farewell was doing his best to placate him. 'But, Father,' he was saying in a soothing voice, 'I know this doesn't happen at the Cape, but this is Zululand, somewhere completely different.'

Fynn busied himself lighting his pipe. Soon, clouds of aromatic smoke were wreathing around his head. Farewell, taking the hint, tugged at Petersen's sleeve.

'See, that's one way to keep the damn things at bay. Light a cigar, for God's sake – in fact, all of you light up, puff your heads off, and the brutes will stay clear.'

Petersen opened his mouth to deliver a testy rebuke. On catching Fynn's eye however, he muttered something below his breath and relapsed into silence.

Fumbling in the depths of his tweed jacket, he extricated a fat Dutch cigar. When he set about trying to light it in the stiffening night breeze, however, it provoked another outburst of muttered curses.

Thirty-five people in all had disembarked at the bay. The potential investors, a mixture of Dutch, German, Danish and English businessmen, were a motley bunch of slightly nervous men; most of them dressed more for an evening in the city rather than an expedition into an unexplored and highly dangerous part of Africa.

Sitting a little distance away from the main group were the others who had sailed north on the *Antelope*. The massive figure of the carpenter, John Cane, could hardly be ignored. A virtual giant of a man, with shoulders as wide as a barn door, he had enormous hands and a look of implacable strength about him.

There was also a father and son, the Halsteads. Like Henry Ogle, they were also farmers who had fled from the frontier lands.

Lastly, there was Rachel, a tall, dignified woman with skin the colour of *cafe au lait*. The presence of a woman in such surroundings, especially one of obvious mixed race, both intrigued and interested Fynn. He thought she'd probably been hired by Farewell as a housekeeper of sorts.

Later, not only did he discover that she had been a slave until the British had banned the practice throughout their territories, but also happened to be the common-law wife of the carpenter, John Cane.

Beyond the camp perimeter, the dark shapes of predators were constantly on the move, patiently stalking those within, both animal and man.

The dozen or so horses brought from the Cape, several dogs and other domestic animals, including pigs and goats, were also housed within the compound. The horses stirred restlessly, disturbed by the feral stench of the predatory hyenas and wild dogs circling in the darkness.

From time to time, their own dogs would start up a round of aggressive barking punctuated by a long, low mournful howling, which would be answered by packs of their wilder brothers prowling about up on the bluff.

And always, always, there were the eyes; glinting in the firelight filtering through the fences, cruel, savage eyes capable of haunting a man's dreams.

Two days later, a handful of terrified amaTuli came running to warn them that a large party of Zulus was heading their way. When Farewell gave the order to prime and load the muskets, the amaTuli took to their heels and scattered into the bush, wailing in terror, fearing an attack.

Half an hour later, Mbikwana arrived with a large escort. Bringing up the rear were several young boys herding a score or so of prime cattle.

Seated in the shade of a tree, waiting to receive them, were Fynn, Farewell and a couple of representatives from among the 'money men.' There was Hoffman, a taciturn, cool-headed Dutchman, who obviously carried some authority with the former lieutenant, with him a stocky blond-haired man in his early thirties sporting a single gold earring, who introduced himself as Pieter Schmidt.

Catching sight of Fynn, Mbikwana threw up his hands in greeting, and with a huge smile on his face strode over to greet him. The Zulus melted silently away into the surrounding bush, no doubt to find water and a place to light a fire.

Fynn, being familiar with ritual greetings, conducted the initial courtesies. He was relieved that Farewell took his cue from him and made no attempt to intervene and rush matters along.

The Chief's eyes flicked over their newly-erected compound and the loaded muskets placed judiciously against a tree a few yards away. Curiosity and some indefinable emotion flashed in the man's eyes for a second or two before he turned to smile at his hosts.

Once the formalities were over, the interpreters arrived, bringing food and drink. Afterwards, Mbikwana announced that Shaka was ready to meet the white men of King George, '*Keeng Jo-Ji*' as he put it.

Fynn's eyebrows shot up in surprise. Now how in the hell did Shaka of the Zulus come to know about George the Fourth?

Later, when he mentioned it to Farewell, the former Lieutenant's reactions were entirely predictable. 'You didn't happen to let that piece of information slip, did you, Henry? Not that it matters a damn, of course. In fact, it works in our interest, the great Shaka knowing we also have a powerful King.'

He swivelled a monocled eye in his direction, a glint of accusation in the cool blue orb. 'You're the only one who's been in contact with these johnnies who even knows that England exists, let alone His Majesty King George. Who else is out here, within a thousand miles or so, who would know that?'

Fynn wisely said nothing. Every instinct in his body told him that, sooner or later, as sure as God made little eggs, they would find out who it was.

Thirty-eight

'Two hundred miles to where we're going, you said?' Pieter Schmidt swivelled round to look at Fynn, his bearded face red with exertion. 'We must have come at least half that way by now!'

Fynn reined in his horse, his eyebrows raised in amusement. He regarded the sweating, blond-haired German on the dappled grey stallion with a mixture of good humour and long-suffering tolerance.

'That's about the third time you've asked me that in as many hours, *meneer*,' he said, 'and the answer's still the same, more or less.'

He grinned cheerfully and gestured towards the distant hills. 'Keep your eye on those, my friend, because that's where we're headed.'

Schmidt shot a scathing look at the silver-haired man astride the roan mare a few yards ahead. 'The old man's holding us up. Why couldn't he have stayed back at the camp with the others?'

Fynn grinned and took a swig from his water bottle. Taking his time before answering, he said, 'Apparently, there's a rumour going around that the King of the Zulus has a virtual forest of elephant tusks around his kraal. He's desperate to see them, so he can to boast to the good burghers back in Cape Town.'

Schmidt groaned. 'Yessus! Like a small boy, wanting to visit a sweet shop.'

Fynn was tempted to say, '*Nix, meneer*, he's here because he's Farewell's pa-in-law. He also holds the purse strings, two very important reasons, especially the last. Yes, I know he's a pain in the arse. If I had my way, I'd give him a boot up the backside every time he opens his mouth to complain. If it's not the heat, it's the flies, if not the flies, the drinking water's too warm, the natives smell, the ground's too rough, too many stones...' but he held his tongue..

Schmidt was right, of course.There had already been a few altercations involving the irascible Petersen, one or two of which had brought the whole entourage to a standstill.

While passing through some dense scrub, the hotel-owner and his horse had become hopelessly entangled in ropes of lianas. Held fast by the sinuous creepers, the more he struggled the more snarled up he and the animal became.

Finally, his temper got the better of him. He started cursing and shouting in guttural Afrikaans, alarming the horse, which reared up, almost unseating him. Seeing the old man's quandary, one of the young Zulus came forward to help him. When he tried to cut him loose, Petersen accused him of trying to stab him with his assegai. Red-faced and apoplectic, he was on the brink of hysteria until Farewell turned up and tried to calm him down.

The next occasion came a day or so later. After crossing a river, they ran into a large patch of swamp. Farewell took one look at it, and said, 'Father, best you get down off the horse now. Go forward on foot. Keep to the clumps of tussocks for safety until you lead the horse on to more solid ground, then you'll be all right.'

Petersen glared at his son-in-law and said nothing, although the stubborn look on his face demonstrated what he thought of such advice. He kneed his horse forward. The animal snickered nervously and tossed its head, its eyes rolling wildly as it smelled the foetid gases rising from the rotting vegetation.

Shortly afterwards, the horse lost its footing and stumbled. Petersen slid over its head and landed in a bog of brackish sludge, which stuck like glue to his clothes, boots, hair, beard, and every square inch of unprotected flesh.

The whole column had to be brought to a stop while a fire was lit, clothes changed, and much coffee drunk, while all the time Petersen's flow of ranting never ceased.

That night, trying to get some sleep, Fynn had to stuff his fingers into his ears and cover his head to block the sound of Farewell and Petersen's quarrelling.

It had taken them almost twelve days of slow, hard travelling but still Mbikwana had made no mention of how far they still had to go before they reached Shaka's settlement.

The pattern was always the same. With a section of the Zulus at the head and the other part bringing up the rear, their route seemed to wander from one military *amakhanda* to another, often changing direction to get there before nightfall.

Since Farewell was more than capable of noticing such tactics, it was inevitable that, sooner or later, he would raise the matter. It came during their mid-day break

'What we have here,' Fynn replied to Farewell's brusque query 'is a carefully-selected tour of Shaka's territory.'

Farewell leaned over and took the coffee pot off the fire. 'I see,' he said, pouring a stream of the aromatic brown liquid into a tin mug embossed with a naval crest and the initials FGF. 'So every day is a demonstration of just how extensive his power is?'

Fynn nodded. Cutting off a slice of dried game meat, he put it in his mouth. 'Partly, though I can see other reasons. After all, he can't be sure of just how much we know about him, or his warlike reputation. This way he's making sure we do.'

Farewell's eyes narrowed. 'What do you feel about us being wedged in between two halves of a small army every day, Henry? Is it because we're actually prisoners, but just don't realise it yet?'

Fynn hissed. 'For God's sake, keep your voice down, sir!' He shot a glance at Petersen who was resting flat out with a chequered handkerchief draped over his face. Then he shook his head. 'The answer to that is no, that's not really what it's about, not all of it, anyway.'

A frown crossed Farewell's face.

'Much of it's for our protection,' Fynn explained. 'Don't tell me you haven't noticed the amount of game that's around, from lion and leopard to rhino and buffalo, not to mention the massive herds of elephant, the ones we're hoping to hunt?'

He drained the last of the black coffee then met Farewell's eyes squarely.

'Let me put it this way, Lieutenant. Here we have five white men, one old and temperamental to say the least, and only one, yours truly, with any idea of bush survival. Mbikwana and the Zulus are doing the right thing by us, believe me.'

Farewell's eyebrows twitched. 'Yes, I see what you mean. So I suppose I've also misinterpreted our nightly visits to his military establishments?'

Fynn got to his feet and stood looking down at the ex-naval officer, his thoughts a mixture of irritation and black humour.

You're not on the deck of a ship any more, my friend, he thought, used to throwing out orders and having them obeyed. In case you don't know it, you are well and truly in another sphere of operation – the African kind.

There was an edge of sarcasm in his voice as he replied. 'At least we haven't had to set up camp every time the sun went down, scavenge for firewood and food, stand guard all night and pray we're still alive come morning.'

As he began to pack away his belongings, he felt he had to add one last comment. 'With all due respect, Mbikwana's orders will have been to make sure the *abelungu* arrive at Shaka's royal kraal safe and well. Every move, every stopping place will have been orchestrated by Shaka himself.'

He closed the bag and handed it to Michael who bore it away. 'I take it you haven't noticed the number of messengers arriving every day?' he remarked. 'He's making sure we're safe. Don't ask me why, but there it is.'

Farewell stood up and tapped his father-in-law's boot with his own. The snoring ended with a muffled snort. Fynn swung himself back up into the saddle. He grinned down at his employer, his brown eyes full of devilment.

'But that doesn't mean His Majesty's benevolence will stretch far if he takes a dislike to us for some reason, or suspects we might be planning to steal his ivory!'

For Fynn, it was not exactly a hardship to travel on at a leisurely pace, protected by warrior Zulus to front and rear. The truth was that he relished it.

With each passing day, he was reverting back to his old ways and the exuberant embrace of Africa itself. It pleased him no end to be on trek again, with only the limitless horizons before him and the ever-changing skies above his head.

The veneer of urban living, which had grown over him like a turtle's carapace during his time in Cape Town, was slowly but surely being stripped away. Day by day, Mbuyasi, the finch, as he was known to the frontier tribes, was beginning to re-appear.

He took to walking instead of riding, often moving up to step it out alongside the young warriors. Engaging them in conversation gave him a chance to come to grips with the cadences and click sounds of the Zulu language.

The land itself was superb, the lush coastal plains across which they travelled interlaced by a network of streams and rivers. Once or twice they had glimpses of a towering massif of mountains to the north-west.

And the game! Never had Fynn seen such herds of animals

and flocks of birds, many species of which he had never seen before. They were so tame they simply stood watching the meandering procession of men and horses passing by.

The easy, ambling pace also gave him an opportunity to keep an eye open as to other aspects of Shaka's kingdom. After they crossed the River Tugela, he realised they had entered Zululand proper.

Before that, the land had felt curiously deserted, with only the cawing of birds, herds of game and the shadows of fish eagles passing across the silent terrain. The few villages they skirted looked poor and almost deserted; their inhabitants subdued and ill-fed.

Whenever their Zulu escorts came into sight, the fear and apprehension in the air hadn't escaped Fynn's notice, either. No doubt the information old Mahamba had given him about the Zulus' ruthless intimidation and the appropriation of amaTuli cattle and crops was obviously being carried out further afield.

Something else provoked his interest. During their wanderings, his keen eye had picked out the occasional gleam of whitened bones lying half-hidden in the grass. At first, he thought they might be animal remains, but after a cautious and covert inspection found that they were indeed human, as he'd suspected.

So many skulls, their empty eyeholes and bared teeth grinning up into the peerless blue of the winter sky, the unmistakable shape of human ribcages and the long bones of thighs and arms. The deeper into the country they went, the more Fynn noticed the pathetic remnants of humanity scattered across the plains, relics of the many battles or massacres that had taken place.

He said nothing, just moved doggedly on. If any of the others noticed, they made no comment; even the voluble Johann Petersen stayed curiously silent.

Later, with the flickering flames of the night fires and the hum of African voices around him, he was reminded vividly of Mozambique and his desperate efforts to gleam information about Shaka along the Maphuto River.

The dark faces of tribesmen floated into Fynn's mind. Whenever he'd brought up the name of Shaka, they'd been transfixed by terror, many sidling away into the shadows to avoid having to voice it.

Shaka, sibilant like a snake, a deadly viper. Lord of all the wars since time began... see his great armies come, like buffalo black on the plains, their sound like thunder on the ground...

Next day, around noon, Mbikwana fell into step beside Fynn. Gesturing up ahead, he said. 'One night we sleep here. Then tomorrow is kwaBulawayo.'

The announcement was accompanied by his usual generous smile, although his watchful eyes still carried the canny glint Fynn had come to expect from the uncle of the Zulu King.

Fynn's heart hit his breastbone with a sharp thud. He returned the smile, and tipped the brim of his hat in acknowledgement. '*Ngiyabonga*, thank you.'

Not that the news really surprised him. The frequency of messengers had greatly increased over the last day or two. And the tantalising ridge of blue hills had been growing ever closer.

The young Zulus he'd befriended had told him that beyond the forested ridge up ahead lay the Umhlatuze River and the valley of Nkwalini, where Shaka's stronghold was situated.

A brilliant shaft of sunlight broke through the clouds and lit up the grassy slopes of the mountains ahead. Fynn's heartbeat steadied. The news of their imminent arrival at kwaBulawayo would keep till later.

By late afternoon, the lowing of cattle and the raucous cries and whistling of herd boys told them they were approaching the military settlement where they would spend the night.

Bathed in sepia light, the whole valley seethed with energy and movement. Vast herds were being moved from the pastures up the winding trails to the kraals that lay sprawled on the hillsides. Clouds of dust stirred by the feet of the milling cattle cast a reddish hue over the scene.

As they came nearer, the sense of discipline and control was evident, order and cleanliness in the neat beehive huts and the well-swept, hard-packed earth around them.

At the unexpected sight of horses, riders and yellow-skinned natives leading packhorses laden with boxes, groups of hard-muscled young men stopped in their tracks and stared at them, open-mouthed.

Judging by the sweat and dust on their half-naked bodies, it was obvious they had been involved in hard training and physical combat. Some carried war shields almost as tall as themselves while others had smaller versions slung over their backs. Most were heavily armed.

The *knobkerries* were clubs ending with deadly-looking balls of metal, which could smash bones or skulls with little effort. There were also short-handled *assegai* with broad blades, honed and lethal, and all manner of spears, both long and short.

Petersen eyed their weapons with some misgiving, but kept his mouth shut when he caught Fynn's warning eye.

Fynn was sure that this *amakhanda* and others like it were the arenas where warriors were either created or young men broken. No place here for battle finery, war paint or swirling ox-hair bands, only hard, ruthless training

No one made any attempt to speak or approach them. The young soldiers just stood silently examining every detail of the strangers as they passed by.

It was patently obvious that these young men were a world apart from the mild amaTuli living around the bay. There was an edge to them, an undercurrent of watchfulness and a kind of ferocity in their dark eyes. Strong and fit, they held themselves with a cheerful arrogance that spoke volumes about the kind of young lions they were. Eventually, the hawk-like stares changed to glances of guarded acceptance.

The man they feared more than death itself, their Nkosi, King Shaka, for reasons of his own, had summoned the people with skin the colour of fish-bellies to come to his great settlement of kwaBulawayo, also known as the Place of Killing.

Before turning in for the night, Fynn told Farewell about their imminent arrival at kwaBulawayo next day. Farewell stared coolly back at him, the firelight glinting off his eye-glass. Then he nodded.

'After our recent conversation, I decided to count the comings and goings of the messengers. Well, you were right about that, but tell me, why so frequent? What does he constantly need to know and have reported back to him?'

Fynn met his eyes squarely. 'You were an officer, Mr Farewell. If the Admiral of the Fleet was coming to inspect your ship, wouldn't you be running up all kinds of flags, making sure every bit of brass and inch of deck was shining and scoured to perfection?'

Francis Farewell's blue eyes gleamed with genuine amusement. He put back his head and laughed.

'I like your turn of phrase, Fynn, really I do, but I mean to say, old chap, comparing a native tribesman with an English officer, a representative of His Majesty's Royal Navy? Surely there's a world of difference between the two, even though the man in question calls himself a king!'

Fynn's scalp prickled. There it was again, that near infallible sense of something out of kilter, an abrasive edge of arrogance which, if handled in the wrong way and at the wrong time, could lead them all to disaster.

You're damn right there, he fumed inwardly. You aren't the same. *You*, sir, are an arrogant ass. Just how the Zulu king will turn out, I don't yet know, but the one thing I *can* tell you, is that he won't play by your rules. Take it from me, he'll have a set all of his own – and you'd best remember that if you want to stay alive in this neck of the woods.

Later, after everyone had retired to their tents, Fynn, restless and too alert to sleep, draped his blanket around his shoulders and set off for a stroll.

The skies above his head were a dazzling blaze of light, the stars rendered brilliant and luminous by the higher altitude and the crisp cold of winter. He drew in a deep breath of air, relishing its tang, redolent of wood smoke and a snap of frost.

Apart from the distant howling of wild dogs, jackals and the occasional roar of hunting lions, the silence was deep and profound. Fynn padded on, his feet scuffing on the dry, hard ground. The tents housing the white men stood a short distance away, their flaps closed. His lips tilted in a grin as he caught the dull rumble of Petersen's snoring.

A blanket by the fire for me, he thought, suddenly cheered by the idea of a night below the stars and the embers of a smouldering fire to keep his feet warm. He shot a glance at the dun-coloured canvas tents, the largest of which belonged to Farewell.

An officer and a gentleman you might well consider yourself, Mr Farewell, he thought. I've met quite a few like you up along the frontier. Not bad men, only with minds closed to what's around them, seeing everything only in terms of control and dominance.

He took out his pipe and lit it, the bite of tobacco welcome in the back of his throat.

One thing I did learn though, often the hard way, was to treat what was around me, both animal and man, with some respect and an even bigger dose of caution. That way, I managed to stay alive.

He stared at the closed flap of Farewell's tent. And I also learned not to pay too much credence to the colour of a man's skin or what tribe he belonged to. Nowadays, I tend to trust only those whom my deep-down instincts tell me to.

Above his head a shooting star streaked across the sky. One moment it was there, the next gone, its fiery tail disintegrating in the vastness of space.

Fynn released a stream of pipe smoke into the cold air. And strike me down dead for saying so, but right now, although I ain't set eyes on Shaka of the Zulus yet, he's personally done nothing to give me any disquiet, whereas, you, Lieutenant – that's twice now you've ruffled the hairs on the back of my neck. And that, in my book, is twice too often.

Thirty-nine

Outside a small hut hidden in the fold of the hills, Langani sat staring into the fire. In the valley not far away the dark waters of the Mhlatuze River flowed, silent and black, beneath a night sky glittering with stars.

It seemed cold, much colder than usual. The diviner wrapped the karosse closer round him and held his hands out to the blazing logs. A sudden movement in the glittering heavens made him glance up. A shooting star was streaking through space, a shower of sparks cascading from its tail.

An omen! A heavenly body trailing fire could only mean one thing – a tragedy, or near-tragedy, for someone.

His mind immediately spun to the white men. They were almost at the gates of Shaka's stronghold. Tomorrow would see them enter it. Did it mean that something was about to happen to one of the group – or all of them?

If Shaka turned against the interlopers, as he could do so quickly if he suspected them of treachery, unfounded or not, his retribution would be swift and terrible, as many had found to their cost.

In spite of his wariness concerning their motives in coming here, the young diviner felt a tug of concern at the thought of Shaka killing any of them.

He looked deep into the leaping flames. Whatever the outcome, his plans to enter kwaBulawayo still remained. Dreams, visions and trance states induced by the effects of *impepho* or *lesedi* were one thing, but to be able to actually see and observe these men in the flesh was quite another.

The quick glances he'd had as they'd stepped ashore at eThekwini had not been enough. They had been too far away to see them clearly, their features indistinct. And besides, there was another very good reason why he intended to breach King Shaka's stronghold.

Langani's shoulders drooped in frustration.

Over the past year, ever since his powerful experiences in the San caves, his periods of meditation and vivid dreaming had been extremely productive, allowing him to move freely between past, present and future. He had even been able to travel briefly out of his own sphere of existence to the cold, northern land where the blue-eyed child of the sea people lived.

But that had been the last time. Since having made the vital connection between the glowing orb dancing so innocently on the sun-dappled roof and the child of the sea people, there had been no visions or dreams, only unbroken, calm and dreamless sleep, his times of meditation confined to routine matters.

It was as if the wind had suddenly changed direction and the world of divination, the universe he had begun to span so freely, became closed to him, the portal to it shut firmly in his face. All his attempts to look into the future had come to nothing.

Perhaps that was all I was permitted to see, he thought. Can it be that my duty is done? Sadness warred with acute apprehension at the thought of it. Tomorrow, or the next day, the *abelungu* would enter Shaka's fortress and come face to face with him.

If my connection to the white men is lost, how can I warn Shaka about what might follow, if I only have half a story to tell?

And if he should ask me 'What dangers do the abelungu bring with them?' I will not be able to say with any certainty, because I truly do not know the nature of these dangers or their duration.

Langani stared up into the star-studded sky until his head was full to bursting with its brilliance. The light streaming down from the heavens was dazzling, almost overwhelming. Suddenly uneasy, he tore his eyes away and looked instead into the soothing darkness of the sleeping land.

A man, even a diviner like himself, skilled in interpreting mysteries, could go mad if he looked too long at the stars.

Unbidden, the image of the small child sprang to mind, and he saw again the red gold hair winnowing about the small face, the delicate skin reddened by the cold wind, the water lapping and sucking below his small feet, waiting to draw him in.

Luckily, the child hadn't come to grief because the storyteller had risen out of the sea to save him. But what about later? Would the sea try to take him again, perhaps in later life? And if so, which ocean would it be – another, far beyond his ken, or perhaps the one currently washing along the shores of Zululand?

Langani shivered, and drew the karosse closer around him. The flames spat, hissed, and sent showers of sparks into the night sky. Once again, there were no answers, either from the heavens, or from any other source.

Tomorrow, he would enter kwaBulawayo, silent and unseen, no matter the outcome. Langani glanced briefly up at the star-filled heavens before turning away from it and closing his eyes.

His thoughts returned to the falling star. It was possible, of course, that it had been a warning, not for the *abelungu* – but for the Nkosi himself.

Forty

It was barely light. The sun was struggling to rise above the
horizon, its single eye baleful and red as the Zulu escorts, the
mounted white men and the servants leading the pack horses
passed through the gates of the *amakhanda* and set off towards
kwaBulawayo.

Even at that hour, the heightened atmosphere among the Zulus was palpable, a mixture of excitement and nervous
anticipation at the imminent prospect of reaching Shaka's citadel.

By the time they'd travelled a mile or so, two separate messengers had come and gone. Afterwards, Mbikwana came up to
Fynn, looking inordinately pleased with himself. A wide smile
wreathed his face and his usual look of caution and keen appraisal had disappeared.

Gesturing to the low-hanging sun struggling to rise from the
mists, he pointed overhead, 'When it is here, then we come to
kwaBulawayo, the Great Place of our Nkosi.'

After he'd gone, Fynn leaned sideways to Farewell and muttered, 'Well, I reckon we're going to be delivered on time just as I
thought we would.' Farewell raised an eyebrow.

Fynn's teeth were white in his bearded face as he laughed. 'Our journey's been as fine a piece of military precision as even the British Army itself could have engineered. No wonder the old boy's looking so pleased with the world.'

Ignoring Farewell's glance of exasperation, he added, 'Just wait till later and you'll see what I mean.'

With a thoughtful expression on his face, Jakot stood on the brow of the hill and looked down towards the pair of massive gates standing wide open at the lower end of keaBulawayo.

A buzz of chatter floated up from below, along with the bawling of cattle and the whistling and beating of sticks as the herd boys took the herds down to the river. A steady stream of women were passing through the gates, balancing baskets of food on their heads, singing and laughing as they headed towards the crowded living quarters. Running through it all was the low pounding of drums adding to the palpable air of excitement coursing like a river through the vast citadel.

Very soon now, they will come, Jakot thought. If all goes to plan, the *abelungu* will arrive just as the sun reaches its highest point. His eyes flicked skyward. A little time yet, he calculated. I wonder who will be first to pass through the gates of kwaBulawayo?

Although he had questioned the returning messengers, even prompting them as to height, colouring and idiosyncrasies of those he expected to be among the strangers, their answers had been a quaint mixture of bafflement and incredulity that he should even ask such things of them.

'How can I tell one from another?' they'd replied, scratching their heads. 'Aiee, such strange clothing, their faces hidden by beards and with such large war bonnets on their heads – truly, I do not know how to tell them apart. They all look the same. One was an old man – that is all I can say.'

In the end, Jakot was sure of the identity of only one. Francis Farewell. The sun glinting off his eyeglass had been distinctive enough to mark him out. Oddly, there had been no sign of the man he knew as Kingi.

He'd explained, 'One of the *abelungu* has hair dark as night, and with a broad streak of white running through it. Did you not see such a man?'

Since the answer had invariably been in the negative, Jakot had come to the conclusion that James King was elsewhere. So, of the reported white men, only one of them had been identified. Who were the other four, then?

A sense of dread had clutched at him. What if the dog, Thompson, was among them?

The shouts of warriors speeding past him brought Jakot back to the present, and he let out his breath with an audible hiss of relief.

Here, he was no longer Jakot Msimbithi, ex-felon, former inmate of Robben Island, bound over to His Majesty King George's naval forces to serve as interpreter until such time as he might be released, or returned to the penitentiary, according to their whim.

In the land of the Zulus, in Shaka's kingdom, he was Hlambamanzi, interpreter to the king himself, a man of standing, with land, cattle, a wife and an expected child. Here, he had a new life, a future. In many ways, he was no longer even Xhosa. I have become a Zulu, he told himself – except in the heart, of course, and there I will always remain Xhosa, no matter how far from my lands and my people.

Jakot smiled, a great and generous smile, his teeth white against his dark skin. The past is over. Even if Thompson should walk through those gates, the red-faced dog has no power to send me back to Robben Island. No one has. This is Shaka's land. And as long as I remain Shaka's man, I will be free.

The tawny jewel embedded in his left eye glowed like that of the great cat it so resembled, the green fire of wild freedom at its heart.

'Hlambamanzi will stand here and welcome you to kwaBulawayo, *abelungu,*' he whispered: '*Yebo,* I will look forward to it.'

A distinct change in mood had taken over. The singing of the Zulus had turned from a lightsome, joyful tempo to a paean of triumph, their voices strong and confident as they came nearer to the heart of Zululand.

Mbkwana was waiting for them up ahead. His mood was almost frivolous. Pointing to a wooded ridge a half mile or so away, he announced, 'Beyond is kwaBulawayo. What do you expect to see?'

Fynn shrugged his shoulders. What other response could he give? Mbikwana cackled softly, then lowered his voice and muttered something.

After he'd gone, Farewell leaned sideways and asked, 'What did he just say?' Fynn kept looking straight ahead. 'I couldn't swear to it, mind, but I think he told us that 'The Place of Killing' is just over the ridge ahead.'

Farewell raised his eyebrows. With steely composure, he tightened his lips. 'In that case we'll have to stop.'

'Why?'

He drew in the reins sharply and fixed Fynn with his piercing pale blue eyes. 'Because, my dear chap, it's *de rigeur* that we dress for the occasion. We're the guests of a king, after all. We don't want to let the side down now, do we?'

Wheeling his horse round, he added, 'In any case, I'll be damned if the King of the Zulus is going to be the only one allowed to dress up!'

Digging his heels into the flanks of the bay stallion, he cantered off towards a clump of trees a hundred yards or so away.

After a muttered consultation with the others, Fynn sent Michael Jantyi up ahead to relay the news to Mbikwana that the white men needed time to prepare themselves before meeting the King of the Zulus.

Even allowing for the brief stop, by the time they were within a few hundred yards of the summit, the sun still had not reached its zenith. Fynn, already changed and spruced up, cocked a calculating eye at it.

'What did I tell you?' he crowed. 'Even allowing time for a lick'n spit and a dress rehearsal, it's not even noon yet.'

His sunburned face creased in a grin as he ran an eye over the rest of the party. My Lord! The cream of Cape society and King George's Royal Navy come to present their credentials at the court of King Shaka... before they try to stiff him for a fortune in ivory, that is!

With his white, starched shirt front, gold cuff-links, formal high-collared dark suit and well-buffed shoes, Johann Petersen looked as if he were about to go to a board meeting or a grand ball.

Schmidt and Hoffman were clad in more sensible garb. Their polished black boots, military-style twill riding jackets, well-tailored breeches and the unmistakable, slouched hat of the Boers spoke of riding excursions around well-tended Cape farms. Fynn's eyes swivelled to Lieutenant Francis Farewell, RN.

Sitting astride the bay stallion with consummate ease, he was dressed in the formal naval dress of his rank, complete with a dark blue frock-tail coat decorated with gold braid and epaulettes, a cream, gold-buttoned front-piece and waistcoat and pale pantaloons neatly tucked into a pair of highly polished boots. On his head he wore a gold-braided cocked hat, while pinned across his chest were the medals he'd received for gallantry during Bonaparte's war.

Fynn, in a clean jacket and breeches, with a blue and white kerchief around his neck, his hair combed and tied back, felt reasonably pleased with his own appearance.

'Not that the King of the Zulus would notice anything amiss if we turned up bare-arsed, with chamber pots on our heads,' he muttered below his breath. 'Still, as the man said, "Why should the Zulus be the only ones allowed to dress up for the occasion!" '

Far below, the Mhlatuze River wound snake-like around the contours of the surrounding hills, its waters silvered by the cool morning light. Wisps of vapour drifted ghostlike along the higher slopes, changing shape as it moved, transforming the broad valley into a magical place, full of other-world mystery and hidden secrets.

But it was not that aspect of it which caught and held their attention. To a man, their eyes were riveted on the huge oval-shaped construction that lay sprawled on the hillside across the river. Even half-hidden in the eerily drifting mists, there was no mistaking what it was.

By its sheer size and strategic importance, it could only be kwaBulawayo, the Place of Killing, Shaka's centre of power. A moment or two of stunned silence followed.

Fynn was first to react. 'Oh my God! I never expected...' His voice tapered off, then he coughed dryly and said to no one in particular, 'What does it remind you of?'

Hoffman's response was immediate and cryptic. 'A wild beast about to spring at our throats?'

No one spoke, either to agree with or refute his description. '*Meneers*,' he sighed, 'I think we might have bitten off more than we can chew this time, hey?'

A squawk of rage split the air. With a face as red as a turkey cock, Johann Petersen kneed his horse round and pointed a shaking finger at his son-in-law. 'Jesus, man, what have you got us into!'

The stubby forefinger made a jabbing motion in the direction of kwaBulawayo. 'Look at it! It's a...a monstrosity, a nest of rats and vipers. We'll be lucky to get out of there alive.' His voice cracked and wavered. 'Don't be a bleddy arse, man! For God's sake, turn back while there's still time.'

The words dwindled away. No one was listening. Instead, they were staring transfixed at their end destination.

The settlement must have been more than a mile across and perhaps a mile and a half in length. Wreaths of smoke coiled lazily into the air from countless cooking fires scattered through the valley and across the hillsides on either side of it. Tiny tongues of flame could be seen flickering through the eerily drifting mists. From time to time, the vapour thinned to reveal glimpses of what lay beneath.

Even from a distance, the sense of discipline and order was evident, both in its construction and planning. A huge oval arena dominated the centre. On both sides, clearly defined fenced-off areas were crammed with countless beehive huts, while the top section seemed to be separated from the main concourse by a selection of high fences.

Fynn tilted his hat back and stared long and hard at it. 'God knows how many people live there. Ten, twenty thousand…or even more?'

Twin rays of sunlight broke through the thinning mist and lit up the hillside. The contrast was instant and stunning. No longer a creation of magical mists, softly blended colours and diaphanous imagery, little by little the true face of kwaBulawayo began to emerge.

An almost tangible vitality sprang out at them from across the river, as if the distance between them had suddenly narrowed, bringing it closer, much closer.

Farewell rummaged in his saddle bag and brought out a pair of field glasses. Adjusting the lens, he scanned the opposite hillside.

A gigantic sprawl of wide-open spaces, huge cattle-pens and the packed density of countless huts sprang to life in front of his eyes. Rivers of small black dots, representing the citizens of kwaBulawayo, could be seen flowing in and out through the massive gates, spreading up into the vast empty oval or trickling back down on to the many paths leading to the river.

'Gentlemen,' Farewell said softly, putting the field glasses away. 'I think it's time we introduced ourselves.'

Patently ignoring his father-in-law, he gave the bay a nudge with the heel of his boot. It snickered and shook its mane. Guided by Farewell, it made a wide detour around Petersen before setting out down the other side of the ridge.

As the others fell in behind him, the man's voice could be heard above the clink of bridles and bits, the clop of muffled hoofs and the shuffle of bare feet.

'I should have barred my door against you the night you stood on my doorstep, shivering like a drowned rat. What a bleddy pity you didn't go down with your ship – it would have saved us all a whole pile of grief!'

As they began to ford the river, a pounding of drums erupted. Simultaneously, a wave of ululating broke out as crowds of people raced along the river bank to greet them.

Fynn cocked a roguish eye at Farewell. 'Was I right, or was I right? In case you haven't noticed, it's almost exactly noon, or as near as dammit, just as I said it would be! I tell you, if Shaka runs his military campaigns the same way he plans the arrival of his visitors, it's no wonder he rules half of Africa!'

He glanced back across his shoulder to where the retinue of riders, horses and Zulus was strung out across the fording place. Ahead of them, up the hill, the massive gates of Shaka's citadel stood wide open, waiting to receive them.

Getting to this stage, however, had not been without moments of high drama; in fact, confrontation had seemed highly likely at one point.

At Mbikwana's insistence, only Fynn and Farewell were to be allowed to enter kwaBulawayo initially. The others were to remain in a meadow with access to shelter and water a hundred yards or so back from the river and wait there until they were called for.

Farewell did not take the arrangement well, to say the least. Neither did Petersen, who insisted in staring somewhat aggressively at Mbikwana, reminding Fynn of a kettle about to boil over and set its lid rattling.

The former Lieutenant had addressed Mbikwana from his superior position on the horse's back. 'Why should we be separated? Protocol demands we be treated with courtesy.'

Such diplomacy, Fynn thought, beads of sweat breaking out on his forehead. Mbikwana was not impressed. He may not have understood the actual words, but the bitter sarcasm of the man's tone was not lost on him.

'*Cha! Cha!*' he'd shouted, breaking into a flood of irate language, so fast that Fynn failed to understand more than a few words. Not that he needed to. The scowl on the chief's face said it all.

The abelungu will do as they are told. This is Shaka's land – and these are his orders!

Luckily, the sudden change in the demeanour of their Zulu escorts was enough to convince Farewell not to pursue the matter. The hardening of the fierce, bold eyes and the stiffening of their bodies was enough to convince him not to provoke further confrontation.

All he could do was shoot a scathing look in Mbikwana's direction before cantering off down the river bank, the bright noonday sun glinting off the gold braid and polished buttons of his immaculate, dark blue dress-jacket.

Johann Petersen, for once, had the good sense to keep his mouth shut.

Fynn, after witnessing the brief but fiery exchange, refused to dismiss the incident as a mere clash of personalities. He saw it more as a statement of fact.

They were now in Shaka's territory and whether Farewell liked it or not, they were well and truly under his control.

Nudging the horse's flanks gently with the toe of his boot, he tipped the brim of his hat in the direction of the investors then cantered off after Farewell.

As they passed beneath the broad arch spanning the huge gates, however, he felt a twinge of apprehension trickle down his back.

The empty eyeholes in the bleached skulls of elephant, rhino and buffalo, along with those of deer, foxes and even a selection of the birds sacrificed for their feathers, leered down at them as if to mock the arrogance of those foolish enough to bring themselves within killing range of the King of the Zulus.

Forty-one

The volume of noise that greeted them as they passed through the gates was indescribable, a wall of sound rolling around them in waves, battering at their senses.

In an instant, they were surrounded by a sea of gleaming black flesh. Shaka's people, in a welter of tossing, feathered head-dresses, paint-daubed faces and bodies, bare-breasted women and girls arrayed in high neck-collars, bracelets of brass and colourful beads, jostled around them, eager to be the first to see the strangers who had come to meet their Nkosi.

Behind him, Fynn heard Mbikwana bellow out an order. The Zulu escorts swung into action and began to push the crowds back.

The horses, alarmed by the noise, the smell of sweat and the close proximity of so many people, began to toss their manes and shake their heads. Sweat trickled down Fynn's back.

As he sought to control the animal, its eyes were wild and staring, on the edge of panic. Oh, my God! he thought, what if the horses rear up, or bolt...

Suddenly, a woman with hair twisted into stiff spirals decided to dart out in front of Farewell's bay stallion. Startled, the animal reared up, whinnying and baring its yellow teeth. With a high-pitched scream, the woman tripped, fell and disappeared below its flailing hoofs.

Farewell desperately tried to rein in the animal, fearful that the woman would be pounded to a pulp. The crowd scattered on both sides, intimidated by the massive bodies of the animals built for speed and stamina.

Fynn's voice was hoarse. 'Where's the woman – where in the hell's the woman?' Cursing, he tried to bring his own mount under control.

Up ahead, there was a wave of displacement, people scattering in every direction, a sibilant cry echoing out over their heads.

'*Fasimba-a-a!*'

A phalanx of young warriors, their paint-streaked faces menacing below a mass of fluttering black and white ostrich feathers, came pushing towards them, manhandling people out of the way. Like the waters of the Red Sea, the crowds parted obediently to let them through. Instantly, the Fasimba formed a protective cordon around the riders.

Once things had quietened down and the horses were back under control, the fallen woman with the stiff spikes of hair was retrieved and sent on her way, a trifle bruised, dusty and ruffled, but otherwise unhurt.

When Mbikwana arrived, agitated, with sweat running into his eyes, Fynn prepared to dismount then changed his mind. On horseback, they would be safer, less likely to be swamped.

Glancing over at Farewell, he noticed that he seemed totally disengaged with what was going on around him. Something up ahead seemed infinitely more interesting.

Fynn's eyes flicked over the heads of the crowd. A tall figure was pushing his way towards them, elbowing people aside as he came. By his dress and confident stride, it was clear he was someone of status.

He whipped a swift glance back at Farewell. A surge of emotion flicked across the Lieutenant's normally aloof features, a mixture of incredulity and a flush of anger, both quickly brought under control.

The newcomer, after giving Fynn a cursory glance, stopped a few feet away from Farewell. He was young and strikingly handsome, his features clear-cut and regular, the finely trimmed beard accentuating the line of his taut jaw.

His elaborate head-dress of scarlet and black feathers was impressive, a perfect foil for his good looks. A cape of spotted genet fur covered most of his upper body while a short kilt of animal tails fell to his knees. At neck and wrists, multiple rows of beads in bright colours accentuated the burnished tones of his oiled skin.

He motioned for Farewell to dismount. For a split second, Fynn thought the Lieutenant was going to refuse, but then swung down reluctantly from the saddle.

Fynn viewed the interaction between the two men with keen interest. Without a word being said, it demonstrated a certain amount of familiarity between them, although not exactly one of friendship or mutual respect.

One a British war hero, an impressive figure in his formal dress uniform, medals pinned to the breast of the dark blue jacket; the other, younger, flamboyant, someone of obvious importance in Shaka's citadel. What possible connection could there be between the two? He didn't have long to wait to find out.

Farewell's voice rapped out, hard and angry. 'Jakot! What in the hell are you doing here?'

Curious eyes flicked from one man to the other, sensing the hostility between them. Fynn stared hard at the man Farewell had addressed with such veiled contempt and was rewarded with a flash of something deep and indeterminate, a frisson of raw anger in the bold eyes.

He was also close enough and observant enough to catch sight of the wedge of colour lodged in the dark brown iris of the man's left eye. A jolt of recognition ran through him, a flash of déjà vu.

I've seen that eye before, but in God's name, where? The answer trembled tantalisingly on the brink of discovery for a moment or two before the relentless voice of Francis Farewell broke his concentration.

'Since we failed to pick you up on the beach along with the others, we assumed you'd been drowned or some other mishap had befallen you.'

Fynn was startled to hear a pleasant, well-modulated voice answer him in passable English. 'Ah, no, Lieutenant Fah-well,' it said, 'after the gods of the sea spared me, I thought it would be best to come and live with my brothers, the Zulu.'

Farewell snorted. 'And what of your duty to those who took you from prison and gave you employment?'

The answer was again delivered softly, with no rancour, a hand briefly touching his breast as he spoke. 'Yebo. Kingi is a good man. He saved me more than one time. I owe him much. For all my life I have only respect for him.'

Farewell opened his mouth to speak, but was stopped short by the man who had once saved him from drowning off the coast of St. Lucia.

'But enough of talking,' he said, with an abrupt nod. 'The Fasimba, they will take you to a place where you can leave the horses and be comfortable.'

With a swift bow, he turned to Fynn. 'Jakot welcomes you to kwaBulawayo. I am interpreter to the Nkosi Shaka. The Zulus call me Hlambamanzi – it means "the swimmer".'

The dark eyes were full of mischief as they met Fynn's. 'If you ask Fah-well, I am sure he will share my story with you.'

Then he was gone, swallowed up by the crowd.

Forty-two

The sun was hot, the sky cloudless and the air still, the last of the morning mists melted away by the warmth. A haze of fine red dust hung over the great arena and the dry taste and the smell of it hung on the air.

A buzz of excitement, much like the sound of wild bees about to swarm, drifted up from below, while the muted throb of drums added to the high expectation spiralling through the crowds.

From their position half-way up the slope, comfortably ensconced in the shade of a leafy fig tree, Fynn and Farewell had an excellent view of the vast parade ground spread out below.

Fynn cocked an eye skyward. 'Have you noticed that time seems to stand still here? I could have sworn the sun was directly overhead an hour or two back, but I'm damned if it's budged since then!'

He half-turned towards Farewell. 'Remember my comments on Shaka's immaculate sense of timing, having us arrive on the stroke of noon? You don't suppose he's got the rest of time and space under his control as well, do you?' Receiving no response, he glanced sideways. Farewell had divested himself of his dress jacket and cocked hat and was in his shirt sleeves, his long pantaloon-clad legs stretched out before him. He was deep in thought, his brows drawn together in a frown.

Fynn decided to answer his own question. Tongue in cheek, he said, 'Time's not standing still, *kerel* – I'm just relieved to be still alive, that's all!'

Farewell came back from a long way away. Then he laughed. 'I take your point, Henry,' he replied, 'but if the bloody sun's still overhead come suppertime, I'll expect another explanation.'

Any further discourse on the subject came to a halt with the impromptu start of the festivities.

One moment, the parade ground lay empty and waiting; the next, the war drums began to beat, their rhythms fast, urgent and commanding. The swelling hum of excitement in the crowd changed to an ear-shattering roar.

This was what the crowd had been waiting for.

Stepping high and proud, legions of Shaka's elite warriors swept into the arena, row upon row, wave after wave; regiments, companies and full brigades, every man knowing what was expected of him, every row moving as one.

Sunlight glinted on spears as they poured into the arena, head-feathers streaming out behind them; buffalo horns, ruffs, cowtails, pom-poms; fringes of ox-hair, creamy white against dark, oiled skin; faces and bodies daubed and streaked with war paint in scarlet, ochre, yellow and black.

Zhee! ...zhee! ... zhee!

On and on they came, moving to the insistent beat of the drums and the deafening rattle of spear shafts on shields, superbly fit, magnificent and utterly terrifying – the legendary army of the Zulus.

Shouted orders and shrill whistling echoed down the ranks. The front rows inched forward a few yards then stopped. Almost simultaneously, the huge war drums rose to a crescendo then ceased on a single beat.

The sudden silence was crushing. One long moment slipped by and then another. The acrid, peppery dust stirred by thousands of feet hung thick in the air, the reddish haze drifting through the sunlight. Somewhere in the crowd, a child wailed and was quickly hushed.

Then, out of the silence a long, low growling began, softly at first, then increasing in strength and volume like the muted rumbles of thunder heralding an approaching storm. It grew and swelled until the hissing chant made the hairs stand up along Fynn's arms.

That sound! The last time he had heard it, it had been like a wild beast purring, chilling his blood and turning his knees to water. Stupefied and more afraid than he'd ever been in his life, he'd watched the columns of returning warriors advance up the beach and head straight towards him.

What he was hearing now was no longer the sound of a purring animal, but the full-throated roar of a truly terrifying entity, primal, savage and totally ruthless. His mouth went dry.

Spear shafts and shields were brought together in a huge rattle of sound. At the same time, thousands of iron-hard feet were brought down on the ground. '*Bayete! Bayete*! Hail the King!'

Unnoticed, the Xhosa interpreter had moved silently into place a few yards away from them and was standing with his arms folded, watching the spectacle. The drums started up again. A tangible wave of feverish excitement thrummed through the crowds.

Fynn got up and leaned against the gnarled trunk of the fig tree. Eyes shaded by the brim of his battered hat, he stared intently into the arena. The aroma of syrupy resin of ripe figs was heavy in the sultry air

Advancing at a fast pace down the middle of the arena was a group of Fasimba warriors, thirty or so self-assured young lions. These were Shaka's elite, his personal guards, their white shields and snowy cow-tails in brilliant contrast to their dark skins and the black and white ostrich feathers of their head dresses.

The breath caught in Fynn's throat. Though the Fasimba were magnificent, they were merely a foil for the man who appeared a few yards behind them.

Shaka of the Zulus, the Warrior King himself.

He was tall and powerfully built, standing barefoot with his feet apart. The single blue crane feather tapering upwards from the circlet of leopard-skin around his brow added a foot or two to his already impressive height, while bunches of scarlet *igwala gwala* feathers provided a vivid splash of colour against his dark skin.

A magnificent collar of leopard-skin accentuated his broad chest and muscular torso. A kilt of leopard tails reached to just above the knee and fringes of combed cow-tails cascaded to his ankles and wrists. In one hand he held a short-bladed spear, in the other a shield of pure white with a single spot of black.

Everything about him spoke of power and authority, a man at the peak of his powers, someone to be greatly feared. Here was the ruthless and skilled warrior of legend, the figure that haunted the dreams of many, a man imbued with the driving force and cool logic of a military genius.

A chill ran down Fynn's back. Even from the distance, he was aware that the eyes of the mesmerising figure were fixed on the fig tree half-way up the slope – or to be precise, on the two white men sheltering below it.

So you're just as astute off the field of battle as on it, hey? he thought. What better way to introduce yourself than in full regalia against a backdrop of your splendid warriors?

He watched, mesmerised, as Shaka dramatically held up both shield and spear. Silence fell. The crowd was hushed, waiting. The scuff of bare feet alerted them to Jakot's presence. He stepped up quietly beside them, clearly about to take up his duties as royal interpreter.

As Shaka's deep voice carried out over the crowd, heads began to swivel in their direction. The buzz of curiosity rose. No doubt as to who he was talking about. Jakot pressed his forefinger to his lips, advising them to wait.

Finally, it was over. Shaka raised his spear and shield in their direction then gestured for the rest of the proceedings to go ahead. Jakot turned to them, smiling. 'What was all that about?' Farewell demanded.

'Nothing to worry you, *meneer*,' Jakot replied. 'The Nkosi was welcoming you to kwaBulawayo. He also said that you have nothing to fear from his people while you are here.'

'That wasn't all he said, though,' Fynn said, 'I did catch a few words, something about being the most powerful King in the world.'

'Very good,' Jakot responded, the corners of his eyes crinkling in amusement. 'The Nkosi was letting you know his people are as many as the stars and his herds of cattle so great it is hard to count them. All this is true, just as he said.'

At just over six foot, Fynn was only an inch or so shorter than the Xhosa. As their eyes met, the sunlight caught the curious distortion in the man's left eye once more. Fynn stared at it. The feeling of déjà vu resurfaced, like an itch impossible to scratch.

Jakot spread out his hands in a gesture of appeal. 'The Nkosi is especially interested in seeing how you ride on the backs of the horses. Never before has he seen such animals -'

An irrepressible grin lit up his face. 'Of course, it is also true he has never before seen *abelungu* either! But this you already know…'

Fynn responded quickly, afraid that Farewell might refuse. '*Yebo*,' he replied, 'we'll be happy to do it.' Relieved, he heard Farewell agree.

'Why not?' he responded. 'After all, we did dress in our best for the occasion. Pity to waste it, don't you think?'

After a brief consultation, Jakot hurried off to make arrangements. In a surprisingly short time, he returned, his bright feathers bobbing in the sunlight.

'*Woza, come!* Now is time!'

Picking up his hat, Fynn set it on his head at a jaunty angle and set off up the slope after him, whistling as he went.

After they'd collected the horses, they made their way down towards the arena. Just as Farewell was about to mount the bay, Jakot put a restraining hand on the horse's bridle.

'*Cha!* Not you, Fahwell,' he intervened. 'First must be the one who raised the dead, then the other – the Nkosi's words, not mine – so please, if you will wait.'

Fynn felt the blood rise to his face, and he stepped away from his horse, hotly embarrassed at such fulsome praise. 'The woman in question was never dead,' he protested, 'and I'm no maker of miracles!'

On seeing the look of acute apprehension flit across Jakot's face, he hesitated. Any delay, and the blame would certainly fall on the interpreter's head. 'One time only around the arena,' he warned, 'then Farewell joins in, too.' Jakot flashed him a relieved smile.

'What was that all about?' Farewell demanded. 'Did I hear him right, Fynn, calling you "the man who raised the dead"? What in hell have you been up to, Henry?'

Fynn swung himself up into the saddle. 'A complete misunderstanding, I can assure you.'

Farewell looked at him appraisingly. 'But a pretty useful talent to have up your sleeve, don't you agree?'

Feeling like a gladiator about to be thrown to the lions, twenty-year-old Fynn took up a position roughly in the middle of the arena and waited for Jakot's signal.

His throat was dry and his mouth and nose itched from the dust. He was acutely conscious of the vast blur of faces and thousands of pairs of eyes on him, staring at the lone figure mounted on a strange animal, both belonging to a species they had never seen before.

Briefly, he wondered whether the *indunas* he'd met near the Umgheni River were somewhere in the crowd, pointing to the strings of beads around their necks, and telling their friends where, how and when they had met the white man on the horse.

A shrill whistling brought his head round. Jakot was waving furiously at him, translation unnecessary.

Fynn edged the horse around until he was facing the brow of the hill. Having guessed that Shaka would be positioned where he could get the best view, he located the high fences guarding the royal quarters, then looked down to the large, spreading tree a short distance below. A small group of people were clustered beneath it.

There you are, Shaka, he thought, his heart pounding. Pulling sharply on the reins, he dug in his heels and urged the horse up on to its hind legs.

With his boots stuck firmly in the stirrups, he raised himself from the saddle, scooped off his hat and bowed low, the horse's front hoofs flailing in the air. Turning round, he repeated the gesture to the spectators, and the crowd went wild.

After that, Fynn set off cantering round the arena, stopping now and then to let the horse snicker and paw the ground before trotting on again.

Oddly enough, once he had settled down, he began to enjoy himself. He cantered, trotted, and then galloped at full speed, the horse's hoofs thundering over the hard-packed ground.

Back in the centre of the arena, he dismounted, removed his hat then placed it on the ground with a flourish, before climbing back into the saddle again. Cantering on for a further hundred yards or so, he turned the horse round, sighted up the place where he'd left his hat, then urged the animal forward, first at a fast trot, then at a gallop.

Gradually, he eased his boots free of the stirrups. After making a swift calculation, he lowered himself down the horse's flanks until the ground was only inches away from his fingertips.

Gasps of excitement rose from the crowds. Timing it to perfection, Fynn snatched up his hat, heaved himself back into the saddle and waved it around ostentatiously, before replacing it on his head.

It was a move he'd perfected some years ago on the frontier, one of the many activities he'd indulged in with the rest of the wild, headstrong youths frequenting the dusty wilderness of the Colony.

'*Oh, Jesus… but I'm out of practice!*' he gasped, as he spat out dust and grit and wiped blood from his grazed knuckles.

At the end of another half hour or so, he and Farewell retired, dishevelled, dusty, but triumphant.

'I reckon that's as good a show of horsemanship as you'll find anywhere,' Fynn said to Farewell as he swung down and patted the horse's sweating flanks, 'and you didn't do too badly for an old sea-dog, I have to say!'

They had ridden separately, then together, racing each other down the length of the arena and back again, throwing in a bit of equestrian showmanship by urging their horses over the make-shift jumps hastily arranged by Jakot and some enthusiastic youngsters.

It ended with Fynn cantering alongside Farewell before abandoning his own mount to ride bareback behind him, waving his hat in the air while his own horse followed behind, riderless.

As the afternoon's celebrations came to a close, the arena began to empty. Shadows crept across the stretch of iron hard ground, changing the colours to amber and grey. The first sharp tang of smoky wood fires came drifting on the air, along with a mouth-watering aroma of roasting beef.

Fynn groaned, and rubbed his belly. 'You realise we've had nothing to eat since supper last night? As the old saying goes "I could eat a horse" – begging your pardon, old girl,' he added with a grin, seeing the horse's ears flick.

'I hope you're not expecting an invitation to dine in regal fashion tonight,' Farewell replied, 'because I have a feeling it won't be forthcoming – not yet, anyway.'

Fynn eyed him curiously. 'Well, no. I'm just plain starving, that's all. In any case, I doubt this particular warrior king goes in much for the social niceties like sitting us down to a formal banquet, do you?'

The Lieutenant slapped dust from the sleeve of his jacket, then prepared to mount the stallion. 'I doubt it. But just let's wait and see. He might surprise us.'

They lapsed into an easy silence on the way back, each preoccupied with their own thoughts of what the day had brought forth.

It seemed a long time since sunrise and setting out from the *amakhanda* in the dawn light. Curious, Fynn thought, the way time seems to stretch and elongate in this neck of the woods. Still a long way to go before the day's over. He wondered briefly about the rest of the party, and in particular, how Petersen was coping with being literally marooned and out of sight, on the riverbank.

A little later, they passed a cluster of beehive huts standing well back from the path. Something drew Fynn's eyes to the one standing slightly away from the others. For some inexplicable reason, he felt the hair stir on the back of his neck. We're being watched...

Nothing unusual in us being stared at, he chided himself, two white men on horseback riding through the heart of Shaka's citadel. But a sixth sense told him to trust his instincts. And they were sending out alert signals...

A swift glance sideways from beneath the brim of his hat was rewarded by a tiny flick of movement beyond the doorway. Someone was standing well back in the shadows. And there was no doubt that either he or Farewell was the object of intense scrutiny.

Fynn clucked softly to the horse and pulled gently on the reins, slowing it almost to a standstill. Casually, he glanced sideways again, narrowing his eyes against the fading light.

The man was young and tall, perhaps a few years older than himself, long coils of plaited hair falling around his shoulders. Fynn stared hard at him. He had only seen hair like that once before, and it had belonged to a Xhosa holy man in a remote part of the frontier.

Their eyes met across the space. In that split second, Fynn recognised something else – a look that spoke of personal recognition, a certain familiarity in the infinitesimal exchange between them.

Just then, a voice hailed them from further up the lane. Instinctively, his head turned in time to see Jakot hurrying towards them... Fynn's eyes flicked back to the doorway. But it was too late. The man with the long, plaited hair had gone.

A moment later, Jakot caught up with them. He was breathing heavily, as if he'd been running, a sheen of sweat on his brow. Just then the last rays of the setting sun slanted between the huts. The interpreter raised a hand to shield his eyes from its fierce glare. But not beforeFynn caught a glimpse of the elusive gold chip in his left eye.

The familiar feeling of *déjà vu* returned. But this time, the answer he'd been looking for leapt straight at him.

After his return from the frontier, Fynn had busied himself trying to find work. On that particular day, he was hurrying along the quayside at the city's busy harbour, hoping for an interview with a ship's master due to sail north within the next week or so.

Currently, rumours were flying about that the Commander of the British fleet docked in the harbour had just negotiated the release of a couple of convicts from the prison on Robben Island. Apparently they were needed to act as interpreters during the Royal Navy's forthcoming survey of the coastline between Algoa Bay and Portuguese East Africa.

The gossip had obviously been true because Fynn almost ran into them that morning. Chained at wrist and ankle and escorted by prison guards, they were shuffling awkwardly across the cobbles towards the gangplank of HMS *Leven*, the British flagship.

Fynn, head down and in a hurry, nearly collided with them. The taller of the prisoners thrust out his manacled hands to stop him. Muttering an apology, Fynn shielded his eyes against the dazzle of early sunlight and stared at him.

He was young, only a few years older than himself, the ravages of prison life echoed in the desperate intensity of the eyes looking into his. Fynn could hardly fail to notice the distinctive, tawny-gold segment embedded in the prisoner's left eye, for it demanded to be noticed – and remembered.

A curse and a savage pull on the chains by the prison guard broke the contact between them, and gestured for Fynn to go on his way. Looking back over his shoulder, he saw that the prisoner was still staring after him.

Fynn stared blankly at Jakot, his mind struggling with the sudden revelation as to the interpreter's past history.

'Sorry,' he muttered, 'what did you just say?'

The Xhosa, completely unaware of Fynn's dilemma, repeated what he'd come to tell him. 'Your friends have just crossed the river. Wait by the small kraal and I will bring them to you.'

With that, he retreated into the rapidly falling dusk and headed back the way he'd come, leaving Fynn bemused by both his recent experiences.

An hour later, the rest of the party arrived, exhausted and extremely hungry. Jakot appeared in their wake, and with his usual good timing, set about arranging for corn, hay and water to be brought for the horses.

Fires were lit and torches brought, for it was almost dark. A stretch of land nearby would serve as a place for Farewell's party to raise their tents.

'I don't know about you people, but my back bone is about to shake hands with my ribs,' Schmidt said, rubbing his substantial middle. 'What in the hell does a man have to do to get fed around here?'

Fynn sniffed the air. 'I doubt we'll have to wait too long. I'd say supper's on its way.'

A few minutes later, a shuffle of bare feet heralded the arrival of women carrying platters of food and several earthenware pots containing generous quantities of *tshwala* beer and fresh water for washing.

The platters revealed enough slices of succulent roasted meat to feed a small army, along with piles of freshly cooked ears of maize, vegetables and a sort of flat, unleavened bread.

The starving men fell on the food with gusto, while Jakot retreated diplomatically into the darkness beyond the outer rim of firelight.

Forty-three

Darkness brought a distinct change to the atmosphere and mood of kwaBulawayo. As the whispering shadows swept in to snuff out the last of the light, their perceptions of Shaka's great citadel began to alter. The air seemed warmer than before, with an edge of sensuality in the drifting wood smoke and muted throbbing of drums. With the encroaching darkness came closeness, human warmth and the exchange of confidences, stories and secrets.

Within the enclosed sprawl of the residential quarters situated on either side of the settlement cooking fires twinkled like hosts of fireflies in the dusk. On the hillsides beyond, the campfires of the Zulu army lit up the night and sent coils of smoke curling up into the skies.

Shaka's people, divested of their bright clouds of feathers, trimmings and warlike regalia, were reduced to black figures silhouetted against the scarlet and saffron of blazing fires, anonymous and faceless, wraiths of the night set free by the coming of the dark.

On the far side of the fences guarding the royal quarters, there were also lights, many lights. Torches and bonfires had been lit and preparations put in place in honour of the *abelungu* who had travelled across the sea in their great winged vessels to meet Shaka, the great Nkosi of the Zulus.

Langani's sandals made no sound as he moved into the shadows on the far side of the fence enclosing the square. Feeling his way along the intricately woven wickerwork fencing, he found the place where he'd teased out a small section the day before. He squinted through the gap, scanning the square for signs of activity.

It was empty, with fires burning at both ends, the leaping flames sending darting shadows into every corner. Below the massive fig tree in the far corner, a pile of rolled-up reed mats and karosses had been laid out, with small lamps and pots of scented oil standing by ready to be lit.

Langani's heart beat faster. If Shaka planned to meet the *abelungu* here, he would be able get a good view of the proceedings. He settled down to wait. It would not be long now.

Drawing the monkey skin cloak around him, he pulled the hood up so that it completely covered his head. Even if someone came up close behind him, he would be almost invisible. His teeth gleamed briefly in the dusky light.

I have become like the chameleon, he thought, even the keen eyes of the watchers at Shaka's gates failed to notice the grey shadow slipping past them.

His decision to breach Shaka's closely guarded sanctum had been made some time ago. Merely entering kwaBulawayo itself was not enough, because it would not bring him close enough to see what happened when the *abelungu* finally came face to face with Shaka.

The bustle and commotion during the preparations for the victory celebrations had made it easy for him to slip in unnoticed just as it was growing dark. The idea that anyone of sane mind was planning to penetrate Shaka's private domain under the noses of the Fasimba would have been ridiculed.

Once inside, Langani left two places strictly alone. The first was the royal *seraglio*, the vast network of twisting lanes and beehive huts where Shaka's women lived. This particular part of the royal domain was of no interest to Langani. It was not that he didn't like women, because he did – but there was no reason to believe that Shaka would invite the *abelungu* there.

'The place of women' was forbidden territory and the last place Shaka would allow any male to enter. Also, the barred gates were guarded by those called *Qwayi Nyanga*, the Moon Gazers, men who were either eunuchs or had no natural interest in the female sex.

The second area he deliberately avoided was the private quarters of Shaka himself. They were considered sacred ground, where no one, not even his close friends or members of his family were ever allowed. Besides, it was not his intention to pry into Shaka's intimate life—that was not why he was there.

His sole concern was how Shaka would deal with the arrival of the strangers who'd had the temerity to breach the shores of his kingdom. Would he honour them as welcome guests, or view them as a threat? In which case, anything could happen.

He already knew that the Nkosi had been very generous to Fynn. Because of his skills in treating the sick, he had rewarded him with gifts of fine cattle and given him every courtesy, but still...

Langani stirred uncomfortably. There were those at Shaka's court who kept their hatred of the Nkosi well hidden. If he continued to be generous to the white men, might it not rub salt into already festering wounds?

His mind swung back to the brief encounter he'd had with Fynn an hour or two earlier. Recalling the sudden awareness he'd seen sparking in the man's eyes, he drew in a sharp breath. It was lucky Jakot had called out to him when he did.

Even taken by surprise, Henry Fynn was fast, alert, his instincts that of the hunter. I must remember that in future, he told himself, pulling the cloak closer around his shoulders. The whooping cry of a night bird drifted in on the cool night air, an unsettling, lonely sound.

He sighed. It had not been part of my plan for the *abelungu* to find out who I am, or that I knew who they were and what had brought them here.

So why did I wait for them to pass by, knowing that they might see me, certainly remember me? Curiosity will no doubt be the death of me, he thought, ruefully.

A burst of laughter and the sound of running feet made his body tense. Gradually, the voices faded, and he relaxed again.

It was true he'd come too close to Fynn. From now on, Langani the diviner, the man of magic, must be like a passing shadow, only watching and waiting, nothing more. But he knew it would never be as simple as that, his connection to them was too great.

A sudden clamour of voices in the square drew him back to the hole in the fence. Peering through, he saw that servants were gathering up the mats, karosses and other items. A moment later, a small gate swung open, and an imposing figure swept through it. Langani's eye followed him as he crossed the square.

Clearly, the tall, dark-skinned man was someone of importance. All he had to do was clap his hands sharply once or twice for the servants to scurry off in all directions, bearing away what they had come for.

After checking all was in order, he went back through the gate and closed it behind him, the hem of his long cloak swirling about his ankles.

The square was empty now, except for the fires burning at each end. Obviously, Shaka had changed his plans. Was it because of the coolness of the night – or some other reason? Langani slowly uncoiled himself and stood up. It was time to become a shadow again.

Stepping away from the fence, he re-arranged his cloak so that it also covered the lower part of his face. With only his eyes visible, he melted away into the darkness.

Forty-four

After dark, the view from the upper part of Shaka's citadel was impressive, to say the least. It seemed as if a great mystical city had been spirited on to the hillside overlooking the Mhlatuze River.

No longer cloaked in mists and illuminated by stray gleams of sunlight, as it had been that morning, it was now burnished by the reddish hues of innumerable fires and torches and veiled by drifting smoke, while above it floated a full orchestra of sounds; bursts of full-throated song, snatches of laughter and the buzz of chatter, the whole overlaid by the earthy and compelling pounding of drums.

So deeply absorbed in the sights and sounds were the four men that when Jakot coughed discreetly to announce his arrival no one seemed to notice.

When Fynn turned round he saw that the Xhosa's earlier finery had been discarded. He was bare headed, with only a chequered blanket draped around his shoulders against the cooler night air.

'The Nkosi bids you come,' he said, addressing Fynn, his eyes gleaming amber in the reflected firelight. 'Once more, he wants only you, *meneer,* 'the one who raises the dead.'

Waving an apologetic hand at the others, he said, 'Tomorrow, in the morning, the Nkosi will see you all. I will come for you then.'

Farewell's father in law muttered something incomprehensible. Jakot looked sharply at him, then at Fynn.

'*Woza!* We must hurry. You would not like to make the Nkosi angry. I can assure you of this, my friend.'

'That I could well believe,' Hoffman muttered as he watched them disappear into the darkness. 'Thank God, His Kingship didn't want to see all of us, hey? Yessus, it's been a long day. Enough is enough. I'm for bed.'

Only the muffled sound of Fynn's boots and the pad of Jakot's bare feet disturbed the silence as they traversed the network of narrow lanes winding between clusters of beehive huts.

Above their heads, the sky was clear, ablaze with swathes of stars. Away from direct light, there was nothing to dim their icy perfection. All was still and quiet, unnervingly so.

Once or twice, Fynn thought he caught a glimpse of someone flitting like a shadow among the huts. So faint that it appeared almost transparent, the wraithlike figure seemed to appear then disappear between one blink of an eye and the next.

Sometimes, a snatch or two of whispering voices drifted out from behind the intricately woven walls of the beehive huts, almost as if the inhabitants were bound in a conspiracy of silence.

Just when Fynn had almost given up hope of finding a way out of the maze, Jakot nudged him and pointed ahead to where a reddish glow lit up the night sky. With a renewed sense of urgency, Jakot hurried him along. As they moved nearer, a rhythmic, melodious blend of women's voices drifted towards them.

The incongruity of unexpectedly hearing soft female voices raised in song struck Fynn like a physical blow. 'Jesus!' he whispered, visibly moved. In a world dominated by men, physical action and rough, hard living, he'd almost forgotten that women existed.

Jakot shot him a crafty glance. 'The Nkosi's 'sisters',' he chuckled, 'or so he calls them.' 'Sisters?' Fynn queried, his curiosity piqued.

'Later,' Jakot muttered, 'no time for talking, now. *Woza!*'

Grabbing Fynn by the arm, he broke into a trot. As they ran through the remaining twists and turns between the huts, the singing grew louder and the flickering lights brighter. Finally, they came out into a wide, firelit clearing.

In addition to two large fires burning at either end, the square was ringed with torches, smoke writhing up from the guttering flames. Fynn looked around, blinking in the light.

When a solid wall of faces turned expectantly towards them, he reacted like a stunned rabbit caught in the glare of a hunter's torch. The singing trailed to a halt. A collective sigh rose, followed by a stir and a rustle of bodies.

Fynn felt like a mole emerging from below ground. The square was packed with people. On one side, there were women, many women and girls, a blur of brass necklets, beads and the gleam of teeth and eyes in the firelight. Opposite them were rows of befeathered chiefs, their dark faces impassive as they viewed the strange white man who had come among them, the one who was said to have the power to bring the dead back to life.

But it was what lay beyond the ranks of curious faces and watching eyes that drew Fynn's attention.

Dominating the square and everyone in it was a domed structure of superior dimensions. Massive, elegant, and beautifully constructed, it was lit from within by the soft glow of many lamps and tapers.

Weathered by wind and sun into a smooth, silvered grey, the thatch was thick, expertly shaped and built to weather a thousand storms. It fell neatly over the supporting framework and ended in a series of neatly cut layers above the high, arched doorway leading into it.

Adorned with skulls and horned heads, the entrance was broad enough, and high enough, to allow the tallest of men to walk through it without bending their headd. Just visible through the doorway were immense wooden posts and the glow of a small fire burning in the centre.

Silhouetted against the soft amber light was the figure of a man sitting in a high-backed chair. Fynn's heart raced. No mistaking the powerful shoulders and the imperious set of the head. Shaka of the Zulus, in person...

Jakot breathed out hard, 'Now we go.' Nudging him forward, he whispered in his ear. 'Only to the door, then we wait.' Acutely aware of the rustling and whispering among those watching their every move, Fynn shuffled forward as if hypnotised, his sense of reality rapidly fading.

The glow of the lamps and flickering tapers were reflected in the vast, shining floor of the interior, creating the illusion that they were about to walk over a sea of soft lights. It was a place of shadows and mysteries, dominated by the enigmatic figure in the carved chair.

'Eyes down, eyes down, not look!' Jakot muttered as he fell to his knees. Fynn remained standing, awkward and uncertain as to whether to follow suit.

The faint smell of honeyed beeswax and woodsmoke drifted out of the interior, along with a whiff of fresh thatch, dried grass and reeds. Minutes crawled by.

Damned if I'll fall to my knees, Fynn thought, struggling with conflicting emotions. *Respect, yes, submission, no...*

Although he was itching to look directly at the figure in the chair, his better judgment prevailed, and he contented himself with allowing his eyes to travel slowly across the gleaming floor.

What little he could see of the interior walls told him they appeared to be finely plaited and exquisitely neat. The massive hardwood posts supporting the framework of the roof were covered with intricate panels of beadwork executed in geometric patterns and woven in bright colours, in themselves works of art.

Everything spoke of skill and craftsmanship, artistry and endless patience. Fynn had never seen anything, anywhere in Africa that remotely resembled such a level of sophistication and expertise.

A deep voice rang out, almost catching him by surprise. Jakot cocked his head, listening to what it said. 'Now is time,' he whispered, 'please to follow me, eyes down!'

Ushering Fynn towards a pile of animal skins, he urgently motioned him to be seated. Fynn dropped a cross-legged position, while Jakot squatted a few yards away.

It was only then he noticed that the chequered blanket, which the interpreter had started out in, had somehow been replaced by a length of soft woven material draped around his shoulders. When or how the exchange had been made, he had no idea.

Fynn raised his eyes a fraction. On receiving no rebuke, he lifted them further and dared a quick glance beyond Jakot's crouching figure.

Shaka was seated in a massive carved ebony chair only a few feet away, his long, muscular legs stretched out before him. A leopard skin cloak was draped around his shoulders, a scarlet flash of feathers at his brow. His eyes appeared black in the soft light, a flickering intensity and clear intelligence in their depths.

He regarded Fynn with open, frank curiosity, unsmiling, but with no trace of hauteur. Conscious of being under his close scrutiny, the hair stirred along Fynn's arms.

The face of the Zulu king was masculine in the extreme, the flared nose and full lips carved as if from dark warm wood, the lightly trimmed beard adding to the strong line of the jaw and the broad neck rising out of a pair of massive shoulders.

Long minutes passed, during which time his eyes never left Fynn's face. When he spoke, Jakot listened carefully then translated. The conversation centred mainly on Fynn's medical abilities. At one point, Shaka scowled and rapped out a string of sharp words. Wooden faced, Jakot translated.

'Are you a doctor of dogs? You were sent here to be my doctor, not to waste time saving the lives of animals.'

Nonplussed, Fynn took it that he was referring to the old woman he had treated in Mbikwana's village. He shook his head, and answered directly, in Zulu. 'It is my duty to help anyone who is sick. I can do no other.'

Silence, while a frisson of something indefinable spun through the air. A look of utter surprise crossed Shaka's face as he heard his language issue from the mouth of a white man. Then he shook a finger at him. 'Then tell me why I am suffering in my body. What is wrong with me?'

Fynn spread out his hands. 'Without examining you, I can not be sure. If you can tell me where you feel pain...'

A scraping movement as Shaka rose to his feet and stepped away from the chair. The leopard-skin cloak slipped to the floor. Apart from a short *umutsha* of animal tails and a pair of bronze bracelets on his upper arms, he was naked. 'If you do not tell me,' he thundered, 'I will have you sent to umGeorge to be killed!' Jakot's face bore a pinched look of despair.

Fynn was so taken aback at the mention of King George that he stared blank-faced at the Zulu king for a moment or two. Then collecting himself, he said, 'If you will allow me to look closer, perhaps I can help you.'

Jakot remained squatting between them, his head moving between one and the other as he waited for the resolution. The quick flare of anger left Shaka as quickly as it had come.

Reluctantly, he motioned Fynn to come forward. After a few paces, he held up a warning hand. 'Enough! No closer!'

Fynn ran a practised eye over his well-developed, muscular body. To all intents and purposes, Shaka was in peak physical condition, the whites of his eyes clear, his skin taut and his body straight, strong and well muscled. The only thing to catch his eye was several patches of dark, discoloured skin above his hip bone.

Ah, probably treated by an *inyanga*, or several of them, he surmised. As that was all he had to go on, Fynn put his head to one side, looked thoughtfully at the dark patches for a few moments, then said, 'You suffer with pain in your loins, Nkosi. I can see it clearly.'

The look of astonishment that crossed Shaka's face showed Fynn that his calculated guess had paid off. When the King clapped his hand to his mouth in amazement, Jakot played to the gallery and translated rapidly.

In response, a scattering of applause came from those watching from beyond the arched doorway.

In the shadows beyond the floodlit square, the near-invisible figure of the diviner caught the swelling tide of approval. Langani nodded, not in surprise, but in acceptance of the accolade.

'So, Mbuyasi, the magical healer, is proving himself worthy of his reputation.' In spite of his forebodings about the eventual outcome, a look of satisfaction crossed his face.

Shaka eyed Fynn with approval. 'Truly, King Jo-Ji has sent me a good doctor, a man of many marvels. It is my wish that you stay with me here after the others return to eThekwini.'

Seeing the hesitant look on Fynn's face, he smiled, 'At least for a time, perhaps from one moon to the next.'

Stunned by the proposal, Fynn readily agreed. A feeling of massive relief flooded through him. Now there would be time and opportunity to broach the sensitive matter of their trading for ivory in Zululand. Some time later, Shaka reluctantly let him go, insisting that he return in the morning with the others.

While he was making his way back through the maze of huts, guided only by the stars and the faint glow of the fires from the crowded living quarters below, Fynn marvelled at the day's events.

Was Shaka really as savage as it was claimed? So far, his acceptance of the white men had been without blemish.

Then he caught sight of something; a shifting, flowing movement somewhere in the shadows. Turning his head sharply, he scanned the area but found nothing, only silent pools of darkness and the brilliance of starlit sky.

A trick of the light, or perhaps it was one of Shaka's spies, keeping an eye on him?

Moments before he fell asleep, wrapped in his blanket by the fire, he reminded himself to let Farewell know that he'd finally solved the mystery of who had told Shaka of the Zulus about King George the Fourth of England.

As he moved cautiously towards the place where he intended to spend the night, Langani shivered and wrapped his cloak closer around him. Away from the warmth of firelight and the hum of voices, the night was chilly, the stars glittering icily above his head.

A few minutes later, he approached a small beehive hut standing near the outer fence. No welcoming fires, no stir of human warmth in or around it, or any of those close by. Although they were fairly new, an air of quiet desperation hung about the huddle of abandoned huts.

As he crawled in through the low doorway, Langani knew he could sleep there undisturbed for as long as he needed to, for people tended to shun places where someone had recently died.

In time, the beautifully woven thatches would sag and decay and be nibbled at by mice and ants. Finally, they would collapse. Eventually, all that would be left of the places where someone had once lived would be the iron-hard circles of their once-glossy floors.

So, tonight, and for as many nights as he needed shelter, Langani could sleep soundly, undisturbed by either the living or the dead.

Gathering up an armful of bundles of reeds and dried grass from the back of the hut, Langani set about preparing a makeshift bed for himself. Then he lay down facing the doorway and pulled the cloak around him for extra warmth.

Apart from the patch of starlit sky beyond the opening, everything was dark. As he gazed at the silent stars, he let thoughts of the last few days slip through his mind.

Once again, the lynx-eyed Fynn had become aware of him. Somehow, he must have caught a glimpse of the 'shadow' keeping pace with him as he passed through the maze of huts leading to the place where Shaka was waiting.

Langani's lips twitched. He was not totally invisible, even at night-almost, but not quite. As far as he was aware, no one other than Fynn had noticed him flitting through the night like a grey and insubstantial wraith.

One thing did strike him as strange, though. Although he'd come within a few yards of Shaka on more than one occasion, a shadow among other shadows, the warrior king had shown no signs of being aware of an unseen watcher close by.

It could mean one of two things. Either Shaka knew, but refused to acknowledge the possibility that someone actually had the audacity to stalk him within his own citadel – or that he, or one of his bodyguards, had already smelled him out, and were only biding their time until they could confront him at a time of their choosing.

Sometime during the night, Langani stirred and turned over. Even through the haze of sleep, his senses told him that something had altered. His eyes flicked open. The way the starlight was filtering in through the doorway wasn't quite right. Something was blocking it...

An animal was crouched in the doorway. By the angle of the head and the intensity of the body, Langani knew it was coiled like a spring, watching for signs of life.

He lay still, feigning sleep, his heart racing. Opening his eyes a fraction, he darted a cautious glance at it. There was only time for a brief glimpse of small rounded ears and the glint of cat eyes before it silently closed the distance between them, after that the coarse rasp of a tongue on his hand, the fishy smell of animal breath and the heat and weight of it across his legs.

His hand came in contact with soft fur. Below it were the vibrations of a rumbling purr, so loud it seemed to fill the hut.

Celiwe? But how could it be? She'd made no move to follow

him, merely watched him lazily from the shade as he'd set off without her.

He had long been aware of the powers inherent in some species of animals. His old mentor, Nthabiseng, had been sceptical of this, but the brotherhood of diviners to whom he belonged had not.

One of them had said, 'Why should humans be the only one of Nkhulunkhulu's creatures to be given a spirit? If so, is it not natural that they might seek to use their powers to communicate with other species, even help them? After all, they can hear sounds we cannot, smell danger, disease and even death, long before it comes. And some have even been known to sense the presence of the amadhlozi.'

The gentle rumbling emanating from the animal was soothing in the half-light. The eyes, now so close to his, began to fill his vision. Soft yellow and amber with a flash of green fire at their heart, he found them powerful, yet unthreatening, fierce and wild, but with compassion in their depths.

After a while, he drifted into a deep and peaceful sleep.

When he woke at first light, no trace of it remained. Had he just been dreaming? Had an animal really been in kwaBulawayo, or was it still where he'd last seen it over a week ago – in his sanctuary, half-way up a mountain, many miles away?

Forty-five

It wasn't until much later in the day that Fynn remembered what he'd meant to tell Farewell about solving the puzzle of King George and Shaka of the Zulus – but too much had happened since that morning, and other matters had claimed his attention.

Jakot had arrived to wake them just after cockcrow, coughing discreetly outside the tents where Farewell and the others were sleeping. Fynn was in his usual place, bedded down by the burned-out embers of the fire.

As the Xhosa bade him good morning, Fynn pushed back his blankets then shuddered as the raw morning air hit him, raising gooseflesh on his exposed flesh.

'Good God, man!' he said, hastily pulling the blanket back up over him. 'Why so early? The bloody cockerels haven't stopped crowing yet.'

Mist writhed eerily around the stakes of the horse pen and drifted along the ground, while faint stars twinkled in the patches of sky visible through the drifting clouds.

Several women appeared, carrying large earthenware jugs of

water on their heads. After they'd gone, Jakot produced several bunches of small twigs that had been sharpened at both ends.

'For the teeth,' he said, mimicking a scrubbing motion. Kneeling down, he stirred the embers of the fire then blew on it to coax it back into life. After a few grudging flames appeared, he scraped about for some twigs and small branches and added them to the fire.

He grinned across at Fynn. 'I know, you need *caffee* to bring you back to life.' As he filled the tin kettle with water and set it on the fire, he added cryptically, 'you see, I already know the ways of the white man too well.'

Then he left with the promise to return to escort them to Shaka later that morning.

Jakot was as good as his word. By the time he came back, they were already dressed and fortified with strong black coffee and a hard biscuit or two from Farewell's supplies. In spite of the activities of the previous day, Farewell managed to look uncrumpled and suave, the others less so, but still presentable.

The horses had been fed and watered, and some of the boxes and packages to be presented as gifts for the Zulu monarch made ready. Michael Jantyi and Frederick, the interpreters, looked apprehensive when told they would have to to carry them into Shaka's presence.

Jakot's arrival soon put paid to their attack of nerves. Putting his fingers to his mouth, he let out a shrill whistle and beckoned to some youths who happened to be passing by. Without a word, they came forward. Jakot gestured to the boxes. The youths picked some up and put them on their heads.

'*Hamba!* Let's go,' he said, ushering the reluctant Michael and Frederick up the slope. The little procession did as they were bid and moved on towards the gates leading to the royal places.

The square was wide and completely fenced along three sides. Dominating the far right-hand corner was a huge fig tree. Below its spreading branches, a fair-sized crowd of people were gathered, either squatting or sitting cross-legged on the ground.

When the white men appeared, heads turned in their direction. A ripple of curiosity spread through the throng. The interpreters and the youths put the boxes down and were instructed to wait where they were. Jakot ushered Fynn and the others forward.

A pathway opened up to allow them to pass through. Curious eyes followed them, taking in every last detail of their strange clothing and appearance.

The sight that met their eyes was unexpected, to say the least. Johann Petersen, caught unawares, made a distinctly choking noise at the back of his throat.

Standing below the fig tree with his arms above his head, Shaka was completely naked, apart from the *umncedo,* the brief sheath-like penis cover worn by adult male Zulus. And what made it all the more astounding was the fact that the monarch appeared to be soaping himself all over...

Around him were arranged a number of servants, including some small boys. Their duty seemed to be to offer up dishes of various soapy unguents and oils, as and when directed by the king, only moving when ordered to. At all other times, they stood as stiff as statues with their dishes and pots held out before them.

Surprisingly, not only was the king of the Zulus actively performing his ablutions, but also seemed to be conducting his business affairs at the same time. Councillors and elders came forward then retreated, as dictated by Shaka.

Jakot ushered them to a spot a few yards away and indicated that they should sit down. For a moment or two, it looked as though Farewell might refuse. Pointedly, he produced a clean handkerchief from the inside pocket of his dress jacket and spread it on the ground. Sweeping back the swallow tails of his coat, he lowered his cream-pantalooned backside on to it. Once he was settled, he removed his gold-braided cocked hat and balanced it carefully on his knees.

Fynn saw a look of amusement cross Jakot's face. On catching Fynn's eye, he fluttered an eyelid in a brief wink before returning to the business in hand.

Shaka gave no indication he had seen them, merely continued with his routine. After rinsing his body, he gathered a lump of red ochre from one of the dishes and began to rub it into his skin. Next, he motioned for one of the servants to step forward with the bowl he had been holding for the last half hour or so.

It was clear the young man was extremely nervous. As he came forward, his hand wobbled, the dish tilted and some of the contents slithered on to the ground. The terrified youth let out a howl of anguish. A petrified silence followed.

Shaka rapped out an order. An instant later, two burly men stepped forward. One of them took the dish of creamy unguent from the young man's hand and gave it to the nearest servant, while the other seized the unfortunate youth.

The loud crack as his neck was broken seemed abnormally loud. The body slumped to the ground and lay there, twitching. The guards dragged it to one side, before taking up their positions again, with their aarms folded.

Fynn felt his stomach heave. Blinking hard, he glanced sideways at the others. Farewell's jaw was set in a rigid line, the cocked hat gripped in fingers of steel, beside him a scowling, almost apoplectic Petersen. Hoffman appeared pale and sickly below his tan, while Schmidt's body visibly shook. The unpredictability and callousness of the act had obviously taken a toll on all of them.

Shaka continued with his routine as if nothing had happened. Dipping his fingers into the fatal dish, he scooped out some of the substance and began to smooth it on to his skin in long, languorous strokes, giving his body a well-oiled, healthy glow.

Fynn's eyes flicked back to the youngster's body. Flies were already beginning to buzz around the head.

When Shaka's ablutions were over, he clapped his hands sharply. Several male servants stepped forward, bearing his costume for the day. With their eyes lowered, they waited until they were asked before presenting him with a particular piece. After he was dressed, a resplendent figure ready for the day's celebrations, he gave a brief nod to the waiting slayers, who came forward to remove the lad's body.

'Heathen bastard,' Petersen muttered, his breath sour on the morning air.

Within a few minutes, the crowds had dwindled away, leaving only a handful of courtiers behind. All eyes were nervously fixed elsewhere rather than the smear of blood still visible on the dusty ground.

Seemingly unconcerned by the effect it might be having on his guests, Shaka sat down on the pile of rolled-up reed mats that served as both dais and comfortable seating, then indicated that they should move nearer.

He greeted Fynn with a smile and asked if he had slept well. When Fynn replied in passable Zulu, the smile grew broader. Jakot stood ready to translate.

'It is good my doctor feels safe here.' Shaka indicated Farewell and the other three men. 'I bid you welcome to my kingdom. I hope you also slept well. If you need anything, ask Hlambamanzi, he will see to it.'

He gestured for Farewell to stand up, which he did, his cocked hat tucked below his arm. Shaka ran an appreciative eye over the gold braid and epaulettes, the pale trousers and leather boots.

In spite of the dust of travel, horse riding and other activities, Farewell still looked every inch the decorated war hero he was. Briefly, Jakot related that he was an important *induna* in the legions of King George's many sea warriors.

Shaka's eyes lit up when he heard the details of his naval service and requested his battle decorations so he could look at them more closely. He directed several question at Farewell. Once he was satisfied, his eyes flicked over the other three men who were then duly introduced to him in turn.

By this time, the sun was well above the horizon, heading for noon. Jakot began to sweat profusely and it was obvious his command of English was being stretched to the limit.

Farewell asked if he could speak. Shaka nodded. 'We would like to present the Nkosi with some gifts,' he said.

The monarch looked suitably pleased. Farewell gave the signal for the boxes and packages to be brought forward. They were duly opened and the contents presented.

Coiled strings of beads in many colours slithered out, glistening in the sunlight, all of a superior quality to those brought by the Portuguese. Tinkling bells, mirrors, and cascades of trinkets, necklets and bracelets followed, along with a selection of children's toys, ladies' lace scarves, hats and ribbons. Of more practical terms, there were woollen blankets, lengths of bright cotton, three-legged cooking pots, jugs, plates and cutlery.

Finally, the *piece de resistance* was produced: a bright scarlet military coat with gold braid and epaulettes. Oddly enough, Shaka's eyes passed over it without comment, his attention already being taken up with the bottles of pills and potions specially chosen for him by Fynn.

After examing them, he flicked a hand at Fynn. 'Very good,' he announced, 'but you can tell me their purpose later. Now it is time for our celebrations to begin.'

He shot a shrewd glance at Farewell. '*Fabana ka ma Jo-Ji, induna* of King George, you know that a victory must be celebrated if the people are to be kept happy.' With that, he indicated that the meeting was over.

As the four men walked from the square towards the gates leading down into the concourse, Petersen lost no time in showing his disgust at what he'd seen.

'Just like that, hey, the poor young native's neck wrung like a chicken,' he said, clicking his fingers. 'And for what, slopping a bit of bloody grease on the ground? I tell you, that man's too bleddy dangerous to do business with.'

If Petersen or anyone else thought that the morning's incident was all they would witness concerning the King of the Zulus' propensity for swift and pitiless retribution, within the next few hours they would be sadly disillusioned.

By the end of the day, a few more dead men had been added to the count. The final incident happened just as they were cantering out of the arena after completing a four-man riding show and a display of rockets sent up to dazzle the crowd.

An old man, no doubt confused and alarmed by the noise, had tried to defend himself against the rough treatment being handed out by the guards attempting to keep the crowds from swarming into the arena. After being beaten with his own stick, he was dragged away, his frail arms and legs windmilling weakly.

Later, Jakot told them he had been taken outside the gates and left barely conscious on the far bank of the river for the hyenas to dispose of.

When asked whether this was a common occurrence, the Xhosa had merely shrugged his shoulders.

'Who is to say?' he answered 'a wise man in the court of the Nkosi must be blind, and keep his eyes only on what is important to him.'

'Like staying alive?' Fynn responded softly, his eyes on the strands of beads around the Xhosa's wrists.

Jakot, on seeing where Fynn's attention lay, nodded briefly. 'A gift from the *amabhuna*,' he said softly, 'but Jakot still lives. Here, in the land of the Zulu, I will also survive.'

The second day of the victory celebrations had been as impressive as the first. After partaking of a substantial mid-day meal, they had taken up their places once again in the shade of the fig tree overlooking the arena.

There was no need for Fynn to explain the importance of cattle in African tribal life. Although Petersen, Hoffman and Schmidt were city-based men, they were also more than familiar with the wider aspects and problems of the British Cape Colony.

As Hoffman put it, 'Don't tell us about how important cattle are to the *muntus* – and to us, the Boers. How many wars have we fought with the Xhosa over land and cattle – five, or is it six, now?'

Nevertheless, they were very impressed by the Zulu herds. They had been arranged by colour and size, their varieties endless. The stars among them were the pure white cattle belonging to Shaka himself. And all of them, from the great snorting bulls down to the smallest of the calves, had been combed and plaited to within an inch of their lives.

Hoffman, especially, was genuinely astonished at the care lavished on the cattle. 'My God, he must have a small army looking after them! To present herds of that size in such condition takes time and real dedication.'

Fynn scratched his chin thoughtfully. 'Well, he's got plenty of both on tap,' he said, 'yet another side of him we know nothing about.'

Silence followed. Then Farewell broached the subject of the killings. 'What's your opinion, Henry?' he asked. 'Did he do it deliberately, or is this kind of thing a common occurrence around here?'

'Both, I think, Fynn answered with brutal honesty. 'I'm sure the rumours I heard up north weren't exaggerated. I've seen at first hand just how terror lurks around his very name. For God's sake, even that was enough to make people cower away in horror – and they'd never been within a hundred miles of either he, or his warriors.'

He glanced round at his companions.'Don't tell me you failed to notice the human bones scattered over fairly large areas during our travels here?'

Judging by their reactions, it was what he'd suspected; everyone had seen the pathetic remains but had kept quiet about it.

'I thought you might have,' he said, 'and as for the rest of your question, Farewell – do I think he had that poor boy's neck broken on purpose? Well, yes, I do, he's ruthless enough, and calculating enough, to do just that. A split second after he gave the order, I watched his eyes flick in our direction. He wanted to see how we would react.'

Pieter Schmidt burst out. 'But, why, for pity's sake – he's in the middle of celebrating a victory! On one hand, he makes us welcome, you especially, Fynn. Gifts of cattle, ivory, assuring us, only yesterday, that we'd nothing to fear in his land – then today, such barbarity, right in front of our noses. What's behind it, tell me?'

'I don't know,' Fynn replied, shaking his head, 'but I'd say he needs to demonstrate the power of life and death over his people on a fairly regular basis. The fact that we happened to be here as well has little to do with it, I feel – apart from reminding us we're also under his thumb, as it were.'

Twenty-year old Fynn then issued a stark warning. 'Don't ever make the mistake of thinking Shaka's a man not so different from ourselves. He's not, he's nothing like us, nor will he ever be. Amen.'

As the sun began to go down, the atmosphere in the arena increased in intensity. 'What's next, I wonder?' Hoffman muttered, looking around.

The sense of expectancy rose. At a hidden signal, the drums began a low pounding rhythm. A group of youths carrying unlit reed torches soaked in palm oil entered the arena and positioned themselves at strategic points around the perimeter.

Once they were in place, a bearer carrying a flaming torch moved from one unlit torch to the next and set the oil-soaked heads alight. In turn, each torch bearer lit the torches on either side of him. In a surprisingly short time, the great oval was surrounded by a blazing ring of fire.

A buzz went up from the crowd. The sound of women singing brought forth a great spiral of ululating and frenetic beating of drums. As a long, undulating coil of women and girls entered the arena. Hoffman whistled, 'Hisst, man, will you just look at that!'

The bodies of the women were pressed close together, a viper made of female flesh. To enhance the snake-like effect, the tallest of the girls had been placed at the front, tapering back to allow the smallest to form the tail.

Except for the 'head' of the python, which was made up of girls dressed in vivid scarlet, all the others wore identical short skirts of green and yellow with headbands of white feathers. Attached to their ankles and wrists were strings of brass bells. With each step, the tinkling added sibilance to their carefully executed movements and seductive singing.

'My God, there must be at least three hundred there,' Farewell said, looking suitably impressed. Schmidt eyed them appreciatively. 'Fine-looking women, these Zulus,' he commented.

'I wouldn't let my mind wander too much in that direction,' Fynn said, with a grin. 'Unless I'm mistaken, I'd say these are choice specimens straight from Shaka's *seraglio.*'

'Which is where?' Schmidt asked curiously, his eyes lingering on the dancers.

'How in hell would I know?' Fynn retorted. 'But let me tell you – that's one area you need to keep your eyes and your mind off – as long as you want to stay alive, that is.'

The winter dusk had fallen and the arena was now totally lit by the flickering light of the torches. Men began to pour in to the arena. This time, there was no display of regimental colours or military trappings. These were dancers, pure and simple, chosen for their skills in a different arena.

It soon became clear that they were to play the part of hunters. Armed with long sticks, they proceeded to bait the python, darting in close then retreating in mock terror.

The reptile's coils moved smoothly across the arena floor, its scarlet 'head' moving from side to side, striking down one group of hunters after another, leaving them writhing on the ground.

As the flames of the torches guttered and flickered, the chase became wilder, the hunters more daring, the python's coils contracting and expanding as it covered ground.

When a lone figure strode into the arena carrying a blazing torch in each hand, a loud gasp went up from the crowd. This time, Shaka bore no royal insignia. Here he was just a dancer like the others. With a mighty leap, he sprang into the fray and thrust the torches close to the head of the python, taunting it with fire.

The voices of the women rose in a siren song of defiance. To and fro the battle raged; the python coiling and retreating, then surging forward to trap the hunters in its coils. The dance was wild and savage, a masterpiece of co-ordination and ingenuity, at its heart the age-old struggle for survival between man and beast.

And always, always at the centre of the dance, was the lithe figure of Shaka of the Zulus, armed not with assegai and shield but with burning torches, his powerful body leaping and pirouetting in mid-air as he fought to subdue the thrashing snake.

The rhythm quickened. The crowd yelled and whistled, urging on the hunters to kill the beast. The long snake began to weaken, its coils less certain now, the shrill ululating of the crowd sounding its death knell.

The lone figure of their King sprang into the air, a mighty leap which brought him close to the creature's scarlet head. Raising the torches high, he held them there for a moment then pretended to plunge them straight into the beast's heart.

Beginning with the 'head' of the serpent, the coils slackened then collapsed; each girl falling gracefully over the one behind until the whole mass lay still and lifeless. The singing petered out then stopped. The crowd was hushed. Only silence and the bodies of the girls lying like crumpled dolls in the dust of the great oval.

One by one, the torches of the hunters went out. Then the heart of esiKlebeni was left in darkness, with only the pale light of the half-moon rising from behind the hills of Nkwalini, to illuminate it.

After supper that night, Jakot came to escort Fynn through the same twisting lanes to where Shaka was waiting for him. This time there were no fires burning at each end of the square, no hushed crowds and watching eyes, only the great bulk of the shrouded dome with its softly-lit interior.

Shaka appeared to be in fine fettle and ordered *tshwala* beer to be brought to them. Jakot sat between them as before, ready to interpret, though Fynn found that he was beginning to pick up most of what was being said on his own.

Time slipped by easily enough, the talk being mostly of King George and how he ruled, how many wives he had and other questions of a more personal nature. It was evident the Zulu king had a lively, enquiring mind and a keen wit to match.

Casting a discreet glance at him from time to time, Fynn found it hard to reconcile his attentive host with the man who had ordered the deaths of three men with a casual snap of the fingers on a day of supposed celebration.

It was well into the early hours by the time a reluctant Shaka allowed Fynn to leave after inviting him to return in the morning along with the others.

Refusing Jakot's offer to accompany him, Fynn set off back to the camp site on his own. As he staggered through the winding lanes, humming to himself, there was no denying the yeasty beer was having quite an effect on him. Not one, but two half-moons shone down at him from a clear sky. He grinned, closed one eye, and squinted up.

'That's better,' he mumbled, 'now there's only one of you.'

Whistling softly below his breath, he weaved his way past the darkened square and followed the path to where the guards stood at the gates leading down into the main compound. Just before reaching the camping place, Fynn passed by the enclosure where the horses were coralled.

His horse snickered and tossed its head, then ambled towards him. Fynn stroked its mane, mumbling drunkenly to it. Then, for no obvious reason, it pulled its head away, snorting, nostrils flaring and the whites of its eyes showing.

He tried to soothe it, but whatever the animal had sensed had spread to the others. They bunched together, snickering and moving about restlessly. Fynn's head cleared rapidly.

Alarm among domestic animals in the African night was rarely unfounded. Their superior sense of smell alerted them instantly to the presence of a predator, or in fact, any presumed danger, specific or otherwise.

A predator? Here in the heart of Shaka's kwaBulawayo? Fynn dismissed the idea as being unlikely. His eyes scanned the area. The camp site was relatively bare and windswept with nowhere for anything to hide. The stakes of the enclosure standing out in the pale moonlight were as tall as a man, and the gate was firmly closed.

He turned his head sharply. For a split second, he caught sight of something – a pale-coloured blur, fairly low down, and moving fast. Could a hyena, or even a jackal, have somehow found its way in?

Stone cold sober now, the effects of the beer rapidly dissipating, Fynn dropped into a crouch. His hunter's instincts had picked up something else – the unmistakable whiff of a cat, and a large one, at that. His fingers fumbled for the short hunting knife in his belt.

Behind the rough wooden stakes of the enclosure, the horses whinnied and milled about. Fynn strained to pick up a sound, any sound. But there was nothing. No predator, no intruder, only the sound of his own harsh breathing.

Gradually, the horses calmed down. As Fynn straightened up, he realised his legs were shaking. 'And it's not from the beer,' he muttered. 'Dammit, there *was* something there! I know it, the bloody horses know it – but just what it was, is another damn question altogether.'

Forty-six

As soon as Fynn opened his eyes, he knew in his bones that the day was going to be a bastard. For a start, the weather had changed. The high, blue skies of the last few days had given way to an oppressive humidity, almost as if the rains were about to start.

He made a quick calculation. It must be about late July or early August by now. The first of the lightning storms didn't usually begin until at least the end of September. While it wasn't unheard of for the occasional storm to blow up out of the blue, what was happening today was strange, out of kilter.

As he went about getting ready for the day, Fynn thought back to what had happened in the early hours of the morning. Had it been the effects of too much grog, or had he really seen something in the half-dark? Had he imagined that pungent whiff of a wild or feral cat?

The thought kept niggling at him. There had been no mistaking that feline odour, sharp yet musky. Even the effects of the beer hadn't been enough to blur either his instincts or his sense of smell to that extent.

Unwilling to accept that his instincts had misled him, after he'd finished his coffee, he retraced his steps back to where the horses were kept.

On reaching the enclosure, he dropped to one knee and scanned the dusty ground. It hadn't rained for months and the ground was baked dry, although soft in places where it had been broken up by the horses' hoofs.

No sign, nothing. Then, just as he was about to turn away, his experienced eye caught sight of what looked like an imprint in the sand a few yards away. Although faint, it was unmistakably not that of a horse, or a man. Squatting down, he took a closer look at it. Then he whistled.

It belonged to a cat all right, but hardly a domestic one. The pad was too large and well-defined. His eyes lit up. Oh, yes! And here was another little detail that interested him, one that told him a great deal about this particular beast. Its claws were set and non-retractable much like those of a dog. There would be no sharpening of claws on a tree for this pussy cat, he thought. He stared hard at the imprint, at a loss for words.

A cheetah! Here, in Shaka's well-guarded citadel? Unbelievable, yet its imprint was there, clear to see, and unmistakable. The way a cheetah's claws were set made them unique in the cat family, large or small, wild or domestic.

Casting about, he eventually spotted a small tuft of hair caught on the rough bark of the hardwood stakes. Holding it up between thumb and forefinger, Fynn examined it closely, noting its colours and soft texture.

It had been a cheetah all right, and a young one, at that. No doubt about it. He whistled softly. But where in the hell had it come from? And, more's to the point, where was it now?

As he made his way to keep the rendezvous with Shaka, Fynn said nothing to the others. There was enough tension in the air already.

He knew that the thought of witnessing another execution was weighing heavily on the minds of his fellow travellers. The news that there might be a predatory animal on the loose would hardly improve matters.

Shaka was busy performing his morning rituals; bathing, scraping his skin clean, ending with a final finish of native butter to give his skin a healthy, ruddy glow. Unlike the day before, this time there was no drama, no horror scene, no body, only the low murmur of voices and the sound of birds twittering.

After the coterie of councillors and headmen had withdrawn, they were invited to take part in an audience with him. When Farewell offered Shaka some more medicines and patent remedies from the boxes, he received the gifts graciously enough, but seemed oddly distracted. He made little comment concerning their properties and merely laid them to one side.

It was at this point that Petersen, no doubt meaning well, and seeking to amuse his host, produced a small music box and raised the lid.

As the tinkling notes trilled out, Shaka, far from being amused, looked distinctly unnerved. When he saw the figure of the brightly coloured ballerina begin to twirl around in time to the music, he gave a visible jump and rose out of his seat with his fists clenched.

He scowled at Petersen, who looked completely taken aback by the aggressive response. Luckily, the old man said nothing, but promptly closed the lid with a snap and put the music box out of sight, behind his back.

Shaka was silent for a while then waggled a finger at them. 'Perhaps you should see some more of my kingdom. Hlambamanzi will accompany you. He knows the places of interest I think you should see.'

Although his smile was open, generous even, Fynn was not slow to detect the flicker of nervousness on Jakot's face as he translated.

'*Ngiyabonga*, thank you,' Fynn replied, 'we will be happy to see more of your kingdom.'

When they left the square, Petersen clutching the disgraced music box, he muttered, 'Well, at least we didn't have to witness any more neck-snapping. Let's be thankful for small mercies, hey?'

After they'd eaten their mid-day meal, they got the horses ready. Although the early mists had cleared, the sun glowered fitfully from behind banks of heavy clouds.

A look of dismay crossed Jakot's face when he saw the horses being brought out of the paddock, saddled up and ready to go. Fynn laughed, and slapped him on the back. 'Don't worry, Jakot! You can hop up behind me and see Zululand in comfort.'

As they set off down through kwaBulawayo with Jakot holding on behind him, Fynn noticed that the light had changed to a strange bronze colour. Wrong season or not, he thought, a storm's on its way. Or something is.

Once through the gates, they set off upstream along the riverbank. The boy herders waved and cheered them on, running alongside the horses for a bit before falling back to take up their duties again.

Although it was officially a time of celebration, the normal work of the settlement was obviously still going on. They passed women cutting wedges of clay from the river bank; oxen dragging loads of firewood; women bearing huge piles of reeds on their heads, small children tagging along behind them.

After following the river for a few miles, they decided to turn inland. The surrounding hills were dun-coloured, the grass tawny and brittle, clumps of aloes dusty after months without rain. Although the land appeared fertile and well-drained, the further they moved away from kwaBulawayo the less there appeared to be in the way of human habitation.

A little while later, Jakot pointed up ahead. A rocky ridge stood out against the skyline. 'On the other side, lives the Nkosikazi, the mother of Shaka.'

After a brief silence, he shook his head, 'Strong womans, every-one afraid of her... even the Nkosi, I think,' he added, somewhat obliquely. Flashing a brilliant smile, he made a snapping move-ment with his teeth. 'Like crocodile. One bite, all gone.'

A mile or so further on, Farewell reined in his horse. They'd left the river behind some time ago and were traversing a rock-strewn valley watered by a small stream. The other horsemen drew up beside him and dismounted. Jakot swung down from behind Fynn and disappeared into a patch of scrub.

The weather had turned breathless and humid; even the tin-kling of the brownish water sounded brassy and muffled in the heat.

To the west, a series of grassy hills studded with outcrops of rock, gave way to folds of high, rolling land. Low clouds hung heavy on the skyline, giving the place a gloomy appearance.

'I don't know if anyone else has noticed,' Farewell said, indi-cating the skyline, 'but there seems to be a great deal of bird activity going on beyond that particular ridge. I've been keeping an eye on it for some time now. They're mainly of the predator variety, scavengers, vultures, that kind of thing.'

Sure enough, flocks of birds were circling lazily in the sky, wheeling and soaring on the air currents.

On his return from inspecting the scrub, Farewell fixed Jakot with a questioning blue eye. 'Have you any idea why those birds are there, and why they're so busy?'

The interpreter was silent for a moment. When he replied, he seemed unsure of himself. 'This is not a good place, Fahwell,' he said, at last. 'Better to pass on, not see.'

Argumentative as always, Petersen piped up, 'I think we'll be the judge of that. It could be something interesting, Francis. Up to now, we haven't seen much, just some natives going about their business, and endless hills.'

Fynn, who had made no comment regarding the circling

predators, was remembering the rather oblique comment Shaka had made when suggesting they explore his kingdom.

What was it he'd said? '*Hlambamanzi will show you the places of interest I think you should see.*' Given the current bird activity, the words had an ominous ring.

He asked the interpreter, 'Did the Nkosi order you to take us to this place, Jakot? What's here that he wants us to see?'

Jakot shook his head, his voice hard and stubborn. 'Never will I take you there, never!'

Farewell stared at him for a moment then gestured for him to climb up behind Fynn again. 'Well now, since we wouldn't want to get you into trouble for disobeying Shaka, we'll make this decision on our own. Agreed?'

Long before they reached the top of the ridge, the smell hit them. Sickly sweet and putrid, it was unmistakably the stench of decomposing flesh.

'Sweet Jesus!' Fynn hurriedly crossed himself then whipped off his neckerchief and held it over his nose and mouth. Swivelling round in the saddle, his eyes met Jakot's, the question in them fairly obvious.

The tawny segment in the interpreter's left eye glowed. 'I tell you not to come,' he said, breathing hard, 'this is a bad place.' The words came out in a rush, as if his mastery of English was suddenly running out.

'A graveyard?' queried Hoffman, trying not to breathe in through his nose.

'I would hardly describe it as that,' Farewell's curt voice interjected. 'At least we have the good sense to put our dead below ground. Gives them dignity, and doesn't bloody well offend the rest of us by having to smell them!'

The valley was a tangled mass of coarse grass, stunted mimosa trees, studded here and there with outcrops of moss-covered rocks. Details began to emerge of what else lay down there.

It seemed to those staring down that they were looking at a field of scarecrows erected by a farmer to scare birds away from his crops. Only in this case, it didn't appear to be working.

'What in the hell's all this about?' Hoffman shouted out.

Down among the scarecrows, the sound of his voice caused a fluttering and a heaving. Before their horrified eyes, the scarlet heads and wattles of hooded vultures flapped awkwardly away while others stayed where they were, too bloated to move. Hoarse, raucous squawks of protest filled the air.

The stakes on which the scarecrows were fixed stood in neat, orderly rows. The tattered caricatures of what had once been human beings were impaled on them, their twisted skeletons and half-picked bones testament to the agony in which they had died.

Schmidt's face was a study in horror. Petersen swayed in the saddle, his face ashen. Jakot, his expression closed and stubborn, turned his back on the charnel house below, and refused to look at it.

Farewell tapped his heels against the stallion's flanks. 'I don't know about the rest of you,' he said, as he started off down the boulder-strewn slope, 'but I need to see the worst this man can do. Gentlemen, if we're considering doing business with the Zulu leader, we owe it to ourselves to see exactly how he treats those who fall foul of him.'

Fynn, Hoffman and Petersen reluctantly followed his lead, leaving Schmidt and Jakot behind, both men silently refusing to descend into the valley.

Even Hoffman's crude remark that 'the stink won't be any worse down there than it is up here,' failed to change their minds.

In that sense, his statement proved less than accurate. On such a strangely still, hot day, the sickly-sweet smell of putrescence was stronger and even more poisonous down in the sheltered valley.

It clung to their skin, hair and clothes. Even the horses were affected by it, snickering, snorting and rolling their eyes. Half-way down the slope, Johann Petersen leaned over and vomited into the stunted grass.

The shining white pates of the more recently deceased glimmered up at them from between the scrubby mimosa roots and boulders of rock. Many of the bones showed signs of having been shattered and splintered with rocks, or heavy objects. It was clear many had either been killed quickly or battered senseless and left to die. The rows of 'scarecrows', however, were a different matter altogether.

Silence as the men's horses clip-clopped past the ghastly bands of victims; the only sounds being the gabbling of flopping, overfed birds fighting over scraps of flesh.

Fynn, hardened by his experiences in the hospitals of the East End of London, was able to view the victims with a slightly more dispassionate eye, while Farewell was no stranger to seeing men blown apart by shell and shot.

Moving in closer, he noticed the sharpened point of the bamboo stake protruding from the spinal cord of one of the victims. It was dark brown, stained with blood. His testicles shrivelled. The stake had clearly been inserted through the anus and driven up into the poor devil's internal organs.

The perfume of the mimosa blossoms was sweet, but not sweet enough to mask the smell of the man who had been impaled, then left to die from thirst, starvation, or the ministrations of scavengers. Not all of the ghastly crew were bone and dust. Some had tatters and scraps of bloody flesh still holding them together.

And they weren't all men, either ...

Horrified, Fynn noticed the flopping, dried-up breasts of more than one woman. Pathetic patches of woolly hair were still attached to the skull, and the empty, flaccid flaps of flesh which had once suckled a child now sagging on to the partially-exposed rib cage.

'Dear Christ,' he muttered,'what kind of crime deserves such a punishment?' But he already knew the answer to that.

His years on the Cape frontier had taught him many things, and not just to hunt, shoot and ride horses. Among the indigenous peoples, the most damning of the crimes punishable by death had been accusations of 'witchcraft'.

Silently, he addressed the pathetic remains. Did you really dabble in the occult, or did some jealous neighbour lie about you, claiming you'd bewitched her husband, or turned her milk sour?

The crack of rifle fire shattered the stillness. The air was full of the whoops and cries of birds as they fluttered up, alarmed and aggravated at being interrupted in their feasting.

Fynn swung round. Farewell and Hoffman stood with smoking muskets in their hands. A short distance away, the remains of several vultures too bloated to flop out of range lay twitching on the ground.

'Goddampt birds!' Hoffman yelled, lapsing into a spate of incomprehensible Afrikaans.

'Likewise,' Farewell responded brusquely, brushing spatters of blood from his cream pantaloons. 'Though at this precise moment, I have to admit I don't know which I find worse, those who carried out these abominations, or the scavengers who feed off their handiwork.'

The journey back to kwaBulawayo was made in near silence, each man too preoccupied with his own thoughts to make conversation. Once they were back, Fynn took Jakot aside. Still withdrawn and sullen, the Xhosa looked at him with a somewhat jaundiced eye.

Fynn stared him down then said quietly, 'If Shaka asks you about the valley and what we thought of it, I want you to tell him this. We, the people of King George, think he is less merciful to his enemies than the King of the Zulus. He rarely kills them, just shuts them up in houses of stone to rot in chains, never again to see the light of day or feel the sun on their faces, not until the end of their days.'

The Xhosa's teeth gleamed in the strange bronze light. '*Yebo*, Mbuyasi, I can tell him this from my heart, true. Hlambamanzi has also seen the darkness of King Jo-Ji's prisons. If it were not for Kingi I would still be there, even now – or dead.'

Grateful to be back in the comparative safety of kwaBulawayo, they lit a fire and put on some coffee to brew. Farewell dug around among the supplies and produced a handful of Dutch cheroots. Passing them around, he sat down by the fire, took off his jacket and laid it to one side, along with his cocked hat.

On the return journey, the atmosphere had been stiff and awkward, most of it emanating from Schmidt, who had hardly said a word after refusing point blank to go down into the valley. Oddly enough, Petersen had also said very little.

Farewell rummaged in the breast pocket of his jacket and took out his gold-rimmed eye glass. Once it was in place, he looked round the circle of faces.

'Since I'm the official head of this expedition – and I mean by that, not just this specific journey to visit Shaka of the Zulus, but the mission that set out from the Cape – after all that's happened, I feel I should make some points clear.'

He fixed Petersen with a stern eye. 'Father, I'm sorry this afternoon's experience distressed you, but you had no need to go down there. You should have stayed with Pieter here and not upset yourself by witnessing such barbarity.'

'You say, that now, Francis,' the old man said, his lips twitching,' but if I had stayed behind, no doubt you'd have thought me an old fool, and a coward, to boot.' He waved away Farewell's denial with a peremptory wave of the hand.

'I know what you think of me, Francis. If I hadn't insisted on coming up here with you from the Cape, you would have been more than happy just to take my money and plunge it unseen into this caper. No, my boy, I'm glad I came, I'm glad I saw that murdering black scum's handiwork for myself.'

Petersen tailed off into a fit of coughing, and buried his face in one of his huge handkerchiefs. Schmidt leaned over, and patted him gently on the back.

'Nie, don't worry yourself, Johann,' he said, 'I fully have sympathy for your views.' Turning to Farewell, he stared at him for a moment.

'I can also, of course, see your point of view, Francis. You were an officer, a man used to action, no stranger to bloodshed and death, and now a trader with a risky proposal, taking daring steps to achieve it.'

He took a sip of coffee. 'For myself, I am a simple businessman, used only to dealing with civilised people. This *trek* has been an experience – but I have to tell you now, I am no longer interested in putting my hard-earned money into such a venture.'

Draining the last of his coffee, he set the tin mug aside and got to his feet. 'From now on, I have no wish to be involved in further discussions of this nature. Also, I will not be coming with you when summoned the next time by the Zulu chief. Never will I look on his face again, for it is the face of the Devil.'

He turned away. 'I am now going to my tent. Maybe if I sleep I can forget what I saw today. It was like Hell itself had come to earth.'

After he'd disappeared, Fynn broke the silence. 'I just knew this was going to be a bastard of a day. The minute I opened my eyes, I just knew it.'

He shot a glance skyward. 'There's something about this bloody light, something's not right about it. I wish this storm, or whatever it is that's on its way, would hurry up, and put in an appearance.'

Long before the day finally came to an end, Fynn's premonition returned to haunt him. An hour or so later, just as the apology for daylight finally ebbed away, Jakot came running to tell him Shaka wanted to see them, all of them.

Leaving Schmidt behind, they followed him through the gates and entered the maze of huts. As usual, everything was very quiet, although they could hear the sound of women's voices and the faint clatter of cooking pots.

When they came out into the wide square and saw Shaka's great house standing in all its glory, Farewell, Hoffman and Petersen fell silent, suitably impressed by its size and the splendour of the exquisite workmanship.

And by the time they finally stood on the threshold of the magnificent arched doorway and looked at the twinkling lights of the oil lamps reflected in the glossy floor and caught sight of the bead-covered, massive wooden pillars supporting the dome, even Petersen seemed overawed.

As Shaka bade them enter, a tall, dark-skinned male servant in a long brown robe slipped quietly past them and out into the night.

The warrior king was seated in his carved chair, a cloak drawn around his shoulders. Arranged before him were some of the boxes of potions and medicines brought as gifts, the day before. Barely acknowledging their presence, he spent a few minutes staring distractedly into the square, almost as if he was waiting for someone to appear. After a moment, he snapped out of his reverie, and bade them welcome.

Two young girls came in, carrying large jugs of beer and platters of small cakes. After serving them, they slipped quietly away. The preliminaries over, Shaka leaned forward, his eyes gleaming with curiosity.

'Hlambamanzi tells me you believe the punishment for King Jo-Ji's bad people is even greater even mine.' He shook his head. 'Ah, but I do not agree with this. I must let Jo-Ji know of my feelings on this matter. To let them live a long time in this way is very cruel. My way is best – quick, finish! What is your opinion, Mbuyasi?'

Jakot's handsome face was impassive and unreadable as he translated, while Fynn wisely responded with suitable platitudes.

Beyond the high arched doorway, the night was dark, brooding and very still; even the shrilling of the cicadas was muted. During the long silence that followed, Shaka again seemed distant and pre-occupied. Below the circlet of padded otter fur and sweep of feathers, his eyes were remote, his thoughts obviously elsewhere.

A moment later, he looked up, smiling, and pointed to the collection of boxes. Some were open, the bottles and jars spilling on to the floor, while others were still in their oilskin coverings. He motioned for Fynn to come closer. Jakot moved nearer, his eyes on the floor.

Shaka pointed to one of the open packages, and indicated that he wanted Fynn to tell him about the contents. Fynn extracted one of the brown glass bottles and read the hand-written label. The purpose of the chalky liquid was easy and amusing to describe.

'For the stomach,' Jakot translated, rubbing his belly and making groaning noises.'For when you have eaten too much food – or drunk too much beer.' Gurgling noises followed, which made Shaka put back his head and laugh.

Fynn was about to move on to the next package when he felt something nudging him from behind. Turning round quickly, he saw Petersen edging forward with a glass bottle, half-full of small green pills in his hand.

Unbidden, he inched towards Shaka, rattling the contents of the medicine phial. Shaka's brow creased in a frown. Fynn tried to deter the old man from getting any closer, first with a warning look and then with a surreptitious jab with the toe of his boot.

Ignoring Fynn's dirty looks, Petersen took the stopper out, shook a few pills into the palm of his hand, and held them out to Shaka.

'I find these very good when my insides are stopped up by too much rich food,' he said. 'One or two at night usually sorts me out.'

Shaka stared at him, the scowl deepening. Jakot was flustered, not knowing whether to start translating or not. Clearly irritated, the king of the Zulus rattled out an order to Jakot, who then turned to Petersen.

'The Nkosi asks you to show him what this medicine does. Please put them in your mouth. And swallow.' He mimicked the action. Petersen's mouth dropped open. 'But I didn't mean them for myself, I was only suggesting…'

On seeing the regal scowl deepen to one of open rage, he hurriedly put a tablet in his mouth then swallowed it. Shaka's finger wagged in irritation. Jakot translated.

Another pill, then another – Petersen by now had swallowed three of the bright green tablets. Sweat beaded Fynn's brow.

He knew only too well what Petersen's pills were for, because hadn't he dished them out himself to ease the man's constipation? That was a double, if not a triple dose he'd now swallowed…

His stomach contracted when he saw Shaka's commanding forefinger rise once more and watched Petersen gulp down yet another pill. Four or perhaps five tablets! Dear God, he would have to step in, such a dose could kill a man of his age, not to mention the effects…

Petersen coughed and gagged on the final pill. The glass bottle slipped from his sweaty fingers. Its contents spilled out on to the glossy floor and rolled away in every direction.

Farewell came forward to help him. He lifted his father-in-law on to his shaking legs and helped him back to where Hoffman was sitting with a look of bemused horror on his face.

As he brushed past Fynn, he muttered, 'We need to get him out of here – and fast!'

Although the day had been a total disaster from beginning to end, it seemed that at last the fates were about to step in – on their side, for a change.

A discreet cough announced the return of the tall, dark-skinned servant in the brown robe. He hovered at the doorway, a look of urgency on his face. Shaka waved him forward. The man leaned in close and delivered his message, his lips barely seeming to move.

The monarch's head came up sharply, and his eyes travelled to the sultry darkness beyond the doorway. The servant, whose name was Mbopha ka Sithayi, and someone whom Fynn was destined to come up hard against in the future, bowed low then backed away as swiftly and silently as he had come.

Shaka rose from the carved chair, his face suffused with a strange look of tension. He announced, through Jakot, that he regretted bringing their audience to a close, but he had urgent matters to attend to.

Much relieved, they scrambled to their feet and with Farewell helping Petersen along, hurriedly made their departure. Just before they entered the network of pathways, Fynn glanced back over his shoulder.

The warrior king was standing in the doorway of his magnificent residence, a dark silhouette framed against the warm glow of the interior, his eyes scanning the night sky as if searching for something.

The next time Fynn looked back, the doorway was empty.

By the time they reached the gates leading from the royal quarters, Petersen was doubled over, clutching his belly. It took all of Farewell's strength to stop his father-in-law from slipping to his knees. Fynn slung an arm around his shoulders to help him stay upright.

Petersen was a heavily built man and by no means either frail or unfit. Nevertheless, it was clear his well-intentioned attempt to introduce Shaka of the Zulus to the benefits of pills made from the ground seeds of the castor-oil plant had been a disastrous mistake.

'What made it come on so fast?' Farewell demanded of Fynn, as they stopped to get a better grip on him. 'It seemed to me those damn pills were no sooner down his throat than they started to work.'

Fynn replied, 'The beer. The damn stuff's full of yeast – and unless I miss my guess, he'd supped quite a bit of it earlier on.'

Luckily, their camping area was separate from anyone else. Petersen found a place as far from the tents as he could. Yanking down his breeches, he squatted, groaning and straining while his insides erupted noisily.

Leaving Petersen to his privacy, Fynn sat down by the fire. 'Thank God, Shaka didn't take any of those pills,' he said. 'Even though his stomach's a damn sight stronger than Petersen's... Jesus, can you imagine!'

He stared into the flames for a moment. 'But what in the hell got into him – Petersen, I mean? One moment, he's calling Shaka every name under the sun, the next he's coming forward to offer him his favourite remedy for stopped-up bowels!'

Farewell set some water on to boil. 'God knows', he said, a trifle wearily, 'you can never tell with Johann.'

Loud moans came from the darkness. Fynn hurried off to check on the sick man. 'I'm pretty worried about him,' he added, when he came back, 'all that straining's dangerous for a man of his age, but I'll do what I can for him.'

An hour or so later, Fynn brought Petersen back to sit at the fire. The man had visibly aged and his usually ruddy face was strained and pale. When Farewell bent to put a blanket around his shoulders, Fynn shot him a warning look, which clearly said, 'Now's not the time for blame. Let him be.'

He made some camomile tea in a tin mug and encouraged Petersen to drink it. The old man's hand shook as he held it to his lips. His jowls quivered as he spoke.

'As soon as I can climb back on my horse, I'm getting out of here. It was a mistake for me to come. I'll go back to the bay as soon as can be arranged, then on to the Cape. No more for me. I'm with Schmidt on this.'

He gestured towards the tent with the closed flap. 'Like Pieter, I refuse to see that black devil's face one more time.'

When his insides began to erupt again, he groaned weakly. As he retreated into the darkness again they heard him gasp, 'Just don't expect one penny piece from me, Francis. This venture's damned...and so will you be, if you persist in going on with it.'

After he'd gone, Fynn, Farewell and Hoffman stared into the fire. The night seemed to have grown darker, no stars or half-moon to lighten the oppressive blackness.

Hoffman eventually broke the silence. '*Ja*, I also have to admit that I am less sure than before about this whole venture – '

He broke off hastily, then as if to re-assure them of his good intentions added, 'Right now, I'm not saying I'm going to pull out for sure, but I need to think about it some more. As soon as he is fit to ride, Schmidt and I will take Johann back to the bay. We will of course need some of your young Zulus to go with us. A hundred and fifty or two hundred miles, with maybe ten, twelve days trek is a long way for us to go alone – too many dangers, especially with the old man.'

Farewell frowned. 'Thank you for your offer,' he said stiffly, 'but my father-in-law is well noted for his quick temper. Once he feels better, I'm sure he'll change his mind.'

Hoffman stood up. 'In which case, he will remain your problem. As for myself, I will stick to my plan to return to the bay. Once I have spoken to Schmidt in the morning, I will let you know what we have decided.'

In the ruddy glow of the firelight, they saw that his face was determined, his lips set in a thin line below the blond moustache.

Farewell eyed him severely. 'Out of the question,' he snapped. 'I won't allow you to go, Hoffman. We can't seem to be running away, man. Good God, we've only been here a few days.'

He got to his feet, his eye-glass glittering in the firelight. 'Be a good fellow, just lie low for a bit and let me see to the rest. You've played your part and most of the celebrations are over. In any case, Fynn and I can't leave yet. We came here to talk of ivory and trading, and by God, that's what we're going to do. '

Hoffman listened carefully then, with a snap, brought his booted feet together in a decidedly military salute and strode off towards the tents.

Alone by the fire, the two men were silent for a while. Farewell reached into his saddlebag and produced a bottle of Cape brandy. 'I'll let Petersen have some in a bit,' he said, 'it might settle his stomach.'

Fynn nodded. 'Add a little warm water to it. It won't do him any harm.'

Farewell poured a generous quantity of the fiery brandy into the tin mugs and handed one to Fynn. 'As you said, Henry, what a bloody day it's been.' Swirling the brandy around the bottom of the mug, he took a hearty swig.

'Amen,' Fynn replied, letting out his breath in a long sigh, 'my sentiments exactly.' Farewell posed a question. 'D'you think the other three will hold out – at least until we can all leave here together?'

Fynn shifted uneasily. 'God knows. Remember, Shaka's asked me to stay on afterwards, so I won't be travelling back with you, in any case. If they're hell-bent on going, best to let them go, in my opinion. Grudges can spread fast. If Shaka senses anything's wrong in our camp, he might easily change his tune. As you said, it's only been a few days since we got here. There's been no opportunity to bring up anything remotely like the possibility of trade with him. We've only just 'broken the ice' with him, as you might say –leaving out the old man's gaffes, of course!'

Francis Farewell grunted, 'But if they do go on ahead, I fear we'll lose the rest of the investors. I know Johann well enough to know what he's capable of. You've seen how stubborn he is. Once he's set against something, it's the devil's own job to get him to see sense. Right now, I don't give a damn if he pulls out or not – it's how he'll bully the others into following his dictum that bothers me.'

He got to his feet. 'I'll best go and see how the old devil's getting on. After that, I'm going to turn in before anything else happens.'

'Amen,' said Fynn, draining the last of his brandy.

Afterwards, he lay wrapped in his blankets by the fire, listening to the night sounds. The darkness seemed impenetrable, and even the cicadas seemed to have stopped cricking.

Turning on to his back, he put his hands behind his head and looked up into the blackness. Events seemed to be moving very fast, pushing and pulling them this way and that. Why did he have the feeling that everything was speeding up, building to some kind of crisis?

Although he hadn't said much to Farewell about Petersen and the others making moves to leave, he knew one thing for sure.

They might well want to skedaddle back to the comparative safety of the bay, but would Shaka allow them to go? What if he took umbrage and saw it as a personal rebuff to his hospitality? After all, they were only here because he had issued them with an invitation.

Petersen, in springing the musical box on Shaka without warning, had obviously irritated him – then, for the second time that day, he had done it again, this time with small green, laxative tablets.

Fynn turned over and groaned. 'Three days,' he muttered, 'it's only taken three days for the cracks to show in the white man's circus. What in the hell's likely to happen in the next three?'

Forty-seven

Even from where he was hidden beyond the outer rim of firelight, Langani could feel the tension emanating from the two men hunched over the fire. Their slumped heads and shoulders told him all was not well.

Darkness and sorrow had been hanging over them since their return from their journey beyond kwaBulawayo. It was clear that viewing the horrors of Shaka's valley of death had greatly disturbed all of them, without exception.

In a way, the diviner was pleased, for it showed him that they were men with no appetite for such cruelty. The obvious distress demonstrated by more than one of the party, and their refusal to even look on it, had greatly moved him, and made him look more kindly on them.

Jakot, who was no stranger to cruelty himself, had especially impressed him. His silent refusal to lead the *abelungu* to witness the results of Shaka's terrible justice had been a brave act of defiance.

Langani shot another glance at the men by the fire. The others were weakening in their resolve to trade with the great Shaka. Did this mean that their mission would fail? Sadly, he feared not.

Farewell and Fynn were different men from the others; strong, decisive, and very determined to find a way to get their hands on the ivory of the great *ndlovu*.

The diviner sniffed the air. The night was full of strange currents, moving and shifting in odd ways. In fact, the whole day had been the same, the air sullen with the threat of a brooding storm.

He had sensed a thin thread of danger running through it, but it was hard to tell where it was coming from and who it threatened. All day, the light had been a strange bronze colour, much like it had been the day before he'd become aware of the swirling currents in the rock pool.

Without warning, a surge of energy crackled around him, stirring the loose strands of his hair and making them fan out around his head. A metallic taste filled his mouth and the skin on his face felt tight and stretched.

What had just happened? He looked around but saw nothing untoward. Whatever was in the air was strong, making its presence felt.

Langani heard the horses snicker nervously. It was unlikely they'd sensed his presence for he was too far away. No wind to carry his scent, but yet something was worrying them. Could it be what had just passed by so silently?

A quick glance told him that Farewell had gone into his tent and closed the flaps, while Fynn was preparing to bed down by the fire as he usually did. Obviously, neither of them had noticed anything out of the ordinary.

He waited patiently for Fynn to settle down. Once he was asleep, there would be no reason for him to stay.

The horses were still restless. He could feel their agitation. The diviner stood perfectly still, listening for a sound, any sound that might account for it. It might only be a scurrying rat, a night bird or some other small scavenger. He waited and listened, but could hear only the faint crackle and spit of the dying fire.

Almost beyond his range of vision, he caught sight of something pale, almost invisible in the half-light. He stared hard at it.

There! This time, there was no mistaking the quick glint of cat eyes, the flash of rangy legs and long, lean body...

The hairs on the back of his neck prickled. He hadn't forgotten what had happened the night before, but having found no traces in the morning, he'd merely pushed it to the back of his mind. Strange occurrences, after all, were part of his life as a diviner, a dealer in mysteries and the inexplicable.

But now, faced with a second sighting of the animal, questions tumbled over one another in his mind. If it was indeed Celiwe, the young cheetah had found her own way there, although his sanctuary was many days away. It could even have followed him, keeping well out of sight, of course.

Given the large numbers of people continually coming and going, for the animal to have come in through the front gates would have been virtually impossible. The opening and closing of the massive gates at sunrise and sunset was strictly controlled, for safety reasons. For it to have scrambled over the high fences enclosing the settlement was also highly improbable...and in any case, how had it known exactly where to find him?

He focused his attention on the tawny shape lurking on the edge of the darkness. There was no doubt it had seen him, for the neat head was turned in his direction. And judging by the way it was already half-turned towards the head of the slope, there was no doubt in his mind that it was waiting for him to follow.

Langani shot a quick glance in the direction of the camp. Fynn was asleep, rolled in his blankets by the fire. The flaps of the tents were still closed. All was quiet.

The animal was on the move. A lithe shape in the darkness, the cheetah was moving up towards the brow of the hill, stopping now and again and looking back to make sure he was following. Where was it going? Only Shaka's private quarters lay up there. Not daring to call out, Langani drew his cloak around him and moved swiftly up the hill after it.

The cheetah always seemed to be just a few yards ahead, its long banded tail swinging gently as it padded along. Where it was going, or rather, where it was leading him, Langani had no idea.

A few moments later, two wraith-like shadows slipped past the nodding sentries and disappeared into the darkness beyond.

As they neared the wide square where Shaka held court, Langani heard the first growls of thunder, distant but unmistakable, the sound adding its own particular menace to the throbbing darkness and the underlying smell of danger.

When the growls of thunder reached him, Shaka instinctively glanced up at the sky. A smile tugged at the corners of his mouth. What he had been waiting for was on its way and getting nearer by the moment.

Tonight, he was bare-headed, no band of leopardskin or otter fur around his brow, no scarlet flash of *igwala gwala* feathers, no regal collar or other decoration – only a plain cloak thrown around his shoulders against the oppressive night air.

After a few moments, his keen ears picked up the faint sound of footsteps. Someone was near the entrance to the square, one person only, moving carefully and lightly. Instinctively, he stepped back into the shadows, not wishing to be seen. When lightning flared briefly overhead, he saw that the square was empty. Whoever the footsteps belonged to had passed by.

Shaka moved out from beneath the tree, his bare feet making no sound among the scattered dry leaves. Retracing his steps, he located the small gate concealed in the thatch, opened it then slipped through.

Shadows, he thought, with some humour, so many shadows in and around the house of Shaka during these last few days. Moving in the night, flitting around me, watching... if I didn't know better, I might think that spirits from times past had returned to haunt me.

A slight frown creased his brows. Strange, though, that I was never aware of such shadows before – only since the *abelungu* have entered my gates, in fact. Could it be that their arrival has disturbed the shades and left them uneasy?

The smile returned. Or is it that there is only one shadow, not many, as I might have feared – but only one of great significance? Another dull rumble of thunder in the distance, though much closer now.

The area beyond the square was heavily wooded and on his orders had been preserved that way. After a day spent with councillors and the never-ending streams of plaintiffs seeking his advice, dealing with affairs of state and the military, he liked to walk in the fading light at the end of the day, breathing in the smells of earth and growing things and listening to the lowing of the cattle in the enclosures settling for the night.

With the ease of long practice, he moved stealthily and silently through the trees, his senses alert to everything around him. Now and again, he stopped to listen, and sniff the air, his nostrils flaring. When he heard the soft pad of footsteps coming towards him along the path, his lips curved in a smile.

Swiftly, he stepped into the darker shadows beneath the trees and stood very still. Lightning flared up again. In its brief but brilliant light, he caught a glimpse of a grey, indistinct shape flowing towards him down the path.

For an instant, Shaka could have sworn he also caught the luminous flash of animal eyes in the darkness, but dismissed it as unlikely. Only small animals of the rodent variety would be scavenging here; what he'd seen would have belonged to a much larger animal.

Keeping his eyes fixed on the shadowy wraith, he waited until it was almost level with him. Then he stepped out from beneath the trees, effectively blocking its way.

As he called out, the unmistakable ring of triumph was in his voice.

'So, Yendane, *we meet again...* '

Langan was stunned to see Shaka suddenly appear without warning out of the shadows.

With a dull thud of awareness, he realised his earlier instincts had been proved right. Shaka, with his well-honed skills and uncanny instincts, not to mention his legions of informers, would have realised that someone, or something, was at large within his citadel, someone who was secretive and potentially dangerous.

Beyond him, the path lay empty. No pale blur in the darkness, no soft pad of animal feet. Only the trees stirring in the rising wind, dark patches of shadow, undergrowth on either side. The cheetah had been ahead of him all the way from the campsite. Surely Shaka would have noticed it?

Langani let out a slow breath, his mind racing. Was the animal really Celiwe, or had he just assumed it was? If not, then what was it that had led him here, to this very spot?

Shaka laughed and shrugged his shoulders expressively. 'Have I surprised you, Yendane? Surely, you did not believe there is anything, or anyone, within my kingdom that escapes my attention?'

He felt a stab of unease. *Could it be he knows where my sanctuary is?* No one knew where he lived, not even those closest to him, and he wanted it to stay that way.

As the warrior king and the man of magic faced each other across the path, forked lightning tore down the sky and illuminated them in its eerie light.

Shaka gestured overhead. 'Seeing it is not the season for storms, do you not think this is strange, Yendane?'

Langani hesitated before answering. Had he made the connection between him, as he was now, and the small boy of long ago? Shaka's next words dispelled any doubts he may have had.

'You say nothing, little brother? I ask you again – do you not think it unusual that we two should meet again with a storm breaking above our heads – just as it did the first time we met all those years ago?'

A flash of surprise showed in Langani's eyes. So the astute

king of the Zulus already knew of the connection between them. With a sigh, he let the hood of the monkey skin cloak slip back to reveal his face and long, plaited hair.

'Nkosi,' he replied, 'I am indeed surprised you know who I am – or who I was,' he corrected himself quickly.

Shaka laughed. '*Yebo*, I know who you *were* – and also who you *are* now, brother dancer. The last time we were face to face, the witch Ntombazi recognised you as being a danger to the devils that lived within her, did she not?'

Serious now, he surveyed Langani for a few moments. 'Although I did not understand it at the time – later, after I found out more about you, it told me clearly that you were someone who opposed evil and who also possessed great powers of divination. Although I was sure we had met somewhere before, I was at a loss as to where it might have been.'

He indicated Langani's plaits. '*Yebo*, after a while, after much searching, I discovered who you were – the small *toto* who danced with me in the storm.'

Shaka smiled, his eyes glittering in the half-light. 'It was a long time ago, little brother, but although much has happened since then, I did not forget you. What a day that was! No doubt you were later told how I had called down the storm on my father's head and destroyed most of esiKlebeni.'

Langani nodded. 'I knew nothing of it – not until very recently,' he explained, 'my grandmother, a very wise woman, told me how you had refused to accept the *umutsha* from your father – and also about our meeting during the great storm that followed.'

The warrior king was silent for a few moments. 'Even then I saw that you were a special child, fearless in the face of a storm that forced grown men to run from it in terror...'

'*Cha!*' Langani protested. 'To be truly brave, you must also taste fear. I had no fear of the storm, I loved its rage, its power and its rhythms – as I still do,' he added, glancing up into the thundering blackness above their heads.

Shaka looked long and hard at him. '*Yebo*, so now tell me, little brother – perhaps you can even command these powers to rise at your bidding?'

Langani shot him a quick look, but said nothing. Shaka went on, 'After I found out that Langani, the powerful diviner and the *toto*, my little brother of the storm, were one and the same, I began to wonder just who had been responsible for the storm that day. By its nature and timing, it was no accident.'

His eyes travelled over the young diviner's long braided hair, the grey cloak and the slender hands that held nothing in them.

'Since I have never believed in coincidence, I had to ask myself just who had raised the storm that day. Was it me? Once before, as a young boy, I had called down the anger of my ancestors on the heads of my enemies – so why not this time? I had always believed that esKlebeni was my doing, until -'

The violent cracks of thunder were almost overhead now, blotting out his last words. 'Or was it you, little brother, the *toto* who loved its rage and fury? You who could dance to rhythms without drums to mark the beat? Were you the one who made the thunder and lightning your playthings, your partners in the dance?'

Langani felt his senses reel. Surely not! A child as young as he had been then could not have summoned up such powers –

With a stab of guilt, he remembered the storm he had deliberately called up, not so long ago, on the headland at eThekwini. Had he not summoned the wind and the seas to rise up and drive the white men's vessels against the rocks, nearly killing those aboard?

Quickly, he thrust the doubts away. But that had been completely different. He was a man now, in full command of his powers, a man of skills and training. To raise such a storm had not been easy; it had taken much prayer and meditation to make it happen. Also, it had not been done for his amusement, or to test his skills – only to try to protect his native land from a threat whose shape he could not see, from a power he did not fully comprehend...

Above their heads, sheets of lightning tore down the heavens, striking the earth some distance away. The smell of ozone was in the air, sharp in the nose, the taste of copper in the mouth.

Langani faced Shaka across the path. 'I was a child, only three or four years old at the time. I had no awareness of such things. And I did not know then that the ancestors would call on me to become what I am now.'

Shaka took a step closer. 'Yes, I do understand what you have become – one of the most powerful diviners in the land.' His face softened. 'Do not be mistaken. I do not seek to remove blame from myself for what happened at esiKlebeni – only to understand the nature of such things. Whether we use them or not, we two have uncommon powers, little brother – that is all I meant to say.'

The diviner responded quickly. '*Yebo*, it is true. We do have powers. But they are not the same, Nkosi. I do not seek earthly power, only to use that which the *amadhlozi* give me for the good of others.'

A wind had risen, bringing with it the smell of dry earth, rustling grasses and stored heat. Around them, the trees swayed and creaked.

Shaka said, 'So, now, Langani, *isangoma*, man of magic – tell me why you have been moving like a shadow around my house? I need to know what is it you are looking for and whether you have found it yet.'

Langani stared at him, hard. 'I search for nothing that can be seen with the eyes, or held in the hands, Nkosi. I look for the truth.'

'Truth?' demanded Shaka. 'There are many kinds of truth. Which one do you seek? Tell me, and I will help you find it.'

A roll of thunder directly overhead almost drowned out Langani's reply.

'It concerns the *abelungu*, the white men who are with you now. I am afraid they will bring much trouble to our land. I have known of their coming for some time, I have watched them from afar, seen them approach in their great ships with the white wings...'

'You saw them from afar, you say?' Shaka responded, frowning.

Langani held his breath. Perhaps he should be more careful. The man's distrust of the occult was well-known. His fears were short-lived, however.

Shaka nodded. '*Yebo,* you are an *isangoma,* and a powerful one. This I know already. And you have very strong powers – powers I know nothing about. But you are also a good man and a wise counsel to those who trust you with their secrets.'

He fixed him with a benevolent eye. 'Have no fear I will mistake you for the other kind, little brother. The Zulu Nkosi knows the difference between the brotherhood you belong to, and those who seek to spread evil throughout the land.'

Langani resisted the impulse to shudder, remembering only too well the cruel deaths visited on Ntombazi, Nobela and those who used the dark powers for their own ends.

Seizing the opportunity to express his fears concerning the arrival of the white men, he went on. 'I am afraid that the coming of the *abelungu* to our shores will be a source of great trouble in the days, or even in the years to come. The matter has concerned me greatly for some time.'

'What kind of trouble do you think a handful of white men will bring me?' Shaka roared out above the cracks of thunder. 'Am I a weak old man, drooling in his beard, to be afraid of a few strangers?'

Putting back his head, he laughed contemptuously. 'I do not need your powers to tell me who among them I can trust, and who I can not!'

Langani gritted his teeth. In spite of his subterfuge, he now found himself in the place he never wanted to be. Face to face with Shaka, and yet unable to tell him exactly what had made him so afraid for his land and its people. Desperately, he sought for the right words.

'I do not think these men are bad men in themselves, Nkosi, but it is what will follow after them that troubles me so greatly. I cannot, as yet, tell you exactly what shape or form this will take, I only know that it is not a good thing, and it is waiting – '

'Waiting for what?' Shaka demanded. 'My *impis* are invincible. You have seen them for yourself, man of magic. What can a few white men do against Shaka of the Zulus and the might of his warriors?'

He waved an impatient hand. 'The Xhosa, Hlambamanzi, has already told me a great deal about them. About their vessels that fly over the sea, their soldiers and the marvels they possess – and much about their great King who lives across the waters.'

His face softened. 'I can see you mean well, little brother. But you need have no fear on my behalf – or for the kingdom of the Zulus. '

A huge crack of thunder rolled round the heavens, followed by jagged spears of lightning that made Langani blink rapidly.

In the split seconds of that vivid searing light, he caught a glimpse of the cheetah. It was padding along the path towards him, a few yards behind Shaka. The warrior king's immediate instincts would be to kill it. In his youth he'd once despatched a leopard with little more than his bare hands – a half-grown cheetah would be nothing in comparison.

The animal's head came up, the luminous gleam of its eyes plainly visible in the eerie light. It was only a few paces away from Shaka now. Not knowing whether to call out to him or not, yet afraid of what might happen if he did, Langani could only stare at it in horrified fascination.

A tingling sensation erupted in his hands and feet. Heart racing, he became aware of his hair rising up to float around his head. What was happening?

The cheetah drew level with Shaka. Langani prayed that no sudden flash of lightning would betray its presence. The only sign of its awareness of the Zulu monarch was a twitch of its whiskers as it caught his scent.

Langani closed his eyes, almost afraid to look. An excruciating few moments passed. But when no shout of alarm or outrage came from the warrior king, he shot a mystified glance in his direction.

Why hadn't he called out? Surely, a man of his instincts would have sensed the presence of a wild animal passing within a hairsbreadth of him.

Instead, Langani heard him ask, 'Is this why you entered kwaBulawayo like a thief in the night, to warn me about the *abelungu*? Why did you not seek an audience with me, as all my people are free to do?'

The brush of animal hair and the heat of a body pressing against his legs made him jump involuntarily. A trickle of sweat ran down his back. Langani managed to stammer out a bland reply, enough to satisfy Shaka for the moment. Caught between several hard truths, he struggled with the reality of what was happening.

Shaka simply didn't realise that a live cheetah had come within a whisker of him. How could he tell him that a predatory wild animal, one he couldn't see, was watching him from a few yards away? The repercussions would be horrendous...

Secondly, he could hardly admit that his powers of prophecy had been failing him of late. His reputation would be destroyed and he would be marked out as inept and weak. So what did that leave him with?

The fleeting image of a small, bobbing orb of light on the roof of a rock-pool half-way up a mountain flashed into Langani's mind with the force of a thunderbolt. It was immediately followed by that of a young boy of no more than three or four years old, tottering above an iron ladder leading down into the treacherous water below.

The truth was that these were the only certainties Langani could swear to at the present moment in time. Those other certainties – Jakot, Fynn, and Farewell, the people he had seen during his 'dreamtimes' – were already here, in the flesh.

There was no way he could begin to explain that a child of the *abelungu*, presently living in a far-off land, would play a part in what was destined to unfold in the land of the Zulus – although how far in the future, he also couldn't say.

Langani dragged his thoughts back to the present. The storm had worsened. No rain, only the turbulence of light and sound and the wind tearing through the trees. His long hair had been shaken loose from its plaits and was floating around his head. The waves of heat from the animal pressing against him were increasing, as was the strong tingling sensations in his hands and feet. He felt a strange lightness in his body, as if he too, were about to defy earthly forces and fly upwards.

Shaka took a step closer, a strange excitement in his eyes as he watched the coils of the Diviner's hair float and twist in the air.

'You see, little brother, I was right. It is because of you this storm has come out of nowhere, the strange weather and the curious light. All day I have felt it, and even the night before. I knew that this was the day I would meet the elusive "shadow" haunting my every step.'

Only a yard or two separated them now. The animal at Langani's side pushed even closer to him, purring in its throat. Surely Shaka could hear it?

A wave of energy surged through him, adding to the sensation of weightlessness. The throbbing in his hands and feet rose to a painful climax.

'Now do you see why I say that we two are men of great power?' Shaka said, 'I have created a powerful army and a great nation. Tribes fall before my warriors and my name is known and feared throughout the land – and beyond.'

He smiled, and closed his eyes briefly. '*Yebo*, soon the amaPondo will fall and then 1 will go further south.' He stared, fascinated, at the mass of hair floating around Langani's head.

'But you, little brother, yours is a different kind of power. You walk in places I can not go, travel in lands I can not see. Is this not so?'

Langani could only nod, for his body was clammy with sweat and trembling as if with a fever. The heat emanating from the animal's body was almost unbearable. Just then, something passed through him. It was as if a fierce animal spirit, unique and powerful, had been completely at one with his own for the space of a few moments.

The wind shook the trees, picking up dust and grit and sending it whirling down the pathway. Langani's cloak fluttered around him. He tried to move the cheetah away from him, to spare him from its heat, but his hand felt only air, a lightness where the animal had been a moment ago.

The path before him and behind him was empty; only he and Shaka facing each other, with the wind gusting around them. The thunder was directly overhead now, the bolts of lightning at their most intense. Langani looked directly at Shaka.

In a voice hoarse with tension, he said, 'Twice of late, I have seen a star fall from the heavens, trailing fire. At first, I thought it was meant as a warning for the *abelungu* – but now I can see that the omen was meant for *you*, Nkosi. There is much danger around you. You must take great care about who you allow to come close to you – that is all I can say.'

Shaka laughed; his teeth and the whites of his eyes luminous in the dusky light. 'Now you see danger coming at me from the skies, *isangoma*! Am I such a weak man to heed all the fears you seem to be gathering for me?'

Langani felt a spurt of anger rise in him. The heat in his body began to generate the need for some kind of action.

First he commends me as an *isangoma* of considerable powers, he thought, and then berates me for trying to warn him about what I know is there!

Whirling round, he roared at Shaka above the noise of the storm. 'No, Nkosi, I do not think you are a weak man, only one who will not listen to me! When I tell you that you have much to fear, take heed of my words. As you say, you have your power and I have mine. While I can plainly see your handiwork, you can not see mine, for I deal in things beyond the ken of normal men – even yours, King of the Zulus, so do not forget it!'

Power surged through his tingling fingers. A bolt of fire shot out from them, setting the leaves and small branches alight and raising puffs of acrid smoke. Globules of liquid fire ran along the pathway, jumping and crackling as they went.

Shaka's face was alight with glee. 'You say well, *isangoma*. I see you are still full of spirit, just as you were as a small child!'

He gestured towards the spurts of fire crackling among the trees. 'Now do you still have doubts about who raised the storm of esiKlebeni?'

Langani's hair was streaming around his head, coiling and uncoiling, while shards of light spun about him. His hands were outstretched, as if he was about to greet someone. His eyes were not fixed on the warrior king, but on something, or someone, far from the forest paths of kwaBulawayo.

But Shaka, energised by the storm and greatly impressed by the effects of the young diviner's show of power, failed to notice such details.

'*Woza*! Come, little brother!' he called out to the motionless figure. 'Why waste a good storm! Now you have created it, let us dance together as we did before. Only this time, do not expect me to carry you on my shoulders!'

Tossing his cloak aside, he took up his stance in the middle of the path, a figure of terrifying strength and grace, poised for a performance that would have no awestruck spectators or cheering crowds to applaud it.

A frenetic display of light and noise split the night sky. Rivulets of fire and sparks ran along the ground in every direction, its source Langani, the diviner. Silhouetted against burning trees, he still stood with his hands outstretched and a smile of welcome on his face.

Shaka, the warrior king, the Lord of the Dance, launched himself into the air. In the space of that one gigantic leap, his powerful body was able to turn round once in mid-air before he landed in a graceful crouch, the tips of his fingers lightly touching the ground on either side.

As his head came up, he looked around expecting to see Langani. But the path before him lay empty. Of his brother dancer of the storm, there was no sign. All that remained were the still smouldering trees and shrubs and the intermittent flickers of lightning.

And just as it had been, all those years ago at esiKlebeni, Shaka of the Zulus found he was alone, with only the dying storm for company.

An hour or so later, all was still and quiet. The thunder had ceased, as had the lightning. Just before entering his magnificent, high-domed palace, the King of the Zulus paused on the threshold and glanced up at the night sky.

The last vestiges of the day's sultry clouds had cleared away, the air was clear and cool, and the stars had come out.

'Ai-i-i' Shaka said softly, 'so be it. Return to your hidden sanctuary, if you must. *Hamba ghale,* little brother, until we meet again.'

Epilogue

Act i

1824 *eThekwini Six weeks later*

F rancis Farewell stood with his hands clasped loosely behind his back, gazing up at the ridge on the far side of the
lagoon. Beside him was John Cane, the carpenter who'd
come up from the Cape with him on the *Antelope*. Standing at
over six and a half feet, he was, literally, a giant of a man.

The former Lieutenant found it difficult to keep the satisfaction from his voice as he turned to speak to the man.

'I'd forgotten how good it is here, Cane, and I'm damn glad to
be back. Tomorrow will be time enough to get down to work. I've
declared today a holiday, as we've much to celebrate.'

The bearded carpenter nodded and tipped a sausage-like forefinger to the brim of his hat before moving off into the trees.
Farewell drew in a deep breath of salty air and cast a last, long
look at the distant ridge before continuing his stroll along the
foreshore.

It was hard to believe that it had only been a few days since he'd stopped on the summit of the ridge just visible through the haze. The sight of the lagoon and its islands spread out below in the late afternoon sunshine had rendered him almost speechless. The thought that it was all his now, had been almost unbelievable…

Not given to extravagant displays of emotion, Francis Farewell was forced to blow his nose several times in quick succession to mask his feelings.

His first sight of Zululand had been from the deck of the ill-fated schooner *Fame,* a few years ago. He had been sailing south, skirting the dangerous Wild Coast, heading for the Cape, before setting out on the long journey home to England. The emotions it had stirred in him had been unexpected and all-consuming.

Thoughts of the ivory and the land in which it lay had eventually changed the entire course of his life – as had the unfortunate shipwreck that had cost him the *Fame* and a great deal of his capital.

He stared out across the empty lagoon. Only a few hours ago, the small supply ship *Julia* had been lying at anchor fifty yards off shore, waiting to sail on the morning tide.

Aboard her had been his father-in-law, Johann Petersen, and the group of investors who had sailed up with him from the Cape. Their abrupt departure was not totally unexpected, for the arrangement had been for them to stay for a short time, looking around the lagoon and its environs and realising its potential.

But because of what had happened in kwaBulawayo, the situation had drastically changed. To say the atmosphere had been somewhat strained before the ship's departure would have been an understatement.

None of the party had officially withdrawn from the project except Petersen, who had been livid to the point of hysteria; Schmidt, dazed and withdrawn; Hoffman uncommunicative, while the rest were confused and at a loss as to what to think.

Even knowing that the entire bay of eThekwini now officially belonged to FG Farewell and Company had failed to lighten their mood, or change their minds to any significant degree. His father-in-law had seen to that.

To hell with the lot of you, Farewell thought, with a spurt of anger. Those who want to stay will stay, while those who don't, will back out. I've no use for doubters and waverers. Only those with grit, backbone and very deep pockets need apply...

A surge of emotion threatened to overwhelm him. He stopped walking and looked out to where the breakers curled in against the headland in long, slow movements.

Not only did this beautiful bay belong to him now, but he also owned the coastline for twenty-five miles to the north and south of it. But that was not all. Shaka had also very generously included territory within a hundred-mile radius of where he was now standing.

Unshed tears filled his eyes. Unaccustomed to such extremes of emotion, Farewell hastily cleared his throat a few times, blinked his eyes rapidly then set off for home.

Earlier in the day, he had ordered bonfires to be lit and food prepared in celebration of his successful mission. None of the workers knew exactly what the 'success' of the mission entailed, for he'd deliberately kept quiet on the subject. He would reveal all, he informed them, at a time of his choosing.

As the sun began to slip down behind the hills, the moment had arrived. The bonfires were blazing merrily with several amaTuli at hand to do the needful and stoke the blaze when required.

Trestle tables and an assortment of up-turned barrels had been arranged as seating, while lit candles set into empty bottles had been placed around to create a festive atmosphere, while a delicious smell of roasting meat and baking bread permeated the air.

Farewell was freshly spruced-up, his blond hair plaited behind in naval fashion, his jacket and trousers immaculate. The first to arrive was John Cane, the bearded carpenter, and Rachel, his common-law wife. Her dusky skin glowed in the firelight, the gold hoops in her ears catching the light as she came forward to be greeted by the Lieutenant.

Also present was Henry Ogle, dubbed 'the singing Yorkshireman' because of his fine tenor voice. With him was Tom Halstead, the rather gormless youth who had come up from the Cape along with his father. Halstead senior had sailed south on the *Julia* along with the others, but would be returning on its next voyage. Last but not least were German Otto and the taciturn Dane, known only as Dupres.

Farewell ushered them forward, bade them all sit down and offered them some freshly brewed beer. 'I have to thank Rachel for helping with the food,' he said, making a small bow in her direction. 'A glass of claret and a drop of best Cape brandy to go with it afterwards.'

After they'd eaten and had something to drink in their hands, Farewell stood up and announced formally, 'I'd like you to raise your glasses. We have something to celebrate tonight, and I want you all to share in it.'

Raising his glass, he said, 'I give you Farewell and Company.' The others duly raised their glasses and joined in the toast.

'Look around you, if you will.' He swept a magnanimous hand around the compound, encompassing both the shore and the lagoon beyond. 'This beautiful bay will be your home for as long as you want to stay.'

His blue eyes glittered in the firelight. 'A week or two ago, it became the property of FG Farewell and Company. It was given to me by King Shaka himself. I should also add that land for a hundred or so miles inland, including coastline for twenty-five miles to the north and south of here, also belongs to me. Not on a short lease, I have to tell you, but in perpetuity.'

Only the crackle of logs and the whining of mosquitoes were audible in the silence. Henry Ogle gave a loud whistle of approval, while Tom Halstead stared into the fire, open-mouthed. Cane and Rachel especially seemed very pleased with the news.

'I give you the bay!' Farewell raised his glass high and drank deeply from it. 'In the morning, there's something else I'd like you to see, but for now – let the good times begin!'

Later, after his employees had all gone, Farewell opened the hardwood chest in his quarters and took out the scroll of parchment he'd carefully wrapped in oilskin against the ravages of tropical damp and insects.

Lord, how ridiculously easy it's all been, he thought, remembering the long months of frustration, sheer hard work and effort it had taken to even find the place.

Only a matter of a month or so from landing here and I've been handed more than I could ever have dreamed possible – probably the only safe harbour on this whole damn' coast and everything within a radius of a hundred miles inland, to boot.

He ran his eyes over the document, savouring every word.

'I, Inguos Shaka, King of the Zulus and of the country of Natal as well as the whole of the land from Natal to Delagoa Bay, which I have inherited from my father, for myself and heirs, do hereby, on the seventh day of August in the year of our Lord eighteen hundred and twenty-four, and in the presence of my chiefs and of my own free will, and in consideration of other divers goods received....

'do grant, make over and sell unto FG Farewell and Company, the entire and full possession in perpetuity to themselves, heirs and executors, of the Port or harbour of Natal, known by the name of Bubolongo, together with the islands therein and surrounding country... the whole of the neck of land or peninsula in the south-west entrance... all the country ten miles to the southern side, extending along the sea coast to the north and east as far as the river now called Farewell's River... being about twenty-five miles of sea coast together with all the country inland as

far as the nation called by the Zulus, Gowagnekos, extend-
ing about one hundred miles back from the shore...'

'all rights to the rivers, woods, mines and articles of all
denominations contained therein, the said land and appur-
tenances to be from this date for the sole use of Farewell
and Company, their heirs and executors, and to be by them
disposed of in any manner they think best calculated for
their interests, free from any molestation or hindrance
from myself or my subjects.'

'I, of my own free will and consent, acknowledge to have
fully consented perfectly understood all the purport of this
document, the same having been explained to me by my in-
terpreter, Hlambamanzi, and in the presence of witnesses,
before the said FG Farewell, whom I hereby acknowledge
as the Chief of the said country, with full power and au-
thority over such natives that like to remain there after
this public grant ... promising to supply him with cattle
and corn, when required, sufficient for his consumption, as
a reward for his kind attention to me in my illness from a
wound. '

At the bottom of the page was printed Shaka's name and those
of his witnesses, the Chiefs Mbikwana, Msika, Mhlophe and the
interpreter Hlambamanzi.

Under each name and rank was scrawled a cross and a thumb
print representing the signatures of the aforementioned.

Mind you, Farewell was forced to admit, if it hadn't been for
young Fynn, things might have turned out very differently. There
had been a point when he feared it would turn into a disaster,
mostly due to old man Petersen's bungling attempts to undermine him.

The atmosphere had become poisonous after Hoffman and Schmidt, the most stalwart of the investors, had threatened to withdraw their support, and their finances. Then, just in time, Fate had seemed to intervene in the shape of an unexpected and dramatic attempt to assassinate Shaka.

Farewell idly stroked his beard while he mentally replayed the events as they'd unfolded. Under cover of darkness, while the monarch was performing an intricate dance, someone mingling with the dancers had taken the opportunity to stab him in the side, bringing him down.

The place had erupted into bedlam, people running with torches, yelling and trying to find out who was responsible. When the search for the assassin failed, the hysteria got out of hand, and the real trouble began.

Fynn had explained it to them all afterwards. Apparently, when a king or important person dies, or is thought to be dying, all hell breaks loose. As he said, 'It's the native way of showing grief, or mourning, if you like. The only trouble is that once the blades and knobkerries come out, anyone at hand will do... '

But, lucky for them all, the miracle-working Henry Fynn had been on hand to save yet another life. This time it had been Shaka's. After the initial treatment and stemming of the blood, Fynn had never left his side and stayed on hand to bathe and clean the deep wound until he was out of danger.

The Zulu King had been so grateful to Fynn that he had freely agreed to hand over the bay for their future project, even promising to supply them with beef and corn on a seasonal basis.

Farewell's thoughts soured when he remembered his father-in-law's remarks on hearing the news. 'It doesn't change my mind one whit, Francis,' he'd remarked, 'this place will likely be the death of you.'

Carefully, the new owner of the bay put the document back into its oilskin wrappings, placed it in the hardwood box and locked it securely.

Once things got underway, he would make a copy of it. Then,

before the *Julia* next sailed south, he would hand it over to Captain Garrett with instructions to lodge it with the Land Registry in Cape Town.

Idly, he wondered how Fynn was faring in kwaBulawayo. Due to his promise to Shaka to stay on for the best part of a month, he had chosen not to return with the others.

Farewell then turned his attention to something else that had been nagging at him of late, another piece of business that needed to be attended to – that of his partner, James King, who was presently in London.

Not that there's much I can do about you right now, he mused, since there's no carrier pigeons or convenient mail boat passing by. So, James, old boy, you'll just have to wait.

His features hardened. But I should tell you, James, now that I've won the race, gained the prize – your services are no longer required.

At sunrise, FG Farewell and Company's full complement of staff, all six of them, turned up as requested. Since the amaTuli were also up and about, a few gathered to watch the strange, yet interesting activities of the *abelungu*.

Farewell, arrayed in his formal naval dress jacket with his war decorations pinned across his chest, arrived shortly afterwards. Beneath his arm, he carried a tightly wrapped bundle.

He looked around the small gathering. 'We won't always be so small in number,' he said, smiling, 'but today is an important day, a very important day, one we'll look back on with pride.'

Taking the package out from below his arm, he unfolded it. The familiar red, white and blue of the Union flag tumbled out. In the middle of the fenced area where they were gathered, a tall post had been erected. Attached to it, top and bottom, was a long double lanyard made of stout cord.

Stepping forward, Farewell fiddled with the cords until he'd threaded the flag correctly. Giving it a shake, he began to run it up the flagpole. Once it reached the top, the morning breeze caught it and set it fluttering. Farewell fastened it securely, then drew himself erect and saluted.

'On this thirtieth day of August, in the year of Our Lord eighteen hundred and twenty-four, I hereby formally take possession of this piece of land. Since it has been bequeathed to me, and mine to do with as I see fit, I now claim it on behalf of the British Empire. God save the King!'

The echoes of their cheering ran round the clearing. Farewell glanced up to where the British flag fluttered in the breeze, his face flushed below the tan.

Looking round the small circle of faces, he added, 'By the way, I've decided to change the name of the bay to Port Natal. I believe this was the name it was given a hundred or so years ago. From now on, it will no longer be called eThekwini. To Port Natal, ladies and gentlemen, and to new beginnings!'

A group of amaTuli fishermen, setting up their nets further along the foreshore, heard the infectious sound of people cheering. Deciding to join in, they set up a round of ululating.

Not to be outdone, a troop of samango monkeys, disturbed by the outbreak of jollity, proceeded to add their ear-piercing screeches to the celebrations.

Act ii

As he passed through the tall gates of Shaka's citadel, Fynn glanced up at the ceremonial arch spanning the massive posts, remembering the first time he'd passed below it and the chill of apprehension that had run down his back.

How long ago had it been? Time had a strange habit of becoming elongated in and around Shaka's domain. He thought back. Was it only seven, or perhaps eight weeks ago? It seemed much longer.

It had been early July, mid-winter, when it had all begun; his arrival in Zululand and his extraordinary meeting with the Zulu army a few days afterwards. Everything had led on from there; so many incidents and experiences, large and small, both trivial and life-changing.

Winter had now given way to spring. The days were longer, the weather hot and sunny. It was also time for him to leave kwaBulawayo. He had stayed the allotted time promised to Shaka – from one new moon to the next, after the others had gone.

Now his bargain was complete. Shaka was fit, well and had fully recovered from the murderous attack on him by person or persons unknown.

It was time for Henry Fynn, also known as Mbuyasi, the finch, to move on. But not back to the bay – at least not to stay. South, he thought, I'll head south. A good stretch of the legs down the Wild Coast is what I need, see what's there. Elephant, lots of 'em, with any luck. Ogle'll go with me, he'll be good company, little York-shire rat that he is. Always good for a sing-a-long is Ogle.

His ebullient mood soured a little when thoughts of Farewell and the land grant crept in. With his usual open-handed generos-ity, and thinking all of them would benefit from such an incredible opportunity, he had been the one to suggest it to Shaka when the monarch had sought to repay him for saving his life.

The change change he'd noticed in Farewell afterwards had not been exactly unexpected, but he had been somewhat shocked and disgusted, by the speed with which the hand-written and impressive piece of vellum had materialised, complete with red sealing-wax and official-sounding legal terms.

It wasn't the first time he'd suspected that the former Lieuten-ant's veneer of outward charm would turn out to be rather thin in certain circumstances – especially where his own interests were concerned. The arrogance of his class he had in plenty, also with-out doubt, its ruthless streak, was Fynn's opinion.

As he urged his horse across the fording place on the uMhlatuzi River, his mood picked up and he began to whistle a chirpy tune.

The only thing Farewell still lacked, vital to his plan, was Shaka's permission to hunt elephant in Zululand. And investors with deep pockets, of course. Until he had both, he would have to find other, simpler commodities to deal in.

Fynn grinned. Please yourself, FG Farewell, he thought. Stay in the bay and gloat over your territory. Fynn won't stay around long. I'll be gone before you know it, bound for the Wild Coast.

His teeth flashed white in his bearded face. And that piece of territory, my friend, does not belong either to Shaka, or to you. If there's elephant there, I'll find 'em – and who knows what else.

Act iii

Mid October

Langani straightened up and viewed his growing crops with satisfaction. As expected, they'd surpassed all his expectations. A little *isangoma* magic goes a long way, he thought, smiling to himself.

His mind went back to that oddly humid morning some months ago. He'd been about to try out a little experiment in the hope of making his vegetables flourish.

That had been the day the weather had changed, or perhaps something even more elemental had altered. It had been the start of his experiences involving the waters flowing from the heart of the mountain and what he'd subsequently discovered floating on the silent currents in the rock pool.

The diviner looked up from his curling beans, fat watermelons and tall heads of corn and glanced over at the water trickling down the rock face. Its gentle sound was as melodious and soothing as ever.

From where he was standing, digging tool in hand, he couldn't see the roof of the small rock pool, but then he didn't really need to.

He knew that the small orb was still there, the tiny spark of light at its core beating steadily. And there it would stay, until the time was right.

A movement in the shrubbery caught his eye. The tawny shape which had been resting in the shade languidly stretched its long limbs then padded towards him, the long banded tail swinging gently as it came.

Celiwe was now almost fully grown. A beautiful animal, the diviner thought, glancing at her sleek pelt and exquisite face markings, just as much a creature of mystery as the mountain waters and the rock pool were.

On his return from kwaBulawayo, she had been waiting for him. Rising out of the shade below the trees to greet him, she had rubbed her head against him. This time no fierce heat emanated from her, only the normal body warmth of a healthy young animal.

For days afterwards, he had been conscious of her eyes following him as he went about his duties. Was her scrutiny keener than before, he wondered, or was just he imagining it?

Had he really seen her framed in the starlight at the doorway of the dead man's hut and felt the rasp of her tongue and the weight of her body across his legs – or was what he'd experienced been the result of something else? Had she led him to the fateful meeting with Shaka of the Zulus, or was what he'd followed been only an illusion?

A series of tingling sensation ran through Langani's hands and feet, a vivid reminder of what had happened that night. More layers of mystery to add to those already there, the diviner thought.

He smiled to himself. But I'll do what I usually do when faced with the inexplicable, or echoes of other worlds, other powers – I'll accept them for what they are, and not probe too deeply into things that can never be explained, for that way lies only madness.

Glancing down at the cheetah, the smile was still on his face. 'If you could speak,' he said aloud, 'I know you would agree with me. I have my secrets, and you have yours. That is how things are. And it is all we two need to know.'

The diviner straightened up and brushed earth off his hands. Soon, the sun would begin to go down; time to feed the chickens and prepare the evening meal. He walked across to the edge of his land and looked out over the bush. It was peaceful out there, nothing stirring, only the silent land stretching to the horizon.

Somewhere to the south, far beyond the Tugela River, lay the bay of eThekwini and far away beyond that, worlds away, lay the cold northern land where the young boy with the bright hair and blue eyes lived.

Langani smiled. Only the child was no longer a *toto*. He was a fully grown boy of perhaps ten years, with all the energy and tricks of boys everywhere.

He knew this was true, because had he not seen him, clear as day, on the night of the storm with Shaka only a pace or two away from him, and an animal the king of the Zulus could not see pressing up against him.

What he had feared lost, his gift of prophecy, had returned – briefly, but long enough for him to catch glimpses of what was to come.

A handful of white men, shivering, cold and at the mercy of the sea, among them a boy with red hair, and with him a dog, a huge dog the like of which he had never seen before.

He had been allowed only a short glimpse into what was to come, but a second had followed, hard on the heels of the first, no doubt released by the surge of flame-hot energy streaming from his finger tips.

It had allowed him to look further and deeper than before. And he had seen the same boy, only older and taller this time, almost a youth, his hair long and braided, much like his own, with birds' feathers entwined in it.

With him were not white men, as might be expected, but Zulus, perhaps an *impi* of young warriors, with the dust of travel and hardship on their bodies, surrounding them the taint of battle and spilled blood.

Langani looked south. Miles away lay the beautiful bay and the white men who now lived there. It was said that Shaka had made Farewell, the man with the look of the wolf about him, the master of eThekwini.

No man owns the earth, or the waters or the air, the diviner thought.They may believe they do, but it is foolishness. . .

He knew it was inevitable that more white men would arrive on the shores of Zululand, but instead of concerning himself too much with them for the moment, instead he would focus his attention on the one he knew whose destiny it was to accompany them.

Once he was here, the boy would play his part – not only during his time in the land of the Zulus, as he had first thought – but for many years beyond that. Then Langani spoke aloud to him, his words carrying across the great divide of lands and oceans separating them.

'When the time is right, you will find me waiting for you at the bay of eThekwini. *Hamba ghale*, little friend.'

Still smiling, the diviner turned away from the gathering shadows of night and headed for home and supper.

END

About the Author

Isabella Bleszynski, the life of...

Isabella was born and educated in the north-east of Scotland. Six years after entering the teaching profession, she took up a contract with the Ministry of Overseas Development, London and left for Ndola, Zambia, with her sons then aged 6 and 4.

It was followed by a move to Chingola, a few miles from the border with the Republic of Congo, where she was appointed as Head of The Helen Waller School. She was instrumental in re-naming it the Princess Nakatindi School, the name it still bears.

Several contracts later, she moved to Lilongwe, Malawi and taught at the Bishop MacKenzie International School. Her final tour in Africa took her north, to Libya, where she worked for Sirte Oil Company in Marsa el Brega.

The year after the Americans bombed Tripoli and Benghazi she left Libya and returned to Scotland. Isabella now writes full time, and spends a part of each year in Australia. She has four grandchildren.

'A DANCE CALLED AFRICA' is her first published book.

Acknowledgements

Many thanks to my son, Nick, a published author himself, for all the help so freely given over the long gestation period it has taken me to get this far. Also to my other stalwart, Tim, for advice on matters relating to computer-based technology and sound business practice – at which his mother is generally useless!

To Captain James Macpherson for keeping me right on ships and sea-faring matters and to Esme deToit and Solomon Sibiya, kwaZulu Natal, on Zulu matters and language.

To the British Library, London for requested materials: also Loraine Noble of Fraserburgh Historical Society for information relating to 'John Ross' aka Charles Rawden Maclean, the source inspiration for these books. I also owe thanks to staff of various Libraries in Durban, also known as eThekwini. The kwaZulu Natal Tourism Board was also unfailingly helpful.

To the various editors, critics and readers whose services I've used along the way – what can I say? I've taken on board some of your advice, have greatly appreciated and agreed or disagreed with parts of it – but have never quite managed to swallow it whole! Consequently, any faults, excesses or suchlike that might show up are solely my own.

After taking the long way around, what I have ended up with – a trilogy – is more or less what I set out to achieve in the beginning. Trying to capture the essence of an epic story and re-create the intriguing life and times of Charles Rawden Maclean, aka 'John Ross' has not been easy, to put it mildly! But one of the great benefits has been that every day I sat down to write, I had a chance to go back to Africa!

Africa, of course, and Zululand in particular, became the co-stars of the tale – as were the unforgettable characters, both black and white, who were involved in the forging of the history of kwaZulu Natal and who consequently left more than just their footprints behind.

Author's Notes

Thank you for spending time in the intriguing world of 19th century Africa. I hope you'll want to come back and read more about the characters and find out what happens next in Book 2 'KINGDOM OF A THOUSAND DAYS.' You will not be disappointed!

If you've enjoyed reading 'A DANCE CALLED AFRICA' I would greatly appreciate it if you would take the time to send a review on my behalf to www.amazon.co.uk. Thank you, in anticipation.

If you'd like to contact me, ask a question, or be notified by e mail about new posts on my blog/ writing/ newsletter, or be kept up to date with news, events or publications, please go to my website: www.stravaig-books.com and leave a message with your name and e-mail address. Your details will never be shared with anyone and you can unsubscribe at any time.

Facebook: www.facebook.com/Isabella-Bleszynski.

Most copyright pages begin with the following declaration, you know the one... *"This book is a work of fiction. Any resemblance to actual events or persons; living or dead; is purely coincidental."*

Not that you'll probably have noticed, but there is no such declaration on the copyright page of 'A DANCE CALLED AFRICA'.
Although it is a work of fiction, I honestly couldn't make the
claim *that 'any resemblance to actual events or persons, living or dead;*
is purely accidental.' No way!

I based all the main characters on the real flesh and blood characters of the time, as I saw them – with the exception of only one.
As for the actual events in the book – apart from the truly mystical – I've tried to keep them as historically accurate as possible
and how they occurred.

Originally, I'd intended to make 'A DANCE CALLED AFRICA' available on 17th August, 2015. This was to celebrate the 200th
anniversary of the birth of 'John Ross' aka Charles R Maclean in
Fraserburgh, Scotland in 1815. Unfortunately, due to technical difficulties, I had to delay it for another month or so. Also in 1815,
exactly 200 years ago, Shaka kaSenzangakhona became King of the
fledgling Zulu state.

And the rest, as they say, is history.

Since I've never believed in 'co-incidence' the deeper I got into the
background and personalities of the characters and the actual writing of the books, the more I realised the profound connection that
exists, even down to the present day, between these two unlikely
protagonists, a young seafarer born in a far-off fishing town in the
north-east of Scotland and the force of nature that was Shaka, the
warrior King of the Zulus.

Though 'John Ross' doesn't actually appear in the flesh in Book
1 – never fear, you will meet him in Book 2: 'KINGDOM OF A
THOUSAND DAYS' and in Book 3: 'LORD OF THE RED FIRE.'

What's Coming Next

BOOK 2

'KINGDOM OF A THOUSAND DAYS'

When former RN Lieutenant, JAMES KING goes in search of his missing partner FRANCIS FAREWELL, disaster follows disaster. Shipwrecked on the coast of Zululand, among the crew is 10-year-old Highlander CHARLES RAWDEN MACLEAN and a Newfoundland dog called Dileas, the faithful.

Stranded without means of escape, the former partners become locked in a feud which spirals into bitter division and tragic endings. To make matters worse, when Shaka, the warrior King, refuses to release their youngest crew member, the flame-haired boy is brought, fevered but defiant, to the feet of the ruthless King.

After meeting the powerful young diviner, LANGANI, JACKABO as Maclean is now called, becomes the unwitting keeper of the most dangerous secrets in the Zulu kingdom, and is led into a web of suspicion and murderous intent.

Not even Langani, it seems, can stem the gathering flood of malignancy which begins to affect the future of Zululand and those involved in the various intrigues. Death, betrayal and near-madness become the order of the day.

In 'KINGDOM OF A THOUSAND DAYS' Charles Rawden Maclean – the young Highlander who becomes *iQawu, Shaka's hero* – allows us mesmerising glimpses into the secret world of the loves, triumphs and betrayals surrounding Shaka and his court.

It is where 'JOHN ROSS'- one of South Africa's most endearing historical figures – steps out of legend, not only to tell what lay between himself and Shaka, the most magnificent warrior king of them all, but of the ill-fated first expedition by white men into the land of the Zulus.

Kingdom of a Thousand Days
Part 2 of 'The 'John Ross' Trilogy'
will be available in spring 2016

If you would like to read the 1st chapter please follow the website link below. Click on CONTACT then leave your details.

LORD OF THE RED FIRE is the final book of the trilogy. It will be available in 2017.

If you would like to READ MORE, about the background to the actual WRITING of the books, in 'JOHN ROSS' AND ME or about the young Highlander, CHARLES RAWDEN MACLEAN or any of the other characters- please visit my website: **www.stravaig-books.com.**